I0661625

Message

from

the

past

Part-02

Table of Contents

1

New associates.

'Human beings cannot only be educated.
He must educate himself, be an educator for himself'.

Ten years earlier,

28 April 2008, London, Fulham Road Kensington, Brompton Cemetery,

12:30pm

Matthiew was standing near the chapel where George's body was located.

He held an umbrella in one hand and a cigarette in the other.

It was raining heavily that afternoon, and the forecast brightening was not due until late evening.

Dressed in a smart black suit and shoes, smoothly shaved and neatly combed, Matthiew looked nothing like himself.

His appearance surprised the other mourners who had come to say a final farewell to George.

It was also a surprise that Matthiew, appeared in the company of two colleagues visibly younger than him.

Men whom neither staff nor George's closest friends had ever met before.

Not yet, because they were Simon and Harry.

This was met with no small amount of disapproval among those gathered, as it was easy to guess that these individuals had come there at Matthiew's request.

There was no doubt that George had had nothing to do with them in the past.

This was even taken by some in a very insulting way, derogatory to George's memory.

There was a quick opinion that Matthiew had invited two of his friends as if he was going out to a bar or some sort of special event.

Thus, desecrating the seriousness of the situation.

Matthiew noticed the mourners looking at them angrily as they entered the chapel together and took their seats in the last pew near the entrance.

However, he completely didn't care.

In his life, such antics were perfectly normal, so he got used to it.

George's friends and staff, had to ignore the situation out of respect for the deceased.

It was common knowledge that George had no immediate family.

However, there was no certainty over the relatives who might still attend his funeral.

Only Matthiew knew that Nattaly, George's daughter, had stated that she would attend her father's burial ceremony.

Given this knowledge, he was very surprised that she had not turned up. Because of this, he felt puzzled and slightly anxious, as he was sure she would have been present at the chapel by then.

During an earlier phone call, he gave her the date, time and address of the cemetery where the funeral would take place.

Nattaly thanked him at the time and said that she would come.

Therefore, the only explanation as to why she did not come could be that she had simply decided not to. This prospect worried Matthiew.

Because such a case negatively affected his further plans for his deceased partner's daughter.

Matthiew looked at his watch and then at the chapel door, concerned. He had hoped, she'll be in the chapel any minute, but that was not the case.

Just in case, he had to start thinking about what he would do if it turned out that Nattaly had indeed decided not to show up at all.

There was going to be a meeting with George's lawyer immediately after the ceremony.

I'll call her as soon as we get out of here. he thought.

Two days earlier, Matthiew had been contacted by a man called Michael Edwards.

He then introduced himself as George Bradley's lawyer and explained the purpose of his phone call.

It was to arrange a meeting at which Matthiew's presence was required. The lawyer also said, "...I am obliged to pass on to you information that my client, George Bradley, has left in my care..."

It was not difficult to guess that this was about George's holdings in the agency.

Matthiew was under no illusion that he should become the owner of the office.

At the same time, he was almost 100 per cent sure that Nattaly would be the one to take over the role.

However, at that moment, doubt was creeping into his head.

He began to consider options that until now, he had not considered at all. - *What if, there is someone else? Someone George had never*

3

spoken of, kept secret; he hadn't known about Nattaly either, after all, until recently. He pondered.

From the very beginning, the seed of his plan had been to manipulate Nattaly to convince her to cooperate.

What he hadn't considered, however, was that there might be another person he didn't know and that she would be his future boss.

This possibility was slowly becoming more and more real.

But at that moment, he had to wait and see what would happen next. "In the worst-case scenario, I will be forced to negotiate with an unknown person." He stated reluctantly while hoping that it would be Nattaly after all.

The thought appealed to him because, in his eyes, he could see how she could help him with his plans.

She was perfect for this.

After the first part of the ceremony was over.

Four stout men carried George's coffin on their shoulders, and the mourners slowly got up from their seats and, one by one, went outside.

The rain did not stop, not even for a moment.

The whole setting looked very depressing.

It was raining, people dressed in black were walking slowly, hiding under umbrellas, holding flowers, and everyone felt an overwhelming sadness. Even the two strangers accompanying Matthiew felt as if they were saying goodbye to a good friend, yet they didn't even know George.

It seemed that few people were bothered by the ugly weather as they stood hidden under umbrellas outside.

Most were too deep in grief to even notice the relentless rain.

Only Matthiew and his companions were looking forward to finally putting an end to the whole spectacle.

It was hard for the men to overcome the curiosity that was almost eating them from the inside.

So, they counted down every minute that brought them closer to the end of the ceremony.

The mourners slowly walked behind the coffin containing George's body, heading towards his final resting place.

In the first line walked Lucy Clarke and Katy Taylor, two secretaries from the agency for whom George was like a father.

Both young women were very attached to him and loved him very much. Behind them were Jack Johnson, Terry Smith, Andrew Harris and Ralph Williams, four estate agents and close friends of George who had worked with him for years.

The others Matthiew did not know personally, but he guessed that they were people from George's private life that he did not want to invite him into. In total there were seven, attractive, women and five men whom Matthiew knew only by sight.

As he watched the unfamiliar women, he felt a stab of jealousy at the thought that George had probably slept with them.

He squirmed at the thought.

It was past 01:30 pm.

Having arrived at the grave, the final part of the ceremony proceeded. People lined up on either side of the pit where George was about to be laid to rest.

The parish priest stood next to a tasteful marble tombstone, ready to be put in place once the ground settled, which bore George's personal details along with the dedication:

"No one dies on earth as long as he lives in the hearts of those who remain".

Matthiew was standing between the agency staff, while his two colleagues preferred to keep their distance, so they positioned themselves at the back. Then, a few dozen metres from where he was, he noticed a person standing alone with an umbrella by a tree.

There would have been nothing unusual about this, after all it was a cemetery, and many people were walking around visiting their dead. However, this person stood out because he was apparently lurking under a tree, and due to the terrible weather, the area was empty at the time.

Matthiew strained his eyes to take a closer look.

Then, he recognised the long brown hair, and the thought immediately dawned on him that it might be Nattaly.

Matthiew's eyes widened as the adrenaline suddenly hit his brain.

There she is! He thought exultantly.

He had just been waiting for her all this time.

Matthiew began to back away slowly, gently poking people in the process, paying no attention to anyone.

For which he received, from some of them, a chastising look in gratitude.

Ignoring this completely, however, he moved towards the person hiding under the tree.

When he was close enough, he noticed that the woman began to move restlessly.

She took a few steps and stopped, undecided whether she should leave immediately.

Clearly unsure what to do, she eventually stayed.

Matthiew approached her and was relieved to find that he had not been mistaken.

Indeed, it was Nattaly, coming to say goodbye to her father.

Although he hadn't seen her for almost four years, since they had met at the Hilton Hotel restaurant, he recognised her instantly.

When he was sure it was her, he quickly put on a face appropriate to the circumstances in which they had met.

"Why are you standing so far away...?" he asked in a caring voice. "... Don't you want to come closer?"

"I'll come closer once everyone has left." Nattaly said.

"There's no reason to worry. There are only friends here..." Matthiew replied. "... Is that why you didn't come to the chapel? Because of these strangers?"

His voice was full of mock tenderness, quiet and friendly.

At the same time, a deep sadness was visible on Matthiew's face. No doubt, he could have become a great actor if only he had been a little better looking.

"No..." she replied briefly. "...I've only just arrived; I didn't make it earlier." She added after a moment.

"I understand, come with me, let`s get closer." Saying this, Matthiew took the umbrella from the woman and grabbed her under her arm. She let him lead the way.

As they walked side by side, Matthiew discreetly glanced at Nattaly's waist, who, despite the wide coat she wore for camouflage, was visibly advanced in her pregnancy.

He quickly analysed all the pros and cons in his mind, asking himself if the fact that she was about to become a mother might somehow thwart his plans for her.

He was not going to give up.

He was also puzzled as to why Nattaly was apparently trying to hide it, having no doubt that the coat she was wearing was not only to protect her from the rain but also to cover her entire body tightly.

7

However, she was six months pregnant, and there was little she could do to disguise it.

The ceremony continued as they approached the assembled people. It was then that Nattaly noticed that she had attracted the attention of some people.

People were looking at her curiously, wondering who she was.

Nattaly felt uncomfortable in this situation and regretted letting Matthiew lead her out of hiding, where she was safe, and no one could see her. In truth, none of the people present had any idea who she was, and Nattaly knew it well.

But just the sight of them, looking at each other and quietly whispering something made her want to get out of there as quickly as possible. If it wasn't for the fact that Matthiew was still holding her arm, and she didn't want to make a scene at George's funeral, further drawing the already clearly focused attention to her, she would have simply turned on her heel and left the cemetery.

She wasn't normally a shy person who was easily frightened, but in this situation, it was different, and at some point, she felt that her confidence had been overstepped.

"Stop..." she said suddenly. "...We are not going any further."

Matthiew obediently followed her command.

They were standing next to each other a few metres away from the other people, making them look like they were a couple.

Which only intensified the curious stares.

Only after a while Nattaly realised what they might have looked like they were together.

She then thought that this was the last thing she wanted to be thought of. Even being completely anonymous, she did not want to be thought of as being in a relationship with this horrible man.

But she didn't let herself be bothered by that for too long.

She was there to say goodbye to her father, not to worry about the opinions of people she didn't know.

Staying until the end of the ceremony, she tried to ignore the people who openly and without much embarrassment glanced at her and her belly.

Adding to it, probably, that Matthiew is the father.

If they want to talk down on me then go ahead, I don't care about the opinion of strangers. She thought and raised her head proudly.

The next few minutes passed quietly; it was past four o'clock.

George's body was lowered into the grave, and the ceremony was slowly coming to an end.

The assembled people were still awaiting the conclusion of the ceremony. Nattaly stood motionless next to Matthiew and looked towards her father's grave, ignoring those trying to make eye contact with her.

Matthiew continued to stubbornly hold her arm and was very comfortable doing so.

Because the circumstances demanded seriousness, Nattaly did not want to behave rudely towards him. Otherwise, under different circumstances, she would have told him to back off a long while ago.

Ten minutes later, the rain began to subside.

It was still dripping slightly, but the weather began to improve noticeably. Once the ceremony was over, those gathered slowly began to disperse in silence in their respective directions.

Including Simon and Harry, Matthiew's companions.

At one point the men wanted to approach him, but he showed them discreetly with his head not to do so, so they headed towards the exit. Eventually only Nattaly and Matthiew were left, at which point the woman was able to come closer and lean over George one last time.

Matthiew noticed tears streaming down her cheeks that hadn't been there before.

He stood patiently behind her as she honoured George's memory with a minute's silence.

When she finished, she straightened up and reached into her handbag to take out her phone.

The time on her watch at the time was 02:10pm.

"In twenty-five minutes, my train leaves." She announced.

She didn't know why she had started the conversation with Matthiew, she didn't really want to talk to him.

But he was the only person there at the time and Nattaly, deep down needed to speak to someone.

She needed to break the agonising silence that reigned in her head, if only to hear her own voice.

"I think you should come with me." Matthiew replied suddenly. "With you? Where?" she quirked a brow and furrowed her brow suspiciously.

To meet Michael Edwards, George's lawyer, haven't you been told?

I know about it, but I don't think I can handle it today.

"Well, he called me two days ago said he had some documents from George that he wanted to hand over immediately."

"Alright, but why do you want me to go with you?"

Because it's about George's shares in the agency and probably, also about the last will.

"If it's about his will then I'll call Micheal and make another appointment, it doesn't necessarily have to be done today, does it?" Nattaly insisted. "True, but aren't you at least a little curious about what he has to say? Besides, this is also about my part of the business, and I prefer to deal with such things on the spot."

"Oh, and that's why you want me to go with you now? Because it suits you? You do what you want. I can't force you to do anything, but I think it would be good for both of us if you came to this meeting, Michael will be expecting us at half past three." Matthiew was playing out his strategy.

Earlier, Nattaly, had not given much thought to her father's will.

In truth, she had received an email from Michael asking her to contact him and listing the details of the meeting, including date, time and address. She also knew that George was the principal owner of a housing agency. However, since she had received the news of his sudden death, ironically from Matthiew, she had not taken a moment to consider the possibility. Matthiew had managed to plant a seed of curiosity in her mind, which quickly germinated.

The way he spoke to her was very convincing and almost fuelled by excitement.

What she heard from him greatly stimulated her curiosity and her desire to know the truth.

"My car is parked not far from here..." He said, snapping her out of her reverie. "...I suppose the meeting won`t be long, then you can go to North

Hill."

Matthiew was forging the iron while it was still hot, he felt he was one step away from convincing her.

Looking closely, he could see it in her face.

At the same time, he was curious to see her reaction to knowing where she was coming from.

It was supposed to be, a kind of revenge after, as she had managed to corner him in the restaurant of the Hilton Hotel, several years ago.

She had known his personal details, which left him stunned.

And now, the opportunity presented itself to try and bite back a little. But Nattaly quickly saw through his game and did not react to these words, at the same time keeping a stony face.

She raised her gaze slowly to him and asked:

"Why would I go to North Hill...?" she declared, feigning surprise.

Matthiew murmured because he knew he wasn't mistaking.

It was the only thing George had ever said to him by accident.

But he didn't see on her face the slightest embarrassment or even slight surprise.

Nattaly was clever and knew that Matthiew had tried to trick her.

But even if he only knew that her town was North Hill, that was one piece of information too many for her.

Her intention was for absolutely no one to know anything about her. Unfortunately for Matthiew, he was a necessary evil for her to deal with later, because of his relationship with George.

But she didn't want him to find out anything more, and since he already knew this one fact about her, she decided then, to have a little fun with him and to lead him by the nose.

"I haven't lived there for a long time." She added after a while.

"You're lying! George clearly said you live in North Hill...." Matthiew replied angrily.

At this point, he felt as if the ground had started to crumble under his feet. *And damn it! What if George lied to me? I've been putting the whole plan together around this most important detail, could it be that the last two years of preparation have just gone to shit?* he wondered intensely at the same time, tried not to let on how nervous he had started to get.

He tried to remain calm.

"...But... Have you lived there until recently? Do you know the town?" He added quickly, already changing his tone.

The man understood that he had let his nerves get the best of him.

Nattaly, on the other hand, saw him squirm inside and wriggle like an eel.

She got immense satisfaction out of this, so she tormented him even more. "Maybe..." She said with an ironic smile on her face. "...Why do you want to know that?"

"It doesn't matter anymore..." replied a resigned Matthiew. "...I'll call Michael to tell him I'm on my way." He added.

Thus, giving himself a moment to think about the situation.

He pulled out his phone and walked a few steps away to make the call, while casting an arrogant glance towards Nattaly, who only smiled in response.

She could see him trying to show off.

He raised his head proudly, put his hand in his jacket pocket and walked around pretending to be a focused, serious businessman.

This sight made Nattaly wants to laugh.

When she was about to meet George for the first time, and he asked if she could come along to meet his partner, she did a little research on Matthiew.

Even then, she concluded that the man would pose no threat.

Looking through his photos and reading personal details on the internet, she concluded what kind of person Matthiew might be.

She also wondered if she would be able to wrap him around her little finger if necessary.

In the end, she decided that it shouldn't be a big problem for her if she really wanted to.

Now she realised that Matthiew had started to play a game with her, the rules for which he had apparently already set himself much earlier.

For her, however, it made no difference.

She decided, out of curiosity, to join in just to see what he was going to do next.

The situation soon began to clarify itself, as the George inheritance was now involved, which was clearly on Matthiew's mind.

After the many conversations Nattaly had with her father, she was aware of his attitude towards his partner, as he had repeatedly spoken negatively about him.

He often mentioned, that it was a mistake to go into business with him and of a lack of trust and even affection.

Thanks to this, over time, her own opinion of him had managed to form. The likelihood that George would one day change his mind about him and give Matthiew a stake in the agency, thus making him the owner, was zero.

Nattaly was aware of all this.

In fact, she wasn't quite sure what Matthiew intended to do.

But at that moment, she could clearly see from him that he had something in mind.

So, she thought it would be good to find out what it was.

It was also a good opportunity to find out more about her father, as she sometimes got the feeling that he was hiding something from her and wasn't being entirely honest.

Spending an hour or two in Matthiew's company during the meeting with the lawyer seemed an affordable price to pay for gaining more information. Especially as she then had good reason to expect a significant inheritance, at that time.

Okay, I'll go with him, it might be interesting. she thought.

As she waited, she watched Matthiew walked around and talk on the phone. For reasons best known to himself, he had already gone so far down the path that Nattaly couldn't hear a word of the conversation, although there was almost perfect silence in the cemetery.

It seemed that Matthiew was trying to create a mystery around the situation or indeed, had something to hide.

Either way, according to Nattaly, it was very childish behaviour.

If it makes him feel good to think, that he has everything under control, I can pretend to comply. She concluded.

When she finally saw him hiding his phone into his pocket, she put on a naively curious face.

She wanted to make it seem to him that he was in charge.

"Okay, it's settled..." Matthiew said seriously.

His voice sounded proud and overbearing, quite as if, a moment ago, he had arranged a meeting with the British Prime Minister himself.

"...So, what's it going to be? Have you decided to come with me or not?" He asked, putting his hands in his jacket pockets and straightening up in front of Nattaly like a movie star straight out of Hollywood.

"Since I'm already here, I'll come with you."

"Perfect, he will meet us at three o`clock, so we still have half an hour, would you like a coffee or eat something?" he asked, while checking the watch on his wrist.

"No thank you, let's go to the car, I need to sit down." She replied, grabbing her stomach.

With this gesture she made it clear that, given her condition, she needed to rest.

By all means, let's go then, my car is parked nearby.

The man replied and set off in the direction where he had left the car, Nattaly slowly followed him.

She didn't feel like going anywhere with him immediately.

At this point, she had to force herself to talk to him and get used to the idea, that she would probably have to spend, at least, the next hour and a half in his company.

There was something repulsive and disturbing about Matthiew's personality, but it was hard to put into words.

At the time, Nattaly still had no idea how he could be useful to her.

She had not yet imagined a situation in which she could see him behaving usefully.

However, she liked to be prepared for any eventuality, so she left that door open in case she wanted to use it one day.

Even though, she didn't know how to use this man back then, that was soon about to change.

It was almost 3 pm when they arrived at the office building of Michael's law firm.

The office was based in the Oxford Circus area, so Matthiew had expected from the outset that he would find it difficult to find places to park his car. He breathed a sigh of relief when it turned out that the law firm had a private car park, for staff and clients, in front of the building.

He stopped the car and got out, then waited for Nattaly to do the same. However, she had a little trouble unbuckling her seatbelt as it was stuck under her belly.

It took several seconds before she finally managed to crawl out of the passenger seat.

Meanwhile, Matthiew stood idly in front of the car and watched impatiently as Nattaly struggled.

It didn't even cross his mind to help a woman in advanced pregnancy. When he saw Nattaly finally get out of the car and close the door behind her, he wordlessly turned his back on her and started towards the building.

After this gesture, the woman measured him with an angry look.

"What an asshole." She said under her breath and headed off following his footsteps.

Matthiew entered the building first and immediately approached the desk where the receptionist sat.

After a moment, he was joined by Nattaly.

The receptionist leaned her face out from behind her computer as soon as she noticed that customers had arrived.

"Good afternoon, how can I help you?" the woman asked politely. "Hi, my name is Matthiew Braddock. I have an appointment with Michael Edwards." He replied in a serious tone.

"Of course, rest assured I'll let him know you're waiting." said the receptionist and looked at Nattaly who was standing a few steps behind.

"This lady is with me." He hastened to explain.

He pre-empted her question when he noticed her looking at Nattaly, she clearly thought they had come separately.

"I understand, please take a seat it won't take long." The receptionist replied.

At the same time directing the guests towards the elegant sofas at the other end of the room.

There was a neat little reception room in the office, decorated in a good, modern style.

An energising citrus scent filled the air, and it was clear at first glance that this was a professional establishment owned by serious people. Next to the sofa on which Nattaly sat with Matthiew, there were two lifts, which indicated that the building was three storeys high.

Something you couldn't quite tell by looking at it from the street.

It took a few minutes for the receptionist to contact Michael.

During this time, Nattaly discreetly silently looked at Matthiew and cursed him in her mind, but he didn't even notice.

She resented him.

After the incident in the car park, she wondered how he could be so devoid of manners and even a modicum of empathy as not to move to help a pregnant woman, who clearly needed support.

A conceited, self-obsessed pig, he didn't even deign to wait for me at the car, let alone get out of it. she spoke to herself in her mind angrily. For Nattaly, such seemingly trivial details made it easy for her to determine a particular person's character type.

She had already found him to be a boor four years ago when they first spoke, but she didn't think he was so shorn of basic human emotions.

It was 3:10 pm, when the secretary got up from her chair and announced that the lawyer was ready to meet them.

"Go to the second floor and head down the corridor to the right. Mr Michael is in room five." She advised them kindly.

After these words, Matthiew rose from the sofa and walked to the lift to summon it.

All the time he gave the impression that he did not notice that Nattaly was next to him.

Eventually, the woman decided that she wasn't sure if he was ignoring her or simply not attuned to the company of women, which left him with no idea how to behave in their company. Eventually, she backed off the second answer.

Maybe he doesn't do it on purpose, and it just seems that way to me? she wondered as she looked at the visibly obese and unattractive man, thinking that even a smart suit wouldn't help here.

No matter how hard he tries, it will be hard to make him look even slightly better in the eyes of the fair sex... she acknowledged without hypocrisy. *...Even if there is a desperate woman who would like to get involved with him, I can sympathise with her in advance, people with a character like his are downright impossible to live with and for the good of society it would be better for him never to marry or have children....* she scowled at him in thought. -*... He probably hasn't slept with any women yet anyway.* she added to herself and involuntarily smiled.

Of course, she had no intention of saying such a thing openly to him, at least until he provoked her.

But in truth, she didn't care for him in her thoughts.

If he knew what I thought of him, I'd probably never see him again. she added and quietly snorted with laughter.

This time Matthiew noticed something was on her mind and looked at her and she had a grin from ear to ear.

Is something amusing you?

"No, nothing..." She lied, trying to put on a serious expression. "...It's the hormones." She added as an explanation for her behaviour.

Matthiew was clearly not interested in her pregnancy; from the moment they met in the cemetery, he hadn't even mentioned a word about it. Any other person, by now, would probably have already asked what month she was in or something like that.

But not him. He just didn't care.

19

Which didn't change the fact that he could undoubtedly see that she was pregnant.

Maybe that's the reason why he's acting so arrogantly? He doesn't like pregnant women? she speculated.

The number 0 appeared on the electronic display next to the lift entrance, signalling that the lift had already descended to the ground floor and the metal doors were about to open in front of them.

Nattaly didn't expect that Matthiew could behave like a gentleman this time and let her in ahead, so when the way was clear, she stood a bit further back, allowing Matthiew to be the first to pack his gussied-up belly inside.

Fortunately for her, she had assessed the situation well.

Because if she had moved straight away, they would probably have collided in the lift doorway.

For without a second thought, Matthiew swaggeringly stepped inside as soon as the doors opened wide enough for him to squeeze between them.

Nattaly slowly walked in behind him and stood at his side.

A few seconds later, they were already on the second floor.

The clock showed 03:15pm as they both walked down the heavily lit corridor, counting down the numbers of the offices to their right. Each room was separated from the corridor by a large solid pane of glass and a door.

Blinds were fitted at the windows.

Some were slightly obscured to make it impossible to peek inside for privacy, while others were completely exposed, but these rooms happened to be empty.

The office they were heading for remained with the window uncovered. So, when, after a short while, they stood in front of the door with the number five, they spotted a middle-aged man sitting behind a desk, apparently busy with his work.

Matthiew didn't think long, he knocked on the door.

"Please come in!" a slightly muffled voice called out from inside the room.

On cue, Matthiew grabbed the handle and pushed the door open wide. Of course, without hesitation, he stepped inside the office, leaving Nattaly behind once again.

There is no hope for that man, he will never learn anything. she thought irritably.

Once they were both in George's lawyer's office, the man got up from his chair and walked over to greet them.

With this gesture, Nattaly had the opportunity to get a closer look at him. A tall and handsome guy of about fifty, dressed in a smart suit that fit him well, dark hair and green eyes, he was smiling warmly.

For a moment she had the impression that in stature and style he resembled her father; they might even have been about the same age. Although she assumed that the man who had just approached her was probably a few years younger than George.

"Welcome..." he greeted them kindly. "...My name is Michael Edwards, you must be Nattaly, right?" he added, engaging in an understanding look with her.

He walked over to her, grabbed her and then, in accordance with noble custom, raised the woman's hand to his lips.

There are still true gentlemen in this world. Nattaly thought, while comparing the lawyer to her temporary companion.

"Of course, it is a pleasure to meet you." Nattaly replied.

There was silence in the room for a few seconds, Michael looking at Nattaly thoughtfully.

It was as if he had known her for a long time or had something more in common, and this was not their first meeting.

Matthiew watched them for a moment, confused, he felt like they had completely forgotten he was there too, so he decided to break the awkward silence.

"Matthiew Braddock." He said, extending his hand to the solicitor. "By all means, good to meet you." Michael said, visibly jolted out of his thoughts.

What could that possibly mean? Could it be that they knew each other? In Matthiew's mind, the first questions began to arise.

Nattaly stood next to him and waited until they had finished exchanging pleasantries so they could move on.

"Okay, now that we're all set, I invite you to take a seat." Michael indicated with his hand the two armchairs at his desk.

"Thank you." Nattaly replied and walked over to the armchair to sit comfortably at last.

She felt exhausted, the pregnancy was making it very difficult for her to continue.

She was followed by Matthiew and finally, Michael.

The lawyer settled down in his seat, then, opened the folder he had prepared earlier with notes and documents.

Nattaly noticed how he looked at them with a discreet, questioning gaze. She concluded by this that he had most likely not expected her to come along with Matthiew.

"So, first, I must inform you that I had another appointment with George Bradley, where, from what he mentioned, we were going to make some amendments to his will, and I know it concerned you..." He paused for a moment, looking at Nattaly. "...But unfortunately, the meeting did not take place for reasons you know." He added with sadness in his voice. *Could it be that he did not have time to reassign the estate to her? But what kind of amendments could it be about? Maybe he had bequeathed the shares to someone else and didn't have the chance to change it?* A wave of questions ran through Matthiew's mind.

At the same time, he knew that his name could not appear in George's will, so he did not even try to lie to himself or give himself false hope. He had already come to terms with the inevitable and, at this point, all he wanted was that if anyone was going to take over the leadership of the agency, it was Nattaly.

Matthiew realised that George's daughter didn't like him, but a thread of understanding had emerged between them, even if Nattaly didn't see it yet. "I don't know what amendments George had in mind at the time, but it doesn't matter anymore ..." Michael picked up the subject again. "...I will therefore present to you an earlier version, his last will."

The lawyer opened the folder and placed it in front of him. At the same time he noticed Nattaly looking at the "Newton spheres" standing at arm's length from her.

A slight smile appeared at the corner of his mouth at this sight.

"Do you feel like pushing them?" he asked curiously.

Nattaly smiled at him, then stretched her hand forward to reach for one of the balls. After which, she set them all in motion.

...TIC...TIC...TIC...TIC... The sound spread around the room.

"My favourite toy, it relaxes me a lot." The woman announced.

"Me too." Replied the lawyer.

Michael slid out his desk drawer and suspended his gaze on the documents, for that moment, there was almost complete silence, distracted only by the sound of Newton's bouncing metal balls.

...TIC...TIC...TIC....

On Nattaly and Micheal, it had a relaxing effect, but Matthiew began to squirm impatiently in his chair.

Nattaly noticed his leg bobbing nervously under the table.

I guess that sound doesn't have a relaxing effect on everyone. she thought.

This behaviour, on the other hand, gave her another clue as to his personality.

This man has chaos in his head, is unable to calm down and constantly looks irritated. This could also be related to alcohol or drug abuse. - She spun the analysis in her mind.

"There it is, we can start." Announced Michael abruptly, who had by this time managed to sort the letters he needed.

The solicitor pulled out a binder with the words 'G. Bradley' at his side, then placed it on the desk in front of him, opened it and began flipping through the pages of documents one by one.

After a moment, with a nimble movement, he extracted one of the sheets from inside the plastic sleeve, closed the binder, pushed it aside and put on his reading glasses.

"Okay then, we can move on." Michael said, breaking the awkward silence.

Matthiew waited impatiently for this moment.

After the lawyer's words, he straightened up stiffly in his chair and adjusted his ears. His leg stopped in place.

Nattaly sat quietly, watching the bouncing balls.

"As I said, this is the last will of Mr George Bradley..." saying this, the lawyer pointed to the document that lay in front of him... "As far as I am aware, George was going to make further amendments to it, but we will never know again what those amendments were to be, so I will now take you through the second version of George's original will." He added.

Matthiew felt confused and furrowed his brow in surprise.

The implication was that George had already changed his will once and apparently wanted to do it a third time.

The question remained, "Why did he want to do this?"

What possible reason could there be that he felt there was a need to rewrite the document a third time?

Only one thing was certain in the circumstances, George took this knowledge with him to the grave and it will never really be known what was on his mind at the time.

Also, Nattaly's attention wandered towards Micheal.

Hearing the lawyer's words, she looked away from "Newton spheres" and, together with Matthiew, looked closely at him.

"I can see your confusion, so I hasten to clarify, the will I have here before me now is final and legally binding, written a year ago by George in my presence in this office..." Michael pointed out. "...The first document was destroyed over four years ago, but the person Mr George Bradley appointed at the outset as first contact in the event of an emergency remained you, Mr Braddock...." The solicitor added, while driving his gaze straight into Matthiew.

"Although, this information alone was never changed, which is why I contacted you directly after my client's death..." the solicitor explained. "...These were the only original guidelines I was required to follow, because, as I mentioned earlier, everything else from the first transcript was rewritten..." He was circling around the subject, Nattaly and Matthiew waited for him to get to the point. "...I mention this because I suspect that this may have been the reason why Mr Bradley wanted to see me a third time..." He added seriously. "...As Mr Bradley's solicitor, I had no right to influence his will or to suggest that I think they may have omitted something in the writing of their own will..." Michael took a short pause to even out his breathing.

"...Nevertheless, I have a strong feeling that Mr Bradley recalled this shortcoming, and this was his purpose for the last meeting with me, which unfortunately did not take place anymore, that's all I wanted to add from myself." He finished, then corrected the glasses on his nose and lowered his gaze to the page.

At last, he's done screwing around. thought a nervous Matthiew.

Still, it might have been some form of consolation for Matthiew. Because it followed that George, after all, had thought of him to some extent in the past.

Even if he was eventually to change it.

Nattaly looked at Michael as he began to read.

I, George Bradley, born 5 January 1953, being of sound mental capacity declare as follows, in the event of my death, my entire estate and 60 per cent share of the value from the Bradley and Braddock Lettings housing agency, bequeathed to.... - Here Michael suspended his voice for a moment, furrowed his brow behind his glasses as if he had to think about something.

Matthiew barely restrained himself from rushing the lawyer.

"...To my wonderful daughter..." He mouthed at last. "...Nattaly Kemp, born 26 March 1986 in London. It is my last wish and my will that Nattaly, as my closest relative and only family member, should take over the management of my business from the day I formally hand over the title to her. My will legally become valid as soon as it is read, signed George Bradley." The lawyer added in conclusion.

...TIC...TIC...TIC...TIC....

There was a clatter of bouncing balls.

Michael took off his glasses and looked at Nattaly, who had gone a little pale.

He noticed that her eyes had widened, and she seemed to be having trouble closing her mouth as it was half open, making her look a bit fishlike.

Matthiew also turned his head towards her.

He couldn't say that he felt disappointed, although he had to admit to himself that he had been slightly hoping for a miracle to happen at the last moment.

"So, we have become partners." He said to Nattaly.

The woman took a moment to cool down and understand what had just happened.

Even though she had anticipated this turn of events, it was still a shock she was not fully prepared for.

"Congratulations Miss Kemp..." Michael spoke up. "...I have something else for you, but I have been advised to give it to you in private." He added, looking suggestively at Matthiew.

He was clearly giving him the impression that he would want to be alone with Nattaly in the office.

"But I don't know anything about running a housing agency." Nattaly, still slightly shaken, spoke up.

She was recovering slowly but had apparently missed the lawyer's last sentence.

"Don't worry, I'm on it, I'll help you." Matthiew said to her sympathetically. Nattaly looked at him closely and thought this was the third time that day she had seen him in a different role.

First, he pretended to be devastated at George's funeral, then he was indifferent and thick-skinned when he didn't help her, and now, he was trying to pretend to be concerned and eager to help. she summed up in her mind.

"What if, for example, I wanted to sell my shares?" Nattaly turned to Michael.

A cold shiver ran through Matthiew, hearing these words, he was completely surprised by the question, he had not expected it at all.

However, Michael calmly and slowly crossed his arms on the desk, leaning towards Nattaly, ready to answer.

"Of course, theoretically, you have the right to do this. However, I would advise you to think twice before making such a decision..." The lawyer began to speak in a calm tone.

"...The agency "Bradley and Braddock Lettings" or "BnBL" for short, is an extremely profitable and growing business, as of today the estimated value of the property and the rental interest in the flats and houses is almost five million pounds a year, forty per cent of this money belongs to Mr Matthiew Braddock because that is the amount of his shares, so in practice after the sale of his shares this would give an amount of almost three million pounds..." Michael continued.

Nattaly listened attentively and curiously while Matthiew was already guessing where the lawyer was going with this.

"...But that, mind you, would be a one-off sum and finding an interested buyer who would be prepared to pay three million pounds in cash on the spot to buy back the management of the agency, which, incidentally, is now in your hands, may not be so easy at all..." He took a short break and then continued. "...There are other housing agencies in the property market, and businessmen in this industry usually start their businesses with their closest associates, from scratch, as your father George Bradley did, while it is of course possible, I will tell you frankly, a potential sale could take a really long time, I do not even rule out years, given that recently there has been a significant drop in investment in the property market due to the housing crisis, this sector of the economy has slowed down considerably, at the moment it is impossible to predict when the recovery will take place, it may take several years, believe me, this will put you in a difficult situation if you decide to make such a move, the agency earns a certain amount of money at the end of each month, depending on the monthly income, which you can only receive as a current shareholder." He summarises exhaustively.

Nattaly thought hard about deciding, she believed it was best to do it here and now rather than postpone it.

On the one hand, she knew there was a huge sum of money at stake, which she would like to acquire, but was deterred by the prospect of not knowing how long she would have to wait for it, which effectively discouraged her. On the other hand, a fixed monthly income, quite possibly for the rest of her life or for as long as she held the title of owner of the 'BnBL' agency. Michael noticed how Nattaly was beating herself up with her thoughts. So, he decided it was the right time to speak to her alone at the same time as handing her the last thing he had for her from George.

"Excuse me, could you give us a moment alone?" he turned to Matthiew.

He reluctantly agreed to this request.

"Yes, of course." He replied.

He rose slowly from his seat and went out into the corridor.

Because the blinds were open, Matthiew stood next to the window and began to watch them discreetly.

He could see Michael, still sitting in his seat, moving his lips while saying something to Nattaly.

Unfortunately for him, the soundproof window effectively prevented spying, and he was unable to hear a word from where he was.

When he saw the lawyer get up from his chair, he quickly ducked behind the door, waited a few seconds and wanted to look inside again.

At that moment, he found that the blinds were already drawn.

"Damn it." He cursed under his breath angrily.

Even though he couldn't hear what they were talking about, he wanted to at least see what the lawyer was handing to Nattaly.

However, there was a small gap remained, between the window and the door, which the blind did not completely cover.

The view from it fell directly on Nattaly, who was sitting in her seat; the lawyer was on the side, not visible.

Matthiew saw Michael slide George's will over to Nattaly and point his finger at something.

"What are you showing her?" He muttered to himself and almost bawled his eyes out.

Curiosity was almost churning him up from the inside, especially as there was nothing, he could do to find out what this was all about.

He was getting angrier and angrier out of helplessness.

This was undoubtedly his weaker side - his lack of patience, which made him act like a spoilt child at times.

He hated it when something was kept from him, he absolutely wanted to know everything, and when he didn't get what he wanted, he became hysterical.

However, in this situation, he had to get his nerves under control. There was not the slightest chance that Nattaly or Michael would tell him what they had discussed in his absence.

All that remained was to accept the fact.

Nattaly rose from her seat and disappeared from Matthiew's sight. The man moved away from the door, thinking that at any moment, it would open, and they would both walk out into the corridor to him, but this did not happen.

He had to wait a few more minutes before he heard them approaching the door.

Then, with one swift step, he moved to the opposite side of the corridor to give the impression that he had been standing there the whole time. "Once again, thank you very much, sir." Nattaly said whilst leaving Michael's office.

"If you have any further questions, please do not hesitate to call, anytime."

Michael replied in a caring voice.

"Don't worry, I won't wake you up in the middle of the night." She joked. The lawyer laughed lightly.

"Of course."

Matthiew stood against the wall and listened to the conversation coming from the office, pretending to be indifferent, he wondered how to take things further.

"I will accompany you..." Michael suggested.

Then, all three of them moved slowly down the corridor towards the lift.
"... Mr Braddock..." Michael turned to Matthiew. "...Miss Nattaly and I have reached an agreement to continue working together, from now on, I will be representing her interests."

"Excellent, great decision." Matthiew replied.

"Yes, due to the complexity of my client's situation, I have agreed to assist in making important decisions in business matters..." said the lawyer. "...Which necessarily means that I will also have to stay in touch with you as well." He added.

Matthiew squirmed at the thought.

He was not happy about having to consult a lawyer on business matters. Nevertheless, he kept a stone face because in his mind, the game was just beginning, and it was up to him to make the next move, which was to present his point of view to Nattaly as soon as possible.

A lawyer could always be useful for something, especially when it came to covering up lawbreaking and loopholes in bending the law. he assumed.

However, at that moment, he did not think he would play a bigger role.

"By all means, no problem at all, it will be my pleasure ..." Matthiew replied.

"...I look forward to us working together." He added.

There was so little conviction in his last sentence that he didn't convince himself, let alone Michael or Nattaly.

Moments later, Nattaly and Matthiew said goodbye to Michael and then entered the lift.

When they were alone, Matthiew thought this was the perfect time to make his move.

Being alone with Nattaly, he needed to start putting his plan into action, with not much time to waste.

Knowing that Nattaly had decided to take over the management of the agency, he had to convince her to work directly with him behind the back of the lawyer, who was apparently going to become the point person for all aspects of the business.

Matthiew could not allow this to happen under any circumstances. A situation where Michael would make the final decision on Nattaly's behalf was unthinkable.

Everything depended on him being in constant contact with Nattaly, who was to be the backbone of his extremely risky but immediately even more profitable idea.

If a bureaucrat like Michael were to find out what Matthiew's intentions were, he could find himself in no small amount of trouble.

Matthiew still thought Nattaly had a similar personality to him, which made her perfect for the role she had been given to her and almost guaranteed success.

However, there were still a lot of questions he didn't know the answers to.

One of them was, 'does she still live in North Hill?'

Up until now, he had been one hundred per cent sure of this, but when Nattaly announced that she had moved out of the city, he experienced a huge shock and didn't know whether she was serious or just mocking him again.

It had to be the location because that was where the most money could potentially be made.

What was needed was someone who was from the area and knew the locals, as well as the entire city.

Matthiew's intuition told him that Nattaly wasn't telling the truth, so he decided to put his anxiety aside and focus on the most important thing he needed to do that day. Namely, entice Nattaly with the prospect of big money.

While the two of them were still locked in the lift, Nattaly had nowhere to go.

He started the conversation, fearing that once they were on the ground floor, Nattaly would go her own way, leaving him behind and thus not having a chance to mess with her head.

"So, I understand that you are not selling shares?" he rattled off.

"You heard what Michael said."

"Yes, and I think you're doing the right thing, the fact is, we don't earn a lot now and employees get an average of one thousand five hundred pounds a month paycheck, we as management mostly get up to two and a half, but it wavers." He said as if in an off hand manner.

He mentioned the amounts because he wanted to make her think about money.

This was enough, as Nattaly immediately started thinking about what she could do with an extra £2,500 a month, plus her standard income. However, Matthiew was just starting out and this was just the first seed he planted in her head.

Hence, not only did he want to make her imagine money, but he also wanted to awaken the deep-seated greed and lust for wealth that he believed is present in every human being.

"Since we are partners, I must acquaint you with a new prospect for our agency, an estimate of the success of this venture, which could triple our monthly earnings." He said calmly and composedly.

The lift stops and the metal doors opened wide.

That much time was enough for Nattaly to start thinking exactly as Matthiew had predicted.

"Of course, I'm listening, go on." She replied.

She was intrigued though she tried not to let it show.

However, Matthiew noticed a gleam in her eyes, a gleam that he knew very well and that was caused by only one thing in this world - the lust for money.

At that point he already knew he had her in his grasp, but he had to strike whilst the iron was hot.

"George and I were planning to open an office in North Hill..." he lied. "...Among other things, that's why I asked you earlier if you were still living there?

"George never mentioned it."

"Yes, it's a relatively new idea, George thought North Hill had huge investment potential, he probably would have told you if he'd had the opportunity..." – He replied. "...You see, it's not quite as Michael said, the fact is that the property industry is going through a huge downturn at the moment, but not uniformly across the country, our experts have found after detailed analysis that interest in buying flats and houses has remained constant in towns like North Hill. Many people are also interested in renting in the area and often ask the agency what we have available. This town is still a very attractive and popular place for people who want to start a family or find a quiet area to live in."

He paused for a moment before reaching for his ace up his sleeve. ...

"And it's not just UK nationals, I'm currently negotiating with people from

Africa, specifically Ethiopia, who are interested in a beautiful villa in North Hill that we own, located in the suburbs close to the city centre. I think the deal will be signed any day now."

Natalie felt her heart start to beat faster. She already knew exactly which house he was talking about, but she decided to keep her cool and calm.

"Why are you telling me about this now?"

"Well, we're partners, aren't we? I thought it should interest you..." he explained. "...Going back to that villa, we started talking about it over four years ago, about the same time we met, it's been a long time coming, these people couldn't make up their minds, they were wiggling and twiddling for a long time, luckily it turns out they didn't find any better offer and came back to me, determined." He added proudly.

"Congratulations, but I still don't know, what do you want me to tell you? You're the head of a housing agency now, you need to start getting used to conversations like this."

"Actually, I don't need to at all, Michael will be running my business, remember?" she replied.

"Indeed, but do you really want some bureaucrat locked in his world making decisions for you? Don't you think you should know everything first-hand? After all, it was George who handed over the running of the company to you and not him." Matthiew was pumping Nattaly's ego.

"Indeed."

"Yes, I'm telling you this because I think we should see the project through to the end and open a facility in North Hill, but right now, it's up to you to make the final decision on this."

Nattaly felt herself bursting with pride; the decision was hers make and everything rested in her hands.

She realised in an instant that she really liked this turn of events. The prospect of power tempted her like the smell of a freshly baked cake.

I can get used to this. she thought.

"Can I take you somewhere for coffee? There's one more thing I'd like to talk to you about." Matthiew asked as they left the building.

Nattaly looked at him arrogantly.

"Not now, I'm in a hurry." She replied.

Matthiew felt the blood start to boil inside him, and he got bumps on his face.

Nattaly's arrogance was driving him mad, but he had to keep his nerves in check.

It was like he had to deal with himself, because Nattaly had a similar personality to him.

This made Matthiew realise how others perceived him.

Nattaly was playing games, and he knew it well.

So, he decided that the best way to predict her next move was to think about how he would behave in the same situation.

The hook was thrown, and Nattaly grabbed it.

She pretends to be indifferent, but deep down, she knows she wants more money than a measly £2,500 a month, it's only a matter of time before she calls me to ask for further details, then we can get started. said Matthiew to himself.

They walked down the street, Nattaly looking around for a taxi, while Matthiew wondered how to get her to talk further.

"Do you need a lift somewhere, maybe, to the station?" he asked.

"No thanks, I'll find a lift in a minute." She replied.

"I really think we should talk some more." He tried again.

Nattaly waved to a black taxi driving down the street, which stopped beside her.

"Next time." She opined as she got in.

Matthiew gave up trying at that point.

Seeing her get into the car, he turned and started walking in the opposite direction.

Nattaly felt remorseful for her behaviour.

"I have your phone number..." he heard suddenly behind his back, when he turned, he saw Nattaly standing next to the car. "...I'll call you and we'll talk."

She added and disappeared inside.

The woman was tired of so many events that day she needed a rest and a moment of respite.

So many things suddenly popped into her head that she was unable to process any new thoughts or longer talk to Matthiew, who was bombarding her with information about the agency.

In her mentally and physically exhausted state, she was confused and did not know if she should even broach the subject with him or even tell him to call her, as the lawyer had clearly told her that she should consult him first before making any decision on the matter.

Nattaly rode in the taxi where, in the peace and quiet, her emotions slowly began to subside.

It was when she realised that Matthiew intrigued her in a way, but she still needed some time to get used to him.

Matthiew, on the other hand, got into his car fully satisfied.

In his mind, everything had been eighty per cent successful.

He knew perfectly well that the seed of curiosity had been planted in Nattaly's mind; the only thing left to do was to water it regularly until it finally sprouted, and Nattaly was ready to join him.

Completing this task was not a problem either, as she agreed to call him, and he already knew her phone number, planning to get in touch soon.

2

David Roberts.

'Yesterday does not belong to you. Tomorrow uncertain... Only today is yours.'

One year later,

29 April 2009, North Hill, Carolin Roberts' home, 07:10am

That morning, Carolin Roberts was getting ready to leave the house. She was starting her shift at the post office at eight o'clock and didn't want to be late.

She had inherited the single-family house she shared with her then 15-year-old son David from her parents.

Forty-five-year-old Carolin, at the time, was a single mother following a divorce.

Her marriage of several years to Patrick Roberts, David's biological father, finally ended a year ago.

The man abused alcohol, and neither David nor Carolin maintained any contact with him afterwards.

Immediately after the breakup, Carolin fell into severe depression, through which she met Dr Susan McKane.

For several long and extremely difficult months, the psychologist helped the woman to cope with her overwhelming emotions.

Like every weekday, Carolin had to drive her son to the local grammar school which he attended. From there, she would continue her way to the post office, that was located just four blocks away.

The morning shift traditionally ended at 5 pm.

David, on the other hand, usually returned from school, at around 4 pm. The teenage boy got around on public transport himself, so there was no need for someone to pick him up. He always got home safely.

In addition, David was a rather rambunctious young man, currently going through a rebellious period in his life and was not someone who would be easily persuaded by a stranger, therefore, Carolin was reassured about her son's safety.

Although no announcement had yet been made about the arrest of the people responsible for the disappearance of fourteen-year-old Magda Richardson, Carolin believed that it was only a matter of time, and, in fact, the threat had passed.

In her mind, everyone knew very well who was behind it.

Carolin believed that through the clues that had been provided to the police, it could even be considered that the perpetrators had been handed to law enforcement on a proverbial silver platter.

However, she believed that law enforcement agencies were so inept that they did not take advantage of this situation, and the culprits were released.

Nevertheless, Carolin was proud of herself for personally participating in the circumstances which led to the arrest of the suspects, even if it was only temporary.

She did this by unexpectedly coming into possession of information that she could later share with uniformed officers and close friends. At issue was a Voodoo doll that police later found in Joanna Richardson's home shortly after Magda went missing.

Consequently, the investigating officers had no choice but to visit the home of Ain and Angelina Hailu, the new residents of North Hill, succumbing to pressure from upset citizens.

According to the public, it couldn't have been a coincidence that the Hailu had moved there a mere six months before the incident and that they came from a continent that is the birthplace and practice of black magic.

At a certain point, it began to be widely believed that everything fitted together like a jigsaw, clearly identifying the suspects.

It was thought that there could be no mistake, and yet there was.

Coincidentally, Carolin had met the couple in person at the post office and had exchanged a few words with them, believing them to be nice people at the time.

But when tragedy struck, she immediately changed her feelings towards them.

She later regarded the newcomers as nothing more than horrible child kidnappers and remained so.

People exchanged thoughts with each other, and Carolin was in her element.

She watched with satisfaction as her friends listened with interest when she told them what she thought on the subject, and when they admitted she was right, she was bursting with pride.

She then felt almost like a detective who had single-handedly solved a difficult crime mystery.

Of course, she didn't yet know how wrong she was and had just stigmatised the innocent, who would later suffer through other people, for that very reason.

But Carolin had no bad intentions and really thought she was helping. She was a simple woman with a big mouth who liked to gossip and could do nothing about her nature.

As is usually the case with information passed from mouth to mouth, it spread like wildfire.

As soon as the claim that Magda Richardson had been allegedly kidnapped by the new residents was accepted, a publicity stunt against the innocent began.

Residents, mainly elderly people, called them kidnappers every time they met Mr and Mrs Hailu.

However, as time went on, the situation became much more dangerous for the young couple.

Then teenagers invaded their house at night, spray-painted offensive inscriptions on the walls and smashed the windows.

But the bitterness finally broke when Mr Ain's car was burnt down.

The couple then left town once and for all.

Carolin had heard about all the incidents, the harassment of these people. However, she did not feel sorry for them, thinking erroneously that they deserved all the evil that had befallen them.

If only she had known how wrong she was, things might have turned out differently.

However, there were no other suspects.

Unfortunately, it is human nature to point out someone who stands out and is clearly an outsider, which is usually, let's face it, very convenient. The residents needed to direct their anger at someone, and those innocent people were ideally suited for it.

People almost went crazy with joy when the news broke that the couple had been arrested.

Forgetting that this was because the police, who had been put up against a wall, wanted to calm the mood in the town.

It was even said that Mr Ain Hailu resisted arrest.

After this, residents breathed a sigh of relief and began to expect that any day now Magda would be found; this never happened.

The eyes of residents and the media turned to the hands of law enforcement.

From the very beginning, the case spread with a loud echo, which at one time even covered the whole country.

People followed the actions of the police with tension, catching every piece of, even unconfirmed, information.

The fate of fourteen-year-old Magda and her mother Joanna Richardson did not go unnoticed.

Shortly after the incident, a devastated Joanna returned to Poland to live with her family. She had previously undergone a nervous breakdown and was unable to bear the stress of the investigation and the uncertainty of her child's fate.

She had lost her husband and daughter and was left alone. That`s why there was no wonder why the woman did this.

No one said a word about her being indifferent or callous when she sold her house after leaving the hospital and left the country.

All in the space of two months.

People who still had the chance to meet her somewhere in the area said that the woman had a poor grip on reality.

She wandered around mindlessly, did not recognise people, did not recognise her surroundings, was always lost and could not sit in one position, still, for more than a couple of minutes.

She was in a terrible state, and there was concern that she might take her own life.

She was then assigned a nurse to visit Joanna at home every day and a psychologist to see once a week.

The only person who was able to strike up an occasional conversation with Joanna was her long-time friend and neighbour, Sandra Jones.

This person close to her was also of the opinion that she should live with her family for her own well-being.

When Joanna left the inpatient ward of the hospital, she began to visit Dr Susan McKane.

The psychologist then placed the victim under her care.

The media quickly sniffed out a potential source of information, but Susan never said anything to journalists about her patient's condition.

Visits were few and far between, however, as within a few weeks, Joan had signed a contract to sell the property, after which her brother came to collect her, and together, they flew to Poland.

The euphoria following the leaking of rumours that the suspects had been arrested quickly evaporated.

For the very next day, it emerged that the couple had been released from custody immediately after questioning.

An official statement released to the public by the police said that they had explained that there was no evidence, or even circumstantial possibilities, linking these people to the crime. Therefore, they could not press any charges.

It was then, the feeling of relief and the hope of finding Magda turned into rage, against the police and the stigmatised couple.

Residents felt that law enforcement had made an unforgivable mistake.

A few days later, articles openly questioning the competence of the local police began to appear in the newspapers, as well as photos of the African couple leaving the police station.

Journalists at the time waited tirelessly, hovering around the police station. When the time came to decide on the case, everyone wanted to get the best possible shot for their editor.

So, there was no way to avoid the photos that would later appear in the newspapers.

But this was not the kind of news the public wanted to read about at the time.

Although residents were disappointed by the decision, no one met Mr and Mrs Hailu ever again in North Hill.

Some people believed they had run away, others thought it was not surprising, and they would have done so too, in their place. Opinions were divided on the subject, whatever the truth was.

However, the fact was that these people disappeared from the city almost as quickly as they had appeared in it.

It was said that a few days after leaving the police station, they were seen leaving the newly opened housing agency "Bradley and Brad Lettings," where they had presumably sold their property.

One thing was certain, Mr and Mrs Hailu were gone, but the most important question remained, "Where is Magda Richardson?"

The police investigation had stalled, and no one had any idea what to do to move it forward.

Time spent combing the surrounding woods and meadows by law enforcement and volunteers, had also gone to waste.

Despite the tremendous efforts, put in by many people who took part at the time, nothing was found.

And now, the only suspects in the case have left.

But, as time went by, everyone got used to such a situation. Emotions slowly subsided until it was almost possible to think, that everything was as the incident had never happened.

Then, the vigilance of the inhabitants was put to sleep and a treacherous sense of security prevailed.

There were still only a few who referred to the subject.

However, the vast majority were happy that the town was calm again and life went on.

In the absence of new information from the police, the still-fresh wounds remained unhealed.

Carolin was also going about her daily routine - work, household chores, looking after David and so on.

She was in her upstairs bedroom, ready to leave, when her watch indicated 07:20 am.

She walked down the stairs to the ground floor and made her way to the kitchen, where David was sitting eating cornflakes for breakfast. She walked over to the countertop where the toaster stood, put a slice of bread in it and then pulled the handle down.

"What are you going to do after school today?" she asked her son, leaning her back against the countertop.

"Actually, nothing...." David replied. "... I'm going to come home and probably, play some video games on the console." He added, chewing his breakfast cereal in the process.

"I don't want you wandering around somewhere, do you understand...?" Carolin said. "... After school, you are to come home straight away." She added in a serious tone.

In truth, Carolin, at this point, did not assume that David could be in any danger.

But still, she wanted to be careful.

David was her only son, and she loved him very much, apart from him, she had no one else.

At the same time, she kept somewhere in the back of her mind the fact that those responsible for the disappearance of a fourteen-year-old girl might still be in town.

And David was only a year older than her.

The case was complicated by the fact that residents were not informed as to what the kidnappers' criteria might be and which people to be particularly wary of.

This was partly because it was assumed that this was just an isolated incident.

But for the most part, no one really knew what to expect.

Not to mention the people who really took Voodoo black magic seriously and warned about the curse.

There was no shortage of such people either.

Carolin chewed her buttered toast and sipped her tea, meanwhile gazing at her son as he sipped milk from the bowl.

When he had finished, he walked over to the sink, put the bowl in it and poured water over it, then pulled his phone out of his pocket. "Twenty-five past seven...." he said. "... We should get going."

"That's right, we're on our way, but first...." Carolin replied, drawing her son's attention to the bowl left in the sink.

He rolled his eyes irritably, then quickly rolled up his sleeves and rinsed it off.

Carolin smiled at him conciliatorily.

Good boy, go first. I'll join you soon.

David didn't need to be told twice. He immediately moved towards the front door and onto the car.

As a teenager, he loved sitting behind the wheel and pretending to drive. He couldn't wait to finally pass his driving licence so that he could have his own vehicle in the future.

By law, he had to wait until he was seventeen, but by then he had already saved all the money he could, to make is wish would come true.

He was proud of himself when, after counting his savings, he came up with £335 with pennies towards his dream car.

One step closer to the goal. He thought.

Carolin was also proud of her son for managing his money so well. At a time when other boys his age were spending their pocket money regularly, David was assiduously putting away every penny proving that he was a truly promising young man.

It was twenty-five past seven, and David was sitting behind the wheel of his mother's car, waiting for her, she, meanwhile, was putting her teacup down on the dryer.

Moments later, she moved towards the door, grabbing her handbag on the way.

When David saw her exit, he immediately moved to the passenger seat and fastened his seat belt.

Carolin walked slowly to the car, opened the door and settled herself in the driver's seat.

She started the engine, and moments later, they were on their way to North Hill town centre.

It was very close to their house, David's school and Carolin's work.

They were always able to get anywhere within twenty minutes, with no rush. Her watch showed 7:50 when Carolin parked the car outside David's middle school.

Immediately after stopping the vehicle, the boy began to hunch over, unbuckling his seatbelt to get out as quickly as possible.

At that point, Carolin turned her cheek towards him suggestively, letting him know that she wanted a kiss from her son.

Of course, David, being, after all, already a fifteen-year-old youth, thought he was far too big for that.

At the same time, he feared that he would embarrass himself in front of his friends, who would laugh at him if anyone noticed him giving his mother a kiss.

Carolin waited, not giving up.

David looked around quickly to see if any of his friends were watching and, in one swift movement, kissed his mother on the cheek. Then he grabbed the door handle and got out of the car.

Before rushing towards the school, he turned to Carolin and waved his hand in acknowledgement.

She responded to him in the same way, not yet knowing that this was the last moment she would see her son alive.

Carolin watched as David moved away towards the side of the building. As he disappeared amidst the rest of the crowded gathering of students, she suddenly felt a feeling of dread overwhelm her unexpectedly.

Her heart began to beat faster, her face blushed, and droplets of cold sweat appeared on her forehead.

At the same time, she felt as if her stomach immediately contracted and began to churn mercilessly.

She couldn't explain to herself why this had happened, but she understood that she had just had a panic attack.

For a brief moment, as she breathed deeply to calm her nerves, she felt like getting out of the car and running after David, getting him back in the car and driving away as fast as she could.

Something told her that this was what she should do.

A deep-seated maternal intuition was ringing alarm bells, knowing that she couldn't let David be left alone.

Carolin should protect him and watch over him, keep him close by her side, especially on this day. She ignored this, however.

Once she had calmed down, she thought it would be absurd to run after her son and make a laughingstock of herself.

Especially as she knew David would be furious with her, if she started calling him out in front of the school, among his friends and the rest of the children.

He would never forgive me for that. She concluded.

She continued to sit in the car, trying to collect her thoughts and finally get rid of this absurd feeling of unreasonable fear.

She waited a few minutes, then decided that she could drive on.

It was already 07:57 am, and she decided that she had to move immediately if she didn't want to be late for work.

The feeling of dread was slowly leaving her, and she felt much better.

However, one nagging question remained:

Why did I suddenly feel so overwhelmed? she wondered, but she could not come to a rational conclusion.

Therefore, she decided it was best to forget about all this irrational behaviour and not worry about it for the rest of the day.

She had a multi-hour shift at work ahead of her, and that was the only thing she needed to focus on.

When she arrived at the building that housed the local post office, the clock struck 8:00 am.

In addition to Carolin, there was another woman named Isabella on shift in the building, as well as four postmen and women who were just getting together to go out into the field with their parcels.

When she came in from the back of the changing room, she greeted all the people.

The staff were just putting on their orange uniforms with the "Royal Mail" logo, and Carolin also went to her locker, from which she pulled out a warm sweatshirt with the logo on it and put it on.

Carolin and her co-worker Isabelle's job was to deal with customers coming into the post office and, in the meantime, four postmen delivered letters and other types of parcels around the town.

The post office was small, and two people in the building were more than enough to handle the customer service efficiently.

For a medium-size town, four "Royal Mail" vans driving around the neighbourhoods were also sufficient.

Unluckily, that morning, an unusual number of parcels were due to be delivered.

In addition, one of the vans going to North Hill with extra items that had to be unloaded later had a delay due to an engine fault.

Therefore, it became obvious that, most likely, two postmen would have to make an extra run, which meant, staying longer at work.

Usually, it was easy to organise everything first thing in the morning, then collect the letters from the mailboxes so that the duties would be completed by 3pm.

However, that day, two of the four men had to work late, and it was up to them to decide to whom the dubious pleasure would fall.

For Carolin and Isabella, the working day started quietly.

The first hour after opening, the post office was empty, so they sat behind the window at the counter and sipped coffee, chatting about all sorts of topics.

Carolin enjoyed talking to her work colleague because the woman was very much like herself.

Just two years older than Carolin, 47-year-old Isabella Evans was a divorcee.

Like Carolin, she had a son, William, who was David's age, and they both went to the same school.

Both were single mothers who lived only with their sons in single-family homes.

What's more, Isabella loved to talk, and that's what Carolin liked most about her.

All this created an invisible bond between the women that made them feel very comfortable in each other's company.

Therefore, at one point in the conversation, Carolin decided to confide in her friend about a very strange feeling she had experienced earlier that day when she left her son at school.

"I don't know how to explain it, but..." she started uncertainly. "...When I dropped David off at school today, after he'd gone, and I was left alone in the car I could swear I had a panic attack."

"Are you serious? A panic attack?" Isabella was surprised.

"Yes, when he got out of the car, I felt the fear come over me, my hands started shaking, my heart was pounding like crazy, my stomach was churning, and I felt like I couldn't breathe." Carolin replied.

"Suddenly and for no reason? Is that very strange?" Isabella replied.

Apparently, she didn't know how to answer her friend.

"Well, yes, I've never felt like that before. It was the first time, but I'm more than sure it was a panic attack."

"Well, you know, people sometimes get overwhelmed by all sorts of spontaneous and strange feelings..." Isabella tried to explain Carolin's behaviour. "...But you're fine now?"

"Oh yes, I am now, it all lasted no more than half a minute."

"That's good, so there's no reason to worry about it." Said Isabella, smiling in a friendly way.

"You're probably right." Carolin replied, reciprocating her friend's smile.

At this point they both noticed the first customers entering the building.

The time for chatting was over and they had to get to work.

One of the first people to arrive at the post office that morning was Nattaly Swanson.

A young woman was pushing a trolley in front of her with a small child inside, on which lay a medium-sized brown box ready to be posted.

The woman lined up third.

Looking nervously around to the side, it was clear that she was impatiently waiting her turn.

Carolin remembered her well, from when the woman was still a teenager. But a lot had changed since then, and Carolin, looking at the woman with the pram on which the package was irresponsibly lying, did not recognise Nattaly's familiar face.

Nevertheless, she immediately thought that it was indecent to treat a pram as a means of transporting luggage.

However, she quickly ignored the sight, after all, this was not the strangest event she had witnessed since she had been working at the post office. Carolin remembered vividly a situation where a lady had brought in a microwave on a shopping trolley from a neighbouring Tesco store, wanted to post it, and moments later an upset manager appeared demanding the return of the property.

The woman smiled slightly under her breath, recalling this memory.

While Carolin was serving the first customer, Isabella was talking to the second person in line, so next up was Nattaly.

As Carolin, at the request of her customer, was picking up a parcel from the window for dispatch she heard a telephone coming from outside the window, so she looked in the direction where the music was coming from. That's when she saw a woman with a pram answering a mobile phone. Undoubtedly, there would have been nothing unusual about this and she probably wouldn't have even noticed it, if it weren't for the woman's strange behaviour during this activity.

Carolin's attention was drawn to the fact, that the woman was visibly panicked at that point.

She quickly pulled her phone out of her handbag and turned her back to everyone, as if she was afraid that someone would overhear her conversation.

The way she, surreptitiously, turned and looked towards Carolin and the cash registers also seemed suspicious.

She looked as if she was checking to see if anyone had inadvertently taken an interest in her.

Despite being extra careful, she didn't realise that Carolin had been surreptitiously watching her curiously the whole time.

The cashier knew every corner of the post office very well, so she performed her duties without taking her eyes off the interior of the room.

While also being out of sight of the customers.

This seemingly trivial situation made Carolin feel a little uncomfortable.

She didn't know what to think about it.

When the cashier had already collected the transaction fee and finally sent the customer away, Isabella was still busy at her window.

"Next please." She called out.

The woman, who had been looking at people impatiently a moment ago, now looked as if she was suddenly in no hurry and slowly approached her. When she stood in front of the window, she took the package off the trolley and placed it on the counter.

The box was so large that, placed in such a position, it covered half of the face of a not-too-tall woman.

Therefore, Carolin had to lean slightly from her seat to the right to get a good view of the person she would be talking to.

"Good afternoon, madam." Carolin said kindly.

"Good afternoon, Carolin." Nattaly replied.

Carolin furrowed her eyebrows in surprise.

Do we know each other? she thought.

She felt strange at this point, to say the least.

An unfamiliar woman, addressing her by name, like an old friend. *First the panic attack, and now this, this day is getting more and more bizarre.* She said to herself in her mind.

"Don't you remember me?" added Nattaly after she saw the cashier beating herself up with her thoughts.

After these words, Carolin's eyebrows furrowed even more and slowly slid down over her eyes, forming little crevices through which she could barely see.

She tried desperately to remember who she was.

Isabella walked behind Carolin's back, holding in her hands another package to send.

"I'm so sorry, ma'am, but I don't..." she paused when she suddenly heard behind her:

"Hi Nattaly." Isabella said.

Carolin opened her eyes wider, then turned her head towards the source of the voice.

"Hi Isabella, how are you?" Nattaly replied.

"Fine, thank you..." Isabella replied. "...Next delivery?"

Correct.

Carolin turned her gaze back to the woman, and then it dawned on her. A moment ago, she still didn't recognise the person, but now the memory had returned.

"Nattaly, Nattaly Swanson...?" she asked quietly.

Hearing this, Nattaly lowered her eyes from Isabella and kept them on Carolin, then, she smiled kindly at her.

"... Oh my gosh, I didn't recognise you at all, I`m sorry." Carolin added, slightly embarrassed.

That would explain why she was looking so strangely in my direction earlier. She thought.

"And I recognised you right away." Nattaly replied.

"You've changed so much, you've grown up, you haven't been with us for, what, three years?"

"Almost four..." Nattaly corrected her. "...I left to study in London shortly after my nineteenth birthday. I came back after this one was born here." She added jokingly, pointing to the pram.

Carolin got up from her seat so that she could look inside. Isabella also came closer to the window at the counter, trying to investigate the pram.

But they were both too far away to see Nattaly's baby.

Why didn't I see you with the baby before? Isabella wondered.

Carolin realised that the women had met at least a few times before.

However, Isabella had not mentioned anything to her about it.

"Have you been back long?" Carolin asked.

Well, it's been quite a while, almost nine months.

Hmmm... It's strange that I'm only just now meeting you. - Said Carolin more to herself than to anyone else.

I often go to London; my boyfriend runs a business there in which I'm a shareholder.

"It sounds great." Isabella said.

"What kind of business is it?" Carolin asked curiously.

"Automotive, but it'll take too long to explain..." Nattaly quickly cut off the conversation. "...I must send him this package today."

Both Carolin and Isabella knew that Nattaly didn't want to share any more information with them about it, so they decided not to insist. As they were alone in the post office at the time, Isabella and Carolin stepped out from behind the counter to take a closer look at Nattaly's baby. As Carolin looked into the trolley, she thought about Nattaly's words earlier about her boyfriend.

She felt offended by the fact, that the woman was unmarried and had an extramarital child.

Carolin had grown up in a traditional family, from which she had acquired old-fashioned values.

One of these was, precisely, the prohibition unmarried motherhood. It was an old-fashioned approach to life, but Carolin was instilled with such principles from childhood and over time, it became as natural to her as breathing.

However, she kept a stony face and refrained from making comments, keeping them to herself. At least, for the moment.

Isabella, on the other hand, was in heaven and immediately started smiling at the child.

She made silly faces and made strange sounds in the process, all to elicit some sort of reaction from the infant.

"Boy or girl?" Isabella asked.

"A boy, Yaqub." Replied Nattaly briefly.

"Oh yes..." Isabella replied. "...And how old is he now?"

"Ten months."

Nattaly's answers were short and cold, giving Carolin the impression that she was not at all happy about being a mother or even, quite the opposite. Looking at the expression on the woman's face as she looked at her child, Carolin thought there was something disturbing about her.

However, she also did not want to jump to conclusions, because she might as well be wrong after all, therefore she downplayed the thought. It was easier to do so, than to try to explain to herself the reason why Nattaly seemed uncomfortable in her role, as a mother.

The baby began to wriggle restlessly in the pram, then contorted its little face and wept loudly.

Carolin and Isabella looked at each other and then at Nattaly, who seemed to ignore the fact that the baby had started to cry.

The women felt uncomfortable, they were both mothers and had taken care of their own children in the past.

The first instinct they felt at that moment was to lift the infant out of the pram and cuddle, so that the toddler would calm down. However, Nattaly did not do so.

Instead, she left the baby alone and diverted by talking about the package she had brought.

"Please send this for me, by priority mail." She said.

"Of course." Carolin replied and went back behind the till to complete the formalities.

Isabella, meanwhile, stayed with Nattaly and rocked the baby's pram.

The ten-month-old continued to cry.

"You don't have to do that; he'll stop on his own in a minute." Nattaly spoke up, seeing Isabella trying to rock the baby.

"Please honey, it will be nine ninety." Carolin interjected from outside the window.

Nattaly smiled at her and placed a ten-pound note on the counter.

Thank you... - Nattaly said then quickly added. -... I need to go now. Carolin put the change from the note in front of her, but the woman did not pick it up.

Instead, she walked over to Isabella and took the handle of the pram from her with the crying baby inside.

"Thank you for your help."

"There you go, goodbye." Isabella replied.

"Goodbye." Carolin added.

"Have a good day, if I may say so." Said Nattaly for some reason, then moved towards the exit of the building.

At this sentence, Carolin felt a shiver run through her.

But Isabella did not notice anything strange about it.

As soon as Nattaly had left the room, Isabella headed behind the counter, to take her place at the window.

Meanwhile, Carolin stared with furrowed brows at the now-closed post office door.

Her mind was trying to clarify the meaning of Nattaly's strange farewell expression.

When Isabella returned to her seat, Carolin quickly approached her.

"What did she mean by that?" She asked her friend.

What are you talking about?

"Have a nice day, if I may say so..." Carolin repeated Nattaly's words. "...Why did she say that?"

"How do I know? Is it important? Maybe just, that's what she's used to saying..." Isabella replied. "...A strange habit or something." She added. Carolin wasn't convinced by this explanation and became concerned again.

The feeling of inexplicable fear returned.

It's been one of the strangest days Carolin has experienced in a long time, but it was about to get worse.

It's not even eleven o'clock yet, and I'm already heartily sick of it all. - She thought despairingly.

At the same time, she hoped that in the course of time everything would stabilise.

Unfortunately, this hope was to remain only in the world of the woman's unfulfilled wishes.

And the day, which had started so uninterestingly for Carolin, was to end in just a few hours in the most horrible way she could imagine.

The rest of the afternoon went on as normal.

A late delivery finally arrived, and Isabella went to the back room to help with the unloading, leaving Carolin alone for the time.

Customers came in and out, and the hands on the clock inexorably moved further forward.

Thanks to her constant duties, Carolin, absorbed in her work, stopped thinking about the awful morning she had experienced.

She also managed to forget the panic attack and the strange encounter with Nattaly Swanson.

It was almost 3 pm when three of the four postmen returned, carrying with them letters collected from all over the town for part of the morning and the rest of the afternoon.

The fourth was still in the field.

For one of them, however, as usual at this time, the working day was not yet over.

Because at the back of the post office, there were still a dozen or so parcels to be delivered.

Fortunately, there were not so many that two people had to take care of it. Theoretically, they could have just left them for the next day, but nobody wanted to postpone their duties.

And staying at work a couple of hours longer isn't the end of the world, after all.

While the men chatted amongst themselves to determine who would sort the rest of the stuff.

Carolin and Isabella were busy serving the next customers.

When everyone agreed on the one postman to stay, the others could now go home.

The two of them, on the other hand, went to the back through the shared cloakroom connected to the canteen and set about loading the car. Together, they loaded the new letters and began packing the parcels into one of the three delivery vehicles.

When they had tackled the loading, the second of the postmen went to change out of his work clothes.

The last one, on the other hand, decided to have a coffee before leaving.

To do this, he went to the canteen, carrying a small brown box in his hand. He set the kettle of water on and then headed towards the checkouts, to talk to Carolin.

He stood in the doorway at the end of the short aisle and waited for her to finish talking to the person she was currently serving.

When he saw the customer, who had been standing at the counter so far turn towards the door, he approached the woman.

"There is something for David." He announced, standing next to her.

Carolin turned slightly in her chair and looked at the box he had brought.

"Oh, he didn't say anything to me about ordering something."

"Do you want to hand it to him yourself...?" The man suggested. "...I thought I'd ask you before I left."

"Take it with you, David should be home before me." She replied, then reached out and took the box from the postman to look at it more closely.

She noticed that the small box was extremely light as if its contents weighed absolutely nothing.

Maybe some clothes? She guessed.

A trained eye also noticed the fact that there was no return address of the sender on the package.

There was only her home address and a few stamps, indicating that it had been sent from London.

"Well..." The postman collecting the parcel from Carolin said. "...I'll be on my way in a little while, if you change your mind, you can find me in the canteen. He added and headed towards the back room.

Carolin watched him disappear behind a door in the corridor.

She wondered what David might have ordered, without mentioning it to her.

That was the only question that came to Carolin's mind.

As they didn't know anyone in London or even have any family there, they had never received packages from the city before.

She figured she would find that out when she finally got home. Now, she still had two hours left at work, so she didn't want to bother herself with it.

"I can't handle anything else today, I feel mentally exhausted." She said to herself.

It was past 3 pm.

If it wasn't for the fact that there were still a hundred and twenty minutes left until the end of her shift, Carolin would gladly have gone home already. However, she couldn't do that because she didn't want to leave Isabella alone at work for that long.

So, she gritted her teeth and remained at her post.

From that moment on, it seemed to her that every minute that followed dragged on ad infinitum.

For two hours, a mere five customers came in, and the time continued to drag on terribly.

At four o'clock, the two remaining postmen returned.

One of them announced to Carolin that he had delivered a package to her son.

He also added that, indeed, David had been home to collect it himself, to which the woman reacted with joy.

Despite her fatigue, she could at least be reassured knowing that David was home safe and she would see him soon.

It was 5 pm when Carolin and Isabella closed the tills, the windows at the checkout and the back and front doors of the building, heading out into the street.

Initially, Carolin still assumed that she would go for a little shopping when she finished work.

But she gave up on those plans; she felt too tired for that.

At this point, all she wanted was to finally go home and rest.

She didn't even offer Isabella a lift, as she usually did, anything to save time.

Outside, she simply said goodbye to her friend and headed for her car. When she finally sat comfortably behind the wheel, she took a deep, relaxing breath.

"Jesus, what a terrible day." She said to herself.

She then started the car engine and carefully joined the traffic. The afternoon sun was still hanging high in the sky, and the weather was pleasant.

But all Carolin could think about was getting home as soon as possible and taking a nice refreshing bath.

As she drove out of the town centre, she glanced at the beautiful house that, until not long ago, had belonged to the locally hated, Mr and Mrs Hailu. The house had stood deserted for some months now, and at the entrance to the property, as recently as that morning, there was a prominent 'For Sale' sign from housing agency, Bradley and Brad Lettings. But now the notice was no longer there, which could mean that new owners had been found.

Not quite twenty minutes later, Carolin was arriving in front of her house. She turned slowly into the driveway and then parked the car in front of the garage.

While she was still inside and looking towards the front door, she noticed something hanging next to it.

From a distance, it looked like a basket, like those used at Easter. It was not an ordinary sight, as it was not how she remembered the porch leaving the house that day.

She hadn't hung anything there herself, and she was sure David hadn't either.

What kind of stupid joke is this. she thought irritably as she exited the car.

She walked closer, not taking her eyes off the unexpected decoration. It wasn't until she was within arm's reach of the

64

mysterious thing, to which she had given her full attention at that moment, that she noticed that the door to her house was slightly ajar.

Before she stepped inside, however, she reached her hand to the top frame of the door and pulled down a basket hanging on a small hook.

When she looked inside it, she froze in horror.

Her hands began to shake, her heart quickened, and the familiar churning in her stomach returned.

She stood still for several seconds, paralysed with fear, staring wide-eyed at the contents of the basket, breathing rapidly.

When she finally came to her senses, she threw it to the ground and took three steps back.

Then she turned on her heel and ran into the house, calling out to her son.

"DAVID!!!" Carolin's desperate scream replaced the hitherto quiet space.

As the basket hit the floor, blood gushed from inside.

But it wasn't until it fell to the side that the already rotting remains of the raven could be seen.

Wings, head, body and entrails.

Carolin ran up the stairs to the floor, all the while desperately calling out to her son.

"DAVID!!! DAVID WHERE ARE YOU!!!?"

In vain.

Exasperated and drowsy, she rushed into his room and saw that it was a mess.

But it wasn't a mess like after a fight with someone, more like the typical mess usually found in a teenager's room, who just doesn't like to clean. Carolin looked nervously around, there was a school backpack next to his bed, and the jacket he left home in that morning, was also lying around. This clearly indicated that he had been here before, which was also to be confirmed by the words of the postman, who clearly stated that David had received the parcel from him personally.

"DAVID!!!" Carolin shouted her son's name deep into the house.

No response.

Her heart was pounding, and she felt as if she was about to faint. Despite this, she consciously thought of phoning him, so she reached into her handbag.

As she chaotically searched through her handy purse for her mobile phone, her gaze was caught by a box lying next to the bed, not far from David's backpack.

It took her a few seconds to recognise. It was the same brown box she had seen earlier in the post office.

There was a flashback in Carolin's mind of the moment when she had spoken to the postman, and he had shown her this very package intended for David.

When she found the phone, she walked slowly over to pick up the package, at the same time she was dialling the number.

She took the box in her hand and sat down on the bed, at the same time putting the phone to her ear.

She heard the call confirmation tone in the receiver and also felt a slight vibration behind her back.

As she turned to her left and saw that it was David's phone, left on the bed. *He doesn't go anywhere without it.* She thought without disconnecting the call, the phone continued to vibrate.

Carolin then reached behind her to pull it out from under David's clothes.

As she did so, she noticed something else lying there.

Something that looked very different from the typical things David had in his room.

This item was unusual, and Carolin noticed it immediately because of the way it stood out.

She first picked up the phone, then the thing that was lying next to it, then pulled them together.

"Dear god." She whispered the moment she realised, what she had just held in her hand.

Then in her mind, images from the past popped up.

She saw pictures of Magda Richardson in the newspapers shortly after she went missing.

She recalled conversations about potential suspects.

Again, for a split second, she found herself among dozens of volunteers searching nearby areas for signs of the child.

Carolin already knew what the strange toy she had just found was. She also remembered, released to the public by the police, photographs showing almost the same doll, which at one time provided the only evidence in the investigation of the child's disappearance.

It was the same Voodoo doll that was allegedly planted by Mr and Mrs Hailu, on the fourth of November, two thousand and eight.

At the same time, that they were accused of practising black magic.

However, these people have long since left North Hill, so if not them, who is still doing it?

Carolin sat on David's bed and looked at the little puppet, and tears came to her eyes.

She was still defending herself against the thought, but it was slowly dawning on her what had just happened in her house. With trembling hands, she dialled the emergency number.

"God please, don't do this, please take me, please, don't hurt David."
She spoke quietly to herself.

She could feel her heart racing and slowly going out of her mind, descending into panicked madness as she waited for the call to be answered.

Sadly, there was nothing left to do but wait and pray for mercy for her son.

"What services to call." A friendly woman's voice rang out in the receiver. - Police, please." Carolin replied.

3

This is only the beginning.

"Two for now, though not yet one. From now on, one, though still two."

Six months earlier,

04 November 2008, London, Canary Wharf, London, "Bradley and Brad Lettings agency office", 16:50 pm.

Matthiew was in George's former office watching television.

It was approaching 5 pm, so he was waiting for the time to close the agency.

Not long after George's death, Matthiew moved into his office. At the same time, he put his existing room at the disposal of two newly hired managers, whom he took on in the very first week after George's funeral.

As soon as the staff returned to work at the agency, the changes, both in appearance and in the running of the business, began to be visible to the naked eye.

He turned the once elegant office where George Bradley had officiated for many years into his restroom.

On the wall, he had himself mounted a large plasma TV, to which he connected video games and a TV package.

In addition, where a chest of drawers with George's papers and books had previously stood, there was now a sizable bar with a variety of spirits. He also replaced the desk with a newer one, put in a comfortable leather sofa and got rid of all the things that might remind him of his former partner. At the time, the agency staff watched Matthiew desecrate the office, George's great memory, and resented him greatly for it; however, they could not alter the changes.

He was now their new boss, and he was setting his rules, the most important of which was rule number one – mind your own business.

Everyone knew that Matthiew never counted the opinion of other people, and certainly not that of his subordinates.

Therefore, there was not even the slightest point in trying to persuade him to respect the wishes of his late partner, who had respected their shared workplace so much and had always looked after his office.

They also resented him for sacking two estate agents, Andrew Harris and Ralph Williams.

They were the people with the most experience, had been with the agency the longest and were the most trusted by George.

And in their place, he brought in, Harry Green and Simon Edwards. They took on a management position, but everyone knew they were just Matthiew's friends.

Two new supervisors who, in the opinion of the other employees, did not in the least resemble serious managers or even someone fit for the job. It was doubted that they were competent people and even whether they had any idea of the housing industry at all to be suitable people fit for the position.

From the day Harry and Simon started working at the agency, most of the time they spent there was limited to just hanging out with Matthiew in his office.

Behind closed doors, loud laughter and chatter could be heard, clearly fuelled with alcohol.

Because of this, it soon became clear that Matthiew simply gave jobs to his drinking buddies to have company to party over during office hours.

But there were also occasions when they didn't come to the agency at all, and no one then knew when they would next turn up.

Such an atmosphere at work made the other employees feel irritated. Because, although their names were on the staff list, it was never really known whether they would come to the office that day.

In such situations, Matthiew also seemed to have no idea where his two managers were.

On many occasions, he had to smile weakly in front of the other employees, usually explaining – they are busy with the clients.

However, everyone understood he simply did not know where they were or when they would return.

Apparently, Harry Green and Simon Edwards were doing their jobs, but more importantly, they were doing them perfectly well.

Despite the transformation of the agency's structures, which at first may have seemed detrimental to the business, everything began to show that business was booming.

At the time, Matthiew mentioned putting together a budget in the finance department to the tune of eight hundred thousand pounds.

This was to be an investment in buying back the villa that had recently been sold by "BnBL" in North Hill for the sum of one million two hundred thousand.

The agency had made £200,000 on the deal, with the remaining £1 million going to the rightful owners of the property.

Matthiew now wanted to buy the villa back, investing £800,000.

This was an unprecedented situation, and the agents involved had difficulty understanding the circumstances in which someone would want to sell a house to the agency they had recently bought it from.

Especially when they were losing £400,000 in the process.

If one had thought about it more, it might have seemed a little suspicious.

However, no one felt like thinking about it.

It was recognised that Matthiew apparently knew what he was doing, while being very confident.

Which only reinforced the agents' belief that it wasn't worth the risk and questioning of his methods in running the agency.

That evening, Matthiew seemed to be in a particularly good mood

He was smiling more and even trying to joke with Lucy and Terry

The secretary and the estate agent, who happened to be doing their shift. It was strange behaviour even for him, and it was not entirely clear what could be the reason for it.

He might as well have been crazy or inebriated.

Whatever it was, deep down, the staff sincerely wished he would not behave like this.

Matthiew's jokes were rude and not funny at all to anyone but himself. Fortunately, it was nearing seven o'clock, and they were about to leave the place.

In the office, there was also quiet speculation about whether Matthiew was now the agency's proxy owner, but no one was quite sure.

Everyone knew that George would never put the management of the business in his hands, but at the same time, they had no idea to whom he might have handed over his shares in the agency.

And Matthiew, apparently, had no intention of informing them of anything.

Remaining in the dark, they had to work as they had worked before, but without asking any questions.

Everything pointed unequivocally to the fact that Matthiew was now the owner and, for their own good, it was better not to challenge it. As the two longest-serving employees found out, they were dismissed without a blink of an eye in the first week by their new boss.

The others had to get used to the new working atmosphere or look around for their next job.

Which some quietly did.

No one at the time was in a strong enough position to challenge Matthiew's authority, for whom it didn't matter which people were in his agency. He knew very well how easy it was to replace even a whole squad in one go with a new one, if that was what he wanted.

However, there was no reason to bother with that for now, Matthiew had more important things to do.

That day, he had received documents from Simon confirming the purchase of a vacant building in North Hill town centre, which was soon to become the new office for "Bradley and Brad Lettings". This was precisely the source of his earlier joy.

But Simon and Harry had another task to complete that day in North Hill, it was far more important to Matthiew, than the purchase of the new office premises.

In the matter of the new office, all that remained was to complete some paperwork so that he could achieve his dream goal.

And although he was doing this on behalf of the agency as an official representative, creating the appearance that he was the owner, he was still only a partner.

He had to come to terms with the fact that, despite everything, he was still just a person who played only a secondary role in the business.

But he no longer had any major problems with this.

It was then much easier for him to consult and make decisions with the new boss who had replaced George.

He wasn't able to implement his plans at a time when George always had authority over him and held back any ideas.

At one point, he even found that he was able to very quickly deceive and convince his new boss of his plans.

He knew at some point that he would most likely succeed, as he suspected this person was very much like himself, and it turns to be the truth. - Everyone softens up when the big money is involved. - He was coming to his senses.

He enjoyed it immensely, pretending to be a big fish and presenting himself as the owner of a housing agency while the real owner preferred to remain in the shadows, the same shadow in which Matthiew, for years, had occupied.

The reality hadn't changed, but seemingly everything was different, and that's what made him glad.

The plan laid out in his head for many years was just coming to fruition, and now, the second part of it was beginning, which had also been initiated thanks to Simon and Harry.

Less than a month after George's funeral.

Matthiew had established a close working relationship in realising his intentions with his new boss, who was then easily persuaded to open a new office in North Hill.

The exact same office that Matthiew had wanted to open for a long time but could never get permission from George, which on many occasions was the reason of arguments between the partners.

At the time, Matthiew was the one who had to step down and give in; he could never quite get the go-ahead.

Now, not only has he been given the green light to expand the agency's operations, but he has also gained a free hand as to how to acquire, new properties and clients.

The silent owner empowered Matthiew to make decisions in practising a method that, for most people with common sense and morals, would simply be unthinkable.

In essence, his ideas were extremely inhumane, and the details of them involved serious offences for which, in the eyes of the law, high sentences of imprisonment were possible.

Only people who were extremely greedy and spoiled would undertake the solutions Matthiew proposed in his plans. The risks could be high, the reward, even higher.

Matthiew was the kind of person who would stop at nothing in pursuit of wealth.

Fortunately for him, the new associates he managed to surround himself with were also unscrupulous when it came to big money.

So, that's exactly how things stood.

In the days when George still controlled Matthiew's inclinations, he knew that if he had even just mentioned his idea, George would have informed the police without hesitation.

Therefore, he held his tongue and waited until he was finally rid of him.

However, now all that was merely a thing of the past which he had put behind him.

Times had changed, and Matthiew was now fully absorbed, with a new reality and unscrupulous plans that he was consistently putting into practice.

His objectives included, first and foremost, realising the potential of North Hill, which had long been on the lips of most people interested in buying a property in a quiet and friendly location.

Homes were not only very attractive to potential buyers, but also relatively cheap compared to other cities in England.

Which made the likelihood of quick and profitable sales, several times greater.

According to Matthiew's calculations, this would quickly pay o and at the same time strengthen the agency's standing and his own.

These were just the initial steps for the coming months and the start of some serious business development.

In his mind, he was looking ahead a few more years from now.

The road to ultimate success from here was still long and bumpy. But then, when he had the right people in the right places, he knew that everything was on the right track.

There was Simon and Harry to do the dirty work for him and a boss who preferred to remain anonymous.

Nothing now stood in the way of him being able to control his puppets from behind his desk, dressed in an expensive suit.

Five o'clock arrived, and the secretary, Lucy, and the estate agent, Terry, began to get ready to leave.

Before they could leave work, however, they still had to inform Matthiew, who was then in his new office.

It was a new regulation at the agency, to report to the boss by the end of the day.

Previously, they had not had to do this.

But Matthiew had requested each employee to personally bring sales documents to his desk, before leaving the agency.

George had never required them to do this, even though the employees said they didn't mind bringing reports to him.

However, he himself preferred to collect documents from their desks on his own.

For some reason obvious only to himself, George felt this could be demeaning to the employees, so he didn't want them to feel exploited in any way, although it never even crossed anyone's mind.

But George was just that kind of person and people respected him a lot for that.

That was just one of the changes, in fact the least significant, that they saw in the new bosses' policy of running the agency.

While Matthiew sat with his feet up high on his desk watching the football game on TV.

At the same time, he had a profound disregard for the people who would quietly come in and put documents on the desk, next to his legs or wherever else a scrap of free space could be found, due to the prevailing mess.

Sometimes completely ignoring them in the process, he did not even look away from the TV screen.

It was also normal for Matthiew not to say goodbye to anyone at the end of their work, once everyone left the agency.

In his mind, this was unnecessary, and he didn't choose to do it at all.

He treated his employees like pawns on a chessboard.

He believed that they were only there because he paid them to serve him, which made him entitled to abuse them.

His ego, inflated to the limit, was becoming a reason for him to feel more important than the rest of the people he interacted with daily, and he had no intention of stooping to the level of a subordinate.

While George, treated everyone as equals, Matthiew walked around with his head held high proud as a peacock.

Therefore, his colleagues and those close to him, despised him and considered him as totally arrogant.

The clock showed 05:10pm.

Matthiew was left in the office completely alone.

Every now and then, glancing at his watch, he felt himself getting impatient. - It should be done by now, what could be taking them so long? - He wondered aloud.

He expected by now, he would know how the North Hill assignment which Harry and Simon had been assigned to begin at twelve o'clock in the afternoon, to be done already.

He could not quite count on punctuality on the part of his new managers or, indeed, try to rush them in any way.

Harry Green and Simon Edwards were great companions for parties and outings on the town, but beyond that, Matthiew couldn't know if they were up to such a difficult and risky task.

Simon was a 32-year-old man, tall and well-built, a handsome, brown-eyed grey-haired man.

A talkative person and possessing a gift for persuasion, he could find his way into any company inspiring confidence.

He was clearly distinguished by his character, which was also often very useful in the company in which he usually was.

Since from a young age, he did not see himself doing a regular job, Simon was involved in various side 'interests.

Starting with robbery, drugs and human trafficking.

Over time, his feisty nature as a young man of 22 earned him respect in the street hierarchy, where he cemented his position as the leader of a neighbourhood gang.

Then he was noticed by influential figures, of the criminal underworld, and joined the so-called 'big shots', thus starting business on an almost global scale.

At one time, he had dealings with representatives of the largest mafia organisations in the world.

He did business with Russians, Turks, Italians and even the Japanese Yakuza.

Unluckily for him, as is often the case in the life of someone leading such a lifestyle, Simon lost himself in sudden abundance.

He quickly began frittering away his money, saving nothing in the process. He became addicted to drugs and women, which, in the eyes of the mafia bosses, meant that he immediately lost all credibility and was cut off from 'business' interests.

Although this was the end of his adventure in the structures of organised crime, he still had many contacts with slightly less prominent criminals to whom he could always appeal.

Harry Green's character was quite different.

Less handsome and reticent, a year older than Simon, 33, of medium height with dark green eyes.

His hair was always cut short, making its dark blonde colour barely visible. Harry was the kind of person; you were better off having on your side when it came to a fight in a bar or on the street.

His menacing gaze, broad shoulders and athletic physique made him look like he was always ready for a fight.

An avid boxing fan, he began training in the sport at the age of thirteen. Showing great talent and an excellent right hook, his coaches in the amateur boxing league saw a great career ahead of him.

Unfortunately, like Simon, Harry was also interested in making as much money as quickly as possible, with as little effort.

Thanks to a friend, he had the opportunity to sample the life of rich gangsters, which soon became his obsession.

Training and a boxing career went by the wayside, and the parties, women, drugs, alcohol and life without boundaries began.

Not long after, Harry lost his fitness and carrying a penchant for psychoactive substances. There could not even be a question of returning to sport.

In the lives of both men, reality soon replaced the exuberant world view and both were living on benefits at the time.

Matthiew met them two years ago at a party.

Despite the considerable age difference, they became good mates and often went out on the town together.

Back then, Simon and Harry would often brag about their exploits when they were still members of a gang called the "Mali Boys."

It was because of this that Matthiew thought it would be good to have such people at his disposal.

As the agency's staff had guessed, neither of them had a clue about the real estate business.

But the staff were wrong about one fact, Matthiew had not hired them just to have company to drink alcohol in the office.

From his point of view, Harry and Simon were to be his soldiers.

People to do his dirty work.

They were to perform tasks with which he did not want direct contact.

However, he had to be sure that the job would get done.

Therefore, he decided that if he paid them well enough, those desperate enough would do whatever he ordered.

Then he would be able to safely sit in the comfort of his office and control everything from a distance.

It was past 05:15 pm and Matthiew was getting more and more nervous. This was only the first assignment, and he wanted to know that everything had gone as it should.

In his mind, there was not even room for making a mistake.

He had carefully buttoned everything up himself.

There was an exact time given, two destinations they should reach without any problems, and they also had pictures and the address of the destination.

At twelve o'clock he got the green light from his partner. When it was possible to start, he relayed this message immediately to Simon.

More minutes passed, and Matthiew tried to control his nervousness, while knowing that he could not call Simon himself.

He had to wait.

When at last, his mobile phone lying on his desk rang, Matthiew jumped to it in a split second.

He quickly glanced at the display, and when he saw the number signed 'Simon E' he answered.

"Talk to me."

"Sorry, Matt for being so late, we're on our way to London." Simon replied.

"How are things going?" Matthiew wanted to know.

"We'll talk on the spot, everything's sorted out, albeit there's been a little complication." Simon stated vaguely.

Matthiew breathed a sigh of relief; he knew that if Simon said so he wasn't to worry anymore.

Even if, things didn't go according to plan, the task was complete.

"You'll tell me about it when you get back, why didn't you call before?" there was no signal in the fucking forest, besides, it was better to wait anyway, until on the way back. - Simon replied. Matthiew thought that, in principle, he was right.

Indeed, it was better to hold o on any phone calls until the very end of the operation.

It could have been an extra precaution in case, the police were to trace their calls at some point.

"Well..." Matthiew said after a while. "...We'll talk when you get back."

Okay, I'll see you then. - Replied Simon and hung up.

Matthiew put the phone down on the desk and rested comfortably in his chair.

At last, he felt that all his nervousness had passed, and he could relax.

So, the first part is over. - He said to himself under his breath.

He sat in a comfortable position for a while longer.

Then he straightened up and reached for his phone, dialled a number with a few flicks of his finger and put it to his ear.

He did not have to wait long, because after just two rings he heard a voice in the receiver.

"Hello."

"It's done." Matthiew replied.

"Did they find the place?"

"They're on their way back." He replied without wanting to go into detail.

"What about the kid?"

"Don't think about it, it's not our concern anymore."

"Understood."

"Now, we need to make sure that all eyes are on these people from Ethiopia, and we need to spread suspicion, that they might be responsible for this." Matthiew said.

"Leave it to me I know the perfect person to do this, he will do it without even realising it."

"Great, in a couple of months the new office in North Hill should be open, and fully functional, then Simon and Harry will settle in there permanently and we'll have them in position if they're needed, so far, they're doing great. They've stayed at the hotel for a week and managed to get around under the guise of estate agents, they've seen to it that the premises are taken over for the new facility."

"You seem to be, very confident."

"Because I am, believe me, I have no doubt about that..." he replied. "... I must go; I'll get back to you with some new information." He added and hung up.

Matthiew not only had no doubt that it would work, but he was also convinced of it.

He could already see how the situation would unfold from now on in the city.

He imagined the horror that would soon befall the people of North Hill.

He knew, that as soon as people began to suspect the new inhabitants of Ethiopia of kidnapping the girl, and it turned out that black magic was also involved, the foolish citizens would be enraged.

He even expected that drastic scenes might ensue, but he cared little about that.

The only thing he cared about most at the time was taking over two houses.

First from, soon to be desperate, African millionaires, who would have no choice but to leave town.

Second from Joanna Richardson, mother of the child abducted that day.

Everything was made to look legal and as law-abiding as possible. And even, to some extent, like helping people who just happened to be in need.

The implementation of these guidelines was supposed to take no longer than a few months.

But this was only the beginning.

4

Nattaly`s secret.

'Those who have not experienced forgiveness themselves
are incapable of forgiving others.'

Four months later,

16 September 2008, North Hill, home of Nattaly Swanson's parents,
01:40pm.

Nattaly Swanson, aged twenty-two, was an intelligent young
woman.

A tall, brunette with long hair and a charming smile.

She was in her room at the time, preparing the next package to be
sent.

The fresh-faced mother had returned from London in mid-August to
the family home, along with her then six-week-old son Yaqub.

Shortly after, she began regularly sending packages to her baby's
father, who lived in the UK capital.

When asked by her parents about her private life, she claimed that
her baby's father had a business in London and she was part of his
team. This was to explain the constant contact and the sending of
parcels.

However, she did not want to reveal any details about either the
packages or the man she was sending them to.

This was the second parcel this month and the third overall since she had returned home.

Immediately after her return with her young child, during her first conversation with her parents, she explained to them that she had planned to become pregnant with the man she called her fiancé, and it was not a matter of chance.

However, her guardians did not give credence to these words.

It was hard for them to believe, because Nattaly was still very young and did not even have an engagement ring. Therefore, to older people to talk about a planned child and call a man their fiancé was absurd, and deeply immoral.

For these reasons, they simply did not believe her.

It also did not fit Nattaly's character, who had always valued freedom and did not at all resemble a woman ready to play the role of mother. Although her adoptive parents were disappointed that she had not completed the psychology degree for which she had left for the capital and that she had become pregnant in her second year in London, which ultimately forced her to return, they were glad that she had returned. To a certain extent, they were relieved that their daughter was with them, safe and healthy, even if they had unexpectedly become grandparents. They had no choice but to accept and love their grandchild, just as they had loved Nattaly when they adopted her almost twenty-two years ago. They also didn't mind that the child was light brown in skin colour, although they had no doubt that this would certainly cause a lot of gossip among some of the neighbours.

However, they feared that Nattaly would become a victim of derision, especially from older people.

They did not want her to be talked about behind her back or made fun of, just because the father was not there, and the baby had a different skin tone.

This is how it was in small and sort of backwoods towns, where practically everyone knows everyone.

As we know, everything can slowly be got used to, and after a while, the gossip will stop as people get used to it.

Nattaly's parents, however, preferred to spare her the unpleasantness, so after their daughter's return, when Nattaly had to go out somewhere, the infant mostly stayed at home with her grandparents.

It soon became apparent, however, their daughter was very happy with this turn of events, and soon found that she had many more things to do outside the home, than just going to the post office a few times a month. She started going out more and more often, and her trips lasted up to several hours a day, she would then say that she was working, and all this time was spent on business-related matters.

This was convincing enough, so her intentions were not questioned, especially as Nattaly's income seemed very decent.

She could afford practically everything, she dressed in expensive clothes and jewellery, the child also had many new clothes and toys, and she always had a fair amount of cash in her wallet.

Therefore, the grandparents were often forced to look after Nattaly's child, very often even for whole days, and yet they never refused her or objected to their daughter.

Natalie's adoptive father, Jamie Swanson, was a sixty-year-old retired physics teacher.

He and his wife Melissa Swanson, a fifty-eight-year-old nurse, led a quiet life in a nice house in the suburb of North Hill.

Nattaly could consider herself lucky to have parents like the Swansons.

As a child, she lacked nothing.

Jamie pampered his daughter, sparing not a single penny.

However, given that they were a wealthy family, they could afford such extravagance.

Money was never a priority for the Swansons, and this was partly the source of Nattaly's problems.

Many years later, Jamie, looking back, realised how badly he had raised his daughter, as Nattaly had grown into a woman who demanded too much from life.

There would be nothing wrong with that, of course, if it wasn't for the fact that Nattaly wanted to receive everything as a gift.

This was her attitude when she returned to her family, after her further education was no longer an option.

To put it mildly, Jamie and Melissa were concerned about their daughter's behaviour from the moment she moved in, her behaviour was very strange as well as mysterious.

She would leave abruptly for several hours during the day and often return late at night, sending parcels with unknown contents to London, and when she was home, she would lock herself in her room and talk quietly to someone on the phone constantly.

However, the worst thing about it all was that she gave the impression that she was not at all concerned about the fate of her child.

It was as if she had handed over responsibility for the child to her parents, whom she had literally saddled with the care of him to get rid of her troubles and regain her freedom.

The parents unfortunately did not know how they could refuse or what to do, to make her change her attitude.

Therefore, they meekly accepted the conditions she put to them and, without asking further questions, took them both under their roof and provided for them.

Apparently, almost three years in London has not changed her much... was Jamie's opinion. *...She's just as demanding as she was before she left, most likely this trait, character-wise, will never change.* he said to himself.

The only difference was that she no longer took money from Jamie or Melissa, as she did when she was growing up and going to school. Back then, she would demand they buy more and more expensive clothes for her, which sometimes she didn't even really need, or which her parents thought "were unnecessary" but nevertheless, they fulfilled their daughter's whims.

At least now, she had her own cash to support herself and the child.

At the time, it was impossible to determine, where the money that appeared in her account at the end of each month came from.

Although she claimed to be working and earning money, her parents did not see her doing any work other than going to the post office and driving for hours at a time, and it was unclear, what was the purpose of that. Nattaly did not consider it as her duty to tell her parents exactly what she did and how much she was paid for it; she had no intention of revealing this or even explaining anything more about her employment to anyone. The woman believed that nobody had the right to interfere in her personal life, even if it placed such a heavy responsibility on them as caring for her child.

Although Jamie and Melissa were now elderly, they quickly deduced that her daughter was earning suspiciously well.

This became obvious when they began to pay attention to how she spent her money and what she bought for herself, from exclusive perfumes to clothes from well-known brands to sophisticated and very elegant jewellery.

Without knowing anything else, they could only rejoice in their daughter's success and, although they had many questions, they were proud that Nattaly was doing so well.

In such circumstances, it was best to leave everything as it is and not to look for answers by force because, why fix something that isn`t broken?

01:55 pm

Nattaly, having total freedom, was able to do what worked best for her, which was, to talk to someone on the phone in her room.

Ten minutes later, she finished the conversation, then grabbed her pack from the bed and headed towards the stairs and then, to the living room, where her son was staying with her parents.

As she walked down the stairs, holding the package in her hands, her phone rang in her trouser pocket.

So, she stopped halfway, put the box next to her and sat down on the step. She pulled the phone out and answered it.

"Hello?"

Meanwhile in Canary Wharf, "BnBL" agency office.

Matthiew walked around his office with the phone to his ear.

He was accompanied by Harry and Simon, who were partly watching a football match on TV and partly, listening to his conversation.

"Yes, it's me…" said Matthiew.

"…Good news, everything's settled, there's a green light…" he added and took a pause, listening to the person on the other side of the phone.

"Yes, the last transfer has just been booked, the building is ours…. he continued the conversation.

"…In a couple of days, I'm sending a team, we'll start the renovation, I think by January we should be ready to start the business… he said. "…Yes, doing business with you is really a pleasure, thanks, I`ll talk to you later." He said and put the phone down.

Harry and Simon took their eyes off the TV and looked curiously at Matthiew, waiting to see what he would say.

"That's right, gentlemen..." he spoke to them. "...It appears that in a few months, you will be packing up your bags and moving to North Hill." The staff had been waiting for this information for some time, knowing that sooner or later it would happen.

Matthiew gave them the details of the plan early on, and they immediately agreed to take part.

Before that, there was still the question of when Nattaly would agree to Matthiew buying a building, where they could open another office. It took some time, but Matthiew knew, after the meeting with the lawyer, that she would eventually accept his proposal.

In addition, the strongest argument he was holding for just such a circumstance also worked in his favour.

Namely, a few days after the meeting in Michael's office, he called her and announced over the phone that he had sold the villa in the suburb of North Hill for one million two hundred thousand pounds.

Everything worked out perfectly and Nattaly quickly made a large sum of money, which left her wanting more from then on.

Just a few weeks after that conversation, Nattaly called him and gave him the agreement to find and purchase, premises in North Hill for the agency's new office.

The search took almost four months, but finally, a suitable space was found, the final payment was made, and now, preparations for the opening could begin.

This was another step towards the real goal of this venture.

Matthiew was proud of himself for getting this far and certainly had reason to be pleased.

02:02pm, North Hill.

Nattaly was sitting on the stairs and speaking into the phone in a halfhearted voice, in fear that someone in the household was listening to her conversation.

The young woman's parents were in the living room at the back of the house at the time, along with her son.

From this distance, they could not hear a single word she was saying. Even if they did hear something, they were not nosy, never spying or trying to find out who their daughter was talking to or what she was talking about, as they always respected her privacy. Despite this, Nattaly was particularly careful.

She was extremely anxious that nothing leaked out of her phone conversations.

Once she had finished, she put the phone back in her trouser pocket, picked up the pack and went downstairs, then headed to the living room.

"I'm going out for a bit; I need to go to the post office...." She announced. She showed the package to confirm her words.

"...I won't be back for a while." She added and turned on her heel towards the door.

There was no point in even asking what time she would be back, because even if she answered, her answer was usually nowhere near the truth. For example, when she said she would be back in an hour it usually meant two.

Therefore, Jamie and Melissa merely escorted their daughter away with their eyes as she disappeared behind the front door, leaving it without comment.

2:02pm, home of John and Susan McKane.

John was sitting at his piano, with several-month-old Nicole Denice lying next to him.

The infant was sleeping peacefully in her carrier and John was playing sleepy tunes for her, all the while watching through the glass garden door as Susan walked restlessly back and forth, holding the phone to her ear. To put it mildly, this seemed suspicious to him, because when her phone rang, she quickly took it out of her handbag and immediately moved towards the garden, where she answered it.

Clearly, she didn't want John to hear what she was talking about.

She had been behaving so suspiciously lately and John didn't know what to think about it.

Instead, he knew that Susan would never tell him directly, what was going on.

In such circumstances, she always said it was the patients calling her, but John was sure she was lying.

As time went on, John began to suspect Susan of having an a air, but he did not resent her for it.

He could not be angry with her, if she wanted to put her life back together.

The fact was that he was dying, and he was aware of it.

He was sad, though, because even if he was right and Susan met someone else, the least she could do was wait until he was gone, before she decided to have a new relationship.

John's only consolation in this whole situation was his daughter. The child was the apple of his eye, and he was overjoyed to spend his last moments in this world with his beloved daughter.

Moments later, Susan returned to the flat smiling; it was immediately apparent that she was in a good mood.

At this point John thought she had received some good news, as the satisfied expression on the woman's face did not disappear, it had been a long time since he had seen her so happy for any reason.

"Are you alright?" he chatted to her.

"Of course, Christopher Wilson called. He's inviting us to his son Oliver's birthday party. - She replied without thinking.

But John sensed that she was lying, but he had no intention of pursuing the subject.

There was no point in trying to get the truth out of her, as she hadn't shared any real information with him for a long time, keeping everything to herself. He was just slowly starting to get used to it.

02:07 pm, Jamie and Melissa Swanson's house.

Nattaly left the house and got into her car.

She put the package on the passenger seat, then opened the glove compartment and pulled out a brown envelope, thickly stuffed with something.

She preferred to hide the money she needed in for the day, and kept the rest in her room, also well hidden.

She opened the envelope to once again count the amount that was inside, to make sure everything matched up.

Quickly running her fingers over the fifty-pound notes she counted out the fifty thousand pounds before slipping it back in and placing it back into the glove compartment.

She started the car and carefully backed out into the street.

Moments later, she was on her way to North Hill town centre.

It was past 02:15pm as she drove along the main street surrounded by houses and greenery.

The weather that day was glorious; the sun was shining brightly from the early morning, and it was pleasantly warm.

As she approached the centre slowly, she passed a beautiful villa that had stood abandoned until recently.

She had always thought that no one could afford to buy this property, because it was too expensive.

However, after a while, she noticed a car parked in front of the house, as well as a man coming out of a large garage, holding a strobe in his hand.

It looked as if he wanted to wash his vehicle.

From a distance, she tried to see his face but could not recognise him. The only thing that stuck out in her mind about his appearance, was the man's skin colour, which was unusually dark.

Nattaly had never seen such a complexion before or since, even while living in London for several years.

She felt a little uncomfortable at the thought, so she quickly ignored it.

Once she was a few dozen metres from the entrance to the centre, she slowed down then turned into the street on the left, that led to the seaside harbour.

Although she had promised her parents before leaving, that she only intended to go to the post office, send a parcel and return home immediately, she had additional plans.

So instead of driving directly into town, she turned towards the small harbour where; after driving a few metres, she stopped the car in a car park, next to a popular restaurant serving mainly fresh fish.

She waited a moment, then pulled out her phone and dialled a number.

The person on the other end picked up after just the third beep.

"I'm here." Nattaly said.

"Génial..." A man's voice replied in French. "...Go where you always go, we'll be there in 15 minutes." He added.

Nattaly put the phone down, took an envelope out of the glove box and put it in her handbag, then got out of the car and set off for the pre-arranged place.

Overall, this was her third appointment in less than two months, but each time she was given different instructions as to the exact location, who she should expect and how to recognise him.

These were basic guidelines to prevent any setbacks.

The area had to be slightly different each time, but it always had to be close to the harbour.

The people who arrived there also changed, and the only constant in the operation remained Nattaly.

North Hill Harbour turned out to be the ideal location for this type of meeting, as it was between the city centre and its suburbs, both close and far from the crowds.

It was therefore safe to assume, that it would be the least suspicious. Nattaly knew the area like the back of her hand, as her stepfather Jamie used to take her fishing there every weekend when she was a child, and it was she who came up with the idea of using the harbour to her advantage. She would be the one to choose the location for the next meeting, then give it to her partner in London, who in turn would send the instructions on to the associates who would then turn up there.

She would then wait for a phone call, with the information regarding the date and time of the meeting, the amount of cash she needed to prepare for the day as well as, who to expect.

Now she had to hand over fifty thousand, but this also varied depending on the order placed, sometimes more or less.

She would then go to the post office, send the previously prepared package and that was pretty much the end of Nattaly's work for the day.

The confirmation of her earnings for participation, would arrive in the mail a few weeks later, also well disguised.

It was approaching 3pm when she reached her destination.

While there, she noticed a small yacht moored and the person she had just spoken to standing on the pier.

The man waved his hand to her as a sign, so she moved confidently towards him.

Once she was a few steps away, she put her hand in her purse and took out an envelope, so that when she came face to face with him, she could hand it to the stranger immediately.

Moments later, Nattaly was already returning to her vehicle, knowing that she would probably return to the same place a few days later, to pick up the order.

She did not wait for the man to count the money, because she knew that if he`ll found something missing, he would contact her partner from London. Even if she doubted very much that any errors would suddenly appear, for her own good she attached special importance to ensuring that everything was buttoned up, it was her duty.

There was no room for mistakes in this business and Nattaly was aware of this.

She also knew the consequences, if she had neglected her responsibilities.

On that day, Nattaly could consider that the first part of her job was over, all that remained was to go to the post office, send the parcel and that was all.

So, she left the man on the pier by the yacht and returned to the car. A few minutes later, she was reversing the vehicle to get back to the main street from where she could head into the centre of North Hill.

The most difficult and most adventurous task was complete, so she could then relax completely.

She put on her sunglasses, turned on the radio, opened the windows more and, breathing in the fresh air deeply, enjoyed the beautiful weather. Then she noticed one of the properties in the distance, and memories came back to her, it was the Richardson family home.

A few years ago, when Nattaly was still at school, once a week babysitting then nine-year-old Magda.

It was a great way, for her to get out of the house and earn some extra money, although she never complained about a lack of money. Nattaly remembered how much Magda enjoyed kicking a football and wondered, if she was now also running around the garden while the weather was so nice.

Back in the day, she and Magda had a bond, which could not be said of her relationship with Joanna, Magda's mother.

The women never got along, but Magda didn't want to stay with anyone else, and Joanna had to leave the house every now and then, so she agreed to these exceptions.

A neighbour, Sandra Jones, sometimes came to look after the child, but the older woman did not always feel able to do so.

For Nattaly, such a situation wasn't much of a problem; Joanna would come back, pay her and she would leave and that was the main purpose. Once she was close enough to get a better look at Richardson's garden, she was pleased to find that she was right, Magda was indeed there again, just as she had suspected.

However, the smile disappeared from her face when she noticed Joanna too, so she turned her gaze back to the road and pressed the accelerator harder.

Just another half hour at the post office and I'm off to do some shopping. She thought.

It was one of her favourite things to do; spending money around town. Now, she had even more free time to do it and, most importantly, cash, so she was spending it left and right.

The situation she found herself in suited her almost perfectly, so she never once considered that someone might suffer because of her actions. Thinking of others has never been her strong suit, and this time was no different.

Although it seemed harmless at first, these actions soon took an unexpected turn and had tragic consequences.

But for Nattaly and her partners this was not yet a problem, as it was easier to downplay the fact and live in ignorance, but everything can only last up to a certain point.

5

Termination of duty.

'If someone or something makes you think that you are already at the end, don't believe it! If you know the eternal

Love that created you, then you also know that within you dwells an immortal soul. There are different 'seasons' in life: if you feel that winter is approaching, I would like you to

know that it is not the last season, because the last season of your life will be spring'.

years later,

January 2019, London, Camberwell Green, Rachel and Danny Davis's flat, 4:30pm.

The day that I had deeply feared for a long time, had arrived.

I had been aware from the very beginning of my adventure with the police psychologist that I would most likely soon have to accept defeat and face the inevitable.

However, I was in no way able to prepare myself to receive the blow that was dealt to me so that I would not feel it so painfully.

When I was in therapy an hour ago, the psychologist said something that made me feel as if my whole world was falling apart around me. In my heart I expected him to ask me about it one day, but I lived with the secret hope that I could avoid it after all.

"Mr Davis..." he said to me in a calm tone. "...Have you considered taking early retirement? "

This sentence painfully spread through my head like an echo, recalling the last word repeatedly – retirement.

It was almost like a death sentence.

Until a few months ago I thought I was fearless and would be able to serve forever. How wrong I was.

The word 'retirement' always recalled images of my grandparents, old and ailing people, when I was still in the prime of my life.

At the same time, I was aware that such an image was not the definition of the word, but I could not resist the thought that this was how I understood being retired.

The moment my mind registered this phrase, I saw myself with a wrinkled face, grey hair and beard, sitting in a rocking chair, slippers on my feet and covered with a blanket, holding a cup of tea in one hand and the TV remote control in the other.

I don't know why my imagination decided to make a mockery of me at the time, yet such a rather stereotypical image seriously freaked me out, and I felt I would do everything in my power not to end up like that.

From that point on, I was no longer able to listen to the psychologist, who later told me something else, but I had the feeling that his words were reaching me from miles away.

From what I was able to grasp, I only understood a few isolated phrases that I couldn't put together into any meaningful sentence, so I nodded mindlessly, having no idea what he was saying to me.

Only later did I realise that he was arguing why he thought I was no longer fit for police service, as he was spouting the usual nonsense that accompanies such situations:

"It's for your own good…" Or also. "…It stems from concern for your health."

I understood my mental condition was not at its best.

I wasn't doing well at home either because Denise's presence was very active all the time and Rachel was experiencing it too.

I couldn't say that I got used to it, but certainly, in a way, it became normal. Above all, I stopped feeling the fear as it was in the beginning. It became a daily routine for me, just like visiting the toilet moments after waking up. Although the situation was far from stable, I seemed to have it under control.

Added to this was my problem with alcohol, which I was also trying to work on.

Despite all the circumstances, I wanted to believe that everything would still work out for me, and I would eventually return to police work. However, at this point I had no choice but to accept that my entire future career depended on this final psychologist's opinion.

What she would write in the report to my superiors was then based on my present and immediate future.

However, I could not harbour false hopes, because I knew perfectly well that a positive diagnosis in my case bordered on the miraculous and the chances of returning to work were virtually nil at that point.

The question he asked me was not out of his curiosity as to what I thought about it, it was a decision he had already made and was slowly starting to prepare me for.

At the time I was sure of only one thing - I could not imagine what life would be like, after leaving the service.

I wondered anxiously and intensely, "What would happen next? Will I be forced to stay at home?"

I sincerely doubted that I would find a job at the age of 52, being a retired police officer who had spent most of his life in a police car and could do nothing else, but deal with the bad guys.

What other job could bring me so much satisfaction?

Apart from police work, I had no other qualifications because nothing else interested me, and I didn't see myself as an employee of the Tesco supermarket chain, stacking products on the shop shelves.

Not that I saw anything demeaning in such a job, but I thought it might be a new job or a part-time occupation for younger people who were studying and getting by, but not for an old cop like me.

Private detective work was also out of the question, as I had always considered it an act of desperation on the part of outdated police officers, rather than a serious occupation.

Nonetheless, I knew I wasn't ready to be left without a job and, consequently, without any responsibilities during the day.

I was tormented by all these depressing visions.

I found it hard to accept that I would soon be unemployed, while Rachel pursued her career.

"And how am I going to tell her this?" the question nagged at me.

The very thought made me sick; it was a total embarrassment to me. But no matter how hard I tried to approach the problem, I always reached a point of no return, at least for that moment.

It was past 5 pm when I got home.

I decided not to put too much pressure on myself immediately and to wait a bit, to see how things would turn out.

At this point I thought my first task would be to somehow tell Rachel, who hadn't come home yet and didn't know anything about it.

I felt terribly depressed and found it very difficult to swallow the bitter taste of defeat.

Even as I sat comfortably on the sofa and sipped my favourite drink, vodka with orange juice, I couldn't shake the feeling of embarrassment. It crossed my mind at the time that I would most likely end up as an unemployed alcoholic.

I sincerely doubted that anything else could happen to make this day even more depressing.

That was until I found out that my colleagues at work, were already planning to throw me a farewell party, while suspecting me of leaving the service.

It was going to be a celebration of my defeat.

I was lucky that news doesn't spread around the office so quickly, so I didn't find out the same day, that is, on a day that I could confidently call one of the worst of my life.

It was almost 6pm and Rachel still wasn't there.

I was waiting for her and wondering how to tell her that I was basically out of a job.

There was no point in pretending that I`ll have one, because I knew very well that the chances of me returning to duty at that point were close to zero

So, it was best to just quickly come to terms with this thought and start planning what I would do next.

No matter how much it pained me to be defeated by my own psyche, which I thought was very strong, I felt very hurt that I had to suffer the consequences of something I could not overcome.

However, this was the final stage of my life as a police officer and with every passing moment that I thought about it, it became more and more obvious to me.

I have always considered myself a strong man who does not give up easily and always goes forward, overcoming the next obstacle, no matter what.

I sat on the sofa, sipping my drink, immersed in my own thoughts. I wondered, how it could be that there comes a point in everyone's life when they must raise the white flag and realise that they need help. No matter how strong a person consider himself to be, at any time in life a crisis can unexpectedly affect literally anyone, regardless of age or the role we play in public life.

The question then becomes, how we deal with these problems.

In the twenty years I have been a professional police officer, I have dealt with many people and observed their behaviour.

From drug addicts and alcoholics to drunk businessmen in posh cars. Over the years I have seen hundreds, if not thousands, of different unpleasant situations, on the streets and in homes, I have seen with my own eyes how people's failing morals plunge into even bigger problems.

Until I was shot and almost killed by one of these people.

That's when I thought that at some point in our existence we must go through some kind of breakdown and identity, as I did then, to come out as a completely new person.

Of course, I never expected (and I wholeheartedly believe that none of us really allow ourselves to think about it) that one day I would hit bottom and must face such a problem.

But when I found myself in such a situation, I had to overcome my fears. I told myself that the most important thing was, to try to let go of feelings of shame and not to be afraid to admit my weaknesses.

I kept repeating to myself that I was only human, trying to keep my spirits up and not let my conscience eat me alive.

I knew that these were only temporary troubles and, eventually, everything would work out somehow.

I was infinitely grateful for having Rachel in my life, someone I loved with all my heart. She always knew what advice to give and what words to use to make me feel better.

It was 6.30pm when I decided I needed to do something to ease my mind, until Rachel returned.

I could no longer sit on the sofa and do nothing, as I felt myself getting more and more apprehensive.

In situation like this, not even alcohol could calm my nerves.

There was one more thing I could do, which would allow me to concentrate on doing something, without thinking about other worries.

I decided that I would go and read my notes on the North Hill incidents, which I had collected on my computer in my spare time.

I had spent a lot of time on this and wanted to properly sort all the information I had.

I therefore divided them into four different folders.

Each contained separate details and descriptions of just one event, covering both my observations and articles I found on the Internet. For my own information, I wrote down separately the names of the victims, then the people associated with them, then noted the time and descriptions of the place and circumstances of the event, to which I then attached photographs.

All neatly organised in secret folders, of which Rachel had no idea, on my laptop screen.

I started doing this, which was almost at the very beginning of my adventure with paranormal phenomena and nightmares, that is, right after the incident in which I was shot.

Something was acting on me like a magnet that was drawing me by an invisible force to the mysterious events, that had taken place in North Hill over the past ten years.

I still didn't know what it could be, but I could be sure of one thing, it was more than simple curiosity.

Of course, I hadn't initiated Rachel into anything, and I thought it was best for both of us.

For some reason, that I couldn't understand myself, I wanted to keep it completely secret.

I didn't even confide in my best friend Connor about it, nor my psychologist. Without knowing why, I felt deeply that this issue only affected me personally, but I didn't feel the need to burden anyone close to me with it. Previously, as I read the same articles again and again, I noticed that the name of only one person appeared most often.

This was a psychologist, Susan McKane, who had dealt with and worked with the affected parents, both before and after the events, as well as assisting the police with the investigation. I noticed that the data on her changed over time.

For example, in 2008 she was described as a 22-year-old married woman with a several-month-old daughter, and two years later one can learn that she was a widow.

Newspapers wrote about her great courage and dedication to patients, as they went through the nightmare of losing loved ones.

Even though, she was a single mother herself, she took risks by meeting the victims, leaving her own daughter in the care of others.

At the time, this was considered exceptionally noble and heroic behaviour as journalists understood, especially the young children were particularly vulnerable, and clearly appreciated Susan McKane's attitude.

This name particularly caught my eye, all thanks to a female medium and last Christmas when I first heard the voice of John McKane.

As it later turned out, this man was Susan's husband until 4 November 2009, when he died of extensive lung cancer, orphaning a year-old daughter and making Susan a widow.

Of course, none of this even remotely explained, why he had tried to contact me or what might have connected the man who had died years ago, to Denise Randal.

Susan was repeatedly described as someone who, "Stands by those most in need, regardless of her own safety."

All this feedback also made me think of her as a wonderful woman if she was prepared to help others without failing in her own welfare. But there was another fact that was a common denominator and clearly stood out in the story, and that was the fact that after some time, the victims' families had left the town, selling their properties.

I wondered, why the parents of the missing children had not stayed behind to help the police find their children?

However, I had to consider that what might seem strange to me was a perfectly legitimate action to others.

I found only one article describing this phenomenon.

However, at the end of the summary it said that the police, having checked this information, had no more reason to pursue the subject.

One could, therefore guess that they did not see any suspicious activities in such a turn of events.

Such circumstances could also be explained by the fact that, during all these events, the victims experienced a serious psychological trauma, which later affected their logical thinking.

I could also believe, that during the times when the town was in turmoil, the inhabitants simply left the town out of fear for their own safety.

It was widely believed that single parents were the most at risk, but when the panic reached its peak, everyone felt threatened.

People were disappearing at different times, intervals and ages, so no one really knew what to expect.

From this, I could conclude that the threat level was still very high, and the lack of results from the police only added to the fear among the residents. Following this thought, I looked up what estate agencies were in North Hill and found only one called "BnBL" or "Bradley and Brad Lettings". Apart from general information such as a website with the address of the place, photos of the properties on offer, customer reviews and length of time in business, there was nothing of interest.

Basically, I just looked at the agency's official website and then closed the window without drawing any further conclusions.

However, I had a feeling that one day I would have to take a closer look at the real estate agents in this city, because a spark of intuition had gone o in my head, I had a hunch that something wasn't quite right.

At the time, however, I had too many problems of my own to deal with, which were effectively blocking me from thinking about something else, without overloading my system.

I read the same article for the umpteenth time in a row.

Each time I tried to catch things that might have somehow escaped my attention.

Then I heard the key sliding in the lock of the front door and immediately realised that Rachel was back.

When I glanced at my watch, I realised that it was already 07:20 pm. I quickly deactivated all open folders on my computer desktop, then closed it and got up from my chair.

Moments later Rachel entered the flat holding a shopping bag, I walked over to pick up the bags.

"Oh, thank you." She said in a tired voice.

"I'll carry it." I replied.

I headed for the kitchen with the heavy bag of shopping in hand, leaving Rachel in the corridor while she took off her coat.

I placed the items on the kitchen counter and after a moment Rachel joined me.

She came over and started taking out the products she had bought.

"I'm going to make pasta sauce for dinner." She said.

She stared into the inside of the bag, carefully pulling things out and placing them on the table.

We needed to have a serious conversation however I didn't want to start that topic right away.

I wanted to give her some time to relax, since she had just returned home, but Rachel initiated the conversation herself.

"How long have you been back from the psychologist?" She asked.

"Over an hour and a half ago." I answered honestly.

"Are you alright? You seem depressed. What did you talk about today?" she stared at me with a concerned gaze, she could see right through me.

We need to talk, but I'd rather put it off until later.

At this point Rachel stopped pulling out the shopping and focused all her attention on me.

"What do we need to talk about?" she replied.

"Come on, let's sit in the living room." I said.

I thought there was no point in delaying it any longer. After all it's not the end of the world, maybe partly mine, but generally, life goes on.

I headed for the living room first and heard Rachel's footsteps following me. Once there, I sat down in the single armchair, leaving room for Rachel, who was to join me in a moment, on the long sofa next to her.

I wanted to put some distance between us, so that she wouldn't sense from my breath that I had been drinking alcohol, before she got home. I tried to stay as far away from her as possible, although she would probably have noticed by then that I was up to something.

Once we were comfortably seated, I decided to get straight to the point, as I could see in my wife's eyes that this was exactly what she expected me to do.

"I'm not going back to the force..." I said.

Rachel just furrowed her brow in surprise, but she didn't answer anything to that, so I continued.

"...The psychologist asked me today if I had considered retiring." I explained.

From this you inferred that it is over?

Rachel knew what I meant, because she also expected it to happen, she just said it so I could continue the topic.

If the psychologist mentions it, it can only mean one thing, she has serious doubts about reinstating me, so the chances of her recommending to management in a report that I am fit to continue are basically nil.

111

Rachel was looking at me intensely.

She could well see how devastated and down I was at the thought of having to leave a job, I had been dedicated to for years and loved doing.

"And what are you going to do?" she asked.

"I don't know if I can do anything at all..." I replied. " ...If the final diagnosis says, unable to work, then it's game over." I added.

Then I saw something in Rachel's eyes that hadn't been there a moment before, and I immediately realised that she had some idea in her mind. For a moment, it might even have seemed that she already knew everything, before I told her about it, yet, at the same time, I was aware that this was not possible.

The expression on Rachel's face also implied sadness, in this situation. Nevertheless, I understood that she already had a plan for such an eventuality.

We have been married for almost twenty years and after such a long time I understand my wife without words, I recognise every expression on her face, I can easily determine what mood she is in. I noticed her gathering herself to reveal something to me.

"Okay..." she started. "...I didn't want to tell you this before, because I was hoping all along that there was still a chance for you to go back to work, but since you're saying now that it's not going to happen, I must tell you something...." she paused for a moment.

She didn't surprise me at all with this confession, because I knew her all too well and I knew that she was the kind of person, who always has a contingency plan prepared for every situation, and this was one of those cases.

I let the atmosphere of mystery remain and waited in silence, curious to see what she would tell me next.

"...I had been preparing for such an eventuality for several months, during which time I planned our budget." She said looking me straight in the eye.

"Budget? A budget for what?" I asked surprised.

"I think we should leave London." She explained.

"But how? We've lived in this city all our lives. What about your job? Yes, I know Danny, but I think it would be best if we lived in a smaller, quieter city, my job is not an obstacle to that, I will get good references and I can practise as a physiotherapist anywhere else, don't worry about that." She replied smiling slightly.

I was completely stunned at this point; I wasn't expecting this at all. I supposed Rachel had some kind of idea for what we could do next in our lives, but I didn't think she would want to leave our hometown.

"Are you sure about that?" I finally managed to croak out.

"Yes, I've thought about it for a long time, we can afford to buy a house, so I think it's a right time to start a quiet life away from all this chaos. - She replied, nodding towards the door to make it clear that she meant what was outside.

I think I need to think about it." I replied, but in my heart, I knew there was nothing to think about.

My life, such as it was, was basically over, so I guess, I just said that to give myself a moment to breathe.

"Think about it Danny, you've got time for that and I'm not going anywhere without you." She said, smiling flirtatiously at me.

I noticed that she wanted a hug and was expecting me to take that first step.

I would certainly have done so, if it wasn't for the fact that my breath stank of alcohol, and I didn't want her to smell it.

So instead of squatting down to her I just smiled, after which I got up from the sofa and went to the bathroom to brush my teeth.

On the way there, I thought there would be time to show my true feelings later.

No doubt she was a little disappointed, but well, I preferred that to her being angry with me for letting me drown my sorrows in vodka, again. As I walked into the bathroom, a question occurred to me that I hadn't thought of a moment ago.

I stuck my head out of the bathroom and called out:

"Do you have a specific city in mind?! Where would you like to move to?!"

"Actually, yes..." she replied. "...I like a town called North Hill." She added. When I heard it, the toothbrush fell out of my hand and into the sink. I felt a shock, as if someone had hit the top of my head with their fist as hard as they could, I froze in place for a moment, motionless.

From that moment, it was just like earlier at the psychologists. Rachel continued to talk, but from then on, I was unable to understand anything.

Memories of articles and pictures from North Hill, that I had read over the last few months popped into my mind, I could literally see them flashing before my eyes.

"Could it be that Rachel knows absolutely nothing about these events?" I asked myself.

"North Hill we will go to North Hill..." I repeated as if hypnotised.

I wasn't even entirely sure, if I was saying it out loud or just talking to myself in my mind.

Rachel, however, continued to speak so apparently, she must have heard my voice.

"I've seen the pictures, it's a beautiful place, you'll love it." She added. *Of course, the city itself is beautiful but that's not what worries me*. I thought.

I had seen a lot of pictures of the town, and I had no doubt that Rachel and I could spend our old age there happily.

However, what worried me was the history of events that I knew all too well. I can say without the slightest shame, that I was afraid to live there, and I had all the right reasons for that.

But it wasn't a fear of the unknown for my own safety, I was most worried about Rachel's welfare.

Despite everything, I still didn't want to tell her about the details of the town, which made my remorse more and more unbearable.

Then I put it all on the line, because for some unexplained reason I felt that I was the one who would get to the bottom of the 'Missing North Hill Four,' case.

My persistence was going to make me look death in the eye again soon. It's a good thing I didn't know that at the time, because I probably would have backed out.

"North Hill, we will go to North Hill." I repeated under my breath once again staring at my mirror image.

This time I was already trying to understand what had just happened.

6

The confusion.

'Evil is always the absence of some good that should be present in a being, it is a deficiency. It is never, however, a total absence of good'.

10 years earlier,

01 May 2009, North Hill, home of Mellisa and Jamie Swanson, 12:30am.

The news of their second child's disappearance hit North Hill residents like a hurricane.

Less than six months after the town was rocked by the news that 14-year-old Magda Richardson was missing, news broke that 15-year-old David Roberts had also disappeared from his family house in broad daylight. As in the first case, the police gave no specific information, just a brief announcement regarding ongoing investigations, followed by instructions for the parents with children, who had been told to 'take extra care' in keeping an eye on their kids.

It was also announced to the public that the police were currently working on both cases with redoubled force and that special law reinforcements had been called to the city.

However, it was difficult for residents to be satisfied with such a statement, as too many unanswered questions remained, and there was no indication of a sudden breakthrough in either case.

As in the case of Magda Richardson, who remained on the missing persons list, the police did not give any additional information about the progress of the investigation.

Therefore, no one knew if the police had any leads or clues as to where Magda might be.

Such a situation could easily be described as hopeless, as the helplessness of the investigators almost threw itself into the minds of the residents.

During the last six months after Magda's disappearance, as emotions slowly began to subside in the city, even though her whereabouts remained unknown, residents were once again shaken into terror fear and chaos, returned to the city.

It was 12:30 am when Melissa Swanson, Nattaly's adoptive mother, heard disturbingly loud screams coming from her daughter's room. Melissa was in the living room with Nattaly's son, Yaqub, at the time. Her husband Jamie had gone downtown to meet someone, leaving the ladies at home alone.

Nattaly was upstairs in her home, from where the sounds of an argument were coming.

Concerned, Melissa put the infant in the child's cot and then headed towards the stairs.

She climbed slowly and quietly to the first floor, where her daughter's room was, wanting to see what was causing the unpleasant noise. When she got upstairs, she saw that Nattaly's door was slightly ajar; through the crack left in the door, she managed to see her daughter nervously walking around the room and talking to someone on the phone. Although she had never overheard Nattaly's conversations or invaded her daughter's privacy in any way, this time, however, she was alarmed by her daughter's behaviour, so she decided to find out who she was arguing so terribly with on the phone.

To do so, she stood against the wall next to the door and listened discreetly. Nattaly was furious, she was walking back and forth in an exasperated manner apparently, unable to control herself.

"I don't care!!" she shouted suddenly so loudly that Melissa twitched slightly.

"Do you know what's going on here right now? The police are all over the place because of these disappearances...!" she said after a moment and paused again.

"...Yes, I know we have a deal in progress, and I will finish it! But we must wait a bit now and I don't care, the police are checking cars, I'm not going to be arrested thanks to you!!" she said.

Melissa furrowed her brow; she was then even more worried than she had been a few minutes earlier.

She had no idea, what her daughter was talking about, but it sounded very serious.

"I've already told you; I don't care, they must leave first! You know perfectly well that if I get arrested, we're going to be in a lot of trouble and it's all, because of these kidnappings." Nattaly added and fell silent, listening to the voice on the other side.

Melissa wondered intensely, what was her daughter talking about? *Why was she talking about kidnappings? After all, the police had never confirmed it, it's true that it's anyone's guess, but why is it so obvious to her? Does she know anything about it? Why is she afraid of being arrested? Is it possible that she has something to do with all this? No, that's not true, I know my daughter and I know she wouldn't be capable of that.* she thought to herself, while shaking her head in denial.

"Money is the least of our problems now, don't you understand? We must wait until this all settles down a bit..." Nattaly continued the argument. "...Tell your people to leave North Hill for a while and not to come back, until all the commotion has calmed down..." she added and paused. "...I don't know how long, probably a few months at least." She opined." ...It doesn't matter, I'm not going to see anyone now, I'm not going to put myself in jail because of your greed..." she added.

"...Remember, if I get caught, I'll tell them straight away that you're behind all this, I'm not going to jail alone, so think carefully about what you want to do next...." she said in a serious yet calm tone of voice.

"...First, we'll wait a few weeks and see how it goes, a couple of months at most and we can start again... " she added after a while. "...Okay, bye." She said in conclusion and hung up then hurled the phone against the bed.

"FUCK!!!" she shouted angrily.

When Melissa heard her daughter just finish talking on the phone, she moved quickly but quietly towards the stairs, then further down and straight into the living room, so that Nattaly wouldn't realise that her mother had heard almost all her conversation.

She sat down on the sofa next to Nattaly's son, who by this time was gleefully throwing plush toys.

The woman thought that she had to act like she didn't know anything. Melissa would never get Nattaly into any trouble; she loved her daughter very much, and always stood behind her like a wall.

Even when, she caused problems at school as a teenager, she always stood up for the child she thought of as hers.

Moments later, she heard Nattaly's footsteps on the stairs, coming downstairs.

When she entered the living room, where Melissa and the child were waiting for her, the woman observed her daughter's behaviour with a studied eye; she noticed that she still looked very upset and shaken. Nattaly, however, had no intention of staying at home with her family, she just took her car keys and announced that she had to leave for a while.

"Where are you going?" Melissa asked.

"I want to get some fresh air; I'll be right back."

"Wouldn't you rather stay with the little one? Look, how nicely he's playing." Nattaly only cast an indifferent glance at her son, who was still happily turning over the toys in his cot.

At that moment, Melissa saw something strange in Nattaly's eyes that disturbed her greatly, namely that she could not see in them the feeling of love that a mother should feel for her child.

Nattaly's face remained unnaturally indifferent as she looked at her baby, and the feeling of coldness that emanated from the woman could almost be felt on one's own skin if one stood close to her.

Melissa was frightened by this sight and a shiver ran through her body. She thought then, her daughter was in serious trouble, and not just because of what she had just discussed on the phone.

She assumed that Nattaly also held an unexplained grudge against her son, who was only 10 months old at the time, and needed his mother's love. It became obvious to her that this affection for the child was missing in Nattaly's heart.

Nattaly immediately turned her back on them without a word and headed for the exit, then slammed the door behind her, leaving the house. Melissa looked at the child with sad eyes, while he continued to play, oblivious to anything.

"You are so innocent and vulnerable; you deserve to be loved." She said, but the child as children are accustomed to do, did not even pay attention to her.

On this day the woman realised, that she would have to be the one to replace his mother, because she sincerely doubted that Nattaly's behaviour towards the child, would change and could even assume that it might even get worse, with time.

If that wasn't enough, everything also pointed to the fact that Nattaly was involved in some illegal and dangerous business, that might soon lead to her being arrested.

"Don't worry, dear, your grandmother will take care of you." She added smiling at the child.

Ten minutes earlier, the headquarters of the agency "BnBL" Canary Wharf,

London

Matthiew was walking around his office, arguing with someone on the phone.

The door to his room was locked, yet the secretary and the two estate agents, who happened to be at work that day, could clearly hear that their boss's conversation was not one of the calmest or most pleasant. "Well, be that as it may Nattaly, my boys have been out of sight for a long time now, but if you insist, I will tell them to leave town altogether and hole up somewhere until everything dies down, just like they did the first time!" he said and paused.

"...Okay, just take it easy, no one will arrest you, and you don't have to worry about anything, everything is under control...!" he continued the conversation.

"...Yes, I know perfectly well what kind of problems we could have, don't worry, don't talk so loud about kidnappings, are you crazy!? Do you want someone to hear you...?!" he said nervously.

Matthiew was lecturing the caller, not realising that he himself was just making the same mistake.

Because the people at the agency could have heard bits and pieces of his conversation at the time, and if they had decided to check what their boss was talking about and then put the facts together, the whole game would have ended for him at that very moment, and he would have ended up in prison for many years, probably coming out of it as an old man or not at all. Matthiew however, was, as usual, luckier than he was wiser, so in this situation he managed to ignore the problem, because the staff didn't hear enough to make them suspicious.

"Okay, I agree, keep an eye on this Carolin, make sure she never wants to come back to this house again, I'm slowly starting to prepare an offer for her, we need to be sure she will be as mentally exhausted as her predecessor...." He continued the conversation. "...Yes, calm down, we'll buy this house and then we'll take a break, yes, others will come forward, I have a way to do it without worrying...." he added pausing every now and then. to give the caller a chance to respond.

"...Yes, to hear from you soon." He ended the conversation and took a deep breath.

The man expected that there would be moments, when nervousness mixed with fear would accumulate, leading to nervous conversations on the subject.

In fact, his method was simple - strike then retreat into the shadows of events and wait for the blow, inflicted discreetly and from a safe distance, to have the desired effect, in the meantime fuelling panic and fear among the locals.

The last task, for the most part, was to be performed by Nattaly, who had the most favourable circumstances for this.

However, patience and mental resilience to stress were key.

By far, the most emotionally unstable was Nattaly, who sometimes became hysterical when she called his office.

Nevertheless, he realised how much she must have feared and experienced the whole situation, so he did not hold it against her. In his mind, the whole organisation was well coordinated, but at the same time he knew how risky it was, so it was his job to keep everything under control.

Mainly for this reason, he had to be sure that he could put Nattaly at ease. It was very important that she finally got used to overcoming her own fear, so that, with her nerves under control, she could focus on completing the final stage of the whole operation.

Her part had to be executed perfectly, if the entire plan was to have any chance of success and financial benefit.

Matthiew believed that she had performed perfectly the first time around, so he knew that she was able to carry the burden of responsibility and, in time, even forget about it completely.

He thought that in time, this would become completely normal for her, no matter how far out of the norm it really was.

The most important thing that gave Matthiew peace of mind, was that his mercenaries were professionals in their field and left no traces at the scene of the crime.

And most importantly, they would never make any deals with law enforcement, even if they were cornered.

So, it was virtually impossible for the police to get on their trail at this point. As a result, there was no way to somehow find clues that could lead them to Matthiew and Nattaly, who stood far in the shadows of the criminal operation.

Matthiew felt completely safe in the knowledge that the investigators would first have to arrest his mercenaries, which at the time (according to Matthiew's assumptions) was still light years away.

And even if that happened one day, there was no guarantee that Matthiew's employees would incriminate him with their testimony, as they were both hardened criminals and had never cooperated voluntarily with the police.

But the calmest of them all should have just been Nattaly, who no one in the agency knew about except Matthiew, and whose name was never officially revealed, even though she was now the boss, she remained completely anonymous.

Matthiew, who continued to play second fiddle and was the brains behind the whole operation, assumed from the outset that this was the way it had to be, when doing this kind of business.

It was extremely important to take a break of several months or even a year, to avoid getting caught.

There was no discussion or even the slightest doubt about it.

Anyone involved in such a dangerous game, must be particularly careful and not let emotions take over.

Once you have the emotions that are tearing you apart under control, you can continue calmly, which is how it had to be in the situation that was arising.

Although neither Matthiew nor Nattaly, officially and directly, had anything to do with the criminal activity, if they had been arrested, their complicity would have been 100 per cent and easy to prove.

Investigators would then have had no problems, and they would very quickly have faced serious charges, which would have guaranteed spending many years in prison.

Matthiew sat comfortably in front of his desk, waited a moment and then pulled out his phone.

He dialled a number and put the receiver to his ear, waiting for the call to connect.

After a few beeps, Simon, one of the two managers he employed, answered. "How is the situation?" he asked as soon as he heard Simon answer the phone.

"It's fine…" the man replied. "…The police are snooping around but they won't find anything, people are going crazy as before, nothing new." He added indifferently. "What about the kid?"

"What do you mean, what about the kid? Don't ask stupid questions, when you know the answer!"

"Well, right, I shouldn't ask..." Matthiew reprimanded himself. "…The boss is freaking out..." Matthiew said after a while. "...You and Harry need to get out of town, later tonight."

"We're staying away, send someone tomorrow to run the agency in our place, like last time."

"We've already got two people going to you, you can take it easy and go back to London, just keep your heads down until then."

"Don't you fucking tell me what to do! You know I can fuck you up, just as easily as these muppets, and I don't give a fuck if you pay me." Simon got angry.

"Alright, calm down, I'll talk to you later." Added Matthiew and ended the call, putting the phone back on the desk and straightening up in his chair. He sat for a moment, staring aimlessly ahead, immersed in his own thoughts.

He understood Simon and Harry, whom he had sent to North Hill as soon as the office opened to oversee business and carry out orders pre-arranged between him and Nattaly, were very dangerous people, long-standing members of an East London gang.

In fact, that was the main reason he employed them in the agency at the time, because he needed people who would not back down and do his dirty work for him, without hesitation.

Simon was the brains behind the duo, with Harry acting as the muscle.

When, in George's lifetime, Matthiew was still a supporting figure with no clear authority in the agency, he spent most of his free time with the two on alcoholic binges.

On more than one occasion, he had the opportunity to see with his own eyes, what these people were capable of.

At the time, he was impressed by the widespread fear and respect that Harry and Simon inspired by their very presence wherever they went, which is why he wanted so badly to be one of them.

Although, they didn't talk about it openly, Matthiew knew that they had also been involved in murders that at one time became notorious in the London, for which they had never been arrested.

The truth is that in the past, they had served sentences for lesser offences such as drug dealing and even illegal possession of firearms. But since then, they have changed a lot and have become extremely cautious, learning from their past mistakes, so as never to be caught again. Their new employer saw these qualities in Harry and Simon, appreciated them most in his new subordinates and felt that they were ideally suited, to the job he was assigning to them.

The only person who stood out from the trio was Nattaly, who at the time still had mixed feelings about the whole situation and was sometimes plagued by remorse, which was later reflected in Matthiew's phone calls.

However, she also saw that the plan had started to work from the beginning, just as he had guaranteed.

She then realised that the agency had begun to take a sizeable toll in terms of clients, cash and new properties for sale or rent.

Matthiew knew that eventually even she would reach a point in her life, when the only important thing she would care about the most, would become counting money and planning her next steps to get as much of it as possible.

Then the remnants of high morals or remorse will fade into the background, until they eventually disappear completely.

However, in the current rather unstable situation, he had to be sure, that nothing new would emerge that could ruin the whole operation.

Therefore, he shared Nattaly's opinion that it would not be wise for Simon and Harry to stay longer in a town where there was so much chaos at the time.

It was certain that, as in the case of Magda Richardson, in addition to the police ordinary citizens would also be involved in the search for David Roberts.

So, from that point on, for the next few weeks, it would be most dangerous for them, as people in the troubled town would be keeping a close eye on others, especially those they did not know very well.

At the time, Simon and Harry were still relatively new figures in the area, although they appeared in public often enough to slowly become recognisable among the residents, and people were getting used to them, there was no doubt that they could easily become the centre of attention. Admittedly, this did not happen after the disappearance of Magda Richardson six months ago, but people learn quickly, so in this present situation it was possible that it would be very different.

The risk was high, even though the whereabouts of the missing people were only known to three people: Nattaly, who had chosen and pinpointed the location, which was also an isolated place from her childhood where Nattaly's father used to take her fishing.

Apart from them, no one else knew about the area.

Matthiew, on the other hand, had never been to North Hill, so in this respect his hands were clean, as he handled all matters to get the business up and running including buying premises for the new office, dealing with the paperwork safely, from his office in London.

There he would also receive new, potentially interested clients and deal with the rest of the business by phone or online.

He did not want to appear in person in the town yet, but he also did not rule out, going there one day.

Besides, he had his own people who were his eyes and hands for the job, so he didn't feel the need to go there.

There was no doubt, that business was going better than ever before. The only thing that remained was the question of security under the circumstances.

At the time, the "BnBL" agency was earning thousands, which was quickly reflected in company and bank account balances, both business and private.

The sums of money being raised from the business, reached record sums and continued to grow.

North Hill township, home of Clare and David Roberts, 01:00pm.

Susan was going to visit Carolin at her home.

The woman had fallen into extreme depression since her son's disappearance and had not left her house for several days.

The two women knew each other well, as Susan had already helped Carolin in the past to overcome the nervous breakdown she had experienced after splitting from her long-term partner.

In this situation, she decided to take care of her former patient again, especially as Carolin refused any medical care and insisted on staying at home, until her son David returned.

At the same time, there were serious concerns that, left alone without care, she might make a drastic decision and one day take her own life. Susan McKane also continued to work with the police as a psychological consultant and had previously mediated conversations between investigators and Joanna Richardson at a time, when they were desperately searching for Magda.

She did her best to help both parties, during this difficult time for everyone.

Even when her efforts in the first case were unsuccessful and Joanna Richardson was ultimately unable to bear the mental burden and left town, leaving the case unsolved. Susan continued to be actively involved in the investigation.

However, David Roberts' case was somewhat different, although undoubtedly related in many ways and circumstances, and his disappearance was very similar to the way Magda Richardson vanished.

The biggest and most important difference between the two cases was that Carolin did not have a problem communicating with the officers handling the case, as was the case with Joanna.

At the time, Carolin was believed to have answered all questions honestly, which left the police in no doubt or suspicion that the woman might be hiding something from them.

It soon became apparent that the victimised woman, did not suspect anyone of wanting to hurt her or her son David, which forced the police to start looking for leads elsewhere.

The only clues investigators were able to glean from the Richardson home, were another Voodoo doll and an open parcel, that David had received on that fateful day.

But little could be established from this evidence, as no fingerprints were found on the doll, other than Joanna's and David's.

The same was true of the parcel that was eventually traced to the Elephant and Castle area of south-east London, but it too was well-prepared and clearly devoid of any trace evidence, leaving no fingerprints or information about the person who sent it at the time.

It was easy to guess that the person who sent the package, from the capital, could have used any postal office, of which there are literally thousands in the city.

At the same time, it was obvious that whoever it was, he or she very much wanted to make sure that no one fell on his or her trail., So by taking such precautions, it was easy to remain anonymous and avoid unwanted attention.

So, once again the police had no leads and, just as they did a few months ago during the investigation of the Magda Richardson case, the investigators hit a dead end.

Everyone involved in both cases knew, including Dr Susan McKane, that the situation was fast becoming hopeless and critical.

Once again, the media took aim at the actions of the police and more and more articles leaked to the press, slinging mud at the law enforcement agencies.

From the moment they were confronted with a second, equally outrageous and sensitive case, the pressure that once again fell on the officers working non-stop was immense.

it was greater than when Magda went missing, especially as this case too was still unsolved.

Everyone realised that the situation they were in required immediate action.

But despite all possible efforts, both now and at the start of the initial investigation, no one really knew how to deal with the problem effectively.

It was few minutes past 1pm, when Susan parked her car outside Carolin Richardson's house.

When she got out, she noticed that all the windows in the house were tightly shut.

The woman had not even left one window open, to let at least some sunlight or fresh air in.

However, Susan had no doubt that Carolin was inside.

Her condition must be bad. She thought.

The psychologist also noticed Carolin's car, which had stood in the same place for several days in a row.

Before moving on, she stopped for a few minutes to collect her thoughts. She hadn't expected to see such a sight, so she felt that talking to Carolin, might prove extremely difficult.

For Susan, such encounters were never easy, especially in these circumstances.

In the case of Joanna, and now Carolin, the extremes of both women's behaviour were mixed with a variety of deep emotions, from panic attacks and crying to uncontrollable, obsessive laughter that would make anyone shudder.

Nonetheless, she remained one of the last people, who were determined to try to establish a dialogue with the grieving women and somehow bring them relief.

On top of that, she knew both ladies well and that they were very lonely as they went through this mental ordeal.

To make matters worse, Carolin refused medical attention and, unlike Joanna, decided to stay home alone, while Joanna let herself to be taken to the hospital.

Susan walked to the front door, rang the bell and heard a tune echoing through the flat.

She stood there for a while, waiting for an answer, but when, after a few minutes, there was no sign of Carolin coming to open her door, she rang the bell again.

More minutes passed with no response, at which point the psychologist realised that nothing was going to happen.

I don't think she feels like seeing anyone today. She thought.

However, just as she was about to turn away, she got a hunch, she instinctively grabbed the handle, and the door appeared to be unlocked, so she pushed it open slightly, and it gave way after a little pressure.

Slowly she stepped inside, looking around carefully.

The house was exactly as she had expected, the rooms were almost completely dark.

The curtains effectively blocked the light, which only came in through small gaps, creating bright streams that cut through the air, and not a single light bulb was lit anywhere.

The sight created a depressing and gloomy atmosphere.

Due to the lack of light and fresh air, there was an unpleasant smell of dust and something Susan could not yet identify.

Carolin had clearly stopped caring about her surroundings, which could only indicate the state of her psyche and how deep her depression was. Susan walked cautiously forward, careful not to step on or trip over anything, but the atmosphere of the place made her shiver.

She felt like she was taking part in a scene straight out of a horror movie. She wasn't even sure whether she should turn on the light or respect the owner's decision and leave it off.

"Carolin...!?" she called out into the depths of the house. "...Carolin! It's me, Susan!"

However, this also yielded no results, so she decided to search the rooms one by one.

First, she went to the living room, which was the first and closest large room to the left of the front door.

Once inside, she immediately went to one of the windows and pulled back the curtain to better see her surroundings.

There were neatly arranged furry decorative cushions on the sofa, there was nothing on the table in the middle of the living room apart from a few colourful magazines and the room seemed perfectly clean and untouched, as if Carolin had never used it.

The situation was completely different in the kitchen next door. Susan found there, in addition to several cups of unfinished coffee, the remains of uneaten sandwiches and a piece of yellow cheese, that was already in an advanced stage of fermentation.

Susan concluded that this was the main cause of such an unpleasant smell in the house, but apart from these few things, everything else was in its place.

At least she is feeding herself. - She summed up in her mind.

Before she left the kitchen, she threw the spoiled food in the rubbish and put the dishes in the sink and poured warm water over them, hoping it would help the air return to normalcy.

"We could use some more air in here..." she said quietly. "...Carolin! Where are you!" She called out again to the flat plunged into darkness, but just like the previous time, she received no answer.

She turned back towards the living room, crossed it and began to walk towards the stairs, being careful not to catch anything as the sun, which was gently streaming in through one window, did not provide enough illumination.

As she neared the door of the room, she pressed the light switch, but nothing happened, as if a bulb had burned out or there was no electricity in the house so, she was forced to walk on in the darkness.

Susan knew Caroline was out there somewhere and she had to find her, hoping she hadn't arrived too late, and that the woman hadn't done anything stupid.

With each passing minute, Susan became more and more afraid that there was a chance she would find Caroline unconscious or, worse, dead As she slowly and carefully approached the stairs, she let her mind push her to think of worst-case scenarios that might explain why Carolin wasn't answering Susan's calls.

In her imagination, she saw herself finding the woman's body with slashed wrists in a bathtub full of blood, then she imagined, as she was walking into Carolin's bedroom and seeing her body hanging inert in front of her. Susan's stimulated imagination began to affect her negatively, she felt cold chills run through her body again, as she was now genuinely afraid that she might witness some sort of drastic scene.

Nevertheless, she continued walking, taking step after step, approaching the first floor.

"Carolin!?" she called out while already at the top of the stairs.

Although she got no response, she heard something.

She stood still and listened; at first, she thought it sounded like a mu led, rattling sound, only to realise after a while that it was Carolin sobbing somewhere nearby.

The sounds came from behind the closed door of David's room which was on the right-hand side of the staircase, right next to where Susan was standing at the time, she just reached out and managed to grab the handle. She waited a few more seconds to take a deep breath before opening it, then pushed open the door, which creaked open slowly, revealing the interior of the room.

Opposite Susan appeared David's bed, on which Carolin lay curled up and wrapped in a blanket.

The woman was lying with her back to the door, so Susan couldn't see her face, but she could hear, she was crying.

But what she felt most from the moment she entered, was the incredible stench wafting through the room and it wasn't until she got closer that she realised the stench was coming from Carolin, Susan immediately thought the woman hadn't taking a bath for a long time.

"Carolin?" she said quietly.

Then she noticed that the woman had moved under the blanket, and slowly began to turn towards her.

After a moment, she put her face out and looked at Susan with concerned eyes, through her tears. "Did they find him?" she asked.

"No Carolin, I'm very sorry, but they haven't found him yet." Susan replied truthfully.

"But they will find him, won't they? Say they will find him."

The psychologist could not then tell the woman what she really thought about it.

She understood there was no chance that David would be found whole and healthy, as was the case with Magda Richardson.

She didn't want to give Carolin false hope.

But it was too early for brutal facts, and she was in an extremely difficult mental state to even start to prepare her, for the inevitable reality.

"Of course they'll find him." She replied after a while.

She concluded that, in this situation, she had to do everything she could to get Carolin out of that bed, so she could start to function somehow. To that end, she decided to simply say what she wanted to hear at the time. "You're right Susan ..." Carolin replied, starting to cheer up. "...He'll come back, I'm sure he'll come back any time now, he will come back home." She added to cheer herself up.

"Yes, Carolin, he's going to come home, so you need to get out of bed and get cleaned up so you're ready for his return."

"I need to get cleaned up." She repeated after her.

"Come on, I'll take you to the bathroom." Susan added.

Carolin pulled her legs out from under the blanket and sat down on the bed, Susan grabbed her arm and helped her up, then they both headed for the bathroom.

What happened to the light?

"I turned off the power." She replied.

"What do you mean you turned it off , why?" Susan asked.

I didn't need it, there's a switch box behind the basement door on the right, if you want it, go and turn it back on again.

Susan thought at that moment that she had to do it immediately, after all she couldn't let a woman walk around the house in almost total darkness, let alone take a decent shower in such circumstances.

"Okay, you wait here for a while, I'll be right back." She said.

Carolin sat down again on David's bed, as Susan left the room and came down the stairs.

She knew the house well because she had been there often, so she knew where to find the basement door, behind which was the fuse box. So, she went downstairs, still trying to move slowly and carefully so as not to hit anything.

She helped herself with her phone, on which she switched on a small flashlight.

It was then that she realised she could have done this earlier, and she regretted a little that she hadn't thought of it as soon as she entered the house, but at least it was easier now.

It didn't take her long to reach the door, beyond which was the basement and the fuse box.

Standing in front of the fuses and all the while shining her phone light, she opened the small door and to her eyes appeared a board, showing all the power switches in every room of the house.

Then she saw that all the buttons were still facing upwards, indicating that they were on.

Except for one at the very bottom, it was the main button that turned off all the power at once.

Susan moved it up and at that moment the light from the corridor fell on her, so she closed the box and backed out of the basement. As she stepped out into the corridor, closing the door behind her, she looked around the other rooms and saw that the lights were on in every room.

At this point she realised that Carolin must have simply switched off the power, not even turning off the lights in any of the rooms.

Once the lighting problem was solved, she was finally able to put her phone in her pocket, and she headed towards the stairs and quickly climbed them back to David's room where she had left Carolin.

When she got there, she stopped like a stone at the threshold of the entrance, feeling every hair on her body stand up and a shiver run down her spine.

She was then able to look carefully around David's room, which was a total mess.

But what horrified her most was the sight of Carolin sitting on her son's bed amongst the scattered clothes, with head hanging inertly down.

Susan tried to look at the woman's face, but it was obscured by her loosely hanging greasy hair.

She slowly moved her gaze down the woman's body, analysing the signs of life, until her gaze landed on her hands, and she noticed that she was holding something in them. She squinted to get a better look.

It took her mind a few seconds to register and recognise the mysterious object.

It was the Voodoo doll that David had received in the post on the day he went missing, it was very similar to the one Susan had seen in photographs when investigators had shown her photographs after Magda Richardson went missing.

She was then asked to try and interrogate Joanna as to how this doll came to be in her daughter's possession.

At the time, Susan was aware of this doll of unknown origin, before officers found out about it.

Because Joanna had told her about it before as well during her last visit, which was exactly at the same time as Magda's disappearance.

Susan looked at Carolin paralysed with fear, unable to move, feeling her hands begin to shake.

The woman sat on her son's bed motionless with her head down and her face covered in greasy, mangled hair holding the last thing her son had touched, before hearing of his disappearance.

Beneath her feet, a small pool of blood had formed and was dripping down her hands in a trickle, straight onto the floor.

There was also a brown box lying nearby and when Susan looked at it through the woman's blood stains, she managed to read what was written:

"For David Richardson, sincerely."

"Oh my god Carolin, what have you done?" the psychologist choked out. At this point, the woman slowly raised her head, her body shaking from the traumatic shock.

She focused an absent gaze on Susan, who could barely see her eyes trying to make their way through the messy hair stuck to her face.

She stared at Susan in silence for a moment, tears streaming down her cheeks.

"HE'S DEAD!!!!" she roared suddenly at full volume.

The tone of the woman's voice made Susan literally jump up in fear. Then, in a split second, she leapt up from where she was sitting and threw herself at her, and a startled Susan fell backwards under the weight of her body.

The psychologist was stunned by this turn of events, as it had never occurred to her that Carolin might attack her.

However, at that moment she apparently lost her mind and became enraged.

Once the two women were on the floor, Susan noticed that Carolin was holding a small knife in her hand.

This sight gave her an adrenaline rush, made her push Carolin with her legs so hard, that she almost landed back on David's bed.

After which, she quickly picked herself up and saw that her clothes were stained with blood.

"Carolin!!! Stop it!!! What are you doing!!!" Susan shouted.

"He's dead!!! I know he's dead!!!"

"Calm down!!! David's alive, they'll find him!!! Just calm down!"

"You're lying, bitch! YOU'RE LYING!!! What have you done with him!!!" Carolin was alternately screaming and crying, kneeling on the floor, covered in her own blood.

Susan, on the other hand, waited nervously, watching what the woman would do, prepared to fend off another attack.

A moment passed, then the psychologist felt her body begin to shake from the shock - a sign that the adrenaline was subsiding and being replaced by sober thinking.

Carolin did not get up from the floor anymore, she knelt, bent her head and touched it against the ground, crying constantly.

There was blood everywhere, the situation looked very serious but not dangerous.

Susan decided that the danger had passed.

She approached her carefully and put her still shaking hand on her shoulder.

"He's dead I know he's dead, I can feel it." Carolin whispered, already calm.

Susan took her hand and saw a deep, long wound on her forearm from which blood was still oozing.

There was a towel on the bed next to the woman, so Susan picked it up and pressed it against the wound to stop the bleeding.

"I'm sorry Susan."

"Come on, I'll take you to hospital."

To her surprise Carolin got up without hesitation and obediently followed her towards the stairs, supporting herself on her arm. "He's dead I know he's dead, I can feel it." She repeated.

"It's going to be all right, press it into the wound." Susan replied, placing her hand on the towel next to the wound.

Susan realised then, that the bond between child and mother is so strong that maternal instinct usually reveals the truth.

She had already known that David Roberts, like Magda Richardson, would never come home, but she couldn't just tell her that, especially as the woman was already on the verge of completing suicide.

However, the psychologist understood it would be best for Carolin and everyone else, if she accepted the truth as soon as possible. At this point, when she answered the question for herself *what had happened to her son* it was very comfortable for Susan, so she thought it was a good start to put her on the right path.

Susan's key task was to help Carolin come back to reality.

From that point on she knew, as with Joanna Richardson, she would have to spend a lot of time with her so that she could start to function normally. Looking at the woman's current state, she had serious doubts that she would be able to do anything by herself.

Susan wanted and needed to make sure that Carolin remained as sane as possible.

Now she needed to get the woman to hospital as soon as possible, as she noticed that the makeshift bandage on her cut hand was starting to turn redder and redder.

Carolin was losing a lot of blood, which dripped onto the floor, leaving a trail behind her as they both left David's room.

Susan's mind was filled with chaotic thoughts, from the towel she had wrapped Carolin's hand with, thinking it might be dirty and contagious, to visualising herself lying on the floor with her throat cut in a pool of blood, if she hadn't pushed the woman away in time.

Clearly, she had not yet recovered from the shock she had suffered when Carolin had jumped on her.

But above all, one fact was the priority, and it was the one that first came to Susan's mind - the sooner she could get the situation under control, the sooner she could continue with her task, and that was crucial at the time.

7

A visit to "Bradley and Brad Lettings".

'It will still be beautiful, despite everything. Just wear comfortable shoes, because you have a lifetime to go.'

10 years later,

15 February 2019, London, Camberwell Green, Danny and Rachel Davis's flat, 3:30pm.

The surprise caused by the news that Rachel was considering moving to North Hill without my knowledge had finally passed.

At first, I wondered why she thought it would be best for us, to move to this particular town?

For a while, I even suspected that she had some other ulterior motive, but I soon realised that she simply liked the look of the place.

The house prices were also very affordable and within our joint budget, which we had put together through years of work and the investments Rachel had made to have a financial base for the future.

During this time, a considerable amount of money had accumulated. As it had never occurred to me to check the balance of our joint savings account or the value of the shares we owned, I was impressed that we had managed to save so much money.

I thought then that we should be able to buy a house without any problems and still have enough cash to last us the rest of our lives.

On top of that, there was also going to be my fixed pension and my recent severance pay from work, guaranteeing additional stability.

During our earlier conversation, when Rachel outlined her plan, it was clear that she had started organising everything several months in advance. This was before I had met the female psychic and before my application for early release from the service, was officially considered.

She told me at the time that she had started thinking about it, immediately after the conversation with Connor, which I did not know had taken place, in mid-December 2018.

She also confessed that by then, she had already checked our account balance and was slowly looking around for a place where we could both find peace and live comfortably for the rest of our lives.

I admit that at one point, I felt sorry for her, because I could see that she really did have good intentions, and I couldn't get her out of the mistake she was about to make.

She didn't know the dark past of this town like I did, she had never heard about the kidnappings that happened there, and I didn't have the heart to tell her about it. For her, North Hill was just a picturesque town surrounded by forests and close to the sea.

I didn't know exactly why I couldn`t bring up the subject with her, but it was partly because, I was afraid to reveal the facts about this place. On the one hand, I was afraid that she might get scared and change her mind, but personally I felt that I should go there.

On the other hand, I could see how much she was looking forward to the move, the new house and our new life, so I had no desire to dissuade her from the idea.

I decided it would be best if I kept all the uncomfortable information to myself, and only broach the subject when it came up on its own.

That way you won't bother her now, let her be happy. my intuition prompted.

It was 03:30pm when we sat together in the living room and looked through the photos of the house listings, Rachel had prepared for me earlier.

I could see how excited she was, so I let her lead me by the hand.

It was her moment; it had been a long time since I had seen her so happy. I obediently followed the instructions and suggestions, going through one photo after another in silence.

It warmed my heart to discreetly observe, how glad she was back then.

I had no intention of disturbing her joy in any way.

This was a very important moment in our life together, especially for her, so I didn't want to spoil anything by interjecting some of my doubts. "How do you like this...?" she asked, pressing me with another offer with pictures of the house.

"...Really nice with a huge garden for 500,000..." she added with delight in her voice.

I looked at more photos in silence, thoughtfully, Rachel was so absorbed in looking for a new house for us that she didn't even notice.

I wondered if I was sometimes looking at the house of one of the victims.

Sure, the adverts included street names and property numbers, but I didn't know any of the addresses where the families of the kidnapped children had once lived.

The articles I read never gave this information, presumably to protect privacy.

But there was one thing I could be 100 per cent sure of after the tragic events, many of the flats and homes were abandoned, so, at that point, the chances of me looking at one of these places were very high, and I felt weird about it.

All these listings that Rachel had, were from an estate agency, "Bradley and Brad Lettings."

I immediately remembered that I had already come across this name in an article.

It turned out, that they were originally from London and had opened their office in North Hill almost ten years ago.

Recalling the information I had assimilated by then about Magda

Richardson, it was apparent that the agency started a few months after the girl disappeared without a trace.

At the time, I thought this was probably the main reason why the police only followed up this lead once, talking to representatives of the "BnBL" agency. Which was also described in the article, but then stopped pursuing the subject.

They were new in town, so they arrived after the incident, it makes sense. My instinct said.

However, every time I recalled this information, I had the feeling that something was wrong.

On the other hand, I realised that this was ten years ago, and police procedures were completely different from now.

All I could do was give credence to the thoroughness of the investigative work at the time and trust that everything was done correctly, especially as this case was considered a priority.

I can imagine how determined the officers were to find the missing people and those behind the alleged disappearances.

Therefore, in the end, I was led to believe that such an important link had not been overlooked, if it existed at all.

But the fact remained, no matter how much pressure law enforcement put on the results and what measures were taken in the investigation, no one was ever arrested on suspicion of involvement in any of the disappearances, of which there were four.

This could only mean that this person or persons remained at large all the time, and could continue to pose a threat to the city's residents. The last person disappeared relatively recently, just over a year ago. Besides, I was not convinced by the widely accepted version, which led some people to believe that black magic and a curse cast on the town was to blame for everything that was happening there.

At this point, I decided to put aside the thoughts I regularly and involuntarily returned to and focus on helping Rachel choose a property that would best suit the tastes of both of us and that would become our new home soon. The plan of action was simple: we were to choose two properties that we thought were the best and then call the "BnBL" office to make an appointment.

After establishing all the necessary information with the estate agents and completing all the paperwork involved in responding to the advert and expressing our interest in buying, the next step was to travel to North Hill to view the houses and to familiarise ourselves with the area before making a final decision.

Rachel decided that when we were sure we were ready, she would resign, and from then on, we would prepare to move.

This seemed perfectly logical to me, so I didn't question her decision, although I still had some concerns about leaving London.

Nevertheless, I was excited about moving, but probably for very different reasons to Rachel.

Because for me, it was about seeing the places I had read about, while Rachel was just happy that we would be starting a new life together in a different, quieter environment.

Although I had decided not to mention the history of the town to my wife, I was preparing myself for it, especially as I knew that one day that moment would come; fortunately for me, it had not yet arrived.

There was also the matter of telling Connor everything, who didn't yet know that we were going to leave, which was also going to be a challenge. Rachel and I thought it would be best to decide everything ourselves. We knew for sure that Connor would try to dissuade us from the idea, so it was better to keep him in the dark for now.

We needed to have a clear and unbiased view of our situation, as this was about one of the most important and serious decisions we would soon have to make.

It was past 4 pm and I was feeling increasingly tired because I had already been sitting with Rachel in the living room in one position for two hours, going through the offers and discussing all the pros and cons.

Rachel meticulously analysed every detail of the houses we were checking out: how many rooms and bathrooms there were, whether there was a basement, what the veranda looked like, what colour the rooms were, whether the floors were laminate or carpeted, whether it had a large garden and, if so, whether it had a patio or heated pool, how far from the centre the property was located, and so on.

All of this made me lose interest with every passing minute and it became increasingly difficult to feign enthusiasm, but I couldn't show it and had to persevere for my wife's sake.

In the end, after two and a half hours, we managed to select two properties.

The houses looked very nice. Both had large gardens, one had a swimming pool, and they were close to the centre, which also made Rachel interested.

"The agency is open until 5pm, why don't we call straight away?" she asked.

"You know darling, I'm not in that much of a hurry..." I replied. "...Can't it wait until tomorrow?"

"There's no point in waiting, we've already made up our minds, so the sooner we start the better."

I had to agree with her, there was indeed no need to postpone it when everything was already decided, but personally, I was in no mood to call the office that evening.

"If you want it so badly, then call them. I really don't feel like it right now." I added, sincerely resigned.

"Don't worry, I'll take care of it myself." She replied and gave me a meaningful smile.

Then she reached for her phone and started dialling.

In the meantime, I decided to go to the kitchen to make us both some tea, in my opinion our task for today, was already done.

When I got there, I saw that my laptop, which I had left on the kitchen counter earlier, was on.

I had used it before Rachel came home, and it had been over three hours since then.

It wasn't even that the computer was just on, although I distinctly remember turning it off and slamming the monitor down.

The lid with the monitor was raised high and I could hear the mechanism working.

As it wasn't one of the latest models, it made a specific sound when I surfed the internet, it was the sound it made then as if it was loading web pages.

I had no reason to believe that Rachel had been using it because, firstly, she had her own computer and very rarely used mine and, secondly, when we were both at home, I didn't see her even go near it.

Nevertheless, the laptop was running arbitrarily at full capacity, apparently for some time.

I can't say I was particularly shocked by this sight, as I certainly would have been just a few months ago.

I was used to such strange occurrences in my house, as they happened regularly.

At first, it was just my emergency phone call, but over time, different situations happened that I had become accustomed to, so I stopped inquiring as to why it was happening.

I slowly walked to the front of the computer because from where I was standing, I couldn't see what was on the monitor.

When I got close enough to see what it was showing, I froze in shock. It was a picture of Magda Richardson from one of the articles I had added to my database on my computer hard drive for my own use.

Although I knew the photo well and had looked at it many times, at that moment, something caught my attention that I had not seen before. The photo, taken on a nice sunny day, showed Magda leaning her hand against a tree in the garden, at the background of various bushes with flowers, but this time, I saw more details that I hadn't paid attention to previously.

For some reason, that I didn't understand, I immediately realised how clear and obvious something was that I should have noticed long ago. I closed my eyes slightly and brought my face closer to the screen to see better.

Then I noticed, Magda`s bracelet has little dolphin-shaped things attached to it.

It was barely visible, because the child was standing in such a position that her hand was almost completely obscured by the tree.

It looked as if the girl was trying to embrace the tree from behind with one hand and at that moment, someone took a picture of her, so she looked as if she was leaning against it.

As I focused my gaze on the bracelet to look closely at its shape, a piece of window surrounded by bright yellow paint emerged from behind the bushes in the background, under Magda's hand.

This was also something I had never seen before, and which could indicate that it was the colour of the Richardson's house.

I looked at a section of the house in the background, trying to fix on as many details as possible and remember them.

It wasn't much, as it was only a small element in the picture, but it was enough for me to realise that I recognised the colour from one of the listings I had just looked at.

After that, I gave up making myself a hot cup of tea, switched o my laptop again and went back into the living room to find that property.

Meanwhile, Rachel continued to talk on the phone.

"Well, of course." She said.

I sat down next to her and picked up the sheets of house photos spread out on the table, then started rearranging them in search of a specific colour. Then Rachel turned her head towards me, holding the phone in her hand, and threw me a questioning look.

"So, we have an appointment, tomorrow at 3pm?"

"Yes, my husband and I will both come. Thank you, goodbye." She said in conclusion and hung up.

"Are you going over it again...?" she asked in surprise.

"... Well, you're not going to tell me that you've changed your mind, are you?" "After all, we've already chosen these two." She added, pointing her finger at the two sheets of paper that lay in front of me.

"No, I haven't changed my mind..." I replied. "...I just want to check something."

"Tell me what, maybe I can help you?"

"I'm looking for a house with a bright yellow colour." I replied.

"Most have that colour, one of the ones we chose too, this one here," she replied, smiling at me in a friendly way, then took one of the two pieces of paper she had next to her and handed it to me.

It was indeed the same house, plus there were also pictures of the garden. However, I was surprised that the property remained unoccupied, after all, it had been ten years since Joanna Richardson had left it.

I thought it would be a good idea to ask the person we were to speak to at the agency, about this place.

I was sure it was the same property, the similarities visible to the naked eye remained, even though, much had changed in the area over the years. Even the tree that had previously stood there and by which Magda had been immortalised, had been cut down, although a trace of it was visible.

I had no doubt, it was probably a house that once belonged to the Richardson family.

So, we came across one of them, just as I suspected.

It was only when Rachel looked at me curiously that I realised I had said that sentence out loud, not in my mind.

What do you mean? - She asked.

"I mean, that we found the house in this colour." I was a bit confused, so I answered quickly and thoughtlessly, but Rachel smiled kindly at me.

151

"You're a weirdo, you know?" she said with a smile.

"Thank you." I replied, returning her smile.

"Where's the tea? I thought you went to make it? Do I have to do everything myself in this house?" She added jokingly, then got up from the sofa and headed for the kitchen.

I remained in my seat, where, still holding the picture in front of me, I stared at the yellow house.

"I knew we would come across one of these." I repeated to myself again. Of course, I would never have recognised the house if it hadn't been for that picture of Magda which appeared on my computer.

Then I realised another thing that explained why I hadn't noticed these details before. I wasn't ready for it.

Again, I was given clues, in this case I had to recognise the colour of the building, which simply wasn't necessary until now.

There was still the question of the bracelet.

It must also lead to something. Sooner or later everything would come together. My instincts were prompting me.

"Tomorrow we'll go to that agency; I've arranged a meeting for us at 3pm!" Rachel called out from the kitchen.

"Alright...!" I replied. "...Where exactly should we go!"

"Canary Wharf!" She replied.

"Oh yes of course," then I remembered everything.

I read once when I was doing some research on the Bradley and Brad Lettings agency, that the seed of their business started there.

In addition to this office, they also had seven other locations around the country, including one in North Hill.

"Who should we meet with?" I asked out of curiosity.

"The secretary said that Mr Matthiew Braddock, would see us. - She replied.

"When I heard that name, a light bulb went on in my head again.

Matthiew Braddock, co-owner and partner of George Bradley, founder of the agency, who died in April 2008. - I recalled the information.

"The owner is to meet with us, interesting." I replied.

How do you know it's the owner! - Rachel poked her head out of the kitchen, curious.

"It says so on the flyers." I lied.

Well, yes, but what's so strange about that? They run a serious business and we're serious customers, who want to leave a lot of money with them, so it's probably about us being served professionally, don't you think?

You're probably right.

"Of course I am!" she replied, and I was once again immersed in my own thoughts.

An interesting chapter was beginning, as the "BnBL" agency had also had a place, in the sad history of North Hill.

You could even say that they were right in the middle of these events.

Events that I also felt part of, even though I was miles away.

I was then about to take the first step to become a permanent part of the town's history.

I felt a great curiosity overwhelm me, I wanted to see with my own eyes the places and houses, where mysterious things happened.

I was also going to try and find and talk to old residents, who had also been there all those years ago when the whole nightmare happened.

From what I knew about North Hill, it was largely inhabited by newcomers in those years.

I also wondered if the courageous psychologist Susan McKane, mentioned in the articles, was still working there and supporting people as she did during the most difficult times, which never really ended, just stopped for a shorter or longer period only to start again.

Besides that, I wanted to talk to the local police chief, even though I was no longer an officer, and find out if I could help in any way with the currently open investigations.

A lot of ideas began to germinate in my head, which I would like to implement after moving to North Hill, but before that could happen, we had to take care of the basics first, such as buying a house.

"Danny!?" Rachel called out from the kitchen, snapping me out of my reverie.

"Yes?"

"Are you still using your laptop?

"She surprised me with this question and for a moment, I didn't know what to answer or why she was asking me this, after all, my computer was supposed to be off now."

It took me a few seconds to realise, that wasn't the case at all.

Shit! It must have started up again! I thought.

"Yes, I'm coming!" I replied and quickly got up from the sofa and went to the kitchen.

"When I got there, Rachel was standing in front of my obviously open computer, leaning slightly forward with a cup of tea in her hand, staring intently at the screen.

"Who is this woman?" she asked.

I had no idea who she was asking about, I wasn't close enough to see what photograph appeared on the monitor this time.

"A psychologist from North Hill, Susan McKane." She read aloud the caption at the bottom.

It wasn't until I stood next to her, I saw that it was indeed, a photograph of Susan.

But why her? First Magda and now Susan, what should I understand by that? Is this a random photo or was it meant to be? A series of questions arose in my mind.

However, out of two evils I preferred this photo to the previous one, it was easier to explain.

"I see you are already seeking specialist support?" she said in a satisfied voice.

At the same time finding an excuse for me, which I'd quickly started looking for in my head.

"Yes, I thought it would be good to find someone a little sooner." I lied. "Very good Danny, I'm proud of you, you need to continue with the therapy, until one day, everything will be fine."

"That's what I think too." I added.

The truth was, I hadn't even thought about seeing a psychologist after moving to North Hill, and I had no idea why this woman's picture had appeared on my computer.

But, just to be safe, I decided to take it off the tabletop before it got me into more trouble.

There were times when I struggled to keep everything a secret, especially as sometimes I really wanted to tell her, but no time seemed right. I thought I would plan a day to explain everything to her, but after I had settled into my new place.

However, at that moment, another thing started to bother me more. *Why the photo of Susan McKane? A widely respected psychologist, regarded as very brave and dedicated, who helped the disadvantaged with all her might, why would I need to see her then?* It gave me no peace of mind.

The next day, I drove with Rachel to the address of "Bradley and Brad Lettings."

As the weather was nice and the distance from our flat to the Canary Wharf business district is relatively short, we decided to use public transport. This allowed us to walk around the city for longer, and not worry about parking spaces for our car.

We left the flat very early, as we had an appointment at 3 pm but had already left the house before 12 pm.

This way, we wanted to give ourselves enough time to travel in peace and be able to spend a nice afternoon together.

In between, we wanted to stop somewhere for lunch without worrying about being late.

Rachel told me that she had taken time off work, especially for the day. For a moment I thought about telling her that I could arrange it myself, but I quickly bit my tongue, realising that she wouldn't agree to that, it was too important to her for us to go to the meeting together.

We decided to walk from our Camberwell Green neighbourhood to Elephant and Castle, which normally takes about twenty minutes. We were then to take the London Underground and continue to Canary Wharf.

As we slowly approached the first stop of our tour that afternoon, dodging hundreds of people on London's crowded streets, we discussed where to stop for lunch.

I was craving grilled chicken while Rachel was talking about a healthy and tasty salad.

Personally, I couldn't put together a sentence where words like "salad" and "tasty" would be next to each other, and I had no idea where to go so we could both find something to our liking, so it had to remain open for further discussion for the time being.

I was happy that Rachel was with me, and we could have a bit of carefree banter, leaving the rest of our problems at home for the day.

However, I couldn't delude myself into thinking that going to North Hill would miraculously put me instantly out of touch with the souls who had become attached to me.

I had no idea why they were attracted to me, as Sarah White, the psychic woman who visited us that first day of Christmas, claimed.

In truth, I had my doubts that I would ever be able to rid myself of this unwanted company, and I began to think that the sooner I accepted it and got used to it, the better.

Even then, walking down the crowded street, surrounded by hundreds of strangers passing by me and Rachel, I had the feeling that one of these people wasn`t from our world and simply, should not be here at this time. I had known for a long time that what I was thinking about and encountering on a regular basis was not just a figment of my imagination but a reality that I had to face.

It didn't matter in the slightest whether I was in my flat or somewhere else. I was never alone, no matter if I wanted to be or not.

At one point, Rachel stopped abruptly in front of a shop window and then walked closer, clearly interested in something on display that had caught her eye and encouraged her to look at it more closely.

I glanced in her direction and wasn't surprised to find it was a shoe shop, so I went with her.

"They're pretty, aren't they?" she said, pointing to a pair of shoes.

"Yes, they are nice." I replied without conviction.

I guess, like any man, I didn't have an opinion on women's shoes, so to stay in the safe zone, I always preferred to say "yes" in such situations. "They sparkle beautifully in the sunshine and only cost £35." Rachel was delighted.

She loved all the sequin-covered shoes.

I used to joke that she was like a magpie who was attracted to shiny things.

"Why don't we go in for a while?" she asked.

"If you want, we have enough time." I replied, not wanting to spoil her mood.

I didn't have to wait long, because Rachel went into the shop immediately after my words, leaving me behind.

As I was left alone in front of the shop window, glancing at my reflection and the people passing by, I noticed two figures standing right behind me.

One was short and shaped like a small child, the other tall and male. I noticed them because, unlike the others, they did not have any colourful clothes or visible faces, they looked grey and blurred.

They were simply figures devoid of human features such as faces, arms and even legs, apart from the fact that their silhouette resembled a tall man and a small girl, there was nothing to indicate this.

As I quickly turned around, my eyes met with an elderly black woman and a dark-skinned vendor at a vegetable stall who was bagging tomatoes for her. My behaviour did not go unnoticed, as the strangers also cast puzzled glances in my direction.

God damn it, one day I'm going to go completely crazy over all this. I thought nervously.

My heart started beating faster, under the influence of adrenaline, so I walked into the shop where Rachel was.

A moment later I found her sitting on a leather sofa, trying on the shoes she had spotted in the display.

When I approached her, she immediately noticed that something wasn't right.

"Danny, is something wrong...?" she asked. "...You look shaky." I saw them again.

"Who?"

"Denise and someone else, I think it was John." I replied.

Rachel looked at me concerned, then shifted a little on the small sofa she was sitting on to make room for me. "Come and sit next to me." She said.

So, I did, sat down and hid my face in my hands, breathing deeply, at which point I felt her put her arm around me, hugging me close.

"Will this ever end?" I said in a resigned voice, uncovering my face. "It will end, you'll see..." She said calmly, pressing her head against mine. "...Everything ends one day."

I really wanted to believe that, but the fact was that neither of us had any idea, if that was going to happen.

As time went on, it became more and more apparent that the key to solving my problems, with the souls that were haunting me, was hidden somewhere in the town of North Hill.

This made me more and more desperate and determined to find it, as it seemed to be my destiny and path to freedom.

I realised this the moment I noticed that the feeling of despondency and constant watching was only leaving me, when I studied articles about the "missing North Hill four".

"Let's go on." Said Rachel, putting aside a pair of shiny shoes.

At that moment, a man working there approached us.

"No buy?" he asked in broken English with a strong Middle Eastern accent. "No, thank you..." she replied. "...Maybe next time." She added, not to be rude.

She got up from the small sofa, grabbed my hand, and we both left the shop. I felt shaky and would have given anything at the time to be able to calm my nerves with a quick sip of vodka.

I had been trying to cut down on my drinking on a regular basis for a few weeks and had gradually reduced the amount of alcohol I was consuming. It was a process, and Rachel didn't mind me having a few drinks in the evenings if I was sober for most of the day, which was often very difficult for me.

On many occasions, I found myself in situations that made me feel ashamed, and I had to admit to myself, this was one of the most difficult times of my life.

The temptation and desire never left me, but I tried my best not to think about it and to banish the feeling from my mind.

It was almost the same feeling as that of the haunting of the souls that were constantly circling around me.

Although I couldn't see them, I could feel that they were there somewhere, hiding in plain sight.

The same with the thirst for alcohol, the fact that sometimes I didn't see it didn't mean it had gone away for good, it was just temporarily dormant, but it was still inside me and waiting to return with redoubled force at some point.

It was now approaching 2 pm.

As we continued our journey, Rachel decided there was no point in stopping nearby for lunch.

So, we went straight away to take the tube at Elephant and Castle station, and then went directly to Canary Wharf and wait there until the meeting time. I rarely used the London Underground to travel around the city, but when I had to, I hated the crowds there.

This time, however, it was very different because, even though it was rush hour, the number of people in the station was not that large.

I felt safer surrounded by people both at the station and on the train. I felt that the circumstances effectively prevented me from seeing something I didn't want to see.

We boarded the "Northern Line" tube and after a few minutes arrived at "London Bridge" station, where we in turn changed to the "Jubilee Line," which took us directly to the "Canary Wharf" business district.

Immediately after exiting the Underground, we were surrounded by some of the largest buildings in London.

It was one of those moments when you look up and realise, how tiny you are compared to your surroundings.

The whole environment and the pleasant sunlight reflecting off the hundreds of windows around us, made me feel completely relaxed. From the tube station we had to walk a few more streets to reach the agency, which was on Trafalgar Way.

When we got there, with still plenty of time to spare as it was only 02:20pm on the clock. We stopped o at the Costa Cafe, which was opposite a building that had a sign" Bradley and Brad Lettings" on it.

Rachel found seats for us by the window, and I went to order a caramel latte for her, which she liked so much, breakfast tea and a baked ham and cheese sandwich for myself.

I then had to wait at the counter for the saleswoman to take my order. After a few minutes, I returned to Rachel, carrying a tray with our hot drinks and my sandwich, then placed everything on the table and sat down opposite her, turning my head towards the agency.

The building that housed the office, was an old building and didn't look as impressive as the modern skyscrapers in the centre of Canary Wharf. From where I was sitting, I could see the windows where house listings with photos attached were displayed.

Inside, just by the office entrance, was a woman on the phone sitting in front of a computer, I thought she might be a secretary.

"Why are you looking at that?" Rachel chatted to me.

"I'm looking out of curiosity." I answered honestly.

An agency like any other.

"I thought the same thing, why did you choose this one?" I asked.

Because they're the only ones with house listings in North Hill.

"Are you sure, they're the only ones...?" I was surprised. "...Other agencies probably have some properties for sale there too?"

I looked at her intrigued.

They don't have any, I've checked with several and found absolutely nothing.

Does it have to be North Hill? We could move anywhere else.

That's how it should be, after all, we had enough money saved up that we could go anywhere we wanted, even to another country.

Although the choice was practically unlimited, it had to be North Hill in the end.

We must live there, this town attracts me like a magnet, and we have no choice, I must go there for my own good, it's inevitable. I thought, looking the truth in the eye.

Rachel looked at me with a watchful gaze, she immediately noticed that something was on my mind, but she didn't try to find out what it was.

"You're right, actually..." She replied after a moment. "... But I was looking through photos of different towns, including the surrounding areas, but when I came across North Hill, I thought it was simply fabulous, so many forests, meadows, close to the sea." She added, clearly daydreaming. "Haven't you thought about another country? Like France or Spain, for example?" I probed the topic out of curiosity.

"My dear..." She said, looking straight into my eyes, at the same time jumping from one eye to the other, she knew perfectly well how much I liked when she did that. "...We lived in England our whole lives, and this is our place, besides, you know how much I hate the heat, and you don't like the French." She added with a smile.

And that's where she got me. I thought, returning her smile.

I had to admit that she went straight to the point, all that was left was to admit that she was right.

"Of course." I replied.

"You don't transplant old roots, it's against nature." She added and we both started laughing.

"You don't regret spending so much money at once?"

"Oh Danny, we were saving for something, right...?" she replied looking at me with pity. "...The time has come in our lives when we must slow down and build ourselves a new nest for our old age."

"You can still work, only I was forced to slow down." I replied.

"And how do you imagine that? I'll go to work, and you'll be bored at home all day? I couldn't leave you alone in the apartment knowing, you're worried and seeing God knows what horrors, my conscience wouldn't let me, besides I think I deserve a well-deserved rest too." She said smiling at me knowingly.

I smiled back and then looked at my phone to check the time.

We still have 10 minutes.

"Okay, I'm ready." She replied.

"Me too, so, shall we go?"

"Since you're not finishing your sandwich, we can go." She replied looking at the plate with half of my meal.

"Okay." I added, at the same time pushing the chair behind me, I stood up from the table.

Rachel did the same and a moment later we were already on the street. When we were walking towards the pedestrian lights to safely cross to the other side, she grabbed my hand.

We entered the agency, where we were greeted with a smile by a young woman, sitting behind the desk placed next to the entrance door. "Good afternoon..." She said politely. "...My name is Lucy Clarke; how can I help you?"

"Good afternoon..." Rachel replied. "...We have an appointment with Mr. Matthiew Braddock, at three o'clock."

"Oh yes, Mr. and Mrs. Davis, is that right?" she asked for confirmation.

"Yes, I'm Danny, and this is my wife, Rachel."

"Of course, I have it listed here..." She replied looking at the computer screen. "...I was the one who spoke to you last night." She added, smiling pleasantly.

Rachel reciprocated the friendly secretary's smile.

Without undue delay, the young woman picked up the landline phone and pressed one of the buttons on the keypad, to announce to her supervisor that the clients she had arranged were already there.

"I'm sorry to disturb you, Mr Braddock, I have with me your three o`clock appointment." She said.

"Please, give me two minutes." She heard in reply.

"Would you like to take a seat? Mr Braddock will be with you shortly."

Saying this, she pointed to a pair of armchairs lined up against the wall. "Thank you." Replied Rachel, and we both walked deeper into the small office.

I then had the opportunity to take a closer look at the place.

The office was indeed medium sized but furnished in a quite sensible way. In addition to the secretary's seat, there were four more desks with computers, set at such a distance from each other that there was enough space between them, for the people to move freely.

However, no one else was there.

It seemed unusual to me that in a real estate office, apart from the owner, only a secretary worked during the day.

I didn't really know exactly how such a business functioned, but it seemed a little strange to me.

As we approached the place to sit, a door with a gold plaque reading "Matthiew Braddock," appeared in front of me.

We were sitting close enough to the owner's office door so I could hear mu led male voices coming from inside. I assumed, they were probably other staff.

A few minutes later, the door opened, and there stood a man of medium height with curly chestnut hair and obviously overweight, dressed in a smart, slightly creased, black suit.

Could this be Mr Matthiew Braddock? My instincts hesitated.

Rachel and I exchanged surprised glances.

Then the man in the doorway looked in our direction, which we took as an invitation, so we got up and walked towards him.

As we got closer, I suddenly realised that the man had not opened the door to let us into his office, but to let someone out of it.

Due to this unfortunate mistake, I almost collided with two huge guys, dressed in elegant suits, who were leaving the room.

I had to quickly get out of their way, as both men were of muscular stature and looked like they lived in a gym and drank protein shakes

165

for breakfast. I didn't stand a chance in a collision that would probably have ended with me lying on the floor.

As I stepped back to let them pass first, I simultaneously grabbed Rachel's waist with my left hand, who was standing right behind me, pushing her gently away to do the same.

As they passed in front of me, I made eye contact with one of them, literally for two seconds.

That was enough for his gaze to freeze the blood in my veins. I thought there was an indefinable evil hidden in his eyes, there was something very disturbing and frightening in them, but at that moment I could not yet determine what it was.

But it was not long before I was to find out, these people carried death in their eyes.

"Please, forgive my staff." Said a proud, obese man to us.

His voice came from behind me, as I watched the two individuals carefully, who were just heading for the exit.

Then one of them turned suddenly in front of the door, quite as if he had subconsciously sensed that I was looking at him, cast another sinister glance in my direction, and then disappeared outside.

This gave me the impression that I had seen him before, but for the moment, I could not immediately recall where this might have been or under what circumstances.

"It's alright." Rachel replied, starting a conversation with Matthiew. Before I turned my gaze in their direction, I saw the secretary looking discreetly at us from behind her computer.

She was clearly embarrassed by the situation that had just taken place, it was written all over her face, almost as if she felt personally responsible for everything.

I winked at her in reassurance, and she smiled slightly and went back to work.

I then turned my head towards Rachel, next to whom Matthiew was standing and grinning in a strange grimace.

It took a few seconds before I realised he was trying to smile at us. I didn't see anything nice or friendly in this sight and it certainly didn't improve my mood, on the contrary, his repulsive facial expression discouraged me instead of welcoming me.

But I quickly ignored this, because it was not the purpose of our visit to the agency.

In addition, the situation became more interesting, because of the two hoodlums who had just left the office, and about whom I was curious. I decided to play dumb for a while and approach Matthiew, so that he could tell me more about the men who almost ran me over in the corridor a while ago.

I was going to simply ask about them, pretend to haven`t heard when he mentioned, that they worked for him.

"Please, come in." Matthiew said.

He was still standing at the door and pointed inside his office with a welcoming gesture, all the while smiling crookedly.

Rachel, without thinking for long, moved forward and I followed close behind.

Once we were all inside, Matthiew closed the door behind us and then headed towards his desk.

I cautiously looked around the room, and although I'd never been in an estate agency before, I thought the place didn't resemble a respectable office, but rather the living room of an old bachelor.

A large plasma TV, a stereo, video games, a liquor bar, a large leather sofa and a couple of armchairs and a desk with a computer, it felt like entering someone's private room straight from the office, because the room we had just left looked very professional.

167

I wasn't expecting this in the slightest, seeing the expression on Rachel's face I could deduce that she was as surprised as I was at that moment. Only Matthiew seemed comfortable in his surroundings, and it was obvious that he was proud of his office.

"I know what you're thinking right now..." he said unexpectedly sitting down in his chair, leaving us standing in a stupor in the middle of the room. "...It may be a little unconventional, but believe me, all my clients love the decor of my office, especially the men..." saying this, he winked at me meaningfully. "...I personally prefer a homely atmosphere, please make yourself comfortable." He added pointing to the two leather armchairs in front of him.

"Customers like the two gentlemen, who were here just now?" I asked. Rachel looked at me questioningly, wrinkling her brow, Matthiew also made a confused face.

"Customers? No, you are wrong sir, they were my managers." He replied, gritting his teeth again in an uncomfortable smile.

"Oh sorry, I hadn't guessed." I replied, feigning embarrassment.

That`s fine.

"Managers you say, I would see them more in the role of bouncers in a nightclub, hehehe." I pulled his leg.

"Yes hehehe, right, they are big but, they work for me, running one of my offices, for almost ten years already." He added with pride in his voice. Matthiew Braddock was clearly a very haughty man with a big mouth who liked to boast about his success.

Embarrassingly emphasising that everything was his.

After just a few minutes of getting to know him, I could tell he was an arrogant and morally rotten man, but I could add to my advantage the fact that he liked to talk, and I had to take advantage of that.

"Is that so? That is long time, and which office? If I may ask?" I drilled down on the subject.

"The one in North Hill." He replied without hesitation.

Hmmm, so these two unnaturally grown gorillas, have been officiating in North Hill for almost ten years? I wondered in my thoughts.

My instincts automatically analysed the statement, while remembering new facts that I was later to add to my notes.

"I understand that you are also interested in one of the houses in this town."

He said suddenly.

"Yes..." Rachel interjected into the conversation. "...Actually, we would like to see two properties before we decide."

"Very well, if you want to see the houses first, then feel free to come to our office in North Hill, just let me know when and I'll arrange the rest." Matthiew replied.

There was a light in the man's eyes.

For a moment I wasn't sure why, but I guessed it was at the thought of the money we wanted to leave with his agency.

"Can we go there tomorrow?" Rachel asked while glancing at me, I nodded in agreement.

"Absolutely, I'll book a member of staff who will be at your disposal all day, you can go anytime and once the decision is made, please come to my office, we'll go through the contract together and complete the formalities."

"Okay, thank you." Rachel replied and got up from her seat, extending her hand to Matthiew to shake it at the end of the conversation, I did the same. "Thank you very much, I'm looking forward to hearing from you." Matthiew replied then the three of us walked to the door.

Before we left the agency's office, we said goodbye to the nice secretary and then went out into the street.

169

It wasn't so bad, although I must admit, he's a very strange man and his office, "I've never seen anything like it before." Rachel started the conversation.

"Yes, and those two guys."

"What about them?" she became curious.

"Generally nothing, but very strange individuals." I replied evasively. "It's alright Danny, don't overthink it, we're going home now, tomorrow morning we'll go and look at houses." She added in a clearly excited voice. I forced myself to smile so she wouldn't see that something was on my mind again.

At that moment I couldn't stop thinking about the man's eyes, their expression was deeply engraved in my memory and every now and then, it appeared in my thoughts.

I had never experienced such emotions, after someone looked at me before.

Besides, they had both lived in North Hill for many years and we would probably meet them again, the next day.

Something is very wrong with these two guys; I need to take a closer look at them. I thought and then I felt, someone's watching me.

I looked around carefully, but apart from Rachel and a few people who were on the street now, I didn't see anything strange.

That's when I knew I was already very sensitive about it, and I couldn't react like this every time, when I have the slightest doubt.

For my own good I ignored this thought, took Rachel's hand and we both headed towards the pedestrian lights, and then continued our way back home.

What I didn't know at the time was that the feeling of being watched was completely justified and wasn't coming from a lost soul, as it always had been, until then.

For as we passed the café "Costa," where we had sat before the meeting, there were Matthiew's two managers inside.

They were visible from the street, and from their position, they had a good view outside and watched us closely from a safe distance.

Goosebumps ran across my skin, but when Rachel hugged me around the waist, I felt calm.

I don't like this at all, we must be very careful. My instincts prompted me as Rachel, and I walked towards Canary Wharf tube station.

8

The circle of life.

'Love has explained everything to me, Love has solved everything -

that is why I adore this Love, wherever it may be.'

10 years earlier, 4 November 2009.

Time: 09:10, North Hill, home of Susan and John McKane.

After battling lung cancer for almost a year and a half, John McKane finally died in his bed on the night of 3-4 November 2009, at around 3 am, according to the pathologist.

Although he knew his final minutes were approaching, he was completely at peace that night, feeling ready to look death in the eye and welcome it with open arms.

Ever since he found out about his illness, he had wished for only one thing and hoped very much that his wish would come true.

Knowing that he would inevitably have to leave this world, he wanted to live long enough to see the day when his child was born, so he could enjoy his little one, at least for a while.

When his daughter Nicole Denice celebrated her first birthday a fortnight earlier, John was overjoyed to witness this moment and felt that the meaning of his life had just been fulfilled.

From that day on, he knew he didn't have much time left in this world.

He accepted the impending end and even began to look forward to it. His only regret was that until the last moments, his wife Susan had been very cold towards him.

All this time, she had not changed her behaviour and since another child had disappeared in the city, she had completely and irreversibly cut herself o from him.

John held a huge grudge against her, and it remained that way until he drew his last breath.

The apple of his eye and the greatest joy in his life was his thirteen-month old daughter, Nicole Denice, whom John simply called Deni.

This child made John determined to fight his illness so that he could be with her for as long as possible.

Thanks to her, he found the strength to bravely overcome the most difficult treatment procedures.

By a twist of fate, the date of John McKane's death fell exactly on the anniversary of Magda Richardson's disappearance, but on that day his loved ones did not remember it.

Susan found him unconscious early in the morning, as she'd slept in the guest room for some time.

She explained this by saying she wanted to give him more room, on their shared marital bed for his comfort.

However, John knew that she simply did not want to sleep in the same room with him.

Of course, he was very sorry about that, but he didn't hold it against her because he realised, how awful he looked at the time.

Very skinny and pale, with no hair on his head, John had changed beyond recognition.

The only person who did not look at him with pity in her eyes at that time, was Nicole Denice.

The girl was the only one who spent the most time with John, during which he didn't have to worry about her asking him unpleasant questions, about his health or wellbeing.

She was simply there whenever he needed her most, and he loved her endlessly for it.

Upon discovering her husband's death, Susan kept her cool, immediately called an ambulance and then, while waiting for the paramedics to arrive, decided to notify Judy and Kevin McKane of their son's death. John's parents decided to travel from London as soon as possible and begin preparations for the burial.

"At least you don't have to suffer anymore." She said quietly, looking into his dead eyes.

In a way she felt relieved, as the last few months had been just as difficult for her, as she had watched John slowly pass away from this world, before her eyes.

On top of that, she'd had a lot more work than usual at the time and living with a cancer-stricken husband, hadn't allowed her to concentrate fully, she felt it was only slowing her down.

As she stood in their shared bedroom looking stony-faced at John's lifeless body, a feeling of freedom swept over her.

She knew that from now on, she would be able to spread her wings completely.

Because the main reason which had been holding her back all along, had just been cut off.

John was not a priority for her, yes, she loved him very much when they met and spent every free moment with each other.

So much so that she really wanted to marry him, and when he proposed to her, she felt like the happiest person in the world.

174

But a lot has changed in the last few years, and Susan has reached a point in her life where she realises how many opportunities she could have had if it wasn't for the fact that she got married and pregnant at such a young age.

Everything she once wanted the most; a family of her own, a loving husband and a child - no longer mattered so much.

She wished she had waited a little longer with all this, and that was the moment when John started to bother her. On top of that, their baby was about to be born.

However, when John finally left this world, she realised that everything would change radically.

She would be able to devote herself to her activities instead of constantly hiding with her phone from the sad gaze of her ailing husband.

In those days, Susan went to the hospital regularly, visiting Carolin Roberts, who was now in a secure mental health facility.

This was the same ward where Joanna Richardson was placed a year ago. This happened just after Carolin had attacked Susan in her home with a knife, having painfully, but not fatally, slashed her veins.

Susan then saved the woman's life by getting her to hospital in time, where she had already been forced to stay for her own good.

During both the first and the second child's disappearance, Susan, disregarding the safety of her own family, pledged her unlimited assistance to the investigators. They had tried by every means possible to obtain information that could lead them to the right trail.

In addition, she received many calls from residents who also needed her support, not only as a psychologist but also as a trusted person.

She was getting calls from former patients but also from new people who were struggling with the stress, worry and fear caused by the events in North Hill over the past twelve months.

Most of them, single mothers who were paranoid about their children, but there were also times when men called her asking for advice.

Susan's hands were full, and she was glad that at least one responsibility was off her mind.

Of course, there was still the issue of Nicole Denice, as the year-old needed her more than ever.

However, she didn't think it was as big a problem, confident, she could deal with it quickly.

After a brief conversation with Judy McKane, she also called her own parents, to tell them about the situation.

So, she dialled the number, then put the phone to her ear, her mother Rita Jankins answered after the second tone.

"Hello?" Rita said.

"Hi mum." Susan greeted her.

"Aaaa, it's you! Well, hello, how nice of you to call." Rita was happy.

"I don't have any good news, Mum..." replied Susan in a serious voice. "...John died last night..." she added.

There was silence in the receiver for a moment.

"...Are you there?"

"Yes, I'm here darling, I'm sorry, I'm stunned, did you call an ambulance?" "They should be here soon..." Susan replied. "...I've also spoken to Judy; they're coming today with Kevin."

"And how are you holding up, love?"

"Fine, I guess, I expected it to happen at some point."

"Your dad and I were getting used to the thought too, poor man..." Rita replied and paused to take a breath. "...He was in so much pain."

Susan heard her mother's voice break slightly; she was clearly devastated. Rita had always liked John and was happy when Susan told her she wanted to marry him.

She thought he was a good and caring man and had no doubt he would look after her daughter well.

She worried a little bit about the future of her granddaughter and daughter if John passed.

It was a beautiful time for them. - Rita thought, thinking back about their life together.

When she found out about her son-in-law's illness a year ago, she was heartbroken.

She thought a lot about Susan and Nicole Denice's life without John. This day was to be the first when they would have to face reality, without John McKane's support.

Rita felt obliged to help her family.

"Yes, at least his suffering is over." Susan replied.

"Where are you now?

"I went down to the kitchen; I'm waiting for the ambulance."

"And Nicole? Is she with you?" Rita wanted to know.

"No, she's still sleeping peacefully in her room, I didn't want to wake her... -Susan heard her mother say something indistinctly.

"...Excuse me?"

"Oh, sorry honey, I'm talking to your dad. He's asking me what's wrong." Rita explained.

"Oh yes, I understand."

"He wants to talk to you; I'll give him the phone," added Rita and handed the receiver to James.

For a moment, the sound of the phone being passed from hand to hand, could be heard, and then James spoke.

"I'm very sorry, love." He said straight away.

"Hi, Dad."

"How are you feeling?"

"Fine, I'm in the kitchen, waiting for the ambulance," Susan replied honestly.

"Your mum and I will be with you shortly," replied a clearly concerned James.

Susan thought she couldn't remember a time, when her usually petulant stepfather had been so upset.

"Calm down, dad..." she replied. "...You don't have to bother. I'm fine. The ambulance will be here soon."

"Nonsense, we're already getting ready to leave. We need to see you and Denice."

Susan flinched at these words and felt anger rising within her.

She didn't like her daughter being called by her middle name, which John had chosen for her. She thought they should call her Nicole, the name she had given her.

However, John always called the girl Deni or Denice in their presence, so her grandparents also got used to it, and after a while, it became a habit.

I shouldn't have agreed to a middle name then. She thought.

"Okay, Dad, if you want it so much you can come..." She started to speak and abruptly stopped. "...Wait, someone is at the door, it's probably the medics."

She added.

"Open the door. Mum and I are getting in the car and we're coming to you." Said James, but Susan didn't hear it anymore, as she put the phone down on the kitchen table and headed towards the front door to see who had come.

When she opened it, she saw two men standing on the threshold, dressed in dark green uniforms.

One was holding a stretcher, which he placed upright beside him, the other a medical bag, and behind them, an ex-ambulance was parked in the driveway.

As she expected, more than twenty minutes after calling the emergency number, they arrived to take John's body away.

"Good morning, did you call us?" one of the paramedics asked.

"Yes, please come in gentlemen." She said and let them in.

As they entered the flat, Susan remembered that she had not disconnected the call to her father, who was most likely still waiting on the line.

"Please head up the stairs. My husband is in the bedroom, first door on the right. I'll join you in a moment." She instructed the men while showing them the way with her hand.

After they moved according to her instructions, she headed towards the kitchen to grab her phone.

The paramedics looked at each other slightly puzzled, then walked up the stairs and into the bedroom, following her instructions.

Meanwhile, Susan returned to the kitchen, picked up the handset and quickly put it to her ear.

"Are you still there?" she asked.

But all she heard in reply was a long beep, which meant that the person on the other end had already hung up.

So, she followed the paramedics to the upstairs bedroom.

When she got there and stood in the doorway of the room, she saw one of the men sorting out the chemotherapy apparatus to prepare John's body to be carried out of the bedroom while the other was setting up a portable stretcher next to the bed to put him on in a moment.

"You don't need to be present for this. We'll take care of everything." Said one man when he noticed Susan watching them.

"Sure, if you need anything, I'll be in the next door." Said Susan and went to Nicole Denice's room.

As she approached the little pink cradle, where her baby had been sleeping peacefully a moment ago, she saw that the girl was already awake and was now looking around the room, with big blue eyes.

Clearly amused, she stretched her little hands upwards as if she wanted to catch something with them in the air.

"Well, what do you see there?" said Susan at the same time, taking the baby out of the cradle.

She put her on her shoulder and patted her gently on the back, then sat down with the baby in the chair right next to her.

The toddler wriggled, and Susan could feel her constantly flapping her arms across her back.

"Why are you so excited?" she wondered.

It wasn't Nicole Denice's typical reaction; the little girl never showed such joy when Susan looked after her.

The mother only occasionally looked after the child, as the little one spent most of her time with John. It was then that Susan could see the same behaviour in her.

For a moment, she thought it was a bit odd but quickly ignored it because no one can really define infant behaviour.

"You probably don't know why you're so happy yourself, maybe you're just in a good mood today?" she said to the little girl.

She sat in silence with the baby, who was constantly wriggling on her shoulder and making happy noises.

DADADADADA...!! - Chattered the baby.

Then suddenly, a voice reached Susan's ears, coming from the ground floor.

"Susan!?" she heard James' voice.

"They came quickly," she said to herself.

Susan's parents had a habit of entering her house without ringing the bell or even knocking. It didn't bother her too much, although it could be a little frustrating at times.

"I'm here Dad!" she replied instinctively, but to no purpose, as they didn't hear her anyway.

So, she got out of bed, still holding the baby snuggled in her arm, and headed towards the stairs.

As she passed what was until recently still their shared bedroom, she saw that the paramedics had already managed to put John on a stretcher and were gathering to take him away.

"Is everything okay, gentlemen?" she asked stopping for a moment at the door.

"DADA! DADA! DADA!" Nicole Denice shouted.

"Yes ma'am, we'll be ready to go down in a minute." Said one of them. At the same time, he raised his head, and from where he was standing, which was on the opposite side of the stretcher on which John was lying, he saw Susan looking at her dead husband.

But this was not what most caught the man's attention.

Because his gaze fell on the child, who was happily waving her arms and looking up, shouting "DADA" while raising her head, as high as if she was trying to look at the ceiling.

The paramedic then thought that his own one-and-a-half-year-old son was behaving in the same way, always reaching out to him when he came home and shouting "DADA", trying to convince him to pick him up and play with him.

The man furrowed his brow, slightly surprised by the child's strange behaviour.

At first, he thought that the girl had noticed her dead father and was calling out to him unaware of the situation, but when he saw that she was not looking in that direction at all, but shouting at the ceiling, he realised that there was something unusual about it.

However, Susan moved on and disappeared with the child behind the wall, so the man went back to his duties, forgetting the incident.

"I'm coming! Stay in the kitchen!" she called out, approaching the stairs. When she joined her parents a moment later, her mother Rita immediately went to hug her, as soon as she entered the kitchen.

"I'm so sorry, my dear." She whispered, with tears in her eyes, into Susan's ear putting her arms around her while being careful not to crush Nicole Denice.

Susan looked over Rita's shoulder and saw that James was also slowly approaching them.

His face looked more depressed than usual, as he usually had a serious expression, so it was hard to tell what mood he was in.

This time, however, Susan saw the sadness in her father's eyes, and thought he was clearly suffering from the loss of his son-in-law. It was one of those moments when nothing needed to be said, to understand the prevailing atmosphere.

Susan was grateful for the care of her parents, who she could always count on in difficult times.

"Come to grandpa..." said James, grabbing the little girl and then carefully removing her from Susan's arms.

"...How are you feeling Susan?"

"Not too bad, the shock is gone..." she replied. "...I was expecting it, but I don't think I was ever quite ready."

"No one ever is." Rita said.

At that moment there was the sound of heavy footsteps on the stairs, the paramedics were coming downstairs with John.

"You stay here. I'll go to them." James said.

He then handed the baby to Rita and walked towards the front door, where the men were heading and stopped next to John's piano to wait for them there.

When the women were left alone in the kitchen, the phone rang in Susan's pocket.

Rita watched her daughter curiously as she pulled the phone out of her trouser pocket and, wrinkling her brow, looked at the display.

"Sorry Mum, I must take this, it's from work." She explained, then turned on her heel and walked quickly out into the garden, closing the door behind her.

Rita had already noticed this behaviour in her daughter at a time when she was coming to John's request to help him look after Nicole Denice. She was not happy about it and condemned Susan when she did it, but there was nothing more she could do, because her daughter claimed it was important professional matters, she had to attend to.

Her mother had always believed that a wife, should always look after her own family first, and only then strangers.

But Susan had a different opinion, she never wanted to admit that Rita was right about that.

Even now, when John has just left us, she is still doing the same thing. - Said Rita in a low voice.

As soon as she finished saying this sentence, while watching Susan who was walking around the garden with the phone to her ear, she heard a piano key.

"DUMMM..." - Coming from the spacious corridor, where the instrument was placed, close to the front door.

"DUMMM..." - After a few seconds, again – "DUMMM..."

Then the girl let out a joyful squeal and began to wriggle exuberantly in Rita's arms.

You must be kidding me. - Said the woman in exasperation.

'DUMMM...'

She looked in the direction of the sound, but there was no piano in sight from where she stood, so she moved in that direction with the baby in her arms.

I wonder which one of them decided, to play with the piano at a time like this. She thought nervously.

When she got there, she saw that the front door was wide open, but there was no one in the house except her and the baby.

She raised her eyebrows in surprise and then looked outside.

There, she saw that one paramedic was already sitting behind the wheel of the ambulance and James, standing at the back of the car and clearly moving his lips, was saying something to the person inside.

However, she couldn't hear anything from this distance because they were simply too far away, so she turned her head and looked confusedly at the piano.

The lid covering the keys was up, Rita hadn't noticed it before, so she didn't know if it had been in that position when they entered the house or not. After all, it's not possible for someone to hit the key and then run off in a matter of seconds, or maybe I've misheard myself? Nooo, definitely not, if it was one time, then maybe, but I clearly heard several bangs. She was talking to herself in her mind, looking for an explanation.

"You heard it too, didn't you, darling...?" she said to the child.

"...Is there anyone here!" she called out into the depths of the house, in an act of ultimate desperation, but received no answer.

While Rita looked around confused, the little girl was bouncing merrily in her arms, tearing towards her father's piano.

"DADADA!!" she exclaimed.

"What do you see there, darling? Your place, isn't it? Come, let's sit down." Said the woman then walked over to the piano, pushed back the small leather stool that stood in front of it, so she could sit on it.

She then seated Nicole Denice next to her, as John used to do, while at the same time holding her back with her hand, securing the child so that she would not fall over on the floor.

"DADADA!!!"

The delighted little girl stretched her short arms towards the piano, but couldn't reach the keys, so Rita sat her on her lap and moved closer, so the child could touch the instrument.

I can't play like your daddy. - She said to the little girl.

At the same time Susan, who had just finished her conversation, opened the door separating the kitchen from the garden, and went inside. As she did not find the mother there with her daughter, she crossed the room, heading towards the corridor.

As she left the kitchen and stood in front of the stairs, she turned her head to the left where the piano stood, at which Rita and Nicole Denice were sitting.

When Susan looked in that direction, she unexpectedly gasped for air.

"What the hell?" she said under her breath.

For a split second, it seemed to her that instead of Rita, there was John sitting at the piano, holding his daughter on his lap and staring at her with a sinister look.

It was literally a moment, so when Susan blinked her eyes, Rita was already there.

Then she shook her head slightly, to get the sight out of her mind, and walked closer.

"Why are you sitting here?"

"She really wanted to play with the keys..." Rita replied, pointing at the girl. – "...You know, this may sound ridiculous, but I could have sworn I heard someone start playing a while ago, when I was in the kitchen." She added.

"What do you mean?" Susan raised her eyebrows questioningly.

"Well, maybe not so much as playing, just pressing the keys." Rita replied. Then she pressed one random key, took a brief pause and pressed it again for comparison.

...DUMMM...DUMMM....

"You could have told them they didn't come here to play my late husband's piano, what a lack of respect and professionalism!" replied Susan visibly upset.

"But no one was here when I came in, a minute later, they're all outside."

Susan looked at her mother in disbelief.

186

Keys don't make a sound by themselves, if she really heard something, it must have been one of those paramedics or she must have just imagined something. Susan thought.

"Never mind, I'll call Judy and see what time they're coming." Said Susan. She turned back to where she had come from again, leaving her mother with Nicole Denice.

Rita followed her daughter with her eyes, as she disappeared around the corner into the kitchen.

As if she couldn't call her here. Rita thought.

"Where has she gone?" she heard James' voice behind her.

Rita turned with the baby towards her husband, who had just returned. James had waited outside for the ambulance to pull away, then went inside and stood behind Rita so quietly, that she didn't even notice him.

"To call Judy, she wants to check, what time she's arriving with Kevin..." She replied. "...I'm very worried about her James."

"It's understandable, she's just lost her husband, but she'll get over it, you'll see."

"It's not about that, what worries me is her constant absence, she's always busy with something." She explained.

"She works a lot, people need her help, I don't see anything strange about that."

"Oh James, you don't understand anything..."

She replied irritated. "...I don't mean that she talks on the phone a lot, but how she does it and how she behaves, she's always out in the garden, at home she never answers, even when I was coming in as John asked me to, I saw her doing the same thing, more than once I tried to talk to her about it, she just dismissed me saying it was important conversations with patients."

"I suppose, that's just the way it is." James replied.

"I don't know, but I'm not entirely convinced and let me tell you more, John wasn't thrilled about it either, you should have seen the look on his face, when he looked at her at the time, he was heartbroken, especially when she finished talking on the phone and came back telling him, she had to go somewhere urgently."

At this point Susan returned, still holding the phone in her hand, and looked at her parents, who had stopped talking at the sight of her.

"What are you two discussing?" she asked.

"And what time are they arriving?" Rita replied, ignoring her question.

"I don't know exactly, Judy said they're on the way, but they don't even know what time their train is yet, Kevin suggests going by car."

"The train will be quicker for them." James added.

"True, but is there a reason to rush? After all, it won't help John anymore." Susan replied.

James and Rita exchanged puzzled glances, hearing these words from their daughter.

"Well, maybe it won't help him..." Rita interjected. "...But it doesn't matter to the parents, whether they can help their child at the time like this or not, they've lost their only son and they're going to get here as soon as they can to see him, none of us know how awful they must feel right now, and I hope we never have to face something like that." She added in a serious tone. James put his hands on his wife's shoulders to let her know that he shared her opinion, while she kept looking at Susan, who didn't seem to understand the point of what she was saying.

"I think everyone must go through grief in their own way." Said James to calm the situation.

"Yes, you're right..." replied Susan after a while. "...So, as I said, they are coming today, just not sure what time. We'll wait here for them." Rita decided.

Susan was clearly surprised by this statement; she had not expected her parents to want to stay at her house, all day.

At first, she didn't quite know how to behave, but she quickly composed herself and adopted a serious expression.

I'm even fine with that, they'll be able to keep an eye on Nicole. She thought.

"Okay, if you want to stay here then feel free, I'll be able to go to the hospital, during this time." She declared unexpectedly. "Why do you want to go to the hospital?" James was surprised. "I've been informed that Carolin Roberts' condition has deteriorated..." She explained. "...I have been asked to see her as soon as possible."

"And are you going to go, now?" Rita couldn't believe her ears either.

"Mum, she's my patient, she's going through a nightmare right now..." Susan explained. "...You know her son David is missing, and nobody knows where he is, she needs me."

"I know about David, everyone knows, just like we know about Magda Richardson, but you have your own issues now, you can't help others when you are struggling with your own problems." Rita replied in exasperation. "Darling, what about John? What about Denice? She needs you." James added.

"Her name is Nicole." Susan replied nervously.

The parents were watching their daughter carefully, but the daughter was trying not to show how upset she was.

She really wanted to go to Carolin Roberts, because she still had unfinished business with her that she wanted to sort out, as soon as possible. *Maybe it won't be as easy with them as I thought, mother is clearly on to something, that's why she's so stubborn, I need to play it differently, I'll tell them what they want to hear and then I'll work something out.* Susan thought.

You're both right, but I also need some time to myself, to sort things out in my head... - She began to speak quietly. - ...John's death came suddenly, I'm still shaken, since you're here I can use this to be alone with my thoughts for a while, stay with Nicole until I've come to peace with myself, later I won't have time for that.

Susan decided to take a different tack, she knew James would back her up and she would be able to go to Carolin, all that remained was to convince Rita.

But Susan had no doubt that with James on her side, Rita would quickly give in.

"All right darling, we understand..." James said suddenly. "...We'll stay with Denice, and you go meet that woman, tomorrow will be a new day, we'll start all over again."

Rita shuddered, hearing James' words, she did not share his opinion and still felt that Susan should stay at home with them and her daughter. "Thank you, it won't take me long, I'll just check what's going on and come back home."

"Don't get me wrong Susan, I really appreciate what you are doing for these poor people, the whole town is grateful to you for that, but you must understand, there are times in life when you must put other people's problems aside and deal with your own, especially in the current situation."

Rita added in a calm voice.

I know mum, so many things have come down on me suddenly, it's going to take time to process, but I promise, it's going to be okay. - Susan replied. - Yes, do what you need to do.... - Rita replied. - ...We'll wait here for you. - She added, giving her daughter a friendly smile.

Susan nodded in agreement, smiling gently at her parents.

I'll go and change. - She added, then turned and headed for the stairs. - I can't invite them here too often; a babysitter will be needed. - She thought, heading towards the bedroom.

Rita looked at James at the same time, sending him a look that meant

"Didn't I tell you?"

Don't even get me started. - James said seeing the look on his wife's face. - That's what I wanted to say to you, I don't know, maybe it just seems that way to me, but is what she's doing really that important? I understand, just like Joanna Richardson, Carolin is going through a nightmare and probably the most difficult time of her life, but do you think Susan has a realistic chance of helping them?

I don't know, if she's so dedicated she must believe she does... - James replied. - ...I'm very proud of her attitude, you know she's intelligent, so if she's doing something she has a reason for it, she knows she's going to succeed.

It's true, her intelligence sometimes scares me. - Rita replied in a resigned voice.

"DUMMM...DUMMM...DUMMM..." - The child struck the keys of the piano and bounced happily on Rita's lap.

"Can you please not make so much noise!?" Susan yelled from upstairs. Rita looked at James, pushed back the sofa and got up from the piano, taking Nicole Denice with her.

"Where are you going?" he asked his wife.

"I'm taking her out, for some fresh air."

Then she went into the garden with the baby, leaving James alone in the corridor.

The man stood for a moment, undecided whether he should follow his wife or whether it would be better if he left her alone for a while.

191

He knew she wasn't in the best of moods, which usually meant it was better to stay away from her.

He looked at his watch, which showed 11:00am, and then decided to go upstairs to see Susan.

When he climbed the stairs a moment later, he investigated the bedroom where John had spent last night and saw that the paramedics had left all the chemotherapy equipment.

"Shouldn't they have taken those instruments...?" he called out to Susan. "...I think so." She replied from the next room. "...I was surprised, they left it there, some amateurs. I'll find out later what I'm supposed to do with it. James stood in the bedroom doorway and looked around the room, which was understandably messy."

The blanket on the bed hung so low it almost touched the floor, there was an IV in the top right-hand corner of the bed, with slightly tangled cables carelessly scattered about.

There was a gloomy atmosphere throughout the room.

"Even if I didn't know someone had died in here, I'd still have guessed it." James stated.

At that moment, Susan came out of her bedroom.

When James spotted her, he saw that she was wearing a long, elegant black coat, stylish high heels and a handbag slung over her shoulder. He also noticed that she had touched up her make-up and thought, she looked very good now.

She certainly doesn't look like someone who is in mourning.

"I know what you're thinking..." Susan suddenly spoke up, standing in front of him. "...I know I've gone a bit overboard with the make-up, but I don't want them to see from me that something is wrong, not today."

James nodded slightly as a sign of understanding.

192

"Don't be mad at your mum, you must understand, she's really going through a lot." Said James in a calm voice.

"I'm not mad at her, but life goes on, I can't help John anymore, but I can still help David and Carolin and hope to find Magda too."

"James looked at her more carefully as he thought that the tone of voice, she said this with seemed not to suit her.

He could not now pinpoint it, but he had the impression that Susan was stiffly reciting a pre-arranged statement.

"You know, my dear, tragedy struck us all when Magda went missing..." he began. "...But you must face it, that was a year ago, you know perfectly well, that the likelihood of her being found unharmed is virtually nil. As a father I don't know what I would do if it happened to you, I would probably lose my mind too, just like Joanna."

"Well, Carolin is in the same state now, that's why it's so important to me to help her cope."

"It's all right, I won't keep you any longer..." James replied.

He then walked over to Susan and hugged his daughter.

"...I hope you know what you're doing." He whispered in her ear.

"Don't worry about a thing, dad." She replied.

Then she slipped out of her father's embrace and walked down the stairs to the ground floor, a moment later James heard the front door close. "Don't worry about a thing, dad, if only it were that simple." He said to himself, recalling her words.

James stood for a moment longer outside the bedroom that had until recently, belonged to Susan and John, then descended the stairs. He walked slowly through the kitchen towards the garden, where Rita was still with Nicole Denice.

James couldn't shake the strange feeling that had come over him, when he had spoken to Susan a moment ago, but he decided not to mention it to Rita and keep it to himself.

He didn't want to cause his wife any more worry, as he knew that she already had enough on her plate.

11:20am,

At this time Susan got into the car parked in the driveway.

She leaned back comfortably in the driver's seat and closed her eyes, breathing deeply and evenly to relax.

All sorts of thoughts were swirling around in her head now, so she tried to calm them down.

"Okay, first, I must start with the most important things." She said to herself, started the engine and carefully drove the car out of the driveway onto the street, then slowly moved forward.

When she reached the main highway after a few minutes, she turned left and headed towards the hospital.

She had at least fifteen minutes from here to her destination, so she decided to use that time.

She slowed the vehicle down to a safe speed and then picked up her phone, which she had placed by the gear stick earlier. When she looked at the screen, she saw that it was 11:15am. Then, with a few taps of her finger on the touchscreen she dialled the number for Nicolas Gartner, John's lawyer.

She switched on the speaker option, to keep her focus on the driving.

After a few beeps, a male voice rang out.

"This is Nicolas Gartner; how can I help you?"

"Hi Nic, we need to talk," She replied briefly.

Susan was almost one hundred per cent sure, that the house John had built for them would soon be hers, but there was still the question of the company, which John also owned, his insurance policy and the rest of the possessions he owned.

So, she decided that it was necessary to notify John's solicitor of his death, as soon as possible.

At the same time start consulting with him about the inheritance, so that she could slowly start preparing for the procedure, to take control of her husband's estate.

Yes, first, I must start with the most important things. she thought.

Canary Wharf, "BnBL" agency office.

It was 11:25am and Matthiew was busy on a business call.

That day, he had a meeting with a client about renting a house which started at 11am, so when his private phone rang unexpectedly, he had company.

Matthiew never took other calls when he was working with clients, even his secretary knew, not to put through anyone else at the time.

But this time it was his private mobile phone, only for close colleagues and emergencies.

So, he apologised to the client he was talking to, as politely as he could, and picked up.

"Hello...?" he said into the receiver. "...Is something wrong...?" he asked after a moment. "...I understand, but does it change anything...?" he listened to the voice on the phone. "...Okay, so get it done..." He added and paused again. - ...Yes, I already have the sales contract drawn up, all I need is her signature... - He continued speaking.

Matthiew turned his back on the client, sitting in his office and absorbed in the conversation, forgot for a moment that he was not alone. "...It would be useful to drop off a new cuckoo egg, do you have any leads...?" he asked the person he was talking to.

195

"Cuckoo's egg" was the name Matthiew gave to the packages he had commissioned to be sent to Harry Green or Simon Edwards from various "Post Office" locations in London.

The parcels contained Voodoo dolls, small enough to fit easily, into the slots of post boxes.

This method was the safest and made it impossible for law enforcement, to trace the sender.

Harry and Simon posted the parcels when they were not in North Hill, as they were in town and delivered them themselves, safely under cover of darkness.

Sometimes, they left them on the porch and other times, they placed them in easily accessible places around the house.

It all depended on the leads Matthiew provided them with, who, having agreed all the details with Nattaly in advance, would give them the details in terms of location, time and circumstances.

In this planned manner, Nattaly played a central role, as she was the one who gave the orders and provided the addresses of the next victims, that Harry and Simon would later focus on.

The effect of these actions was to keep the residents of North Hill in suspense, by systematically reminding them of the missing children. Matthiew felt that in this way, he could terrorise the town from a safe distance and keep the emotions of the town under his control.

Which apparently had the impact he expected, because people wouldn't stop talking about the curse and black magic that the Ethiopian couple, had brought up on them a year ago.

Since then, more and more people, came to the agency wanting to sell their houses for cash and leave the town forever.

Matthiew, on the other hand, had no problem finding buyers for his newly acquired properties, among interested clients.

In those days, few people had heard what really went on in North Hill and, as a result, virtually no one knew the history of the town.

Even if anyone had doubts, the picturesque scenery and the location of the town came to the rescue, for the town itself, was a truly beautiful place that was hard to resist.

It was ideal for people, who wanted to escape the hustle and bustle of London's crowded streets.

At some point, the agency started acquiring more and more flats, and up to three properties were acquired in one week, which is a really big number in this industry.

At that point, Matthiew, instructed his staff in all "BnBL" branches, to encourage clients to move to the area.

In addition, agency staff in North Hill were constantly on the lookout for new attractive properties and their owners to whom, they could make an offer to sell.

When such people turned up, often motivated by the atmosphere in the town, they would move on to the first phase of purchase negotiations, but the finalisation of the deal was already taking place in Matthiew's office. The businessman would then receive them at his office in Canary Wharf, while forcing them to make time-consuming trips to London. The agency's North Hill office had three other staff in addition to Harry Green and Simon Edwards.

There were two estate agents, Daniel Hughes and Clarence Taylor, and it was these two men who did all the work of running the firm, along with Barbara Martin, the secretary.

Harry and Simon, on the other hand, were doing completely different 'jobs' and had no idea, how to run an estate agency.

Nonetheless, Matthew Braddock had placed them in management positions in his company.

Neither of them knew they had a different employer, because Nattaly was no ordinary office worker.

She was the principal owner, who benefited most from a well-functioning agency, followed of course by Matthiew Braddock, who officially claimed to be the boss and was widely recognised as such.

Nattaly allowed this to be the hierarchy in the business, because from the first day she became owner, she decided that it would be safest for her to manage in the shadows.

Matthiew proved to her within a year, that he could run the agency efficiently, thanks to him they managed to open four offices in twelve months.

But the biggest success came after his plan was implemented, because thanks to him, properties in North Hill were quickly bought and then sold, raking in millions in profits.

During this time, thanks to Matthiew's scheming, the agency acquired, among other things, a villa that once belonged to an Ethiopian couple, as well as the Richardson family home, bought back from the already mentally unstable, Joanna Richardson.

Time 11:35am.

While Matthiew was on the phone, he turned towards the office. At this point, he trembled, as he realised that a client had been sitting behind him the whole time, listening to the conversation with an intrigued expression on his face.

Slightly confused by this fact, he decided to end the call immediately.

"...I'll talk to you later, I'm with a client right now..." he said.

Still holding the receiver to his ear, he sent the visitor a smile.

At the same time, he quickly tried to analyse in his mind, whether he had said anything suspicious in this relatively short conversation. "...Forgive me, Mr Donovan, business matters, so, where were we?"

the man sitting in the chair opposite him, sent him only a crooked smile of disapproval in reply.

He was visibly disgusted by Matthiew's behaviour, who, as a serious businessman, should have known that it was inappropriate, to take a call from another person while talking to a client.

Whether it was a colleague, a client or even family, a professional should defer such conversations.

As Matthiew sat down on his side of the desk and put the phone down, he was relieved to discover that, apart from using the term 'cuckoo's egg,' which might have seemed an odd term to the uninitiated,

He had not revealed anything else, that might have piqued his client's curiosity more.

Matthiew had reason to be concerned, because the matter was extremely sensitive.

He understood, due to his unruly temperament, he was often careless with his words, especially when he was alone in the office, talking to Nattaly on the phone.

There were times when Matthiew would lose his temper and, in his anger, say things like: "fuck those brats" or "I want the entire North Hill" when he knew, no one was listening, he could afford to be completely honest.

This was also the case here, when for a moment he forgot he wasn't alone in the room; fortunately, the conversation with Nattaly was so smooth and calm, that Matthiew had no reason to get angry.

Otherwise, however, by saying two words too many, he could have quickly sunk in the eyes of the man.

Who, probably driven by curiosity, would have tried to connect all the dots as to what this was all about, and that could have meant that the entire game, would have ended at that point.

Matthiew was only strong verbally, but that was it.

He wouldn't be able to force the man to keep quiet, if necessary, as his mercenaries Simon or Harry would have done.

One day I'm going to have a heart attack from all this, but now, I just need to get rid of this sucker quickly and I can have a drink. He thought. - Ah yes, so as I told you, the offer on this flat is very favourable… - He said, getting back to business.

North Hill, Nattaly Swanson's family home,11:25am,

Nattaly had once again placed her son in her mother's care, so that he would not interfere with her running errands.

Her mother Melissa had already decided to take responsibility for the care of Nattaly's son, the then 16-month-old Yaqub, as her daughter was clearly not concerned about the child's fate.

Still, she tried to influence Nattaly to awaken her maternal instinct. To this end, she tried to force the young mother to spend as much time as possible, with her baby.

Melissa was concerned about her grandchild, so she looked after him when Nattaly could not, or did not, do that.

On another note, she also wanted to make it difficultfor her daughter to go out for hours at a time, making Nattaly feel that she had increasingly limited freedom.

During this time, Nattaly was locked in her room, talking to someone as usual.

"…Nothing happened, I just wanted to say, I must stay home with my son in the evening…" she said into the receiver, pausing to listen to the caller's reply. "…It's just that I won't be able to be in two places at once today, I'm going to pick up a parcel, I'll be out in a minute…" she added and listened. "…Okay, have you sorted everything out yet…?" she asked the person on the other side.

"...No, not today, I told you just now, the parcel must wait, there is no need to rush, everything is under control..." she said after a while.

"...I understand, alright, so take care of it, we'll talk later..." she added at the end.

She ended the call and put the phone in her purse, then walked over to the dresser where she kept the money she was collecting.

Today I need seventy-five thousand. she said to herself in her mind. She pulled out the envelopes in which she had sorted the previously perfectly counted money.

In each of them, was an amount of five or ten thousand pounds, to streamline the process when exchanging.

This was money just to run the business and Nattaly did not spend it on her own pleasures, as the share of the profit she later received was more than satisfying.

Over time, Nattaly became accustomed to her role in the business. At first, she had trouble acclimatising and accepting the great responsibility, that rested on her shoulders.

But when she finally got to grips with her emotions and remorse, everything was going smoothly and could have been even better had it not been for the fact that her ambitions had recently been stymied by Melissa, who forced her to stay at home with the baby.

At the time Nattaly could not, but also did not, want to tell her parents about the activities she was doing with her partner, who was currently transacting business in the London.

She knew well that her elderly parents Jamie and Melissa would never condone the methods and way, their daughter was making money. The moment it came out what she was doing, everything would fall apart, and Nattaly couldn't let that happen.

Her business was taking off , she was making colossal money, and she had no intention of giving it up.

No moral values mattered anymore, she didn't care about inflicting suffering on other people and destroying someone's life.

The most important thing and the only thing that made the young woman feel satisfied at that moment, was to make as much money as possible.

Even if it meant walking over dead bodies to achieve her goal.

While at the beginning of their collaboration, she had had trouble turning o her feelings completely and was often tormented by her conscience, this problem had long ceased to exist.

Nattaly realised that with time, everything can become acceptable, helped by the fact that she did not have to look at the people, she was destroying with her actions.

"What the eyes do not see, the heart does not regret." She said to herself and smiled widely.

She then stuffed eight thick brown envelopes into her handbag, put on her shoes and coat and was ready to leave.

If only I could send this shit away today, because of this brat I'm going to have to leave it home. she thought nervously as she left the room. She quickly ran down the stairs and left the house, without saying anything to her mother.

Melissa looked out of the living room at the sound of a slamming door. But as she approached the window overlooking the veranda, all she saw was Nattaly's car already reversing out of the driveway.

This made the woman furrow her brow in a nervous grimace.

Where are you going in such a hurry? she thought.

Melissa had caught Nattaly talking before, which worried her greatly at the time.

But she didn't know what to do in this situation, because at the same time her job as a mother was to protect her daughter, but on the other hand, she felt that something bad was happening.

Nattaly never allowed herself to be persuaded to talk to her parents and tell them what she was currently doing.

She always dismissed them by saying that her fiancé, runs a car repair shop in London for rich people.

Both Melissa and Jamie suspected that their daughter wasn't telling them the truth, but there was no way to get her to be honest with them.

Ah well, let her do what she wants if she's so stubborn, and if she gets into any trouble, as God is my witness, I've tried to do everything I could to protect her. Thought the elderly woman resignedly.

She waited another moment until her daughter had completely disappeared around the corner, then returned to the living room where Nattaly's son was waiting for her.

9

Criminal practice.

'Human life is priceless because it is the gift of God, whose love has no limits. And when God gives life, he gives it forever.'

4 years later,

15 June 2013, London, Lewisham, Matthiew Brown's flat, 12:35pm.

Matthiew was in his flat, recovering from last night's party.

He had decided not to go to the office that day, because he had spent the entire previous night in a club, abusing alcohol and other psychoactive substances.

He was simply unable to think soberly while still having intoxicants in his bloodstream.

Instead, he called one of the secretaries first thing in the morning, asking her to come and meet him, to the collect the keys to the office.

The woman agreed to her boss's request, but was not happy about it at all, because she thought that the fact that Matthiew had the audacity to call her, at eight o`clock in the morning, waking her up and on top of that, asking her to come to his flat, was simply rude.

Nonetheless, the boss had no intention of leaving the agency closed that day, as it would have entailed unnecessary costs; he would have had to pay his employees for the day off.

It would most likely also affect tenants and clients, which for Matthiew, as a very greedy and money-hungry person, was unthinkable.

While he was recovering in front of the TV, finishing the rest of the cocaine he had left after a night, drinking beer to soothe his hangover, Nattaly was getting ready to make a phone call.

She had important information for him, which she needed to share immediately.

She had found another victim, in whom she saw an easy target for a relatively quick and good income.

In fact, the money the agency brought in was already good enough, that Nattaly would not have to work for the rest of her life.

However, it had been almost four years since the last kidnapping, and Nattaly felt she was missing the adrenaline she felt, when the police were roaming the streets and people were locked in their homes with their children, out of fear.

At the time, she observed the situation in the city and was happy to assess the consequences of her actions, with impunity.

It was like an addiction.

It was possible to live sober for a while, but in the long run it became increasingly difficult, until finally the urge to return to the bad habit won, and she had to give vent to her accumulated desires.

When she contributed to the kidnapping of Magda Richardson, not directly of course, but by standing behind deliberately determined actions. She felt the fear that she would soon be caught, arrested and consequently imprisoned for many years, if not for the rest of her days.

However, over time this fear turned into excitement and an adrenaline rush that was as addictive as the strongest drug.

So just before the second incident, when fifteen-year-old David Roberts would disappear six months later, the woman was eagerly awaiting the moment when the storm would break loose in the city again.

So far, everything had gone perfectly.

Neither the police nor the residents knew where to look for the perpetrators, which filled her with extra satisfaction.

She felt a sense of euphoria, talking to ordinary people about the events and then to the investigators, seeing the trust in their eyes for her. She knew perfectly well that these people had no idea about, and no one even though, that she was to some extent behind these terrible events. This made the emotions, that pierced her at the time so wonderful, that she wished they could last forever.

At the very beginning of the crime spree, she was most horrified by the way people disappeared.

She wasn't a murderer and never became one, because she never personally hurt anyone.

Harry and Simon were doing it, so she made excuses for that fact. However, deep down she knew that she was just as guilty as Matthiew and the two men.

But she had managed to control the feelings of remorse and then, push them out of her consciousness completely over time.

The task was made easier by the fact that she had never seen anything with her own eyes, so she had no memories to haunt her.

She became accustomed to this ignorance and never wanted to change it. Over time, one of her favourite pastimes became going out at night and discreetly tossing Voodoo dolls to pre-selected people.

Later, she could hear it being talked about and people would shudder in fear, thinking that they or their loved ones, would be the next victims.

It turned into a small obsession.

So even though she had to look after the baby, she couldn't stop herself from leaving the house at night and walking into town, unnoticed by anyone.

On that day, she decided it was high time to shake up the town again and began to prepare the ground for it, still without Matthiew's knowledge. Nattaly assumed that she, as the person with the larger percentage of shares in the agency, had the last word, and that Matthiew would have to comply, at the same time bearing in mind, that it was his idea.

Nattaly knew that he would agree to anything she said, because she was carrying out his intentions.

Matthiew, on the other hand, saw no need to risk another kidnapping, at the time.

In his opinion, business was going very well and for it to stay that way, all he needed to do was to keep the people of North Hill in fear by placing Voodoo dolls, which had become a kind of symbol of misery and terror in the town. What he could not have predicted, however, was that Nattaly, who at the start of their partnership seemed shy and unsure about this way of doing business, would turn from a person with doubts into someone who would plan on her own.

Although Matthiew was not afraid to take risks, he was convinced of his invulnerability by two very important facts that worked in his favour. Firstly, he had so far managed to avoid detection after the first two kidnappings, and for the last five years there had not even been the slightest threat of anything coming to light.

And secondly, he had two professionals on his side, Harry and Simon and were extremely cruel and very well organised, hardened criminals. So, if something went wrong, they would be the first to caught, but even then, the chances of them co-operating with the police and dragging Matthiew with them were nil.

He could have always just as easily denied all accusations.

It was a brilliant plan in its simplicity, given that he had never been to North Hill and there was no evidence to directly link him to the crimes, so the police would never be able to prove anything against him.

However, Nattaly may have felt safest as she did not officially exist as the principal owner of the Bradley and Brad Lettings agency chain, a fact known only to Matthiew and her late father George Bradley's lawyer, Michael Edwards.

Time 12:40pm.

Having worked out all the details, Nattaly was ready to inform Matthiew to pass on the assignment, to Harry and Simon.

So, she locked herself in her bedroom, taking precautions even though she was alone in the house with only the baby.

She sat down on her bed and grabbed her phone, Matthiew answered after a few beeps.

"Hello?" he said in a scratchy voice.

The cocaine and alcohol he had consumed, was having the opposite effect of what he wanted, and Matthiew felt sick.

"Am I calling at a bad time?" she asked.

"No, just speak quickly."

"We have a new location..." she replied. "...I'll give you the details to pass on."

Matthiew had the feeling that the cocaine was only now starting to kick in more strongly, because of receiving an extra dose of adrenaline. He hadn't expected to hear this, the feeling of surprise mixed with the psychoactive agents.

"Do you mean to tell me that you have a target?" he asked, barely containing his dizziness.

"Yes, a widower with a son, a nice big house." She answered briefly.

"And what do you want to do?"

There was silence on the phone for a moment, as if Nattaly didn't know what to answer.

"What do you mean...?" she finally asked.

"...I want you to get Harry and Simon up and running."

"Do you really think that's necessary? Because to be honest, I don't think so."

"I don't care what you think..." she replied firmly.

"...Call one of them and tell them to get ready, they must be ready in three days, by then I will give you the rest of the information as I always do."

"What if I don't?" Matthiew replied.

"Then I'll put you out of business, you know I can afford to buy your shares, and you'll end up with nothing."

Theoretically she could do it and Matthiew was aware of this, although it wouldn't necessarily be that easy.

Nattaly had considered this option before but hadn't taken any steps yet, because she knew it would involve a lawyer, and she didn't really want to do that.

This whole conversation was more to show who was in charge and to scare Matthiew, than to make any real threats.

It was intended to remind him, not to try to defy his boss's will.

"Easy target, widower, I know him well, lives in a big house with his ten-year-old son, goes to a psychologist once a week..." she began to provide details. "...He's already found the cuckoo's egg, so he's scared, he spoke to the police a few days ago, so any moment now they will lose interest in him, then it will be our turn."

"I see you started everything without my knowledge." Matthiew replied. "I'm only doing what you asked me to do, this property is worth a lot..." she replied. "...I've done my part, now it's time for you to do yours, notify those psychopaths and make them get ready to work."

"Why are you so determined? Where did the remorse and fear go?" Matthiew, stop asking unnecessary questions, I'm sticking to your plan and don't worry about my conscience, we're in this together, and very deep. "Okay, then I should tell them that the trip must take place in three days?" he asked.

"Yes, the father will be with a psychologist at that time, his son should be unaccompanied when he returns home..." she replied. "...Tomorrow, I will give you the address so they can check the area they are going to."

"Okay, so I look forward to your call."

"Speak to you, soon." he added in conclusion to Nattaly.

Matthiew hung up the phone and straightened up on the couch, stretching his arms high up to stretch his back.

"Who would have thought I would create a monster?" he said to himself. He had first met Nattaly almost nine years ago, when he had followed

George to the Hilton Hotel to supposedly help him with a predicament. Matthiew had found himself involved, on the grounds that some unknown woman was trying to blackmail George by pretending to be his daughter, and Matthiew was convinced George couldn't do without his help.

210

It was then that he had the dubious pleasure of talking to her alone, while George left them at the table to go to the bar for drinks.

Even though it had been almost nine years since, he had first felt that this woman was extremely sophisticated and ruthless.

He still remembered the exact moment when he thought she was very much like him, because it was these character traits that set him apart, and he felt that he and Nattaly might have something in common.

However, he now realised that she was not only similar in personality to him, as he had once suspected, she was far crueller and more devious than Matthiew might have expected.

On the one hand, it didn't make much difference to him, and it even made him more comfortable, because the days of her hysterically calling him while the police circled the town looking for missing children, were gone irretrievably.

But on the other hand, he had to admit that he hadn't expected Nattaly to start revealing the darkest side of her personality over the years. In any case, they were both involved up to their ears, so he couldn't back out of it anymore.

20 minutes later.

Matthiew was still sitting on the sofa staring dully at the TV, his head pulsating from the cocaine-induced adrenaline and feeling cold chills running through his body.

Despite taking the drug, which manifests itself by stimulating the body and creating a false feeling of not being tired, Matthiew was becoming more and more sleepy by the minute.

Spending hours and hours of intense time away from home, without being able to rest and lack of sleep, was taking its toll on him.

At such moments, he reminded himself that he was no longer a young lad who could stand on his feet for days in a row, but an almost fifty-year-old man who was very overweight.

"Well, this needs to be sorted out as soon as possible." He said to himself in a tired voice.

He then leaned over the table on which he had placed the phone, picked it up and found Simon's number.

Although Simon and Harry were inseparable business partners, so they carried out assignments equally without much division of roles, Matthiew preferred to discuss such matters with the former.

He saw Simon as the more organised and responsible man, whereas Harry was mainly a walking sack of muscle for the dirty work.

"The perfect soldier, dumb, strong and without an opinion of his own, blindly following orders." Matthiew smiled to himself at this thought. When he dialled the number and heard the dial tone, he didn't have to wait long for Simon to answer.

"What do you want?" Simon asked immediately.

"How are things going?" Matthiew replied.

"What do you mean?"

"How are things going at the agency, is everything alright?"

"And how do I know that...?" Simon quipped. "...If you want to ask about business, call the secretary or one of your agents."

"Sure, how about Harry?"

"Look, maybe you'd better tell me what you want straight away? We both know you're not calling just to chat."

"Okay, there'll be a job to do..." Matthiew began to say.

"...I have news of a new destination, be ready to travel in three days, I don't know the details yet, but I'll find out everything soon."

"Hmmm, so we're back in business?"

"It looks like it." Matthiew replied.

"We haven't been active for four years; don't you think it would be safer to leave it as it is?" Simon asked reasonably.

"It's not entirely up to me."

"But I suppose you have something to say?"

"Never mind, three days, be ready..." Matthiew replied.

"...Tomorrow you'll go for a look around when I get the address."

"Good, Harry will be pleased, he was already starting to get rusty here."

"What's he been doing lately?"

"Not much, he's only just got back from London." Simon replied.

"Why don't I know anything about it?"

"You don't need to know about everything."

"You should keep me informed about such things, after all, you work for me..." Said man angered Matthiew.

"...I hope you at least look good as the head my office?"

"We moved into this dump five years ago at your request..." Simon began firmly

"...Since then, everything has been fine and there have been no fuck ups, so fucking stop talking shit! Don't forget who you're talking to! Neither me nor Harry are one of your pussy ass agents you can speak to like that!"

"It's okay, calm down, I just need to make sure everything is alright..."

Replied Matthiew quickly, this time with clear fear in his voice.

"You're lucky you're not talking to Harry right now, he's not as calm as me."

"I'll call you tomorrow with the first details, for now start preparing slowly."

"Don't worry about it." Simon replied and hung up without saying goodbye.

Matthiew straightened up on the sofa again, staring at the ceiling.

He took a few deep breaths, feeling his body shake with nerves.

"Fucking psychopaths!!!" He cursed under his breath.

He knew very well that Simon was right about Harry.

Because the man was simply a fury with an impulsive temper, he hated it when anyone tried to tell him what to do.

Matthiew had once seen with his own eyes Harry massacre a man outside a club with his bare hands, just because the man looked at him.

Therefore, he had no doubt that he would not have stopped himself, from doing harm to him as well.

Although he was their boss and paid Simon and Harry good money, he shouldn't forget what a dangerous environment these two came from, especially, what they were capable of.

Let me finally get those details so I can pass them on, and I'll have peace of mind again. Matthiew thought, closing his eyes, and a few seconds later sleep overtook him.

At the same time, Nattaly was scanning photos of ten-year-old Oliver Wilson onto her computer to send to Matthiew later, and he in turn would pass them on to Simon and Harry.

Now that Matthiew had fallen asleep from exhaustion, leaning back on the sofa with his face to the ceiling and snoring loudly, Nattaly was preparing another blow aimed at the residents of North Hill, so that they would once again be unable to sleep peacefully, overcome with fear.

Just three more days, everyone would remember that the nightmare had never really ended, and soon, it would continue.

10

Goodbye John.

'May our hope be greater than anything that may oppose
that hope.'

4 years earlier,

7 November 2009, North Hill, City Cemetery, 02:10pm.

It was a nice, sunny day; the time has come for John's family, to say
their final goodbyes to him.

Kevin and Judy McKane had arrived from London late in the
evening three days earlier, having received news from Susan of their
son's death, and were staying at the hotel until the funeral ceremony.

Susan, for reasons known to herself, did not want John's parents to
spend this time with her in their shared home, so they obediently
respected her wishes.

On that day, John's entire family gathered at his home a few minutes
after 2pm to go to the cemetery together, as the ceremony was due
to start at 3pm.

Kevin McKane and his wife Judy arrived to meet Susan almost an
hour before the ceremony started, with Rita and James joining them
shortly afterwards.

All dressed in sullen black clothing, they were ready to embark with
John on his final journey to the place where he was to rest forever.

Even little Nicole was wearing a black dress that Susan had bought her, especially for the occasion.

When James and Rita saw Susan for the first time since their last visit a few days earlier, they immediately noticed that their daughter looked very miserable.

Her eyes were bloodshot, as if she hadn't been able to sleep for a long time, and underneath them were dark bags that she had tried to hide under thick layers of make-up.

However, given that she had lost her husband only three days ago, her condition seemed justified, as she was someone who was currently experiencing the death of a loved one.

So, neither Rita nor James initially wanted to ask Susan about the rather obvious reason, why she now looked so weakened.

The parents decided that the best course of action was to give their daughter a little more time, to recover and only then try to talk to her. Kevin and Judy, on the other hand, seemed not to notice the sorry state their daughter-in-law was in, because when they arrived on the scene, they greeted her kindly on the doorstep and then immediately went inside, leaving her alone in the corridor for a while.

Once they were all together, Kevin and James went into the kitchen to pour themselves a stronger drink and talk manfully in private, while Judy took little Nicole out into the garden with her to get some fresh air.

Rita, in turn, took a visibly tired Susan by the hand and led her into the living room, so that she could sit on the sofa and relax.

"How are you feeling today, darling?" she asked, sitting down next to her daughter.

"I have a bit of a headache, but otherwise, not too bad." She heard in reply. Rita did not want to ask directly about the bags under her eyes, which clearly indicated that Susan was having trouble sleeping.

"Can you manage to go to the cemetery?"

"Yes..." Susan replied. "...I'm not ill just, I didn't sleep much last night. Rita knew exactly that this was the case, but she was also interested in the reason for her daughter's lack of sleep."

"Does she cry at night? Or is she not sleeping out of despair? Or is Nicole keeping her awake?" there were many possible explanations.

"I understand, you must be experiencing the loss of John very much."

"Yes, it's true, I miss him a lot, but." Susan was silent for a moment.

"But what?"

"But there is something else..." she added after a moment.

"What do you mean?"

Susan searched her mind for words of explanation, which made her look slightly confused, Rita could see that her daughter was having trouble gathering her thoughts.

"It's the piano..." She finally said. "...I heard it playing last night." She added in a slightly trembling voice.

The woman stared intensely at her daughter, and her eyes took on the shape of coins as they widened at what she heard.

Susan's mother immediately recalled a moment when she had been alone with Nicole Denice in the kitchen three days ago, and she had also heard someone tapping on the piano keys, but when she went to check it out, no one was there.

"Oh, darling." She said, putting her arm around her daughter and hugging her tightly.

Susan let herself be drawn close without resistance, hung her head and for a moment they sat in silence.

Rita knew her all too well and that Susan would tell her in a moment exactly how the previous night had gone, once she had gathered her thoughts. She had no intention of rushing her or asking unnecessary questions, like "are you sure you didn't dream that?" or "or maybe it was just your imagination?"

In fact, Susan's mother was a little surprised when she heard her daughter start talking about the piano playing, which must have been loud and intense enough to keep her awake at night.

But on the other hand, she wasn't completely surprised by this, as she herself had witnessed this strange and inexplicable phenomenon before.

"Shhh... It's all right." She whispered in her ear.

Susan leaned against her mother's chest, in such a way that her head was under Rita's.

"First, I was woken up by Nicole, when I checked the time, it was exactly three o'clock in the morning..." Susan began to speak quietly and uncertainly.

"...At first, I thought she was crying, but when I got up to check on her, she was standing in and bouncing happily..." she talked and Rita listened attentively. "...When I took her in my arms, I heard a piano from downstairs, then the door to our bedroom opened and I was terribly frightened, I immediately thought someone had broken into our house, so I put her back in her cot, took the phone and dialled the emergency number..." Susan paused to calm her nerves. "...But the sounds, they were so pointlessly monotonous, pum, pum, pum and so on continuously, at intervals of a few seconds, when I got to the stairs and turned on the light in the hallway, then they stopped."

"Did you call the police?"

"No, admittedly I had already dialled the number, but when I stood by the stairs and listened to the sounds coming from downstairs, there was complete silence and I thought that if someone was there, they wouldn't be drawing attention to themselves by mindlessly making those noises." Susan replied.

"Yes, that makes sense."

"Even so, I slowly and cautiously made my way downstairs, still holding my phone at the ready, and looked around the house, checking the front door, the garden door and all the ground floor windows and nothing, everything was locked and there was no sign that anyone uninvited could have broken in."

"It's very strange." Rita replied.

"I went back to bed but couldn't sleep until morning, Nicole had no intention of resting and for the rest of the night she was strangely agitated, I even dare to say that there was something unnatural in her behaviour, especially since it was the middle of the night.

"It's true, she can at least afford a nap during the day, with you it's worse.

"Exactly, I feel exhausted, but now I can't lie down." Susan confessed.

"I'll help you, don't worry." Rita hugged her daughter tighter.

"I'm just not sure." Susan began to wonder.

"About what, sweetheart?" Rita wondered.

"When I went back into the bedroom and closed the door..." Susan explained. "...Nicole was making noise all the time, shouting dada like she did when she was playing with John, because of all of it I'm not sure if the piano stopped playing completely."

"Of course..." Rita replied. "...It's not important anymore, don't think about it now, try to gather your strength for the rest of the day."

"You're right, it's going to be a long day." Susan agreed.

Rita continued to hug her daughter, trying to comfort her in this way. They sat together for a while longer, when James came into the living room, followed immediately by Kevin.

"We'll have to get ready shortly." James announced.

"It's nearly twenty to three, I'll go and get Judy and Nicole." Added Kevin, then turned back into the kitchen and continued towards the garden.

"Are you two alright?" Susan's father asked.

"Yes, Susan is just a bit tired."

"I'll go and get my bag." Said Susan and slipped out of Rita's arms. James and Rita watched their daughter as she quickly reached the stairs and hurried up to the first floor.

As soon as she was out of their sight, James looked at his wife.

"Are you sure she's alright?" he asked.

"What do you think, is she? She's got a lot on her mind right now." Rita replied.

"That much I know, I mean, why does she look so tired?"

"We'll talk about that later..." Rita replied.

"...Now is not the time for that."

"Can't she sleep at night?"

"It's a lot more complicated than it sounds, I'll explain it to you tonight, when we get home."

"Well, if that's what you prefer." He agreed with his wife.

"She's going to need our help,,," Rita began. "...We need to support her, as best we can."

"What do you want me to do?" James asked.

"I want you to be by her side all the time today don't leave her side for a moment."

James nodded in agreement.

"I'll watch over Denice, so Susan doesn't have to." She added.

"Alright."

"Are you still sitting here? We've got to go." Said Judy, entering the living room with Nicole Denice in her arms.

James and Rita looked in her direction, right behind her was Kevin.

"Yeah, we were just about to get up." Rita replied.

"I'll be waiting for you at the cars." Kevin called out from behind his wife, then turned around and headed for the front door.

"And where is Susan?" asked Judy, looking around.

"She's gone to get her bag; she should be here soon." Rita replied. "It's already twenty to three, we don't have time..." replied Judy and walked closer to the stairs. "...SUSAN!" she called out deep into the house.

"Don't call her...!" angered Rita. "... She'll be back shortly!"

"I'm going to go outside now too." Whispered James in his wife's ear.

"Okay honey, I'll wait for Susan, and we'll join you." Rita replied.

"Just don't be nervous, everything will be fine..." added James and tenderly kissed her on the cheek.

At the same moment, Susan appeared at the top of the stairs and started to walk down quickly.

"Well, there you are, love..." Judy's tone of voice softened. "...Come on, we have less than twenty minutes to get there." She said, at the same time trying to grab Susan's arm so she could follow her.

However, Susan nimbly freed herself from Judy's embrace then took step back, at which the woman furrowed her brow in surprise.

"Excuse me Judy..." she replied.

"...Could you take Nicole into the car with you? I want to go with my parents." Susan explained her behaviour, sending Rita a conciliatory look.

"Yes, of course, just hurry up, there's really very little time left." Judy replied, and without waiting for a reply, headed for the exit.

When they were alone in the house a few seconds later, Rita got up from the sofa and walked over to her daughter, then put her arm behind her back, gently embracing her at the waist.

"Come on, darling..." she said in a calm voice. "...It will all be over soon." She added and they both moved towards the door.

As they passed John's piano in the spacious corridor, Rita stared suspiciously at the instrument.

It was as if she expected the piano to come alive at any moment and start playing itself.

It took her a moment to shake o this thought and concentrate on getting her daughter outside, as she was barely able to stay on her feet.

Rita was still reflecting on what Susan had told her, and she couldn't shake the feeling that her daughter hadn't told her everything.

She suspected that she had deliberately left out some important facts from the story.

But now it wasn't important enough for her to try to revisit the subject with her daughter.

Especially as she knew that Susan herself, would turn to her whenever she felt the need to do so.

When they reached the cars parked in the spacious driveway in front of the house a short while later, Rita let Susan take the passenger seat next to the driver seat, already occupied by James, and sat in the back seat herself.

Kevin, Judy and Nicole were in the other vehicle, ready to go.

Once they were all in their cars, James gestured for Kevin to go first, then started the engine and carefully began to follow his lead.

A few seconds later James turned the vehicle to the left, heading towards the main street, at which point Rita felt a strange, irresistible urge to turn around and look back.

She was a little surprised by this unwarranted feeling, but she knew she had to do it, whereupon she involuntarily turned her head towards the house.

Just then, above the front door, where there was a balcony and below it the four ornate pillars that supported it, where the large windows of John and Susan's once shared bedroom, she caught sight of a dark figure.

When the woman squinted slightly to see better, as the sun's rays reflecting o the glass made it difficult for her to see, she saw the figure of a man standing behind one of the windows, which deceptively reminded her of John.

He was standing next to the curtain and seemed to be watching them drive away.

"John?" she said quietly as the car pulled into the street and the house disappeared around the corner.

"Did you say something?" Susan asked.

"Nothing important dear…" Rita replied. "…I'm just thinking out loud."

The funeral ceremony, scheduled for 3pm, started on time.

All of John's family arrived a few minutes early and took their places in the front row in the small chapel, where there was an open coffin, next to which was placed a large photo of John from his school years, and the whole frame was decorated with red roses.

The people gathered were mostly John's friends and acquaintances from work, but there were also people Susan had not expected to see that day. Although the small chapel was almost full and slowly starting to run out of seats, it seemed that more and more people were steadily arriving. Both Susan, her parents and John's parents were a little surprised at how many people John had known during his lifetime, and who had now come to say goodbye to him.

At one point, Susan noticed that Nattaly Swanson was also among the gathered people, wearing a beautiful black dress, elegant high-heeled shoes and a large hat with a veil, transparent and hanging from her head, falling over her face, covering it.

She looked exactly as if she were a widow.

Susan felt anger sweep over her at that sight.

Nattaly, dressed in what looked like very expensive clothes from some famous fashion designer, entered the chapel and slowly walked past the people sitting in the back pews, heading towards the coffin.

She gave the impression that she was deliberately trying to draw all the attention to herself.

Susan and some of the guests followed her with their eyes, but Nattaly pretended not to notice.

However, she knew exactly what kind of impression she would make when she appeared at Susan's husband's funeral, and in that moment, she had achieved her goal.

She felt like she was on a catwalk for models.

It was for this purpose, that two days earlier she had specially ordered the most expensive and exclusive gown from the collection of the London based fashion house, "Gucci."

Although the dress itself, for which she paid more than three thousand pounds, was more suitable for an elegant party or banquet, Nattaly thought she would compensate when she added a traditional hat with veil. This wasn't necessary, as Nattaly herself was already the subject of much gossip, in ways other than she wanted.

Mostly it was said behind her back, that she had been forced to drop out of her psychology studies, because she had become pregnant and returned to her parents with a bastard child was now broke and raising the child alone.

It was this opinion of a disliked schoolmate that most resonated with Susan and she enjoyed listening to it.

Nevertheless, she didn't enjoy it for too long because her opinion of Nattaly's circumstances quickly changed, since she had the opportunity to learn about her real situation.

In a town like North Hill, with a population of less than twenty thousand, rumours spread quickly.

So, when Nattaly bought a new Porsche, it was impossible not to notice.

She also knew that Nattaly was doing exceptionally well in life.

She realised this when she accidentally bumped into her in "Café Orbi" one day after which they arranged to meet for a longer time.

Susan then noticed that her rival had an expensive watch, lots of gold jewellery and exclusive clothes.

That is, all things she hadn't noticed the first time, when, after a brief conversation she hurriedly left.

It wasn't until their second meeting, when they both had a little more time, that Susan was able to get a closer look at Nattaly.

It was then that she realised how wrong she had been in judging her former rival too hastily.

From then on, she tried to avoid Nattaly like the plague, because she couldn't bear the thought that she was doing better than she previously expected.

In fact, many North Hill residents knew that Nattaly Swanson was not poor, but even in such a small-town gossip has its limits.

So, no one asked where Nattaly got her money, and she only mentioned that her fiancé was a rich man and that they had a business together in the car industry.

This explanation convinced everyone, and no one tried to pursue the subject further.

Nattaly did not like to talk about her life with strangers and preferred to surround herself with a small group of a few friends from school.

But even to them, she didn't divulge facts they didn't need to know.

Susan watched as Nattaly slowly approached the first pews in the chapel, intended for the immediate family.

She wondered if she would approach first to offer her condolences or go straight to John.

Nattaly looked at the floor as she slowly walked forward.

She seemed to be in mourning, almost as great as the loss of someone very close to her, which was not the case.

"Damn it, couldn't she have stayed home and given up this show?" Susan cursed the woman, which she had skilfully avoided for a long time, until now.

She didn't call her and didn't pick up the phone when she called. When she saw her somewhere in the town centre, Susan would quickly cross the street or enter the nearest shop unnoticed.

But now she had nowhere to hide and knew that in a moment, she would have to grit her teeth and politely accept her insincere words of condolences.

Susan knew Nattaly all too well and knew how selfish and sophisticated she was.

For those reasons she assumed, she had come here for a purpose other than saying goodbye to John.

Which might seem an obvious goal, was the last thing Nattaly was thinking about.

"What a bitch! After all, she didn't even know him! Did you come here to show off your new dress?! Unbelievable!" Susan was annoyed almost boiling with anger.

Nattaly theatrically walked over to the open coffin, stopped in front of it, then stood next to John for a moment.

Susan didn't take her eyes off her, she noticed that Nattaly's lips were moving slowly, which meant she was saying a prayer.

When the woman finally turned to face her and made eye contact with Susan, a barely visible mischievous smile appeared on her face.

Susan understood her former rival had hated her since school.

Although, she could never quite figure out where it had all really started, because there was a lot that those two women had in common.

They had a similar past, they were both orphans and grew up in foster care, from an early age.

So, in theory they should have more in common.

But the relationship between two young, beautiful and intelligent women, has always resembled a cold war they fought with each other. To the uninitiated, they might have looked like mere acquaintances, as neither of them ever openly harassed the other.

But this was only a pretence, because they sincerely hated each other. Susan supposed that Nattaly had always envied her intelligence, because when it came to beauty, neither of them lacked anything.

At school, however, Susan had always been better than Nattaly, due to her high IQ, she was called "the child prodigy" by the teachers, who spoke of her only in superlatives.

Still, she had never imagined that her eternal rival could hate her so much, that she would relish her grief as she mourned to say goodbye to her husband for the last time.

Susan turned her gaze towards the chapel's main entrance in disgust, then her gaze fell on another person who made her feel a sudden surge of inner warmth.

The woman's reaction to the accelerated heartbeat warmed her stomach. The adrenaline rush immediately replaced her nervousness about Nattaly, which she quickly forgot.

Her full attention turned to Mark Brown, the local police chief, who had just arrived on the scene.

Mark calmly walked between the pews of St Paul's Chapel with his wife Amy.

Mark Brown was forty-nine years old at the time.

Tall, stately and well-built, with pale skin and white hair.

He resembled Leslie Nilsen somewhat, except that he was much taller than the actor.

He looked and acted like a police chief, even when not on duty, dressed in civilian clothes.

On the job for more than twenty years, he was promoted to chief five years ago when, under his command, the drugs squad smashed a gang of heroin and cocaine smugglers.

The dealers had smuggled Type A drugs from France between 2000 and 2004 and then distributed them in and around the North Hill area.

For several years, there was a real epidemic of addiction which was stopped thanks to Mark.

He was an excellent commander and investigator, and, thanks to his diligence and commitment, the first arrests were made and the whole operation was eventually stopped.

However, despite his many strengths, Mark's experience in missing persons cases was nil at the time.

So, when young people began to mysteriously disappear, his competence was put to a huge test which, despite his best efforts, he was unable to cope with.

The indescribable stress and pressure that fell on Mark, during these years, affected his mental and physical health.

Which was obvious at first glance to those who had known him for years. Twenty years of experience as a police officer, did not make it any easier for Mark to solve an extremely difficult task.

A task, which it was already known in the early days after the first disappearance, would be extremely complicated and time-consuming. The priority of the police and everyone involved, was to find the missing persons as quickly as possible and bring the perpetrators to justice.

It was now past 03:20pm.

Susan stared at Mark and her heart did not slow down.

Although she did it surreptitiously at one point, Mark managed to catch her gaze between people.

It only lasted a fraction of a second, because Susan quickly turned her head in the opposite direction and a blush appeared on her cheeks. The fact that Mark was a handsome man and Susan had always liked him, was not the only reason for this reaction from her.

The answer was much more complicated, but she didn't have time to think about it at the time.

"Susan." She suddenly heard a familiar voice close to her ear and it immediately brought her back to earth.

She looked in the direction of the voice and saw, Nattaly. She approached her unnoticed, while Susan was immersed in her thoughts.

"How are you feeling, darling?" Nattaly asked thoughtfully.

Susan, not entirely convinced that this was genuine concern, took a deep breath.

"Hi, I'm fine, thank you."

"And how are John's parents? How are they doing?" she continued to ask, her face expressing interest.

"Ask them yourself, they're sitting right here." Susan replied and moved a little to the left, revealing Kevin and Judy, who were sitting behind her. Kevin was whispering something in his wife's ear, and she listened intently. "Okay, be strong darling, everything will be fine." Nattaly added, and then walked closer to Susan to kiss her on the cheek.

It was a gesture Susan had not expected, despite the circumstances and when Nattaly leaned towards her, she instinctively bent to the side to avoid her lips.

Nattaly, seeing this, stepped aside and took a step backwards, returning to where she had stood a moment before.

A look of surprise was painted on her face, but it quickly changed to a gentle smile.

"Good." She repeated, then passed Susan and approached John's parents. "Please accept my sincere condolences..." Susan heard Nattaly in the distance greeting Kevin and Judy.

"God damn it." She cursed under her breath.

The funeral ceremony continued for less than an hour, as John's wish was cremation, so there was no burial.

Everyone was gathered until the very end, including Nattaly and Mark. It was past 04:10 pm when some of the mourners began to slowly leave the chapel.

People were getting into their cars and leaving, and those who lived nearby simply started walking towards their homes.

Susan stood outside the entrance and finished smoking a cigarette, while looking at familiar faces.

Some smiled at her gently and with understanding, and she responded with the same.

Susan estimated that just over 50 people might have come. This was quite a lot, given that, according to Susan, John wasn't very popular in the town, and she didn't expect more than 30 guests. "Maybe there's something I don't know?" she asked herself, threw the cigarette butt on the ground and then put it out with her shoe. She pulled her phone out of her handbag and looked at the screen. There were no messages or missed calls on it and the clock showed 04:15pm.

She waited for her parents and John's parents, who were still inside with her daughter Nicole.

She left on the pretext of getting some fresh air.

She didn't need to rush anywhere that day.

In fact, she had an appointment with John's lawyer, Nicolas Barter, at his office, but since he was also present, they agreed to go together after the ceremony.

Susan refused to attend a vigil for the deceased after the funeral that John's father, Kevin McKane, wanted to organise.

She thought the idea was unnecessary and her adoptive mother, Rita, supported her in this decision.

In the end, only James, Judy and Kevin, along with a few men who were John's former co-workers, were to go to a small pub near the cemetery, for a symbolic drink.

Susan, Rita and year-old Nicole were to go with Nicolas to his office. In fact, there was paperwork involved in John's death, such as his construction company, bank accounts, property and insurance policy. James, Kevin and Judy didn't feel they could do it straight away, they were too devastated and distraught to listen to his last words, written down on paper.

Only Susan insisted that they go to the office immediately after the funeral, but when John's parents firmly refused, she stopped urging them.

While James and Rita seemed indifferent to the situation, they did not really want to get involved in Susan's argument with her in-laws.

Consequently, it was decided that Susan would go first, accompanied by Rita and Nicole Denice, with the rest joining them a little later.

Lawyer Nicolas Barter didn't mind, as he planned to spend the rest of the day at the office anyway, so he accepted such an ultimatum without hesitation.

"Are you sure you don't want to come with us, to honour John's memory?" Kevin asked Susan, stepping outside and standing beside her.

"Please, let's not go back to that..." she replied. "...You know my opinion, I think of John every day, thus honouring his memory, I don't think it is appropriate to consume alcohol, we should all go to this office and bring this matter to a conclusion."

Kevin took a deep breath of resignation and then, turned his head and looked towards the entrance to the chapel, where the other family members were waiting.

He felt o ended and even disgusted by Susan's insensitivity.

He really couldn't understand why she thought John's last wishes, were more important than honouring his memory with friends, having a small drink and reminiscing about the times they had spent together.

An awkward silence fell.

Fortunately, a few seconds later Rita approached them, carrying Nicole in her arms, and Judy walked beside her.

Judy and Kevin were the last to leave, talking to Nicolas, and then they all headed towards Rita, Nicole, Kevin and Susan, who were standing nearby.

"Finally." Whispered Kevin under his breath.

He said it loud enough for his voice to reach Susan's ears, who sent him an angry look.

When Kevin noticed her looking at him, he smiled slightly and then ignored her completely, which made Susan even angrier; she hated being ignored.

Kevin was aware of this, but he didn't care.

Maybe it would impress John, but not me. he thought.

John's father had once been very fond of Susan, but his attitude had completely changed during his son's illness.

John complained very often to Kevin about Susan, during this time. On more than one occasion, he told him how his wife had become insensitive, cold and moved away from him, when he needed her most. Kevin knew full well, that if his son had overcome his illness and lived on, he would undoubtedly have, separated from Susan.

However, as befits a gentleman like Kevin, he decided not to start an argument with his daughter-in-law.

Although, he had a great desire to tell her everything he had heard from his son.

The very fact that his daughter-in-law was so interested in John's inheritance now and had no interest in honouring his memory, convinced him that she was incredibly sophisticated and greedy.

Kevin could almost feel his blood boiling with anger, but he didn't show it, remaining calm and serious.

After a while, the whole group was complete.

"So, the ladies are welcome to come with me, and I will meet you later, as we agreed." Nicolas announced.

"Or have you changed your minds, and will you come with us after all...?" Judy turned to Susan. "...It would be nice; we could all use a moment to relax."

"Save it, I've already tried that." Suddenly Kevin replied.

"That's for the best." Added Susan, simultaneously taking Nicole from Judy's hands.

"Then follow me." Said Nicolas, pointing with his hand to the cars parked nearby.

For a moment Kevin, Judy and James watched as Susan carrying Nicole in her arms moved away with Rita and Nicolas.

Then, they too turned around and slowly began to follow the rest of the guests, towards the cemetery exit.

At 05:10pm, two cars were parked on "All Saint Road", opposite the recently renovated historic red brick building.

Nicolas got out of the first one, buttoned up his suit and walked over to Susan's car, to open the driver's door for her.

Nicole sat in a child seat at the back, with Rita right next to her for safety.

"Thank you." Said Susan, stepping out into the street.

Nicolas smiled at her, then opened the back door and slipped inside, to help unbuckle the baby from the seat.

"I'll do it, thank you." Rita said.

"Of course." Said Nicolas and stepped back.

Meanwhile, Susan was looking at an office building owned by a lawyer. A display in the window listed the services the law firm specialised in, available for special occasions 24 hours a day, seven days a week. Above it, was a sign with blue letters forming the firm's logo, "Nicolas & Partners, Solicitors."

"It's a bit silly, don't you think?" she said, pointing to the few pictures of smiling people.

"Ah yes, hehehe, but I`m not working here alone and this wasn`t my idea." Nicolas replied, half-jokingly, half seriously.

"Do they work all day?" she asked, referring to the sign in the window.

"Yes, and no, actually..." he replied vaguely.

Susan's eyes narrowed signifying a lack of understanding.

"...I only work with a few clients and they hardly ever contact me out of office hours, but generally yes, my colleagues and I are available on call 24/7, occasionally, we may get a call asking us to go to the police, but these are rare cases, there have been times however, when I have needed to go to the police at 4am to meet a client, who has been arrested for drink driving."

"I understand." She said briefly.

"What are you two talking about?" Rita asked, coming up with Nicole in her arms.

"Just chatting." Answered Susan.

"Can we go now, ladies?" asked Nicolas kindly.

"Yes, please." Replied Susan.

"Great, in that case, follow me." Added the lawyer and moved towards the entrance of the building.

Nicolas opened the door for the women to enter first and allowed them inside.

As Susan entered the spacious room, a modern office appeared before her eyes.

To the left, along the wall, two elegant black leather sofas were placed side by side.

To the right stood three desks separated by a small space, each with an expensive PC.

Behind the desks were cabinets with shelves that presumably held files of documents.

This place was solidly organised and in good taste.

"Jannis, let me introduce you to Mrs McKane." Nicolas said suddenly.

Susan felt confused as the office seemed empty.

Only after a moment did the smiling, slightly freckled face of a young girl with curly ginger hair, blue eyes and a penetrating gaze, emerge from behind the first computer and look at Susan.

The psychologist realised that the large screen completely obscured the woman of delicate stature.

"Good evening, ladies." Jannis said kindly.

Her voice sounded a little squeaky, as if someone was slowly scraping on the blackboard with a fork.

"May I offer you something to drink, coffee, tea? Or perhaps something cooler?" The lawyer offered.

"I'll have a cup of tea..." Rita replied. "...With a little milk and one spoon of sugar."

"I'm fine." Added Susan.

"How about something for the little one? Would you like an orange juice, sunshine?" Nicolas looked at the little girl, who quickly hid her face in Rita's shoulder, embarrassed.

"No, thank you..." Susan replied. "...We're trying to limit her sugar." She explained.

"I see, Jannis, can you make tea for the lady? I'll have a cuppa too." He asked his colleague in a friendly voice.

"Of course, please give me a few minutes." The red-haired woman, got up from her chair and moved towards the door, behind which apparently was the kitchen.

"Thank you, very much!"

Nicolas' office was deceptively like the previous room.

The same medium-sized leather sofa next to the door, a desk with a computer, three comfortable armchairs, two for clients and one behind his desk, and a cupboard with binders.

Once everyone was comfortably seated, Nicolas took one of the binders he had clearly prepared earlier from his desk drawer.

"So, here we go..." he began to speak. "...Before we start, I was instructed to hand this in first..." he added and pulled a small, sealed envelope from the binder.

"...John wanted you to read it first." He explained and then held out his hand with the envelope towards Susan, who furrowed her brow questioningly.

She wasn't expecting this at all and felt a strange uneasiness, not knowing what to expect from the contents.

She thought Nicolas would simply read John's last will, instead of giving her some sort of secret envelope.

Nevertheless, she took the letter from the lawyer and looked at it for a moment, before deciding to open it, at which point there was a knock on the door.

"Yes, Jannis! Please come in!" Nicolas called out.

The secretary stepped inside with a tray in her hands, then walked quickly to the desk and carefully placed it on the countertop.

On the tray stood two cups, a mug of milk, a pot of tea, sugar cubes and two teaspoons.

After setting the tray down, her gaze paused for a few seconds on Susan, who was holding the envelope in both hands and examining it carefully, before turning on her heel and leaving the room.

Susan took a deep breath and in one deft movement, opened the envelope with her fingernail and pulled out a folded piece of paper.

She opened it and began to read the first two lines of text, then froze for a moment.

It was John's handwriting, no doubt, but that wasn't what shocked her the most.

She felt her face grow hot and her hands begin to shake.

Disbelief mixed with great anger.

She closed her eyes for a moment to calm down, while Rita and Nicolas waited patiently, only Nicole was indifferent to the circumstances. Here were John's last words addressed to her:

"Dearest Susan,

I know you are not expecting what you are about to read.

Unfortunately, it is with a heavy heart I must inform you, that you will not become my heir..."

After reading the first two lines, she fell silent and read the rest in her mind.

11

Oliver Wilson.

'Children are the hope that blossoms again and again...,
the future that remains always open.'

4 years later,

18 June 2013, North Hill, 03:30pm.

Christopher Wilson was feeling very strange that day.

He had been very restless since the morning, an unreasonable feeling
of unease mixed at times with occasional bouts of fear.

He had just finished work at the car repair shop, then had an
appointment with Susan at 4pm.

He had been seeing her regularly once a week, following the tragic
death of his wife Maria in a car accident a couple of years ago, when
a drunk driver lost control and collided head-on with Maria's car,
who later died in hospital.

As is often the case in unfair situations, the perpetrator of the
accident escaped with his life whilst Christopher Wilson world
literally collapsed.

He was then left alone with his 13-year-old son, Oliver Wilson.

Susan helped Christopher cope with post-traumatic stress disorder,
but he found the greatest relaxation and rest when he was tinkering
with cars. So, he tried to pop into his friend Andy's workshop every

spare moment, where he could roll up his sleeves, and spend the next few hours fixing damaged cars.

It seemed that after two years since the death of his wife, Christopher had finally found balance in his life, until that fateful day.

School classes ended at 3pm and Oliver was in the habit of going out with his classmates.

They would kick a football around or go out for pizza, usually together under the watchful eye of a supervisor, often the father of one of the teenagers. On this day, everything followed a pre-arranged pattern, with Oliver and his friends running around the field kicking a ball.

At the same time, Christopher was arriving at the building where Susan McKane was waiting for him.

Canary Wharf, London, 03:32pm.

Matthiew was nervously walking around the office, during the phone call. "Is everything clear...?" He said and waited for an answer. "...Yes, that's right... Do what you need to do... Yes... Remember, your time is between four and five... Let me know how it went... Good luck."

North Hill, 04:05pm.

"Good afternoon, Christopher, how are you feeling today?" Susan greeted him.

"Thank you, I'm not complaining, the workshop is full, but I'm really enjoying it." He replied.

"Great, I'm glad to hear that, would you rather sit down or rest on the sofa?" I'm going to lie down for an hour, when I get home David is probably coming over with his friends to play computer games, so I'll rest here for a while.

55 minutes later, the therapy session ended at 5pm sharp. "So, I'll see you next week?" asked Susan, just to make sure, as Christopher was getting ready to leave.

"Of course, as always, thank you and see you later."

"Goodbye, please say hello to your son for me."

"Thank you, I will." The man smiled warmly at her and, on his way out, closed the door behind him.

When he left, Susan leaned back in her comfortable chair, breathed deeply.

Christopher pulled into the driveway in front of his house at 05:25pm. The mixed feelings of anxiety and fear that had been with him since the morning, had not subsided and had even grown stronger.

Despite meeting Susan, he felt no better.

Then, sitting in the parked car in front of the house, he felt as if his heart was trying to break through his chest and jump straight onto the steering wheel.

"What is happening to me today...?" he asked himself.

"...Maybe I should call an ambulance?"

Christopher waited another two minutes, then opened the door and got out of the car.

A wave of fresh air flowed through his nostrils and mouth soothingly, like the pleasant aroma of fresh flowers.

It wasn't much, but it was enough to make him feel blissful for a moment.

However, it was to be the last such moment of his life.

Because, in a few minutes another nightmare was about to play out for him, from which Christopher, sadly, would never be able to recover. Just as he had managed to do, after the tragic death of his wife Maria. When he was a few metres from the porch steps, he smelt a terrible stench in the air, and then from a distance he saw a small brown box standing outside his front door.

Immediately a feeling of fear, panic and anxiety fall on him like a ton of bricks, overwhelming him completely.

The rapid heartbeat and adrenaline pounding in his head, were so strong that Christopher could barely stand on his feet.

"No..." he said quietly, then shouted with all his might, "NO... GOD PLEASE NO!!!"

He quickened his step towards the door, although he had not yet seen the contents of the box, he knew exactly what it represented.

His subconscious knew very well what he should expect, even if he himself was still trying to dismiss the thought.

He approached the box, from which a thick, red liquid was leaking; it was blood.

Christopher covered his mouth with his trembling hands for a moment, and tears gathered in his eyes. "No..." he repeated quietly.

He knelt on one knee in front of the door, then slowly and uncertainly opened the box, which was not sealed at all.

Large, disgusting flies flew out from inside, feeding on carrion.

When the man bent down to look inside, his eyes were met with the bloody remains of a raven, including its head and claws.

But it was not this sight that frightened him the most, for it was a tiny woollen doll that had done so.

A doll that had the top of its head painted with yellow colour to imitate blonde hair, the same as Oliver`s.

His intuition had been giving him signs all day, warning him that something tragic was going to happen that day.

But it was only at that moment, he understood why he felt that way. He slowly straightened up on his feet, reached into his trouser pocket and with a trembling hand pulled out his phone, then dialled a number.

- Emergency call centre, how can I help you?

-        Hello, please connect me to the police.

12

The ground beneath.

'The rich is not he who possesses, but he who gives.'

4 years earlier,

7 November 2009, Nicolas Bartner's office, 17:25pm.

"...I have decided to leave all my money, collected in the bank account, house, construction company and insurance policy to our daughter, Nicole Denice.

At the same, time I hope you`ll understand and accept my decision. Of course, until she reaches the age of majority, you will manage her assets, with the help of my lawyer Nicolas Bartner, who is already paid and committed to ensuring the rule of law. He also has the power to mediate and prevent adverse decisions, regarding our daughter's estate to safeguard her future...'

Susan read, at times not believing what she was seeing.

She had the feeling that John was slowly stabbing her in the back from beyond the grave.

She was completely taken aback, as she had never expected John to leave her nothing of his considerable fortune.

Even the house they had designed, built together and then furnished with such care, was to belong to Nicole Denice.

Susan was to be at her daughter's mercy, as soon as she reached an age where she could make her own decisions.

"What if she didn't want to live with me? What should I do then?" all sorts of thoughts were running through her mind at this point.

Like a gust of wind that blew fragments of potentially negative scenarios into her consciousness, which could inevitably happen soon.

But what could she do about it? Absolutely nothing.

At least, for now.

So, she decided to grit her teeth, keep calm and put on a brave face.

...I want you to know, Susan, that I loved you very much, have always loved you, from the day we met.

I know that my decision regarding my estate will come as a great shock to you.

But I hope you will agree with me, that the future of our child is the most important thing.

However, this is not the only reason why I decided to change my will. I did it because, we had become almost strangers to each other since the beginning of my illness and during my treatment.

Those were the times when I needed you the most, it broke my heart, when I did not receive your support.

Those were the most difficult times in my life, and I felt you ignored me. I understand, your work is very important not only to you, but also to the people you help, plus the terrible things that have started to happen in our town, have made everything even more complicated.

But I expected from you, as a husband, long-time partner and friend, that I would be your priority, the person you would want to help and support above all else, out of turn and sincerely, until death do us part.

246

But that didn't happen, and I deeply regretted it, in the last months of my life.

You are a strong, beautiful and extremely intelligent woman, Susan, I have no doubt you will cope with the rest of your life. Please take care of our little girl, I love you both....

...Yours forever, John.

Susan placed the letter on the desk and pushed it away from her. She froze for a moment, looking out of the window, and the room fell into complete silence for those few seconds.

Even Nicole Denice sat quietly on Rita's lap, almost as if she understood the seriousness of the situation.

Susan looked at the baby, who was looking back at her with big, curious eyes, sucking on a dummy.

"Okay then..." Nicolas broke the silence. "...Do you have any questions?"

"No, I don't think so, I think I understand everything." Susan replied. Susan knew, the lawyer was aware of the contents of the letter and was undoubtedly already properly prepared for everything.

"Great, here's my business card..." he handed Susan a card containing the details. "...Please, don't hesitate to let me know if there are any doubts or you just want to talk to me, about something." He added, smiling kindly. "Of course, thank you." Susan replied, getting up from her seat, at the same time grabbing Nicole Denice under her arms.

"Thank you, goodbye." Rita said.

"Thank you, goodbye ladies." The lawyer replied.

The women left the office.

Susan's adoptive mother, looked at her impatiently, waiting for her to finally speak and tell her, what was going on.

Rita was the only one of the three who was not yet aware of anything, apart from Nicole Denice of course, who was not at all interested in all this.

A few minutes later the women got into the car.

Rita again in the back seat next to the child seat, while Susan was in the driver's seat, feeling irritated by the situation.

The sensation of nervousness was interspersed with helplessness, disappointment, bitterness and all that was associated with her partner's betrayal.

That's right, Susan felt betrayed by John.

"Will you finally tell me, what happened in that office?" Rita's words reassured Susan a little.

"Nothing happened, he bequeathed everything to Nicole, as we agreed before." She lied.

"What do you mean, she's only a year old..." Rita couldn't hide her surprise. "...Are you sure? Did he leave you some money?" she asked. "Don't worry about it, everything is fine."

Nothing was fine, the whole situation was absurd, in Susan's opinion. Unacceptable and should never have happened, but now, that was the reality, she had to deal with.

She started the car and headed towards the bar, where her adoptive father was staying with the other attendees of the ceremony.

She had no intention of staying there, or even going inside for "one", she knew full well that Rita wouldn't hesitate to share new information with James, and she wanted to avoid unnecessary questions and additional stress.

"I'll leave you here and take Nicole home." She said to her mother when they got there.

"Don't you want to go in, even for a while?" Rita asked without conviction.

"No..." she replied briefly. "...I'm tired, Nicole needs a rest too."

"Okay, call me when you get back and don't worry, everything will be fine." Rita knew her daughter intimately and immediately sensed; she was not in a very good state after all.

"I will."

After a while, Rita was left alone on the pavement.

It was past 7pm, the sun was slowly setting, and it was getting darker outside as the streetlights began to illuminate the street.

Susan was driving and Nicole Denice was sitting quietly in her car seat, at the back.

She was so quiet that at one point, Susan thought the baby had fallen asleep, so she looked at her through the rear-view mirror.

Not only was Nicole awake, but she was happily waving her little arms around as if playing with someone.

Susan turned her gaze back to the road and furrowed her brow.

"Why are you so happy?" she asked rhetorically, obviously not waiting for an answer.

After a few minutes she looked in the rear-view mirror again.

However, this time a shiver ran through her body, causing goosebumps.

The girl was not alone in the back seat.

This time, there was a figure sitting next to her, disappearing and reappearing in the light of passing lamp posts for the few seconds Susan saw her in the mirror.

The woman turned her head abruptly, completely taking her eyes off the road, but found no one there, except the baby.

"AAAA...!!DA... DA... DA...!!" the girl made happy sounds and waved her arms.

249

"What the fuck?" Susan cursed under her breath and focused on the road, pressing the accelerator harder.

13

A new chapter.

'Freedom cannot be just possessed, but must be constantly acquired, created. It can be used well or badly, in the service of real or apparent good'.

10 years later,

2 April 2019, North Hill, Danny and Rachel Davis's new home, 12:37pm.

The move took just one day, the weather was glorious so there was nothing to stop us getting the job done, without too much trouble.

Sta from the Bradley and Brad Lettings agency arrived early in the morning at the agreed time of 09:00am, in two spacious vans.

Four burly men managed to load our furniture and personal belongings within an hour, under Rachel's watchful eye, moments later we were on our way to North Hill.

The whole journey from London took us about two and a half hours. Once we arrived, the staff quickly began unpacking the cars, with Rachel directing which rooms each box and piece of furniture should go into. As far as I was concerned, I didn't have much to do with the whole endeavour, as Rachel had forbidden me to strain myself, besides, there was still the matter of unloading the numerous boxes, so my task was still waiting for me.

We moved into a one-storey detached house with a garden and a large porch, which Rachel and I had chosen from a wide range.

It was here, a new chapter in our lives, was to begin.

It turned out that this agency had ten other properties like ours, as well as flats in or near the city centre, for sale or rent.

At the time, I had no reason to ask myself, *where did they get all these properties?*

It didn't make me wonder for two reasons, firstly, I know nothing about the business, and secondly, after talking to Matthiew Braddock, who offered us a very good price and provided all the amenities, I was determined to move. You could even say, the guy pulled the wool over my eyes a bit, but I must admit he knew exactly what he was doing.

Then all it took was one trip to North Hill to see the house and I was 'sold.'

Of course, there was also my personal reason for wanting to settle in North Hill, and the fact that Rachel herself came up with the idea was just a perfect coincidence.

"Rachel!" I called out to my wife.

"…And with those boxes, up the stairs and into the bedroom on the left, please be careful, there are delicate things inside." She was conducting the staff, completely ignoring me in the process.

"Of course, ma'am." The man replied and walked into the house. "Rachel, I'll take the car and go have a look around the town." I shook her out of her trance-like organisation mode.

"Oh yes, yes, of course darling, go ahead if that's what you want." She replied thoughtfully.

"I'll check where Susan McKane's office is and buy us something for dinner, on the way back." I suggested.

"Great! You know what I like..." she replied cheerfully. "...I'll stay here and take care of everything, you go and relax, we'll both be hungry in the evening." She added jokingly with a smile.

"Indeed, I'll be back soon." I said and headed for the car.

I had the feeling that Rachel was really enjoying the whole moving situation, or maybe not so much the moving itself as ruling other people.

As for me, I was glad that I wasn't the one getting paid that day, for being Rachel's subordinate for a few hours.

I got in my car and drove towards the town centre to find Dr Susan's office, where I was due to start a therapy session in a few days' time. Apart from that, I wanted to see where everything was, the shops, restaurants, town hall, post office and of course the police station, which I planned to visit soon.

The town itself made a good impression on me, it was clean, peaceful and extremely picturesque.

The undoubtedly beautiful villa, just o the road into town, also caught my eye.

But just the all-round setting of numerous trees, grass and greenery made me feel very peaceful.

Being used to the endless chaos of a big city like London, where I had lived and grown up since childhood, a place like North Hill was almost like stepping into another reality.

I found it hard to believe, that such terrible things could happen in such a beautiful place.

The human suffering, due to the loss of loved ones, hung in the air somewhere and I could feel it.

However, with the passage of time and circumstance, it was naturally overlooked and partly forgotten, the new residents unaware of North Hill's past, even as recent as a few years ago.

I wondered, if the story of the missing four from North Hill was still prominent, would young people be so keen to come to this place? There was no doubt in my mind that it was still an uncomfortable and controversial topic, especially for the town council authorities, and such topics are most likely to be swept under the carpet, because they are bad for business.

For me, it was a very current subject, mostly because it was never officially closed.

But also, because, after the shooting, when ten-year-old Denise Randal tragically lost her life and I miraculously escaped death, I feel mysteriously connected to this city and responsible for solving the case of the missing four.

01:05pm

Nattaly Swanson was sitting in the café "Café Orbi" sipping her customary midday cappuccino.

She had to run a few errands in town that day, but she couldn't resist the temptation to stop by the most popular café in the area, for a moment of relaxation.

Her ten-year-old son was at school and Nattaly was busy with business duties.

Despite the years, she successfully kept her London partner identity, and her role in the business run by him, a strict secret.

Nattaly's parents and her friends knew only that he ran a successful car company.

Nattaly herself dismissed uncomfortable questions about her son's father with "You'll meet at the wedding," and became furious when anyone tried to find out more.

In time, even her adoptive parents Jamie and Melissa stopped asking about it and accepted that their daughter was a very secretive person.

01:10pm.

Susan left her office a few minutes after one and wondered, where best to go for lunch.

She felt terribly sleep-deprived and tired, which was clearly visible on her face.

She often found it difficult to relax at home after work, especially in the evenings, when she would hear John's occasional piano strumming and sometimes feel someone's presence in her bedroom.

This had been going on for a long time and was very distressing for Susan, although she tried to ignore the unwanted incidents.

The woman was convinced that when she first saw the mysterious figure in the back seat of her car, as she was driving back from her solicitor's office with Nicole Denice, she had brought "something" home with her and strange things had started to happen since then.

At one point she even wanted to get rid of the instrument from the house, but the lawyer did not agree.

Arguing that the piano belongs to Nicole Denice, as does the whole house, and only she can decide if she doesn't want such an heirloom of her father. Susan was incredibly frustrated but had to comply anyway.

As she approached the "Café Orbi," she saw a "Porsche" parked on the street.

She knew immediately that Nattaly was inside, as she was the only owner of this model of car in town.

Susan stopped and, after a moment's hesitation, decided to go inside after all.

She had no desire to see Nattaly, even if their relationship had improved a little over time, she simply felt too tired to listen to her baloney.

She thought that if she went in secretly, then maybe Nattaly wouldn't see her, that way she could order a coffee and something to eat, then take a table in a secluded spot.

However, her plan and hopes, for a moment of relaxation were in ruins, even before Susan entered the café.

Because Nattaly was sitting at a table by the window and spotted her immediately, before she had time to grab the door handle.

The huge smile that appeared on the woman's face announced that she was pleasantly surprised by Susan arrival.

Well, let's get this over with. she thought, resignedly.

"Hello, dear!" Nattaly greeted her cheerfully.

"Hi."

"Why do you look so miserable? Are you ill?" Nattaly got straight to the point.

That's what Susan preferred to save herself, she didn't feel like explaining herself to anyone, especially Nattaly, who looked as stunning as ever. She was wearing a yellow, airy, knee-length dress, a pearl necklace glittered around her neck and her hands were adorned with numerous gold rings and bracelets.

Susan, on the other hand, was wearing yesterday's grey business suit, slightly creased because she hadn't had time to freshen it up in the morning.

Standing side by side, they looked like a sunny day and a cloudy night, and Susan knew it well.

"I need a coffee." She replied, ignoring Nattaly's question. "Of course, come back to my table, we'll talk."

"Sure." She replied reluctantly.

Susan began to regret not having walked past the coffee shop.

At the same time.

I drove around town for another two hours before deciding it was time to go back.

During this time, I wanted to get as familiar as possible with the place I was to call my new home from now on.

I walked into the clinic where Susan McKane worked, I was quietly hoping for a brief familiarisation chat before my first appointment.

However, I was out of luck, as when I got there, she had just had her lunch break and the nice lady at reception, invited me to come back in thirty minutes.

I politely declined, as I didn't want to waste my time waiting half an hour, so I left the building and got into my car.

As I drove down one of the streets, I noticed three flat rental offers from the agency "Bradley and Brad Lettings", they were stuck in the ground on wooden posts in the gardens in front of the houses, close to the street. The highly visible "BnBL" logos were very conspicuous and hard to miss. I realised that only the listings of this agency were visible to lure potentially interested parties, I didn't notice any other competing advertisements. As a Londoner, I was used to sometimes seeing up to four different housing agencies displaying their listings in one street, so for that I thought it was a little strange.

However, I quickly dismissed this thought as I figured that, it could just be a case of a small town or simply, some other agencies might be hiding somewhere further away.

I couldn't resist the temptation to visit the homes of the families of the abducted children, I had no doubt that this was about abductions. From the articles I read, it seems that local law enforcement agencies also approached the case from this point of view.

Only superstitious residents leaned towards the black magic-related theory, and the proof of this was supposed to be the rag dolls, found at the crime scenes.

I, of course, didn't give the slightest credence to this, but I had to admit, that something very strange was going on here and I felt it myself. After an hour of wandering through the narrow streets of the town, I managed to find the house where Magda Richardson lived, but I saw no one there.

It wasn't long before I arrived at the property, not far away, that once belonged to Jessica Murphy's parents.

There I noticed a young woman, unloading groceries from her car. Just as I thought, there was no indication that not so long ago, in that house, a huge tragedy had taken place.

Tragedy which had forever and irrevocably, changed and destroyed the lives of innocent people.

To someone who had no idea about anything, these houses might seem average, and at the same time cosy - perfect for settling down with a family. It made me wonder, what did the people occupying these properties, know about the former residents?

The likelihood that they knew anything about it was slim to none. They may have heard rumours, circulating around the town from people who still remembered the events, but from what I was able to ascertain, there were not many of them.

In the past, the matter had been cleverly covered up so that no one would seek the truth, but I intended to change that.

There was another reason I wanted to look around more carefully, so Rachel wouldn't know - in a few days I was due to meet Susan McKane, once quite famous, I wanted to ask her some questions.

Back in the day, the woman was a local heroine of sorts and had become a permanent part of the town's history.

A legend as someone who, took no care for her own safety and helped others by being actively involved in the search for the four missing teenagers.

I read a few articles, mostly from the time of the incidents, but there was also one that told a little more about her and her personal life. I was very curious about Susan as a person and was looking forward to getting to know her.

At times I felt a sense of excitement, as if I was about to meet my long-time idol, but I had to wait a little longer for that.

I finished my rounds, then picked up the pre-ordered food from the pizzeria and headed back home, where I still had a lot of work to do, unpacking boxes of stuff.

Susan glanced at her watch, she still had 15 minutes left of her scheduled lunch break. The conversation with Nattaly wasn't really ticking over and time seemed to drag on longer, with Susan feeling an increasingly strong desire to get back to her office.

"And how's your London partner? Is business going well?" For lack of topics to talk about, Susan stepped onto shaky; ground.

Nattaly momentarily fixed an alert gaze on her.

"Well, you know, he's fine and business is like business, sometimes better, sometimes worse..." She replied evasively. "...We had some problems recently, but things have calmed down now." She added unexpectedly.

"Oh, I hope it's nothing serious?" Susan picked up on the subject. "No, it's nothing like that, there was a problem with the staff for a short time, but things are back to normal already." She explained.

"Oh, it's good for all problems to be solved so easily."

"Exactly, it's fortunate that there is peace in North Hill too."

These words caused goosebumps to appear on Susan's skin. "Yes..." She replied quietly. "...Apparently the special detectives from

Scotland Yard have left temporarily, but I don't think it will end there."

"They've left, as apparently there's nothing left for them to do here, although no results of their investigation have been officially presented." Nattaly concluded reasonably.

"That's the whole problem, I think this nightmare is not over yet."

"What makes you think that?"

In a split second, Susan's mind brought back images from the past, memories that flew before her eyes like a speeding bird.

First, she saw the moment Joanna Richardson fainted in her office after taking a call from Sandra, then the car, when she first saw the figure next to little Nicole Denice from a few years ago, then Carolin's blood dripping onto the wooden floor.

She heard Joanna neighbour scream in her head, from the time she answered the phone in her office after Magda's disappearance and finally, the sound of the piano key, the same one that rang out in the middle of the night, for no reason at all.

It all took exactly as long as it takes to blink an eye, but Susan seemed frozen in the past for several long minutes.

"Susan?" Nattaly brought her back to earth.

She woke up visibly embarrassed and looked at her.

"I've got to go..." she said immediately. "...I must go back to my office." She added, then immediately got up from the table and grabbed her bag in one movement.

She then hurriedly headed towards the exit, without saying goodbye to Nattaly.

"Yes..." Nattaly said under her breath. "...The nightmare is not over yet." She added taking a sip of her, already cold, coffee.

14

Jessica Murphy.

'It's not enough to cross the threshold, you have to go deep.'

2 years earlier,

05 March 2017, North Hill, 07:25

Harry and Simon were sitting in a van belonging to the agency "Bradley and Brad Lettings."

It was a plain, almost inconspicuous, apart from the "BnBL" logo on the side of the van, white, spacious van.

They had, as usual, detailed instructions in advance from Matthiew. They then began their next task, watching the house through the rear-view mirrors in the safety of strategically parked van.

The fact that they didn't stand out, even if the car had a logo, made their job easier.

There were several other similar cars of this type in the town, and the fact that they had brought six more, since the opening of the office in North Hill, quickly made them blend in with the crowd.

Residents were also used to the sight of the agency's staff, who often carried out some sort of hire, minor repairs and removals.

In the back of the car was a neatly packed "cuckoo's egg," which they were to deliver as the first part of the job.

It was approaching 07:30am, in a moment Alexandra Murphy and her daughter, were about to leave the house.

Simon and Harry knew their schedule very well, almost to the minute, although they didn't need such detailed knowledge, the approximate hours were enough.

The times they left and returned home, the times they started and finished school, the times Alexandra started and finished work and, of course, the times they could expect Jessica to be alone.

"There they are." Harry spoke up at the sight of the door to the house opening.

Jessica came out first, carrying her school rucksack, followed by Alexandra, dressed in a long brown coat and with her handbag slung over her shoulder. Harry and Simon watched as Alexandra took her keys out of her handbag and locked the front door, then followed her daughter to the car.

"Looks like there won't be any complications, we'll drop off the present and let the old man know we're moving on to phase two." Simon concluded. This was already a pre-determined standard procedure, the term "phase two" meant to mean nothing more than simply sensing the right moment, to put the girl in the car without any eye witnesses present.

As in previous cases, this window of time was to fall between 14:00 and 15:30pm, as this was when Jessica was due to be o at school.

Alexandra, on the other hand, had an appointment with Susan from 14:00 to 15:00pm, after which she was to pick up her daughter from the prearranged location and return home in half an hour.

It was all perfectly timed as Jessica now attended dance classes once a week, which ran from 03:15pm to 04:15pm, so Alexandra was at peace with her daughter and was able to go about her business without worry, while having a little more time to herself.

Alexandra Murphy became a single mother after her husband Gregory, tragically died five years earlier while working in construction.

Jessica was ten years old at the time.

Gregory had been working renovating private homes.

On one unfortunate occasion, he fell from a scaffolding from a height of the third floor, when one of the planks broke underneath him and the pipe that served as a barrier, failed to support his weight.

The man collapsed to the ground, and, despite the rapid arrival of an ambulance, he could not be saved.

Both mother and daughter were very traumatised by the loss of Gregory, and because of the girl's age, the whole incident was presented to her in the gentlest possible way.

Alexandra had to start going to therapy to face the existing and upcoming reality alone.

This is when the invaluable Susan McKane, once again came to her aid. She took care of the woman, with full commitment and professionalism, and together they faced the hardships of life.

"You're good to go." Said Simon as Alexandra's car disappeared around the corner.

"Yeah." Harry replied.

He shot a cigarette butt through the window with his fingers, then got out of the vehicle.

A moment later, Simon heard the back door of the van opening, which closed with a bang faster than it opened.

He then looked in the rear-view mirror and saw that his partner was already heading towards the house, with a quick and confident step, at this sight he pulled out his phone and dialled Matthiew's number.

After a few beeps, a voice rang out in the receiver.

"Hello?" Matthiew answered.

"It's me…" Replied Simon. "…We've started work on the new house, I'll let you know when we're ready to proceed with the transaction."

"Of course, I'll be waiting for the call."

Simon hung up and put the phone on the upholstery of the car, he looked in the rear-view mirror again.

Harry was coming back, already a few steps away from the car.

Then he turned the key in the ignition, as Harry got back in.

"Done, we're good to go." He announced.

The van with the "BnBL" logo moved ahead to join the other cars on the street.

At the same time.

Matthiew placed his mobile phone on the desk and leaned back in his luxurious leather chair.

He was in an excellent mood, even though he should be at least a little stressed, about the upcoming events in "North Hill".

However, he had no doubts about the competence of Harry and Simon, who had proved to him on more than one occasion, that they knew their stuff.

His humour was also improved by the fact that business was better than ever.

The agency had grown from one to nine outlets in the U.K. and its value had almost quadrupled.

And he himself, in George's lifetime, would never have imagined that so much income could come from being a co-owner of a housing agency. He never even dreamed that he would become such a rich man, even though wealth was always his priority.

He was a great egotist and didn't hide it at all, what's more, he was proud of it.

The saying "over my dead body" fit him perfectly.

For him, it was a day like any other, and the fact that in a few hours more innocent lives would be ruined, didn't matter at all.

Now, he just had to get the message across - the next stage had just begun.

So, he picked up the phone from the desk and searched for a number. "Hi Nattaly, we're going to get started." He said.

02:10pm,

Susan was waiting for Alexandra, who was already ten minutes late, nervously glancing at her watch every ten seconds or so.

She was beginning to worry about the woman, as she had never come late to a meeting with her before.

They had been seeing each other regularly for several years, this was the first time something like this had happened.

Susan wondered whether to wait a little longer or try to call her.

What could have stopped her? She wondered.

She pulled her phone out of her purse and held it in her hand as she began scrolling through her contacts looking for Alexandra, a knock sounded at the office door.

"Yes?!" she called out.

Then Alexandra, out of breath, entered the office.

Susan was relieved and smiled at the sight of the woman.

"Here you are dear, I was just about to call you." To prove her words, she raised her hand holding the phone.

"Yes, I'm sorry..." Woman replied. "...I got a call from a client, and we talked for so long that I lost track of time."

Susan knew that Alexandra, as a hairdresser, had mostly female clients, so it didn't surprise her that one of them, was on the phone for a long time. "Nothing's wrong, please sit down and relax." The psychologist pointed to the sofa.

"Thank you." The woman took o her brown coat and hung it on the hanger by the door.

"At most, we'll finish a bit early today and you'll go home to rest, you've had a hard day, haven't you?"

"Oh, you have no idea." Alexandra admitted.

"Okay, so take a deep breath and tell me, how your week has been?" Susan began her therapy in a warm and caring voice.

The school in North Hill.

Jessica and her friend Martha left the school a few minutes after 3pm.

Martha's mother, Sophia, was already waiting for them outside the building. Once a week the woman took both girls to dance class, otherwise they would have to walk through the park separating the school from the rented rehearsal room, and today was no different.

Sophia stood by her car and watched as Martha and Jessica approached her.

The woman was worried about her daughter, because the day before she had complained of stomach pains, for which not even herbal teas and stomach drops had helped.

The teenager claimed that the pains just came and went, for no reason, but she decided not to miss school anyway.

However, Sophia had doubts that the child would be able to practise dance that day after a sleepless night, she thought it would be too much for her.

Martha looked very weak, and it could be seen from a distance. Sophia's watch was showing 03:07pm, when suddenly the phone her handbag rang, she quickly took it out and looked at the screen, it was Susan calling.

Sophia immediately remembered that she had spoken to her the previous night but had completely forgotten about it, due to her daughter's overnight health problems.

"Hello, my dear!" she said into the receiver.

"Hi Sophia, how are you today? How is Martha feeling?" Susan asked thoughtfully.

"I'm fine, and I'll ask Martha about it in a minute, she's on her way here."

"Oh, so you let her go to school after all? I thought she was going to stay at home?" Susan was clearly surprised. "I wanted to, but she insisted on going."

There was a momentary silence on the phone, obviously that answer was not what Susan was expecting to hear.

"I'll be honest darling, you have a strange child, any other kid would be delighted to stay at home." Susan joked.

"Yes, I know, but what can I do about it?"

"My Nicole could sit in her room all day and play with her toys, but never mind, that's not why I'm calling, I wanted to ask if I could still count on your help today?"

It was only then that she realised that, indeed, she had agreed to help Susan the day before with preparations for their mutual friend Karen's birthday party.

With all the stress and fatigue, she was all confused, and she hadn't expected Martha to want to go to school, which further complicated the whole situation.

"Listen, Susan, I'm sorry, but I completely forgot about this..." she replied humbly. "...Couldn't you ask someone else...? Well, hello girls." She added, at the same time turning to Martha and Jessica.

"Yes, I understand, of course, if you don't have time then by all means." Susan replied.

"Wait a second Susan..." she said suddenly.

Susan held the phone to her ear and could partly hear Sophia talking to the children.

"...But you look so poorly..." she was saying. "...It will be better if we go to the clinic... You will come to class next week..." she was clearly talking to Marta now.

A few seconds and a crackle on the line later, Sophia spoke up again. "...You know what dear? I'm just going to take Marta to the clinic for an appointment and I'll come to you soon." She announced.

"Great! So, I'll be waiting for the call, say hello to the girls for me." Susan was clearly overjoyed.

"Of course, so I'll see you later."

"See you later."

Sophia put the phone back in her purse and looked at the teenagers, who were watching her with frowning faces.

Martha was not happy with her mother's decision, but she clearly looked disappointed, and Sophia had no intention of giving in to her teenager's whims.

"She's only fifteen and she must do as she's told, at least for now." She motivated herself in her mind.

"Do you want a lift to the hall Jess?" she asked the young woman kindly.

"No, thank you ma'am, I don`t want to cause a trouble." Jessica replied.

"But darling, it's no trouble at all!" Sophia urged.

"Thank you, but I'll take a walk, it's nice weather and a walk through the park will do me good." She smiled broadly.

"All right then dear, just take care of yourself, and you, young lady, welcome to the car." Sophia said goodbye to Jessica, while turning to Martha.

"So, I'll see you at school tomorrow, then?" Martha asked.

"Sure, if you can sort out the mess in your belly." Jessica joked. "Very funny, take care, I'll call you later, bye!"

"Bye."

Jessica stood on the pavement in front of the school for a while, waving to her friend as she drove away.

As the vehicle turned into a side street, disappearing from her sight, she looked around on both sides of the street, to make sure the path was clear.

She then crossed the road to enter the park, on the other side.

At the same time, Simon and Harry, sitting in a car parked near, watched the teenager and waited, until she was finally left alone.

They had changed vehicles before, to camouflage themselves, something they always did in such circumstances.

They left the company van at the agency and changed to a personal car, designed for this type of work.

They knew that sooner or later the teenager would be unaccompanied, because they had prior confirmation from Matthiew, and he was never wrong.

And so now, Jessica, after a brief conversation with her companions was just entering the park, by herself.

The time was 03:12pm.

"Go." Commanded Simon, and Harry turned the key in the ignition. WRUMMMM...! The sound of the engine starting, came from under the bonnet of the black "Citroen."

269

Harry drove around the park and stopped on the other side in front of the entrance gate, so that he covered it with his vehicle.

From now on, they only had a few minutes before Jessica was due to arrive, which was more than enough time to get ready.

Simon opened the box that held the fast-acting insulin, chloroform and microfibre cloths normally used for car care.

He then dipped one of them in the chemical liquid and got out of the vehicle.

Harry followed him, he was to observe the area and warn of any potential witnesses, if necessary.

The massive man climbed out of the driver's seat, stood near the bushes at the park exit and looked around.

People could be seen walking in the distance, but they were far enough away that they posed no threat.

Simon looked carefully towards the path cutting through the park where Jessica appeared on the horizon, she was no more than 2 minutes away from them.

"It's clear." Informed Harry.

Simon waited another minute for the teenager to approach.

"Okay..." he said to Harry. "...Get back in the car."

03:17pm,

Alexandra left the building that housed Dr Susan McKane's office a few minutes after 3pm.

She now planned to do some shopping, then head to the training room to pick up Jessica.

The woman enjoyed coming in a few minutes before the end of class to watch her daughter's exploits, it gave her great joy and, apart from meeting Susan, it was a pleasant way to escape from everyday reality.

However, the moment she sat behind the wheel of the car, a penetrating feeling of dread overwhelmed her.

Alexandra had no idea what could have caused it, but she had an irresistible feeling that something terrible had just happened. Guided by her intuition, she took out her phone and, without a second thought, dialled Jessica's number; when the voicemail went on, she hung up and in turn found Sophie's number, who answered after the second tone.

"Hello, darling." Sophie greeted her.

"Hey, listen, is Jessica with you?"

"Oh, sorry, I've been very forgetful lately, hasn't she called you? I had to drive Martha to the doctor right after school..." Sophie explained. "...But Jess went to class."

"What do you mean she went! Alone? Didn't you take her?" Alexandra was upset.

"No, I wanted to, but she refused, she said she'd rather go for a walk."

"I must go there." Alexandra replied, as if to herself.

"Darling, I'm sorry, but why the nerves? Has something happened?"

"I don't know yet, maybe nothing, I'll call you later."

"Please call me, darling, I'm starting to get scared." Sophie replied. Alexandra ended the call and straightened up in the driver's seat, she was very cranky but didn't want to let her emotions get the best of her. Although her instincts told her that something was wrong, she knew that acting on impulse was wrong, and she needed to stay calm.

After a few deep breaths, she picked up the phone again and this time dialled the number of Mark Brown, the local police chief and a long-time friend. - Hello?

"Hi Mark…" she said when he answered the phone. "…Listen, this may sound strange, but could you send a patrol to my house?"

There was silence on the line, Mark was surprised by her request.

"Do you need help, Alex? What's wrong?" he asked finally.

"I'm not sure if anything has happened, I'm worried about Jess…" she explained. "…Her phone is off, and Sophie said she went to class alone today…" The woman paused to catch her breath and calm the nerves that were starting to take over her again. "…I can't explain it Mark, but I have a bad feeling, I'm about to go to her class, but I would like someone to check my house at the same time, I can't be in two places at once."

"Of course, I understand, don't worry, go look for her where you need to, and I'll send uniforms to your address."

"Okay, will you be able to inform me straight away if they find her?"

"Absolutely Alex, don't worry, I'm sure everything is fine." He added to comfort the woman, but deep down he didn't quite believe what he was saying.

"Oh, I hope you're right." She replied and ended the call.

Then she put the phone on the passenger seat, buckled her seatbelt, started the car and hurried towards the training room, where Jessica should have been at that moment.

03:42pm,

Mark kept his word and fifteen minutes after speaking to Alexandra, a police patrol pulled up outside the woman's house.

Two officers exited the vehicle, one moving to the main entrance, while the other, started looking around the house and from the backyard.

"Nick…!" The first officer called out to his partner. "…Nick! Over here!"

272

"What have you got?"

"Look at this..." The policeman pointed his finger at a cardboard box standing in front of the door, from which red liquid was leaking. "...I think we need to notify the chief officer."

"What about the girl? Have you checked to see if she's inside?"

"No one's answering the bell, looks like there's no one inside."

"Okay, hold on a minute, I'll call Mark."

"This is Mark Brown." Mark answered a minute later.

"This is Sergeant Nick Brack, chief constable."

"Ah yes, what is it? Have you found the girl?"

"No sir, but we did find something..." Nick replied. "... I think, we've got another one."

At these words Mark Brown's blood ran cold

He knew exactly what Nick meant by "we have another" missing person, victim, vanished, wanted, kidnapped, all the words boiled down to one conclusion - we have another ruined life and a lot of work to do.

Whoever the people responsible were, they had not left town as previously thought, they had been in hiding for the last few years, only to strike again.

"Wait a minute..." Mark finally replied. "... Are you sure about this?"

"There's a box, sir, from which a red liquid is pouring out, I think it's blood." Stay where you are, don't touch anything, I'm sending forensic technicians to you.

Mark ended the call and closed his eyes for a moment, his head began to spin, and he felt his blood pressure rising.

He wished with all his heart, this would never happen again, even though previous investigations were still on going and had never been completed, therefore the perpetrators had never been caught.

Mark was simply deluding himself; it would never happen again.

In a human sense, he hoped so.

But once again, he had to face the avalanche that was heading his way.

Of course, he had to start with Alexandra Murphy.

"God almighty, how do I tell her this?"

15

The new reality.

'You must demand from yourselves...'

2 years later,

5 May 2019, North Hill, 10:25pm.

It's been four weeks since I moved to North Hill with my wife.

The first few weeks were very strange for me, because of the difference to the busy, crowded and endless dynamics of a big metropolis like London. Rachel settled in very quickly, she liked the peace and quiet and I got the impression that she was happy here.

During this time, I had the pleasure of meeting Mark Brown, Chief Constable of the Police, and met Susan McKane three times for therapy.

I have to say, after the first visit I already felt very positive about her.

In my opinion Susan was a very calm, professional and balanced person. She was able to pass on this calmness to the people she spoke to with ease.

The effect of this was that I felt safe in her company and could afford to talk about things that I would otherwise find extremely awkward or embarrassing.

During my second meeting with Dr Susan McKane, I gently tried to introduce the subject of the history of North Hill.

At the time I mentioned that I had read many articles and expressed my sympathy for the situation.

I hoped Susan would talk to me, perhaps tell me more about it, from her point of view.

But I was wrong, as she clearly had no intention of elaborating on the matter, briefly dismissing me - "Yes, it's a real tragedy, but let's focus on you, Mr Davis."

At the time I thought this was due to her dedication to the patients, the fact that she was probably bound by some sort of confidentiality clause, regarding the privacy of those involved.

I gave up that day, but I had absolutely no intention of stopping.

Susan knew almost every detail of these cases first-hand, and I was dying to know what it all looked like from the perspective of, finally, an eyewitness.

"...Have you been fishing yet?" Connor asked.

"That's my plan, I'm still putting together my gear for now, I'm thinking about buying an inexpensive boat." I replied.

"Brilliant! When my holiday starts, I'll come to you, and we'll go together." "You're welcome, it'll be good to meet up, I'm having a hard time getting used to retirement life." I confessed.

"Don't even joke, I'd love to swap with you! Unfortunately, I still have a few years of service left, well, unless someone takes a shot at me too...." He laughed into the receiver.

"You must be crazy, don't say words like that! These jokes of yours will one day turn against you and kick you in the ass, you'll see."

"Of course, I'm fooling around, but I must go, I'll get back to you soon, say hello to Rachel for me." He said.

"I'll pass it on, take care." I added and tapped my finger on the red handset on the phone screen, then put it on the bedside table, next to the "mini." It was almost 11pm and Rachel was still bustling around the bathroom, brushing her teeth and getting ready for bed.

After a few seconds, she turned off the light in the room and closed the door behind her.

"Does he miss us very much?" she asked me when she returned to the bedroom.

"Yes, he plans to come for a few days, when he'll start his holiday."

"That's great, it'll be nice to see a familiar face, especially for you, old man." Joked Rachel, at the same time coming over to my side of the bed, to kiss my forehead.

"Thank you, let's go to bed now, my eyes are closing themselves."

"Good night, love." She replied laying down next to me on her side of the bed.

"Good night." I replied and turned off the bedside lamp.

I closed my eyes and seemed to fall asleep almost instantly, only to wake up in a place I already knew well.

My subconscious, again, transported me to a gloomy forest in the middle of the night, there was a wooden shed and Denise at my side, holding my hand.

Here we go again. I thought resignedly, it had been a long time since I had returned to this dream.

Everything looked the same as it always did when I had this terribly disturbing dream.

Yes, everything was the same, except this dream was completely different from the others.

The surroundings seemed to be the same, only this time, the circumstances were completely different.

The time was 11:15pm, Soho, London.

Matthiew was standing outside a club on a crowded street, talking on his phone.

He had been out partying for hours and his condition could be described as, to put it mildly, intoxicated.

"But what are you afraid of...? It's just one guy, what can he do to us...? So, what if he snoops, let him snoop! He won't find anything anyway... No... I assure you; the boys have taken good care of everything ... I can talk to them if you want...? Okay... To be honest, I don't like the idea of doing anything with him, after all he's a cop, never mind retired...A cop is a cop, you don't touch them... Okay, I'll talk to them so they can keep an eye on him, and you relax, if necessary, we'll get rid of him too... Sure, be in touch."

He added at the end and hung up.

"Stupid bitch." He said under his breath, while simultaneously dialling Simon's number.

"It's me!" he said as it was picked up.

"I hear, what do you want?" Simon's voice expressed displeasure at the dubious distinction of talking at 11:30pm on a Saturday night with a drunk Matthiew.

"Yeah, listen, I need you to do something for me..." he stopped talking to take a break for a sip of beer, Simon waited patiently. "... There's a guy called Danny Davis hanging around town, I need you to keep an eye on him."

"Is there anything else I should know about him?"

"He's an ex-cop." Matthiew replied.

"Now listen to me carefully, we don't mess with cops, they'll let go after a while, quicker than if we make one of them disappear, do you understand what I'm saying to you?" Simon's voice seemed more animated, but not in a good way.

278

"Don't worry, rest assured, he's no longer on active duty, he's retired."

"It doesn't make any difference."

"I'm not telling you to get rid of him, just keep an eye on him, there's a suspicion he might mess us up." Matthiew explained.

"I can't let the pigs poke their noses into my business. Okay, I'll talk to Harry and get back to you."

"That's all I'm asking." Matthiew breathed a sigh of relief and was about to hang up, when he heard Simon on the phone.

"Just one more thing." He said.

"What?"

"Don't ever call me in this state again!" said Simon and switched off the phone, before Matthiew had time to answer anything.

"WHAT A BUNCH OF FUCKERS!!! Do you guys see who I must work with!!!!" Matthiew turned to the group of people standing nearby, who were now looking at him like he was some kind of madman.

"Fuck this!" he shouted and grabbed a bottle of beer, then emptied it in one gulp before staggering slightly and heading towards the entrance of the club, he had come from.

"The night is still young!" he shouted cheerfully to a familiar security guard.

Sunday 09:15am, North Hill,

I woke up wonderfully rested that day, for some unknown reason, it was one of the few mornings I could count as so restful.

Although, I had the same dream last night, after which I often woke up in a cold sweat, last night was very different.

This time I felt as if I belonged to the environment I was in, even though that space was still completely alien to me.

279

I felt as if I had been in the right place at the right time to put it simply. Anyway, I started the day with the feeling that everything was on track, and I was where I was supposed to be.

The hour, 10:30am London, Canary Wharf,

Matthiew woke up sitting in the armchair in his office, his head resting on his desk and just beginning the painful punishment after an all-night binge, commonly known as a hangover.

As he looked around the room, he saw beer bottles lying around, a few cigarette butts, and a small mirror on the desk in front of him, on which cocaine trails were still neatly arranged.

When his still foggy mind managed to recover a little, he noticed a woman sleeping on his couch.

The man could not recall who this person was or how she had ended up in his office.

Overall, he remembered very little of the previous night.

"Thank God it's Sunday." He said to himself.

Matthiew was aware of the scandal that the sight of boss with drugs, alcohol and, most likely, a sleeping prostitute on the couch, could have caused if it had been a working day and his employees could have turned up, at any time.

Although he was known to be a party animal and did not shy away from alcohol, this would be a huge exaggeration and even a vain man like him, seemed to understand this.

By now he had skilfully separated his social life from his professional life, although he was having a drink practically every day.

"Well, let's clean up this mess..." he said, walking over to the couch. "...Rise and shine baby!!" he started poking the woman. "...Wake up!"

11am, North Hill, Nattaly Swanson's flat.

Nattaly was getting ready to leave the house, Sundays were usually days when she had a lot to do.

She had an appointment at the harbour at around 1pm, before that, she needed to drop o and then pick-up her son, from her mother's care. When she was still living in her parents' house, the whole procedure was much simpler, but since she bought her own flat, she had to plan her schedule in advance.

Of course, not every week looked identical, but that was usually the case. The woman was earning very good money for her share of the business, and this meant that she needed to be on top of her game, always.

She only contacted her partner in London for a few reasons:

"To set up a date and place, for the next meeting."

"To inform him about the planned delivery of the consignment."

"And regarding any complications."

Therefore, the last conversation she had with her partner, took place in a heated atmosphere.

Because it turned out that the retired police officer, who liked to ask a lot of questions, had recently moved to the city.

Nattaly had a feeling that he might come across something he shouldn't, and thus draw his attention to the whole operation.

Although, everything had been done over the years to avoid detection, a curious police officer with too much free time on his hands and, on top of that, living in the area, did not bode well.

Under the circumstances, steps had to be taken to safely hide the source of income and keep the nosy policeman at bay.

They both agreed, an intervention was necessary, as soon as possible.

11:45am, the home of Nicole and Susan McKane.

Susan was sitting in the kitchen, sipping coffee and reviewing home surveillance footage on her laptop, while Nicole Denice, was over breakfast and playing with toys in her room.

This day, Susan had no plans for the rest of the Sunday, she wouldn't even be able to think of anything creative, due to the terrible headache that was bothering her.

Last night, the woman barely managed to sleep for a couple of hours, but that too intermittently, because every now and then some sounds coming from inside the house, would rouse her from sleep.

These were the sounds of footsteps on the stairs, the sound of a door closing or the tapping of the keys of the piano.

Every night she made sure that the piano lid was closed, but almost every morning when she went downstairs, she found it open.

So far, she had been able to cope with the strange phenomena that occurred in the house, especially as it wasn`t something that happened every night.

But the last few weeks had been completely unbearable, with Susan napping nights and feeling exhausted during the day.

She had no doubt that the activity had intensified over time, and she had no idea how to deal with it now.

The strangest thing about it all was, that Nicole Denice seemed completely unaware of what was going on at home, or at least not in the least bit concerned about it.

The girl was already ten years old, and Susan expected her to complain about noises or even situations where mysterious occurrences made her feel frightened in the middle of the night, which would be perfectly understandable for a young child.

Despite this, not once did she come to her mum for help; hardly once did she even say a word about these events.

Susan wasn't sure whether this was a good sign or not.

She thought that maybe, it was better that Denice was not aware of anything and just slept peacefully at night, without any problems. But on the other hand, should she be worried that her daughter remained indifferent?

It was as if it was a normal experience when she too was awakened by these noises.

In the end, she decided that she would accept the first version of her thoughts as correct, besides, she wasn't well enough to think about it anyway.

"One problem at a time." She said to herself, looking at the laptop screen. Recently, because of what had been going on in the McKane house, Susan had been watching more and more videos on the internet, where people had shared their experience, claiming their houses were haunted. Initially, the woman was negative about this kind of "evidence" of the afterlife.

She had a very good reason for this, because anyone who watches videos on the internet knows, there are many such recordings that have been expertly prepared or initiated by a specialist, just to make them look authentic.

Susan herself was more sceptical until she experienced these phenomena herself.

She had never considered or delved into the subject of supernatural phenomena before, which made it a completely unfamiliar area for her. However, the more she watched the videos, the more she began to believe that what she was seeing, was indeed real.

Some of the circumstances in the videos, resembled the situation in her home, so she was able to compare what was happening in her flat with what other people had captured.

It all came together at the end.

Faced with the events, she also decided to install a home monitoring system a few days ago.

To do this, she hired a company whose representative was able to install and connect a set of five cameras, within a few hours.

The first overlooked the entrance to the house, the second overlooked the living room, also reaching the piano and the front door, the third overlooked the kitchen, the fourth overlooked the garden and the fifth covered the stairs to the right of the door to Nicole's room and in the hallway, to the left of the entrance to Susan's bedroom.

That Sunday morning, the woman intended to spend several hours reviewing the footage recorded by the cameras the previous night. She focused most on the footage from cameras 2, 3 and 5, as these showed the locations from which, she believed the most activity was occurring.

The woman quickly realised that reviewing several hours of video, plus looking for the smallest details, was no small task.

After just two hours of sitting in front of her laptop and drinking her fourth cup of coffee in a row, she caught herself scrolling through the footage as if it were a boring TV series or movie she had already watched and couldn't wait for it to end.

However, that wasn't the point of the project, and she knew it well, but she didn't have the energy to follow every point in the house, from every minute recorded by the cameras, so at some point she started to give up and question the point of what she was doing, to put it simply, she'd had enough.

That was until the footage showed 03:05am, at which point the woman went into shock.

She stared at the laptop screen in disbelief, her mouth dropped open, and her eyes were the size of a two-pound coin.

"Oh, shit." She said under her breath and rewound the video to 03:04am to watch it again and make sure, her eyes weren't deceiving her.

284

Playing back what she had just seen, she realised that there was absolutely nothing wrong with her eyes, no matter how much she wanted to be wrong, her suspicions were correct.

At exactly 03:05am, the lid of the piano keyboard opened, and what's more, when Susan checked the footage from camera number 4, her eyes saw a faint, white, hazy figure appear to walk through the door and into her daughter's room.

"Oh, shit." She cursed again.

She straightened up in her chair at the kitchen counter and lowered her arms, frantically wondering what she should do.

She had never imagined she would find herself in such a situation and had no idea how to go about it.

Under the circumstances, only two things were certain.

Firstly, whatever was in the McKane house was becoming more brazen by the day, and secondly, whatever it was, it didn't belong in the world of the living.

After a few minutes, she calmed down a little and then, prompted by the moment, typed into Google: North Hill paranormal investigations, which resulted in several related sites popping up on the screen.

Unfortunately, none of them were directly from North Hill or the surrounding area.

The nearest address for paranormal enthusiasts, was in London. For lack of better options, Susan decided to contact an association called "London Ghost Hunters."

So, she went to their website and, after a quick read of some basic information, copied the email address, then opened her mail and began to write a short message:

"Dear Sir/Madame,

My name is Susan McKane, I am a psychologist.

I do not believe in paranormal phenomena, but I would like to share with you a video that was recorded by my private monitoring system. I am attaching the video file below and ask that you pay particular attention, to the image from cameras 2 and 4 from 03:04am onwards. I have never encountered this phenomenon before, and I think it should also be of interest to you.

I am asking for your advice as I have no idea what I should do, thank you in advance for your attention.

Best regards, Susan McKane."

16

Let us go back to the beginning.

'Suffering is also in the world in order to release love in us, that generous and selfless gift of our own self in favour of those affected by suffering.'

10 May 2019, North Hill, 13:34.

I had an appointment at 2pm at the Café Orbi, with Mark Brown. I was pleased, the commander had found a free afternoon for me and had agreed to answer some of my questions.

Given that I could not reach Susan McKane, who was adamant and would not be persuaded to have another conversation outside of the therapy sessions, I had to look elsewhere.

I didn't take it personally that the psychologist didn't want to talk to me or resent me, I could understand that and put myself in her shoes.

So, I decided that I had to keep trying and Mark was the next person on my list.

Besides, we had already established a thread of understanding after our first meeting, so I could immediately see that the commander would be willing to cooperate, which was perfect for me at the time.

01:34pm, "Café Orbi,"

I arrived half an hour too early, excited about the meeting.

I almost felt like I was about to interview someone famous, but perhaps in a negative sense of the word.

Because there was no doubt that the story Mark Brown was involved in, from the very beginning was shrouded in dark notoriety.

I sat with my coffee and replayed the course of the conversation in my head, or you could say, I was putting together a scenario for the meeting.

Under normal circumstances I didn't do this, as I know from experience that in real life, the conversation takes its own course, and I usually preferred to see where it would lead.

However, in this case it was different, because I knew that there was no breakthrough in the investigation in these cases, otherwise it would have been made public a long time ago.

So, I decided to focus on the beginning, going back to Magda Richardson and 2008, rather than trying to find out anything about current events, which in this case, would have given me nothing anyway.

I had a feeling that the key to solving this case, lay at the very beginning.

Mark Brown arrived a few minutes before 2pm.

From a distance I saw a distinguished man, impeccably dressed in a black suit, but as he came closer and extended his hand to greet me, I saw again the face of a person tired of life.

It then slowly dawned on me, that this was due to years of carrying enormous stress and the constant pressure that the North Hill police chief had endured.

Mark was only four years older than me, but if I hadn't known that I would have thought, there was at least a ten-year difference between us, and I don't say that maliciously.

"Mr Davis, good afternoon." He said approaching my table.

I stood up hastily to show my respect.

"Good afternoon, commander." I shook hands with him and bowed gently. "But please, commander, this is how my subordinates address me, call me by my first name." He announced unexpectedly, sitting down in his chair.

"When I met him, he didn't correct me and we remained on formal terms, so

I had to admit that I liked the change, as he started treating me as an equal." "Thank you, Mark, Danny..." I replied and shook his hand again to seal the familiarity. "...Can I offer you a coffee? Or would you like to have something else to drink?"

"Ah... No thanks, I won't be here too long, my wife is waiting for me at home, I promised her I'd be back soon."

At this point I felt a little disappointed, because I was hoping for a longer chat.

But I could also understand him, because I'm married myself and I know the pressure women can exert, when they make up their minds about something.

"I understand, no problem, my Rachel stayed home alone too..." I said, making it clear that I too was walking in those shoes. "...So, I'll get straight to the point."

"Please, how can I help you, Danny?"

"I would like you to tell me, about the circumstances of Magda Richardson's disappearance in 2008." I've started to replay difficult memories.

"Yes, from what I remember, it started in the afternoon ...." He began to recount "...At the time, Magda was at home with Sandra Jones, a retired, elderly woman and neighbour, who occasionally looked after her, while her mother Joanna Richardson, had an appointment with Dr Susan McKane...." He took a breath. "... As a retired police officer, you probably know that in cases like this, we place the family and immediate community, under the microscope first."

"Of course, what about Sandra Jones?"

"The woman testified that she spent the whole afternoon with Magda, while she was playing in the garden, until the phone rang, then left her for a few minutes to go into the house to pick up, this was the time she disappeared, according to Sandra, when she returned there was no sign of her..."

"This subject was clearly weighing on Mark's mind."

"...We had no grounds to accuse the woman of any negligence, because she even agreed to a polygraph test, the results of which completely cleared her of suspicion."

"Where is she now? Do you think I could talk to her?"

"She doesn't live in North Hill anymore, she sold the house about a year after Magda disappeared, I think she couldn't bear the unpleasant memories and depression, I don't know where she is now, like most of those people who had something to do with the "North Hill curse'.'" He replied. "The curse?"

"That's what they said about the dolls appearing, they were supposed to represent black magic, or something like that..." he began. "...First there were dolls and then, boxes of bloody animal remain, birds, rats, foxes and the like, they would appear out of nowhere and then tragedy would ensue."

"Was it the same with Magda?"

"Yes, Sandra talked about the doll that the girl had found that day in the garden, she also said that it frightened her, because she had already come into contact with such practices, she was absolutely convinced of their power and the real danger to the lives of the people, who came into their possession, especially someone to whom such a doll was dedicated, but the little one was stubborn and, apart from Sandra, no one believed that something bad could happen, maybe things would have turned out differently, if she had been taken seriously then." Mark's face became even more distressed.

"And you never established their origin? Those dolls?" I pursued the subject, even though I was beginning to feel guilty for pestering him like that, but I needed to know, that's why we met here.

"We had a few leads that turned out to be blind, no fingerprints, no DNA traces, nothing, there were also packages from London..."

"From London?" that caught my attention.

"...Yes, sent from post boxes, Scotland Yard agents tried to trace using CCTV cameras to see if they could identify anyone, without success."

"So, they were addressed from out of town, just what purpose could someone living that far away have? And how did they know where to send them? It doesn't make sense."

"I think so too, but only some of the parcels were delivered that way, it was enough to cause panic among people, most of them were found already here, on the spot." He added.

"It appears that we are dealing with an organised operation, both external and internal." I thought out loud.

"You don't have to tell me something I already know..." Mark interjected. "...Scotland Yard are still on the case, and we have our eyes on the case, but everything has gone quiet and for the second year we have no new leads, the investigation has stalled."

It wasn't until this conversation that my eyes were really opened to the whole situation, I learnt more in the last few minutes than I did in months of reading articles.

Such facts are not told to the press and only talking to someone, who had direct insight into all the details of the case, could shed a different light on the circumstances.

291

However, the real bombshell was prepared by the commander at the very end, without even realising it.

"But going back to the beginning, as you wanted to, you must also know that the first accusations of Magda Richardson's disappearance, on the part of the locals, were directed at, God forbid, an Ethiopian couple who had only lived here for a few months, after the rumour of black magic spread, people went crazy and there was almost a lynching. Soon after that the couple left North Hill and never came back here again, poor people." He said.

After those words from Mark my heart started beating faster, I don't know why as it wasn't any breaking news.

Nevertheless, I was excited, and I knew at that moment that I had to track down this couple and talk to them, wherever they were at the time. - Tell me more, do you remember any details about these people? Name and surname would be of course, perfect.

"I can't tell you from memory, I can look it up for you, but there is a possibility that you can find out anything of interest about them yourself, for all I know they registered with our health clinic, at the time." He replied.

"Great, only will I be given such information?"

"I will give you a personal authorisation card, as a police consultant, and you will have no problem with that." He replied.

"Thank you, Mark, I am obliged." I said frankly.

"No problem, I'll be the one obliged if you can work something out." He confessed.

"I'll try, that's why I'm here." I replied, taking myself a little too far in my words.

Mark looked at me slightly confused, but after all, I couldn't tell him that the soul of the murdered girl had brought me to this town.

I didn't quite understand it myself and I didn't want to end up in a mental hospital, spreading such statements around.

So, I kept silent about the awkward situation and got up from the table, at the same time extending my hand to the commander.

"Thank you very much, for talking to me." I said.

"Come to the police station tomorrow morning, your pass will be waiting for you at reception, it should open some much-needed sources for you."

"Alright, thanks." I added as a goodbye.

So, the plan for the next day came into its own, in the evening I wanted to call Connor and share the news with him.

I needed someone to talk to openly, but I couldn't discuss it with Rachel yet, so as not to worry her.

I parted from Mark and headed for the car, I was in the great mood and on top of that, the evening was warm and pleasant.

I wonder, what Rachel has come up with for dinner. I thought, smiling to myself.

17

A paranormal investigation.

'Man cannot live without Love. Man remains a being incomprehensible to himself, his life is meaningless unless

Love is revealed to him, unless he meets Love, unless he touches it and makes it his own in some way...'

6 May 2019, North Hill, home of Nicole and Susan McKane.

The response from the "London Ghost Hunters" came much quicker than Susan might have expected.

The very next day the return message she received sounded remarkably enthusiastic and the woman named Marta Bishop, who wrote it, seemed very excited by the circumstances.

Susan read:

"Dear Susan,

We have viewed the footage several times with my team, and we have to say that we have not the slightest doubt about its authenticity, it really is an amazing capture!

We would very much like to investigate at your home, of course, if we get permission to do so?

We have equipment such as an EVP (Electronic Voice Phenomenon) radio, motion detection equipment and thermal imaging cameras.

We are able not only to determine whether there is an 'unwanted guest' in your home, but also to find out who he is, how to get rid of him, and in the meantime collect tangible evidence of his presence!

If you are interested in our services, please contact me at: 0756844578.

Regards, LGH Director, Marta Bishop."

Susan, however, initially had doubts that inviting a handful of unknown people, into her home, was a good idea.

She also didn't want the news to spread around town, which could cause a lot of interest in her home among curious locals.

In short, she did not like the idea of taking the risk of turning the place into a tourist attraction, which posed a real threat to her and Nicole's privacy. However, after carefully weighing all the pros and cons, she decided to call the LGH director.

After a brief conversation with Marta Bishop, who was with her team as she said "set and ready" sealed the decision, to finally agree to such an experiment.

The agreement Susan made, was to be printed and signed by both parties, included, above all, discretion and that the recordings would not be published anywhere else, except in an archive on the LGH website. The plan was for the three paranormal investigators to stay at Susan's home with their equipment for the night, while she and Nicole will stay in a hotel, with costs covered by the "London Ghost Hunters."

Martha Bishop also assured Susan that the results of the investigation and the most appropriate steps to take, once it was established what they were dealing with, would be presented to her by LGH staff the following morning, in a discreet place to talk.

Susan liked this idea, as she was alone with Nicole Denice and had little opportunity to leave the house for the night.

So, she was almost relieved at the thought of spending the night, elsewhere.

All the details had been agreed including the date, time, payment and the mode of transport the LGH were to use.

The deal was done and was to be delivered in writing, on the day of the investigation.

After a few days, the time came when the investigators were supposed to show up, according to the contract.

13 May 2019, 6:05pm.

Susan was in Nicole Denice's room, helping her to pack a small backpack with the essentials for her one night in the hotel.

They both had less than two hours until their guests arrived, so Susan thought it would be a good idea to have dinner at home, so she wouldn't have to buy unhealthy takeaway food in town for her daughter later.

At 07:30pm, the intercom at the gate on the McKane property rang. Susan picked up the phone and saw the young man's face on the camera screen; he was wearing a baseball cap with the LGH logo on it. Therefore, without asking unnecessary questions about his identity, she simply opened the gate with the magnetic button and went out to wait for visitors.

After a while, a dark maroon van drove up to her and stopped in front of the entrance.

The man in the cap she had just seen on the intercom screen, got out of the driver's seat, followed by a woman and another man, who got out of the other side of the van.

They all looked very young, Susan thought, they couldn't have been more than thirty years old.

"Dr Susan McKane?" the man in the cap asked.

"That's right."

"Excellent, nice to meet you, my name is Thomas Martin, or just Tom, this is Pamela Stewart and Adam Miller." He added, pointing to his companions.

"Good evening, I'm Pamela." The young woman shook Susan's hand.

"Adam." The other man did the same.

"Susan McKane, as you already know, you're welcome to come in."

"Thank you, we'll unpack our equipment first." Thomas replied. "By all means, I'll wait for you inside, until you're ready." Said Susan and headed back to the door.

"Of course..." said Thomas, then began to direct his colleagues.

"...Adam, jump in the back and start handing me the instruments, start with the computers, and you Pamela, take the papers and follow the lady, we'll join you in a minute," added the man who clearly had to be some sort of group leader.

Thomas and Adam busied themselves frantically, moving everything they had brought inside the house as quickly as possible, while Pamela sat down at the kitchen counter with Susan and presented her with every point, of the legal agreement on paper.

"...Here is your booking for tonight at the Millennium Hotel, with all the details..." Pamela said.

"...The reservation is already made, so you can check in with your daughter at any time, just show this confirmation, valid until twelve am tomorrow, and you also have breakfast included in the price, if there are any questions, here is my private phone number that you can call at any hour, I will be available all night A all that remains is

297

to sign in these places and that would be it." Pamela added with a smile on her face, pointed with her finger, where to sign.

Meanwhile, Thomas and Adam had finished unpacking everything they needed from the van and were now standing slightly out of breath, by the pile of electronic equipment stacked next to the front door. - I assume you would like a coffee, gentlemen? - Said Susan good naturedly.

"Oh yes, with pleasure." Adam replied with relief in his voice.

"I'll turn on the coffee machine for you." Susan got up from the countertop and went to set the water for the coffee.

"So, this is the piano, you know, I've watched the video a few times and I could swear I saw not only the lid opening, but also the keys being pressed." Thomas suddenly turned to Susan, stood by the instrument and looked at it curiously.

"Oh yes, that's the next thing..." she replied. "...Unfortunately, my cameras don't record the sound, but I can often hear it in my bedroom, upstairs."

"Playing piano?" Adam was surprised.

"Yes, I mean, not so much playing as the monotonous, sounding of the keys."

"Fascinating." Pamela added, packing the documents into a special folder.

"I've never seen anything like it before, plus, that figure on top of it, amazing." Adam said.

"We have a lot of footage in the archive, moving things, doors closing and opening by themselves, cutlery and crockery falling or flying around the kitchen in all directions, dark figures and so on, but the footage from your house is special, I think we're in for an interesting night." Thomas was clearly starting to get excited.

"Well, to be honest, it's hardly a compliment, I'd rather nothing like that happened."

"Of course, I understand you..." Tom spoke up. "...But this is a phenomenon that doesn't happen to everyone, which is why most people are rather sceptical about it."

"Anyway, you are here to help me, come, I will show you around the house." Said Susan, after which she started by showing the exit to the garden, then through the kitchen, the living room, the downstairs toilet and the garage, before leading the guests to the first floor.

There she first showed them Nicole's room, as it was closest to the stairs, the large, shared bedroom where John made his living, then they went through the second toilet, and finally the guest room, where Susan slept.

By the time they had finished their rounds and returned to the ground floor, the clock was showing 20:22pm and Susan decided it was time to say goodbye.

She took Nicole Denice, who by this time was sitting politely in the living room watching TV, by the hand and they both headed outside to get into the car.

If you need anything, get in touch. - She assured the guests before driving away.

The ghost investigators waved goodbye to the hostess and, as she moved away, they returned to the house and began to get on with their work. - Adam, grab your cameras. - Tom said as he walked over to the luggage with the equipment. - ...Living room, kitchen, upstairs and hallway, I'll get the computers up and running in the meantime.

"Well, let's get this party started." Adam replied, then energetically began his task.

"Pamela, take care of the motion sensors, and when you're done make sure, we have enough coffee…" Tom turned to his friend jokingly.

"…It's going to be a long night." He added in a more serious voice.

At 8:40pm, Susan and Nicole Denis arrived in front of the "Millennium Hotel".

As soon as she stopped in front of the building, a hotel employee immediately approached her car.

Being a four-star hotel, it had its own car park, so Susan handed over her keys to the valet so that he could escort the vehicle, to its allocated space.

She took Nicole Denice by the hand and they both went inside.

As they approached the reception desk, a smiling young woman, as befits a receptionist, greeted them warmly.

"Welcome to the Millennium Hotel, how can I help you." She said enthusiastically, while showing unnaturally white teeth.

"We have reservations." Susan replied and slid over the printout, she got from Pamela.

"Of course, let me have a look." The receptionist took the piece of paper, and placed it next to the computer keyboard, then began tapping details rapidly.

Susan at this point looked at the receptionist's name badge pinned to her chest, which read "Linda."

"How long are we staying here, mum?" Nicole Denice suddenly asked.

"Just for one night, like I told you before."

"I know, but I would prefer to sleep in my room, these people in our house, can they handle the pests in one night?" the child referred to the reason, they had to call in the alleged exterminators, as Susan explained to her. The woman couldn't think of a better explanation for the strangers in their house, so she decided to lie.

Firstly, she didn't want to scare her, and secondly, how can you explain to a ten-year-old girl that her house is most likely haunted by a ghost, a demon, a ghoul or, who the hell knows, what else? - I don't know, darling, we'll find out tomorrow.

"Please, here is your card for suite 203 on the second floor..." said the receptionist and held out her hand towards Susan, in which she held a blue square resembling an ATM card. "...Madam let me inform you, our bar is open until three o'clock in the morning, but the reception and kitchen are open all night, you have menus in your room both food and drinks are included, so feel free to enjoy, please let me know if there is anything else I can do for you, to make your stay with us more enjoyable, have a good night." Added Linda at the end, almost in one breath, clearly repeating this line for the thousandth time, which made the words come out of her like an automatic voicemail.

After that, she smiled broadly again and the glare of light reflecting off her artificially white teeth almost blinded Susan.

"Thank you very much…" Susan replied. "...Come on Nicole."

"Meals and drinks are included, please let me know if there is anything else

I can do to make your stay more pleasant..." Susan mischievously repeated Linda's words under her breath. *...I wonder if she also says that after the shag too.* She added in her mind and smiled slightly.

PIMMMMMMM...! A sound communicated the arrival of the transport, then the lift doors opened wide.

"Come on in Nicole." The girl stepped into the lift after her mother's words.

"You can order room service if you're hungry." She turned to her daughter.

"I'm not, I'm sleepy." She replied.

Susan had expected this answer, as it was already 9pm and her daughter usually couldn't last beyond ten o'clock without falling asleep. If the child was exhausted from the day, then even a little earlier.

Well, maybe not room service, but I like the idea of a bar open until three in the morning... the woman thought. *...Pamela didn't mention anything about a free bar, so it seems like I will be able to take o the edge, after all.* she added in her thoughts with a smile on her face.

00:35am McKane's house.

The ghost investigators had been working for a good few hour.

Just setting up the equipment, took them more than two hours, after which they proceeded to test for supernatural phenomena.

Thomas, overseeing the whole operation, sat in the living room in front of the set-up computer screens, connected to the thermal imaging cameras. As an experienced computer scientist, he quickly set up three PCs, thus making the living room a temporary and makeshift headquarters for the expedition.

He sat in one of the armchairs and watched his companions walking around the house.

He looked out for unnatural movements, malfunctions in the technical instruments or generally, anything that stood out from the normal. Pamela and Adam were conducting their first investigation upstairs. They went from room to room, with the very popular EVP device in their environment, a Dictaphone that is particularly sensitive to sounds which cannot naturally be heard by human ear.

"If you want to say something, now's your chance!" said Adam loudly, then stopped to give a chance for a potential answer.

"You have a chance to speak up, we will be able to hear you, thanks to this device." Pamela echoed him.

"We came in peace; we want to help you." Adam continued.

The pair walked cautiously from one room to the next in almost complete darkness, shining only a torch at each other.

They started at the end of the corridor, the guest room, and moved down towards the stairs.

They stopped in each room for ten minutes or so, asking questions, then exited, leaving the door open behind them and activating pre-set motion detectors at the doorframes.

In this way they could hear if anything moved behind them, while not accidentally setting o the alarm themselves.

"Alright come on down, we'll see if you've picked up anything," said Thomas over the walkie-talkie as Adam and Pamela finished checking the last place, Nicole Denice's room.

The comrades obeyed the order and headed down the stairs, with only

Adam stopping for a moment, to turn on the detector at the bedroom door. On the ground floor in the living room, Thomas was already waiting for his companions with mugs and freshly brewed coffee.

"Sit down, we'll listen to the recordings." He said and Pamela and Adam sat down next to him.

"Here." Pamela handed him the recorder.

"Well, here we go." Said Adam, adjusting his ear at the same time, as Thomas pressed the button that said 'play.'

"SSSSSSSSHHHHHHHHHHHH..." an annoying sound came from the small speaker. "...HHHHHHHH If you want to say something, now's your chance!" Adam's first clear words came from the player.

The time is 23:45pm,

At the Millennium Hotel, Nicole Denice had fallen asleep before 10 pm as expected.

The girl was in the habit of sleeping hard all night, occasionally waking up, to use the toilet.

Susan therefore left the room an hour after her daughter had gone to bed, making sure, however, that the child had her phone with her, so that she could call her if she needed to.

The woman was sitting comfortably on the sofa in the bar, sipping another white "Martini" and reading a book, about the adventures of her favourite action novel hero, Jack Reacher.

Apart from her, there were also a handful of hotel guests, who were awake at this hour and sitting quietly with a drink, each relaxed and preoccupied with their own affairs.

Suddenly, she was snapped out of her idyllic mood by the loud, almost hysterical laughter of a woman, coming from inside the bar.

Susan, slightly dazed by the alcohol, the quiet atmosphere, the late hour and the reading, felt almost as if she had been plucked from a deep, pleasant sleep.

Immediately her heart began to beat faster, due to the sudden surge of nerves, there is probably not a person in the world, who would not be upset after their blissful reverie was interrupted.

She abruptly tore her gaze away from the book, to see who was producing the awful noises.

To her surprise, the loud laughter turned out to be coming from a completely drunk, Natalie Swanson who was in a company of a man, who was a stranger to Susan.

"For God's sake ..." She said to herself angrily. "... One evening, I wanted one quiet evening, is it too much to ask for?"

But the fact that Nattaly had interrupted her nice evening was not enough. The situation was about to get even worse, as the woman, barely standing on feet, spotted Susan sitting nearby.

"I CAN'T BELIEVE MY EYES...!!!!" she shouted across the bar, her voice reverberating off the walls in every nook and cranny of the silent room. "...SUSAN?!!! And what, what, are you doing here!!!" she added without mercy, heading shakily towards where she was sitting.

There goes my reading for tonight. she thought resignedly, putting the book back on the table.

"Susan!!! AAAA....And what are you doing here!" she asked again, forgetting while travelling the last five metres that she had already said it. "Nattaly, it's almost midnight, shouldn't you be home with your son?" Susan replied.

"No...!" fired up Nattaly and she paused for a moment, to control the alcohol gashes coming out of her stomach. "HEE...He's at home with my mum, AAA...AND I! I have, a meeting, a business meeting." Saying this, she winked at her awkwardly. Susan rolled her eyes in disgust.

"AAA...BUT YOU! What are you, here doing? Do you have a business meeting too?" Nattaly smiled derisively then sat down heavily and rather intuitively on the couch, which saved her from falling to the floor, on the other side of the table.

"No, I'm here with Nicole because we're disinfecting the house overnight." She lied without any fear, that Nattaly would remember anything from this conversation, the next day.

Estimating her condition, she probably won't remember upon waking how she got here, or even where she is. Susan thought.

"AAA YES! Yes, right, you have to dis... in... fec... ting sometimes, you must..." She choked out. "...AAA BUT, YOU KNOW! You know, this new policeman, this pensioner..." she tried to start another sentence.

"Danny? Danny Davis?"

"YES! THAT ONE! This Davis, I think he's some kind of spy!!!" she said suddenly.

Susan squinted her eyes in surprise, wondering what the woman was trying to say by this.

Nattaly, you are drunk, what are you even talking about? Susan thought it would be a good idea to dig her brain a bit.

"NNNN NO! I'm telling you! He's supposedly retired, BB BUT! He's asking around about everything I saw him! With Mark Brown! He's snooping around here, and I don't like it!"

"Okay, stop talking rubbish and go get some sleep." Susan nodded to her companion, who had been watching them from afar at the bar the whole time, signalling to him that it was time to get going.

Fortunately, the man immediately understood the allusion, put down his beer bottle and, also with a wobbly but steady step, approached her table. "Madam, let me escort you to your room." Said the stranger, grabbing Nattaly under the arm and lifting her, in one movement.

"AAAA! What are YOU doing here!?" she mumbled, barely conscious.

"Let's go, good night." The man said to Susan.

"HEEE HE IS, some kind of spy Susan! DOO NOT trust him! I don't like him!"

She said while still walking away.

"UFFF..." Susan breathed a sigh of relief, glad to finally be alone again. At the same time, this unexpected conversation with a drunken Nattaly, made her slightly intrigued by what she had just heard from her.

Firstly, Danny had never mentioned to her during the session, that he was still working with the police, she only knew that he was retired.

In truth, she had noticed that he had tried to start a wider conversation with her, about events that had been going on for years, but he never pressures her, and when she didn't engage in conversation, he let it go.

Therefore, she did not suspect that he was investigating these matters in any way.

And the second question that popped into her mind was, *why was Nattaly so concerned that Danny was working undercover? And what, if anything, was she possibly risking if that was really the case?*

She wouldn't be saying these things, if she really wasn't afraid of something... Susan thought, taking a sip of Martini. "...I'll have to investigate this a little further." She added, reopening the book and went back to reading.

McKane House, 01:35am.

Thomas, Adam and Pamela finished listening to the recordings in rapt attention, with no results, although they went back several times, to moments where they thought they had captured something.

How immense was their disappointment, when it turned out that, the time spent had been in vain.

"Nobody said it would be easy..." Thomas comforted his companions. "...These things take time."

"That's right, it's still early, let's go through the CCTV footage now, maybe something showed up, while we were here?" Pamela suggested.

"It's quiet upstairs, the motion detectors haven't signalled anything." Replied a discouraged Adam.

"It doesn't matter now, we need to see the footage, better sooner than later," decided Thomas.

"Okay, let's check the cameras, there's no time to waste." Pamela got up from the sofa, followed by Thomas and finally Adam.

"Let's see each one individually, there are three of us, so we'll split up, you take one and I'll take the other two, it'll be quicker that way, we've still got plenty of time before the sun comes up..." Thomas put together a plan.

"...Later, you'll do the test again on the floor with the EVP, and at the very end we're left with the ouija board, we'll do a séance."

"Good idea, this ouija board really works, I know because I've experienced it firsthand." Pamela said.

"Let's do it." New strength had entered Adam.

The initial intention of the research team was, to stay at McKane's house overnight, at least until 7am.

It was already approaching two o'clock, at this moment none of them suspected that they would soon have to flee the property, in a panic. The night had initially promised to be dull and there was no indication that Thomas, Pamela and Adam, would experience the biggest shock of their lives, especially as the first tests had proved unsuccessful.

Until now, the night had still been quiet, but this was about to change dramatically.

Millennium Hotel 02:35am.

Susan felt sleep engulf her, no matter how much she enjoyed sitting up late in the bar, sipping drinks and reading a book, it was inexorably coming time to end this break from reality and return to the hotel suite.

Lazily and without much desire, she closed the book leaving a bookmark between the pages so as not to lose the thread, set the now empty 'Martini' glass down on the table, picked up her phone and glanced at it out of habit, then slowly got up from her comfortable chair.

"Aaaa..." she yawned loudly while stretching her arms and back.

"Ups." She said quietly covering her mouth.

Only when she stood up, did she realise how dazed she was after drinking alcohol, also the fact that it was already early in the morning, didn't help her keep her mind sober either.

Slowly but firmly, she moved towards the lift and waited for it to arrive a moment later.

PIMMMMM... The bell rang and the doors opened.

When she reached the second floor, she still had a short distance to go, just three rooms, before she reached the coveted bed.

Her eyelids grew heavier and heavier, but the knowledge that she was so close to her goal, gave her courage.

In cases like this, magnetic hotel cards are invaluable; there used to be all sorts of problems with keys, but in the modern world Susan could simply touch the card to the reader, the door magically opened, and she found herself back in the hotel room.

"Almost there." She muttered under her breath, pulling off her shoes in the process.

The woman passed the bathroom, then walked through the master bedroom and into the smaller room, where her daughter slept. There was no sign that the child had left the room, while she was gone. However, once she was within arm's reach of her room, she noticed that the door was slightly ajar.

She raised her eyebrows slightly at this sight, but could not for the life of her remember, if she had closed it before she left.

"Perhaps, she had left the room after all." She said to herself, and her alcohol-frazzled mind quickly, let go of the doubt, then pushed open the door with her hand to see if her child was asleep.

The room was small, but it had a balcony overlooking the street and a large glass door, through which the light of streetlamps streamed in, gently illuminating the interior.

The room was well lit, enough for Susan to see almost everything in the middle of the night, but this did not prevent the girl from sleeping.

The door quietly opened wider and to her eyes appeared first, the balcony windows then a small bedside table and after a while, the bed on which Nicole Denice lay buried in the sheets.

The child was sleeping tight, and Susan had no reason to worry.

Just as she was about to turn back to her bedroom, her gaze landed on the floor, and she momentarily felt herself sober up.

Thanks to the light coming through the numerous windows, she saw someone's shadow reflected on the carpet.

She looked to the place where, logically, someone should be standing for such an effect to occur, it was right next to her daughter's bed, but there was no one there.

Then she looked at the floor again and the figure had disappeared. She stood still for a few seconds that seemed like an eternity, until finally the paralysis left her.

Immediately after she recovered from the shock and left the room, closing the bedroom door behind her.

She then leaned against it and covered her mouth with a trembling hand. "Oh my God." She said quietly and drops of tears ran down her cheeks.

Susan and Nicole Denis McKane's house, 02:57am.

"Nothing." Thomas said.

"The same here, I got nothing." Adam replied.

"Nor did I." Pamela added.

"Two hours with the EVP, an hour of watching video footage and we got nothing." Adam made no secret of his frustration.

The whole team had approached the task with excessive enthusiasm, which proved disappointing.

However, the footage sent to them by Susan was very promising, so Adam Miller, Thomas Martin and Pamela Stewart had, as it turned out at the time, overly high hopes for the success of the expedition.

The irritation caused by the lack of results, could be felt especially in Adam's voice.

"We'll try the EVP one more time, leave the ouija boards for last, that should take us through until dawn." Thomas suggested.

"I agree, if we don't find anything then so be it, at least we`ve tried." Said Pamela clearly addressing a despondent Adam.

"Sure..." Adam muttered and got up from his seat, in front of the computer.

"... We're going to have to stay here until the morning anyway, although I can already tell you, we won`t find shit." He added mischievously, simultaneously walking over to the piano while Thomas and Pamela watched him.

"Don't act like a child...!" Pamela angrily added.

"...Is this your first day on the job!? We have nothing to lose and besides, you volunteered yourself to come here, how did you imagine it would be? That it would be like the Ghostbusters movie?" she added, watching Adam with pity.

"I've already said I agree, let's do what we're supposed to do and get out of here, waste of time, maybe the piano will start playing again?" saying this, Adam lifted the lid on the keys.

Then, without thinking twice, he nervously struck one of them hard. "PUMMM...!!!" a sound rang out and all hell broke loose in front of everyone present.

Within seconds, there was a series of sudden events, each successive one a consequence of the previous, like a domino effect, and the temperature dropped dramatically to such a low level, that breath turned to steam in the blink of an eye.

First, the heavy wooden lid closed with such force and speed, that Adam did not have the slightest chance to withdraw his hand.

The lid crushed three of his fingers, instantly breaking two of them.

"AAAAAA!!!!" the man screamed in pain, pulled his hand away in a state of shock, then clutched it to his chest while squeezing with his other hand.

At the same time, all the doors began to close violently:

BOOM!! BOOM!! BOOM!! BUM!!! Activating the motion sensors in the process.

TUUUU!!!... TUTUTUTU!!! TUUU!!!!! .... Which, one by one, were now howling asynchronously and so staggeringly loud that the only human action left in such a situation, is to cover your ears and run as fast as possible without looking back.

Pamela and Thomas looked around in confusion, their pupils dilated to maximum size, and, like terrified caged animals, they stared wildly around with their mouths open.

Only Adam was able to ignore the noise, as all his attention was then focused on the pain in his hand.

"FUCK!! MY HAND!!" he shouted.

Thomas was the first to recover from his shock.

"LET`S GET THE FUCK OUTTA HERE!!" he yields to Pamela.

"WHAT!!!"

"RUN!!! NOW!!!" Thomas grabbed Adam's arm, whereupon they all dashed running for the exit.

312

When they were a few steps away from the front door it also opened wide for them, so they ran outside unhindered and made their way to the car.

"Jesus! What the hell was that!" said a breathless Pamela.

"We'll talk about that later, first we need to get him to hospital." Thomas replied, also catching his breath.

"We'll have to go back in there, to get the equipment." She added after a while.

Adam slumped to the ground, leaning against the car, still holding his injured hand.

"Are you alive?" asked Thomas, poking him with his foot.

"I'm alive, but I think my fingers are broken. - He replied, slowly recovering. - We've got to turn these sensors o somehow, they can't be howling like this until morning. - Pamela suggested.

"They'll turn themselves off in a minute, they're timed..." Thomas said. "...But we must close the door, we can't leave it open."

Thomas had not yet finished speaking, when the house was suddenly silent.

"They are off, I'm going to go lock the doors and we're going to the hospital, get in the car, I'll be back in a minute." Thomas set off towards the house without thinking.

"Be careful..." Pamela replied. "...Well, get up, we're going to go and treat your hand." She turned to Adam grabbing him under the arm. "Oh..." The man struggled to get up. "...I never liked pianos; I prefer guitars." He said jokingly.

"Well, who would have thought?" Pamela replied.

Millennium Hotel, 07:45am.

Nicole Denice woke up a few minutes before eight in the morning, quickly did her morning routine and watched cartoons on TV.

Susan, on the other hand, was finishing getting ready to go down for breakfast.

Despite a slight hangover, she was feeling decent, even had a good appetite, and was beginning to be more and more interested, in how the night had gone at her house.

She also remembered last night's conversation with a drunken Nattaly, which she wanted to analyse properly in due course, and as for Nattaly herself, she didn't expect to see her any time soon, and certainly not at breakfast today.

"Are you ready?" asked Susan after coming out of the toilet.

"Five more minutes!"

"But if we go now, it's all fresh, there's pancakes and waffles for sure. "It'll be over in a minute." Replied the child without looking away from the TV.

"Okay, five minutes." Susan agreed.

She then walked over to the bedside table where her phone was plugged into the charger, picked it up and searched for Pamela Stewart's number, she expected the group had long since left her house and decided to confirm a meeting time, to hear their story.

"TUM TUUUM... TUM TUUUM... TUM TUUUM... The person you are calling is unable to take your call... She heard the automated answer. She pressed the red handset on the screen and furrowed her brow in surprise.

"This is strange, she had said she would be by the phone all night." She wondered aloud.

"We can go now." Nicole Denice interjected suddenly, getting up briskly from the sofa.

"Okay then, turn off the TV and let's go."

As instructed, the girl switched off the TV and then quickly went to put on her shoes.

Ten minutes later, they entered the restaurant, which was still almost empty.

Apparently, the hotel guests were still asleep, and the people who had come to eat so early in the morning, could be counted on the fingers of both hands.

Of course, everything was already prepared, and the smell of freshly brewed coffee and toasted bread filled the air.

The richly laid out buffet also filled the room with pleasant smells, from fresh scrambled eggs, both soft and well-fried, to sausages, bacon, grilled tomatoes, beans in tomato sauce, mushrooms, pancakes and waffles with maple syrup and various types of breakfast cereal, a continental breakfast with a selection of fruit salads, different types of fruit, cheese and cold cuts arranged neatly and aesthetically, on oblong plates also added to the charm.

There were also separate drinks, orange and apple juice, half-litre mineral and sparkling waters, coffees and teas were served to order by waiters, roaming around the restaurant.

There were stars in the ten-year-old's eyes at this sight.

Nicole had never seen such a large amount of delicious-looking food at once before, and certainly, not so early in the morning at breakfast time. So, she immediately felt that she was very hungry, and the typical sound made by a stomach demanding food, rang in her stomach. Susan was also impressed by the professionalism of the restaurant, knowing full well that someone had put in a lot of effort and work, to achieve such a stunning result.

Moments later, one of the waitresses approached them with a smile on her face, that was not typical for the average person at eight o'clock in the morning.

"Good morning, ma'am, a table for two?" the waitress asked.

"Yes, please." Susan replied.

"Please, choose the seat that suits you best."

"How about here?" Susan asked her daughter and she nodded in agreement.

"You're welcome..." The waitress added "...May I offer you coffee or tea?"

"Coffee, please." Susan replied.

"Of course, here's the coffee menu." The waitress handed her a cardboard card.

"And you, young lady? Would you like tea, hot chocolate or maybe some juice?" she turned affectionately to Nicole Denice.

"I'd like some orange juice, please." She replied politely.

"Very well, so what kind of coffee for you, ma'am?" the young woman turned her gaze to Susan again. - I'll have a cappuccino, please.

"Excellent, I'll bring the drinks in a moment and in the meantime, please come to our buffet." She announced and turned on her heel to then disappear, behind the door to the kitchen.

"Shall we go?" Susan asked the girl, who did not need to be asked twice.

She momentarily jumped off her seat and almost ran towards the buffet.

Susan took a moment to join her daughter.

When she stood next to her, they both started to put their morning meal on their plates.

The time was 8:17am.

Ten minutes later they were eating breakfast to the accompaniment of pleasant classical music.

Susan was tempted to eat more wholesome food, namely a bowl of fruit salad, a small, scrambled egg with two pieces of tomato and brown toast with a little butter, sipping this with a sugar-free cappuccino coffee and a bottle of mineral water.

Nicole Denice, on the other hand, had the perfect opportunity to go wild. Especially since her mother had decided that this time, she would turn a blind eye and let her eat whatever she wanted.

So, the girl, without thinking much about it, threw herself at the treats, devouring four thin pancakes with "Nutella" cream and an entire waffle with maple sauce, sipping this with a large glass of orange juice. "Just eat slowly..." Susan cautioned her. "...If you feel you can't eat any more then leave the rest, or you'll get a stomach-ache." She warned.

The restaurant was gradually starting to fill up with hotel guests. That didn't stop them having a pleasant morning, so Susan completely forgot that she wanted to call Pamela Stewart earlier, to ask about the exact time of today's meeting with her team.

Just when she was about to take her phone out of her purse to make another call to her, she looked ahead and noticed, with some surprise, that Pamela was standing outside the entrance to the restaurant.

The table where Susan was sitting with Nicole Denice, was close to the entrance, and Susan was sitting facing that way.

So as soon as Pamela turned up, she saw her straight away, which was quite a surprise though, as she was sure they wouldn't meet until early afternoon at the earliest.

It never occurred to her that she would see her at 8:18am in the hotel restaurant, during breakfast.

When the woman entered the room, Susan could see her face more clearly and immediately realised that something was very wrong with her.

There was something very disturbing about Pamela's appearance. It's normal for a person's appearance to change a little after a

317

sleepless night, but that wasn't the point, this was something else entirely. Pamela didn't look like a tired person, because she had been up all night, she looked more like someone who had just survived a car accident, in which the rest of the passengers had tragically died on the spot. The woman was walking ahead, looking around confused, like someone who was lost in the street and looking for the right direction.

Her gaze seemed dim and her face expressionless.

Even when Susan managed to make eye contact, she didn't recognise her, as if she had never met her before.

"Hey Pamela!" Susan called out to her, when she was close enough. The woman apparently heard someone calling her name, because she stopped and looked around trying to locate where the voice was coming from, she still seemed stunned.

"Pamela Stewart!" she repeated, this time raising her right hand up to be more visible.

Only then, did she see the table where they were sitting and a modest smile, appeared on her face, then she directed her steps towards them.

"Good morning." She said upon arriving at the place.

"Good morning!" Nicole Denice quickly replied with a chocolate-smeared face, through which a satisfied expression shone.

"Hi Pamela, please join us..." Susan indicated a vacant chair at their table. "...Forgive me for asking so directly, but what are you doing here at such an early hour?"

"Yes, the boys and I had to come here, for the rest of the night." She sat down in a chair and began to explain.

"Good morning, madam, can I offer you something to drink, coffee, tea or maybe some juice?" she was interrupted by the voice of the waitress, who appeared at the table as if she had sprung from the

318

ground. "I'll have a black coffee with a little milk, no sugar." Pamela replied. "Certainly."

The waitress smiled and disappeared, as quickly as she had appeared.

Susan waited impatiently for the conversation to continue, while her daughter carelessly devoured more and more pancakes, as if the world around her did not exist.

"Are you feeling alright? You look very tired?" she finally picked up the subject to get Pamela to converse.

"Yes, I feel fine, quite fine, Adam not so well." She replied.

"Why? What happened to him, where are they?"

"They're still sleeping in the room upstairs, we just got back from the hospital a few hours ago." Pamela explained.

"From the hospital? For God's sake, what happened?" Susan was now completely terrified.

"To be truthful, I don't really know what happened, or at least, I can't be entirely sure." Her answer was convoluted and made little sense, but she spoke the truth as best she could.

"Pamela focus please, after all, you were there." Susan was starting to get irritated.

"Please, your coffee." Again, the waitress interjected, but this time she just put the cup with the hot drink on the table and seeing the serious faces of the two women, quickly moved away.

"Yes, I was, but it happened so quickly..." Pamela began to tell the story. "...First the piano lid slammed into Adam's hand and then everything came crashing down on us, as if some kind of bomb had exploded, the slamming door, the alarm from the motion detectors, Adam's screaming, all-round chaos in general, there wasn't even time to collect our thoughts, and we had to run away." She said shakily.

319

Susan watched in disbelief as the woman lifted her coffee cup to take a sip, her hands visibly shaking, needing both to prevent the hot liquid from spilling over.

This was proof enough; she was not telling an imaginary story and was genuinely still emotionally unstable.

Therefore, Susan had no reason not to believe her.

"But did you record anything, did you manage to find anything?" she asked.

She needed to find out everything, immediately.

"No, I mean I don't know, all our equipment was left at the house and we're still going to check it, by three o'clock in the morning we had nothing, we did two EVP examinations and then, we looked at the footage from the cameras and nothing, we were just about to start walking again with the EVP when it happened, then it was the hospital, and we got here after six o'clock in the morning."

Both women were silent for a moment, Susan was deep in thought and Pamela was sipping hot coffee to calm her nerves, only Nicole Denice was indulging in sweets without a care in the world.

"You said, before three o'clock this morning you were supposed to walk with that EVP again?" Susan finally asked.

"Yes, I remember when I looked at the time on the computer, it was exactly 02:55am."

"What time did you leave the house?"

"Let me think..." Pamela reached back in her memory. "...We still had a little conversation before the whole thing happened, maybe ten minutes. So, if you're not mistaken, it follows that at about 03:05am you were no longer there?"

Susan thought out loud.

"Well, yes, that seems about right, including the chaos and circumstances through which we escaped, approximately ten

320

minutes." Pamela lowered her gaze, it was only when she said the words aloud, it occurred to her how confusing it sounded.

"Between three and three-thirty in the morning."

"Excuse me? Do these times tell you anything?" then the investigator was curious.

"Yes..." Susan replied. "...According to the doctors, around that time, my husband John died in our upstairs bedroom, between three and three-thirty in the morning...."

Pamela cast an attentive gaze at Susan as she continued.

"...At three zero four on my recordings, the activity starts, you've said it was three zero five in the morning, but equally, it could have been a few seconds earlier, which is three zero four. - Susan thought aloud.

"I think I know, what you are getting at." Pamela interjected.

"Yes, and I think I know exactly, what time my husband died, and who is responsible for the paranormal phenomena in my house."

18

First accused.

'And here is nothing but trembling, except words
retrieved from nothingness - ah, you are left with a
particle of that wonder,
which will be the whole content of eternity.'

17 May 2019, North Hill, home of Nicole Denice and Susan McKane.

Susan waited a few days for LGH to contact her, wondering in between, what she should do.

Eventually she received a brief and useless message via the internet, which read:

"Dear Susan McKane,

We regret to inform you that we are unable to assist you in this situation. As we have not encountered a similar case before, our current knowledge is uncertain.

However, I would advise you to consult a priest, I think it would be a good idea to consecrate the house with holy water.

I would also like to add, our computers and other electronic devices were irreparably damaged during our stay in your house and are now only suitable for disposal. Therefore, we do not have any videos or other material from that night.

I regret that we were not able to meet the challenge, I wish you good luck and all the best for the future!

Best regards, LGH Director, Marta Bishop."

On the one hand, Susan assumed that if it was indeed John's soul that remained in their home, then neither she nor Nicole Denice were in danger. However, looking at the specifics of the whole situation, she would have been happiest to completely forget that such a thing had ever happened. As a rational person she expected, the problem would not solve itself, simply because she ignored it.

But she also expected that the "London Ghost Hunters", who were clearly overwhelmed by the task, would not take the initiative to help her in any way.

Put simply, she was left alone with a late-night visitor.

02 June 2019, North Hill, home of Danny and Rachel Davis, 10:35pm.

"...Ain and Angelina Hailu, both 45, with two young children, he is a banker, she a housewife, live in a house in Kensington Palace Gardens, whose postcode starts with W8..." Connor relayed the results of the investigation.

"...Incidentally, they've done well here." He added jokingly.

It took Conner a week to track down the Ethiopian couple Danny was looking for.

The task was not easy, as they were not listed on the police database, so he had to escalate the search area and use his police authority, to get this information from the UK immigration department, risking his own head in the process by taking on a case, he was not officially assigned to. Unlike Danny, who, with a bit of luck and thanks to an official pass from

Mark Brown, got the information he needed from a kind receptionist at an NHS clinic, when he went there to enquire about patients registered ten years ago.

"I need to contact them somehow..." Danny said. "...Do you have any idea how I can do that?"

"Let me think, I can't turn up on their doorstep without authorisation, I'd need a good reason for it..." Connor wondered. "...I think, the best way to meet face to face would be to arrange a visit."

"Making an appointment? It's not like a dentist s I can find a phone number on the internet and book an appointment." Danny was irritated. "A dentist maybe not, but the guy's a banker, right? Give me a bit more time, I'll try to find specifically what bank he works for, then we'll think about how we can meet him."

"Yeah, that makes sense." Agreed Danny who felt a bit silly for doubting his colleague.

"Unfortunately, I can't tell you right now exactly, how long that might take ..." Connor immediately cooled his enthusiasm. "...I don't have an update here as to where he's currently working, from what I can see, he's some sort of higher-up and not just a banker you might meet in front of a computer at a bank every day, I think he's a big shot.

"I understand, see what you can do and let me know, as soon as possible, I'll be waiting."

"Sure, but remember, it could take days and maybe weeks, I'm telling you right now not to get too excited, because he might not even be in the country." Connor made it clear.

"I understand everything, thanks for your help, I am in your debt." Danny replied.

"You still owe me a fishing trip, adds another favour to the list."

"If you help me unravel this case, I'll take you on a cruise across the ocean in a luxury yacht, you'll fish until your hands swell."

"It's a deal, I've got to go, I'll get back to you shortly." Connor said.

"Sure, be careful out there."

Damn it, so close and yet so far away. Danny thought as he put the phone down.

Although he was feeling a little frustrated, he knew he was on the right track and that things just took time.

His years in the police force, had also given him the ability to suppress his emotions, while most people have trouble managing their patience, Danny was perfectly capable of calming his nerves and, like a predator hunting prey, waiting for the perfect moment to strike.

This knowledge often came in handy at work, in public life as well as in private, and it served him well in these circumstances too.

The only problem was, Danny didn't realise the trouble, he was getting himself into.

07 June 2019, Nattaly Swanson's flat.

In the meantime, Nattaly was about to leave "North Hill" and move to "London" for a while.

She had recently become uncomfortable in her hometown and wanted to take a break from it.

However, it wasn't as easy as it might seem, because of her role in the organisation she was needed all the time where she was, which was right there, in "North Hill."

But she wasn't going to bother, because firstly, she hated the restrictions, and secondly, she could afford to go to Hawaii and spend a few months in the most expensive hotel she could find, if she just wanted to.

What bothered her most, was that she kept bumping into Danny and she had the impression that the retired policeman was watching her closely, even stalking her.

But the man didn't really pay much attention to her, yes, he had seen her a few times in town, but he didn't care at all.

Still, that was enough to put Nattaly on the verge of paranoia, fearful of being detected, even though "North Hill" was a town where it was easy to hide, without attracting too much suspicion.

But remorse led her to believe that Danny was watching her, and she decided to disappear from his sight, at least for a while.

Also, protests from her associates did not influence her decision, so the whole operation had to be put on hold for the duration of Nattaly's absence.

After some negotiation, an agreement was reached and she was given a week to go to "London" and calm her nerves, but then she had to return to "North Hill," and everything would return to normal.

The woman was then looking forward to her holiday.

She was longingly counting down the time left, before she got on the train and left everything behind.

This included her son, who was due to stay with his grandparents for a week, so in her mind, everything was already ticked off.

It hadn't even occurred to her that the last person she would want to meet on the streets of "London" would be Danny, who was also due to be there at that time.

Danny and Rachel Davis's house, on the same day.

Armed with patience after my last conversation with Connor, I decided to focus on my day-to-day duties, without thinking in between about my friend's doings, or when I would receive the next call from him on the matter.

The first item on my calendar, was an appointment with Susan McKane, scheduled for Wednesday afternoon.

In addition to this, on Mondays I went to the swimming pool with Rachel, on Tuesdays to the cinema or shopping, on Wednesdays I met Susan for therapy while Rachel usually stayed at home, on Thursdays I attended an hour-long meeting for "Alcoholics Anonymous," at which I also managed to meet many interesting people.

On Fridays Rachel and I tended the garden together, and weekends were spent mainly at home, occasionally going out to dinner at a restaurant or simply ordering food delivered to the house.

This was how I spent my days in retirement, and I also had plenty of free time to attend to other things that didn't involve Rachel, such as trying to get to the bottom of the mystery of the missing North Hill four.

I was already getting used to the thought of returning to my standard weekly routine, and my mind was starting to prepare for the next parts of it, when unexpectedly Connor called and completely turned everything upside down.

"I've got him." He said as soon as I picked up the phone, without even giving me a chance to say hello. "...He has an office in the Barclays bank headquarters at E14 Churchill Place." He said in a proud voice. "I'm impressed that you found him so quickly..." I said truthfully. "...How did you do it?"

"I have my ways..." He replied immodestly. "...It turns out that his father has a long history with the establishment, it seems that Ain has inherited a significant stake, you could say that the guy is born into wealth.

"At least, I think everyone would like to be born into a rich family and have everything handed to them on a silver platter..." I replied. "...Now, the only question left is how to arrange the meeting?"

"As always, I'm two steps ahead of you, I called their headquarters directly and the secretary redirected me to his office, as soon as I said I am a police officer and gave her my badge numbers."

"Brilliant! I understand you spoke to him, what did he tell you?"

"Nice guy..." he started to report. "...But when he heard that there was someone who would like to meet him to talk about North Hill, he immediately changed his tone of voice, he clearly doesn't have good memories of this town, I had to do a lot of nagging to get him to agree to a meeting."

"And he agreed?" I interrupted him out of impatience.

"Yes, tomorrow at lunchtime at Canary Wharf is the only free date he has, he said he was flying to Berlin later that day, there was no telling when the next opportunity would arise."

"Sure, I'll take the first train tomorrow and give you a call." I replied.

"What do you say Rachel?"

"I don't know yet, I'll think about it." Really, I haven't thought about it before.

"You can tell her you want to meet me, you do, so you won't be lying." He gave me an idea.

"She thinks you're going to come to us."

"But she knows I'm waiting for a holiday, I told her about it before, just say you miss me, she'll understand."

"Alright, I'll get back to you tomorrow, take care and see you." I added and ended the conversation.

I decided that I would follow my friend's advice, I didn't want to lie to Rachel and yet, the fact was that I would see Connor.

In the process I was also going to meet a wealthy banker, who was an important part of this puzzle, but I was going to keep that to myself.

8 June 2019, 08:10am.

The conversation with Rachel went exceptionally well, she was delighted to hear that I was going to London to meet Connor.

I could even say, she encouraged me on this point, saying "It would do you good, to see him."

So, that day I woke up very early, at 05:30am, without waking my wife. I wanted to have enough time to get ready, have breakfast and go to North Hill railway station, to catch the train leaving at 08:00am.

It took two hours to get to "London Charing Cross".

From the time of arrival to the time of the meeting, there was roughly another two hours to manage, assuming of course, that Mr Ain Hailu would leave for lunch on time, at 12:00am.

Anyway, that was the plan of action in my mind, and I intended to stick to it. I didn't take traffic jams into account because London, contrary to appearances, is not that crowded in the morning.

Even if something would stop me on the way, I had enough time in reserve to deal with it.

Once I was on the train, I called Connor.

"Hi, I'm on my way, I'll be at Charing Cross at ten, where do you want to meet?" I asked directly.

"Okay, go directly to Canary Wharf, we'll meet there." He replied.

"Sure, I'll call you on the spot." I replied and hung up.

I didn't want to talk too much because it was just eight o`clock in the morning, and I knew that Connor liked to lounge in bed for as long as he could, on his days off.

Besides, he was doing me a huge favour and realised it, so much so I was beginning to have serious concerns, about him keeping his word and reminding me of the promised ocean cruise on a luxury yacht.

One problem at a time. I thought, slipping my wireless headphones into my ears.

I still had an hour, and a half left of the train journey, I didn't want to spend it thinking.

I turned on my favourite 80s playlist and closed my eyes, gathering my strength for what promised to be an interesting day, to put it mildly.

Suddenly, I felt someone tapping on my shoulder.

When I opened my eyes, I saw a young woman moving her lips, she was clearly saying something to me, but through my headphones with music playing all the time, I couldn't hear anything.

When I reflexively pulled one out of my ear, I realised that the train was at Charing Cross station and the woman was poking me, to tell me just that. "Oh..." I said, still slightly sleepy. "...Thank you, miss, I didn't expect to fall asleep so hard." I added somewhat embarrassed. "No problem, it can happen to anyone." She replied kindly.

"Excuse me, how long have we been here?" I asked before I thought to check the time on my phone.

"Not long, a few minutes." She replied.

"Thank you again."

"You're very welcome, have a nice day!" she added, walking slowly away.

"You too!" I said already to her back.

"Damn it." I reprimanded myself in my mind.

Indeed, this nice young woman had saved my old arse, I didn't even want to think about what would have happened if I had slept on.

After all, trains stand at the station for up to fifteen minutes and then set off again.

I might well, have woken up at another station, just in the opposite direction.

But there was no point in wondering any longer, *what if?*

I quickly got up and picked up my hand luggage, which contained a few essential personal belongings, as well as the documents I wanted to show Mr Hailu, then hurriedly exited the train.

I walked outside in front of Charing Cross station and checked the time on my phone, it was 10:15am.

Despite the sunny weather, I thought that the best way to get to "Canary Wharf" quickly, would be to take the underground train after all, instead of making my way through the city on buses.

Duty first and pleasure later. I thought and dialled Connor's number.

"Talk to me." He said after picking up.

"I'm at Charing Cross, changing to the Tube." I replied.

"Alright, I'm already heading in that direction too."

"Okay, then I'll see you there." I replied and hung up.

I stood outside for a short while longer to get a breath of fresh air, before heading down into the underground tunnels of London.

I then moved towards the "Underground" sign located in the same building as the overground train station.

Pushing my way through a wave of new people, who happened to be pouring out a crowd from several trains, that happened to arrive at the station.

After passing through the electronic gates, touching the reader with my, "Oyster" ticket, I arrived underground via the escalator and here my journey became a little more complicated, as I needed several transfers to reach the "Canary Wharf" station.

Fortunately, for someone who was born and raised in this city, this was not too much of a problem.

I quickly found the tube line connections I needed to use to get there. I first got on the brown "Bakerloo" line to later change at "Baker Street" station to the grey "Jubilee" line, from where I already had direct access to my destination.

The whole journey, including transfers and walking through twisted tunnels, took me 45minutes.

So, when I saw daylight again, it was just past eleven in the morning.

Perfect. I thought contentedly.

The streets between the skyscrapers in the new financial heart of London, were almost empty, as most people were busy with their duties in their offices.

You could see a few tourists, people going in or out of buildings, people working in local cafes and restaurants, and those just keeping the streets tidy.

Without thinking much, I decided to go to a beautiful park in the heart of the "business district" to sit comfortably and call Connor.

I had to check how far away he was.

"I'll be there in twenty minutes." He announced after picking up the phone. "Okay, I'll be waiting for you in the park." I replied, slightly amused by his behaviour.

"Sure, I'll find you there, see you later." He added and hung up. "I can't say I was particularly surprised by the lateness; it was totally his style.

But I didn't really care about getting here quickly either, but it wasn't because I didn't miss my friend, I just missed the city too and was now revelling in its charms.

I had always liked the "Canary Wharf" area; it was neat and quiet even though it was home to some of the biggest corporations in London, with thousands of people working there.

I also had a sentimental connection with the place, because it had the lowest crime rate, and when I was still a police officer, I remember always patrolling these streets in peace when I was assigned to do so.

At the time, I imagined the whole city looking like this, without fights, thefts, burglaries and murders.

Where people live and let others live in harmony, without hatred for others.

I consider myself a good person, to put it immodestly.

That's why I became a police officer, believing in these values, wanting to uphold the law and justice, hoping that my work and actions could one day make a real difference to someone's life.

The world is a huge and cruel place, but it is the people closest to us who have the greatest impact on our lives, making it better and at least a little friendlier, so that everyone can live the rest of their days in dignity and peace.

11:27am.

I sat there for ten minutes, enjoying the weather and the peace around me. Connor hadn't turned up yet, so I thought a hot cup of coffee would do me good.

I got up from the bench and slowly made my way towards a nearby Starbucks, where I ordered two medium sized cups of latte to go, one for myself and one for Connor.

When I looked at my watch again, it was almost 11:30 and then I saw Connor approaching me, a smile appeared on my face.

It felt like I hadn't seen him for a few years, not a few months.

"I knew I'd find you here, not in the park." He said, hugging me tightly.

"You're just in time, take that." I replied and handed him a coffee. "That's what I'm talking about!" he replied contentedly, and together we started walking back to the park from where I had come. "...You look great, I can see that retirement is doing you good." He added jokingly.

"Sure, it's not as bad as I expected, the only thing that worries me is, the cause I came here for today." I said openly.

"I understand, I honestly admire your dedication and determination, you're under no obligation, yet you've taken on a huge responsibility and you're persevering towards your goal, as far as I can see."

"I owe it to Denise..." I started to say when he interrupted me.

"Denise? Denise Randal?"

"Yes." I replied.

"Wait a minute, can you explain that to me? I don't think I understand something here, I know you've been very traumatised by her death, and I don't blame you at all, as I've had a hard time recovering from it myself, but what does this have to do with the missing four? After all, as far as I remember, the last person went missing there in 2017, and there were no more recorded cases after that, what link do you see between Denise Randal and those circumstances?" he asked a very good question. Worse still, I had no explanation for it, perhaps because, there simply wasn't one.

I didn't see any similarities in the cases or any other connections myself, at that point I just had an instinct and a hunch that I was on the right track, to finding a common motive.

"I don't know yet, but when I find out, you'll be the first person I explain it to."

"I answered as best as I could."

My friend looked at me confused and shook his head disapprovingly, then took a sip of coffee.

"You know what, let's just go to that park." He said.

"It's getting to twelve o'clock, where do we meet him?"

"He'll call me when he goes out for lunch, I think any minute now.

We managed to get back and sit down for a moment, when Connor's phone rang."

"PC Declan O`Connor…" he said in a business like tone into the receiver. "…Yes, of course, we are at Jubilee Park... We'll wait here for you... Goodbye…" He added and ended the conversation. "…He will be here shortly."

A moment later Connor stood up.

"He's coming." He said in my direction.

I did the same, at the same time looking curiously, trying to pick out Mr Ain Hailu from the small group of approaching people.

Then my gaze stopped on one man, and I knew immediately that he was the one we were waiting for.

A man of medium height with a dark complexion, short, cropped hair, a smart blue suit with a white shirt, black tie and black shiny shoes.

At first glance you could tell he was a classy man.

But only when he was close enough could I see the gold Rolex on his left wrist, which must have cost him a small fortune, and was like the icing on the cake of his presentation.

"Good morning gentlemen, Ain Hailu." He said standing in front of us, extending his hand to greet us.

"Good morning, my name is Declan O`Connor, we spoke on the phone, and this is my partner, Danny Davis." Connor introduced us and we shook hands.

"Is there somewhere you'd like to go to sit down and talk?" I asked politely. "And most of all something to eat, it's finally lunch time." Connor added.

"I don't eat lunch..." Ain replied. "... We can sit in Starbucks, but I'll warn you in advance, I can't spend more than half an hour with you, because I have a very busy schedule today and I'm flying to Germany tonight."

"Of course, we won't take up too much of your time and we are grateful, that you have agreed to talk to us." I said, meaning every word.

"I'll try to help you as much as I can, you can address me by my first name."

He replied.

"That's very kind of you." I added, then we started on our way back to the café.

We had walked a few metres when I decided to address the businessman.

"Nice present."

Connor looked at me confused as to what I meant, but Ain knew immediately as he reflexively looked at the watch wrist, on which I had noticed the inscription "To my dear husband, Angela," earlier.

"Ah, thank you, I see you are perceptive..." he replied.

"...A gift from my wife for our wedding anniversary, personally, I don't like expensive things, life has taught me that it is better not to stand out from the crowd."

I smiled slightly after these words.

"And this is said by a person, wearing a suit worth several thousand pounds." I summed up my thoughts with a sneer.

When we arrived, I immediately thought that there was no chance of us finding a table for three inside, as the café was packed with people, almost to the brim at lunchtime.

True, most of them were ordering takeaways, but that didn't change the fact that all the tables were occupied, at least from my point of view. Nevertheless, Ain was walking straight ahead, unconcerned about the number of people, so Connor and I walked behind him.

"Is there something I don't know about?" I asked Connor in a low voice, and he just shrugged his shoulders.

Ain walked in first, ignoring the people, he started squeezing through the crowd.

When we finally managed to pass through, everything became clear, because at the very end of the café we saw the only free table, on which there was a sign saying "reserved" along with four empty chairs.

"Take a seat, gentlemen." Ain indicated the chairs to us with his hand, occupying one of them himself.

"Do you always reserve a table here for lunch?" I asked out of curiosity.

"Not always…" he replied. "... Today I asked the secretary to do it, because I expected to need space to talk, unfortunately silence is already harder to come by, but this is the best place we can find now." He explained. "Indeed ..." I replied, then opened the briefcase and pulled out four pictures.

"...I would like to thank you again, for meeting me and assure you that I do not represent any authority, I am conducting a private investigation on my own and I am just looking for some clues, you are not accused of anything, so please do not misunderstand my intentions... I have made it official. Do you recognise any of these people?" I asked, handing Ain the photographs I had brought with me.

I tried to do it as discreetly as possible, for the sake of all the people present.

Ain took the photos from me and started looking through them. "I understand that you have lived in North Hill in the past." I asked in between.

"That's right..." he replied without taking his eyes off the photographs, he kept browsing. "... About ten years ago, my wife and I bought a house there..." he added, at the same time handing me one of the photographs. "...I remember this child..." he declared. "...Her name is Magda, unfortunately I can't remember her surname. Then a man working in the café approached us.

"Here you go, a double espresso." He said placing a small cup on the table.

It looked like the banker's receptionist had not only pre-booked a table, but also something for the boss.

"Magda Richardson..." I added the name. "...The first missing person in North Hill, the other photos belong to three children, who have also gone missing in the town over a ten-year period." I explained.

"I'm sorry to hear that, it's really a huge tragedy, I had no idea that there were more cases like that, to be honest, after I left, I didn't follow the fate of the place anymore." Ain said, a look of clear concern on his face.

"Could you tell me, from your point of view, what happened then?" I asked.

"Of course, but I won't add anything new that I didn't already say in my testimony, at that time..." He began to tell the story. "...So, my wife and I were still relatively new residents in North Hill, as we had only lived there for five months, but we had already started to slowly settle in, then news of Magda Richardson's disappearance went through the town and the police knocked on our door..." He paused for a moment to take a sip of espresso. "...We then learnt that a doll of unknown origin had allegedly been found to be linked to black Voodoo magic, due to my and my wife's background, the colour of our skin and the fact that we were still new in town, the police and locals assumed that we were behind the incident, because, who else...?" he asked rhetorically, slightly irritated. ...*I thought it was incredibly racist, but we gave a statement anyway, immediately afterwards the police put us at ease, because we had an irrefutable alibi.*

"Let me ask you out of curiosity, what kind of alibi was that?" Connor interjected.

"We were not in the country at the time." Ain replied briefly.

"I see, but something else happened, didn't it? Something that made you decide to leave North Hill for good." I asked another question.

"Yes..." Ain thought back again to the events, ten years ago. "...Despite our alibi and the fact that the police had no reason to link us to the case, the locals decided not to let it go, they literally went mad. To them we were guilty of Magda's disappearance and nothing would change that They passed judgment on us and at first ineptly tried to enforce it, pointing fingers and calling my wife names in town, they broke our windows at night, but when my car was set on fire I decided it was too much and we decided to leave North Hill out of fear for our lives. I couldn't allow anyone to play with me and my wife any longer." He finished his story.

"I am extremely sorry about that; it never should have happened." I sincerely sympathised with him at that moment.

"It is true, but it happened, fortunately we were able to leave quickly and settle in London, we are happy here, we have two children and a third on the way." Said Ain already cheered up.

"Congratulations, I'm glad this story has a good ending for you and your family, unfortunately for those children whose pictures you saw, and their families, this story continues, that's why I'm here today..." I said. "...Apart from the events that happened to you personally at the time, did anything else happen? Something that caught your attention or stood out from these, already extraordinary, complicated circumstances?" I tried to dig further.

"Unfortunately; firstly, it was a long time ago and I was trying with all my might to forget the nightmare, and secondly, everything was happening so fast and was associated with so much stress and fear, both for me and my wife, that we were unable to focus on anything else but our own safety..." He took a moment's pause to check his phone and reflect.

I was slowly beginning to realise that I would receive no guidance from Ain on which to base further action.

Reality was staring me deep in the face, and I could feel myself becoming depressed.

"And what am I going to do about it next?" I wondered.

"...I'm going to have to go..." Ain announced.

These words were like nails in my coffin, all the hope I had placed in this conversation had just burst like a soap bubble, the feeling of defeat was overwhelming.

"...my time's up gentlemen..." He added, getting up from the table. "...I'm sorry if I wasn't very helpful, but I really don't know what else I could add, except perhaps that we eventually sold the house to the agency we originally bought it from."

At this point my eyes opened wide, these words were like music to my ears.

"Excuse me, what agency was it?" I asked curiously.

"Oh, I don't remember very well..." He paused momentarily, but I could see he was searching his memory for the name. "...Something like, brad lettings?" he said uncertainly. "Bradley and Brad lettings?" I added.

"Yes, exactly..." he confirmed my suspicion. "...I must admit that they were extremely helpful, because thanks to them we bought the house we still live in today, as well as agreeing to buy the one in North Hill, but the price was in my opinion way under priced, fortunately, money has never been an issue in my life so I didn't pay much attention to it, for me the most important thing at the time was safety, mine and my wife's, and the price didn't matter." He said immodestly.

"Do you remember what amount we were talking about?" I pursued the subject.

"The difference was probably, two hundred thousand rounded down..." He said, impatiently. "...Well, gentlemen, it was a pleasure talking to you, I hope I was of some use to you after all, please keep me informed about the progress of the investigation and I wish you good luck."

After this he shook our hands and hurriedly headed towards the exit, without even giving us a chance to reply.

Connor and I were left alone at the table with two mugs of already cold coffee.

"Do you have anything?"

"Yes, I think I do." I replied, still thoughtful.

"Great, we'll talk about it over dinner, I'll invite you to a private club, House of Barnabas in London's Soho." He announced cheerfully.

Connor was talking about the historic Gregorian-style house at 1 Greek Street in London Soho.

The property, built between 1744 and 1747, was famous for its beautiful St Barnabas rooms and gardens, which featured in Charles

Dickens' novel about London and Paris during the French Revolution "A Tale of Two Cities," published in 1859.

The site is now home to a charitable employment academy and a not-for-profit members' club, "St Barnabas House."

The club offered its guests the luxury of spending time in colourful rooms steeped in history, a modern bar and restaurant, a tranquil garden and a beautiful cathedral adjacent to the building.

Before I parted company with Connor, after meeting Ain Hailu, we arranged to have dinner at 7pm in Soho Square, near "Tottenham Court Road" station, opposite "St Barnabas House."

In the meantime, he still had some errands to run, and I also felt I needed a rest, preferably a nap, so 7pm suited perfectly.

I thought the best place to find a room for one night would be the "Queensway" district, which is literally filled with hotels.

So, that was my next destination, which meant I had to go underground again to get there.

01:45pm.

On arrival I only found a free room in the third hotel I visited.

It took me more than half an hour but given that I wasn't in a hurry to get anywhere, I had no complaints.

So far, I was happy with how my trip to London had gone, and I could also count the meeting with Ain Hailu as a success, although at one point I thought it wouldn't be.

What puzzled me was the issue of the missing money that the agency had withheld when buying back the house in North Hill from Mr and Mrs Hailu. As a result, they received significantly less money than they had originally paid the agency for the house, which they had to vacate after half a year. Despite my gut feeling that this was a breakthrough piece of information, I could not yet see the link.

Because firstly, £200,000 might seem like a good motive to the average person, but for an estate agency it's not a lot of money and I doubted, anyone had the business or resources to go to that much trouble for such a profit.

Secondly, the "BnBL" agency was not based in the town at the time, so organising everything remotely would have been impossible, and thirdly, what role was Magda Richardson supposed to play? She, after all, had nothing to do with either Mr and Mrs Hailu or "Bradley and Brad Lettings." I felt that keeping everything in sync and working perfectly together might have been too complicated, if not downright impossible.

Because how can you plan something like this and be sure, that it will work in exactly the right order:

1. Magda Richardson disappears.

2. People blaming this on the Hailu family.

3. Mr and Mrs Hailu can't stand the pressure, therefore resell the property, at a loss of 200k.

Add to this the Voodoo dolls, black magic and subsequent incidents, my brain was struggling hard to put this puzzle together.

I couldn't rule out the possibility that it was all just a confluence of unfortunate events.

However, at that moment it was the only clue I had, and no matter how absurd it seemed, I had to stick to it, because I had no other ideas. I decided not to torture myself any longer and closed my eyes for a while, I needed rest both mentally and physically.

So, I lay down on the single bed in my temporary bedroom.

As sleep engulfed me a moment later, my subconscious decided to take over and once again, review the information I had managed to gather so far. Information that had been stuck somewhere deep in my mind and, until now, lay patiently waiting its turn to be recalled at the right time.

It was one of those dreams after which one has the feeling that it played out on waking, and almost everything remains in one's memory even after waking up.

In this dream I went back to a conversation with Mark Brown, who was talking about Sandra Jones. ...she sold the house about a year after Magda's disappearance, I think she couldn't bear the unpleasant memories and depression, I don't know where she is now, like most of those people who had something to do with the North Hill curse... I didn't pay attention to the message of this statement at the time.

I then realised that Mark clearly meant that it was not just Sandra Jones who had sold her house, but also the rest of the people who were in the spotlight back then.

Indeed, I had never considered what happened to Joanna Richardson, Carolin Roberts, Christopher Wilson and Alexandra Murphy, the parents of the missing persons, afterwards.

For a while I assumed that if the police were not in touch with them, it meant that they had nothing new to add and therefore no reason to talk to them.

I knew that these people didn't live in North Hill anymore and frankly that didn't surprise me at all, after all I had left the town where I had spent most of my life seeking solace, when my personal problems began to overwhelm me.

The fact that I still had something to do in North Hill was a separate issue. But at that moment, the one common denominator that linked them all began to become more and more obvious, it was: sales.

New questions began to arise in my mind that I could not answer for myself.

Firstly: Should I try to find the relatives of the missing?

Second: What is the probability that the first disappearance was planned for someone to obtain £200,000?

Third: Is it at all possible that these cases are connected or is it just pure coincidence?

It was imperative that I consult someone else about this, and so I was glad to meet Connor that evening.

I had no doubt that a friend would be able to help me, clarify a few things.

07:10pm, Soho, London.

I arrived in Soho Square a little early that evening, but I didn't have to wait long because Connor turned up exactly at the agreed time and we both headed towards St Barnabas House.

A three-storey brown brick building, surrounded by a black metal fence with a large wooden door with no intercom or electric bell, just an antique knocker, all added to the atmosphere of this unique place.

I was standing next to Connor when he knocked on the door, a few seconds later it was opened by a smiling young woman from reception. "Good evening, gentlemen." She said stepping aside to let us in. "Good evening, my name is Declan O`Connor, I have reservations for two people for dinner."

"Of course, you're welcome." She replied, while pointing the way to the restaurant.

Without thinking for long, we walked deep into the building.

Although I had been here a few times with Connor, I was always impressed by the place, with its modern look and atmosphere that harmonised with the Georgian style.

Which made me smell history in the air, like the aroma of freshly baked bread.

We found a table in the middle of the room, there was a relaxed atmosphere as there were only a few people in the restaurant at that hour. "Tell me, what's on your mind..." he asked me directly, just after we sat down. "...You seem thoughtful."

"I know first-hand, since 2008 someone in London has been involved in the disappearance of these four, has been sending parcels of allegedly cursed dolls there."

Connor stared at me intently in silence, clearly expecting me to elaborate on the subject.

"Commander Mark Brown, told me that between 2008/2017 there had been dozens of recorded reports of mysterious packages, four of which involved the disappearance of children. It had never been established who had sent the parcels, and now Ain Hailu was claiming after the first incident, he had resold the house at a loss of two hundred thousand pounds., I think others were also selling their properties to the agency at a discounted price, I just don't know how to check, if I am right." I explained.

"Motive?"

"Of course, there must be a reason why these children disappeared after all, nothing happens without a cause and until now, it is not known what happened to them."

"It would be difficult to prove, let alone have any evidence, especially if it was an isolated incident, but even if it is as you say, how could anyone be sure that the Hailu family would sell the house, on top of that for less than they bought it?" he confirmed my doubts.

"Good evening gentlemen, may I take your order?" the waiter suddenly interjected.

"Yes, for me I'd like a beef burger, medium rare and a beer." Connor replied.

"I'll have the same and a diet coke, please." I added.

"Of course." He replied and walked away to place our order.

I too find it difficult to find parallels, but what if this was not an isolated incident but a series of carefully planned events? Then it starts to stick together. I returned to the subject.

"Don't you think detectives would have investigated the case, given that the motive may have been money? Evidently it must have been a dead end if they didn't pursue the investigation, maybe it was just about the cost of repairing the house? Ain said they had gone through a series of attacks." Connor wondered.

"That's true, but he also said they moved out a couple of weeks after Magda Richardson went missing, which means they were giving evidence even before the house was sold, then no one spoke to them again, which is why that issue never saw day light."

"It makes sense, but it doesn't change the fact, that it's just conjecture. I still think that for this to have happened, someone must have been extremely lucky or put in an extraordinary amount of effort, with no guarantee of success." Connor had his doubts.

I couldn't blame my friend for finding it difficult to recognise that what I was talking about could be possible.

To be honest, I could hardly accept this version of events as plausible myself.

But at the same time, I had nothing else and had to believe that there really was something to it, without trying to justify it by force.

I felt like I was balancing a bit between reality and illusion, with the almost constant feeling that Denise Randal was watching my every move, I tried not to get paranoid.

"That's what I think too..." I agreed with him. "...But I can't rule it out, I'm wondering if it's worth trying to find other people who have also moved out of North Hill in these circumstances, what do you think?

347

"I think it will be a time-consuming and complicated undertaking that, will probably prove fruitless, but I agree, it is the only way to test your theory." Before I knew it, fifteen minutes had passed when the waiter returned with our food.

It wasn't until I saw the delicious-looking burger in front of me that I realised I hadn't eaten anything all day, bogged down with emotion, I was terribly hungry.

It was the perfect time to take a break from the conversation for a meal, only to return to it when I had recovered.

10 minutes later.

"We'll have to find these people." I said already with a full stomach.

"We?"

"I can't find them myself, only you now have access to a wider base of citizens." I explained.

"You know I'll always help you as much as I can, I'll see what I can do, but like I said, it's going to take a long time, I don't think it's going to work like it did with Ain, there was a lot of luck there." He replied.

"We have four names, and we don't even know if these people are still in the country, but if you help me, I am ready to take up the challenge, even if I must go to meetings every weekend, when it turns out, as in the case of Ain Hailu and his wife, that these people also sold their properties to the "BnBL" agency, then we will have grounds to officially report the suspicion for a professional investigation." I was thinking of the distant future with only conjecture, but sometimes that's all you need for success, a good nose for detection.

"Yes, but remember, if we don't find all these people, or at least one of them admits that they didn't sell the property to an agency or, for example, gave the house to someone of their own free will, then your theory will crumble like a sandcastle. It only takes one exception to undermine the whole motive..." He stated aptly. "...Of course I'll help you, but I have my doubts that anyone would be able to plan all the details so precisely, there were so many events that had to be based on pure chance, such as Ain Hailu's decision to leave town and sell the house."

Connor was thinking sensibly, as befits a police officer, and I couldn't disagree with him in any way, especially as I had the same opinion myself. However, in my mind, the decision had been made and I was going to follow this path to the end, regardless of whether it turned out that I had wasted both my own and my friend's time.

Besides, there was something else that gave me confidence that I was on the right path.

Oddly I hadn't had nightmares for a long time, and the dreams that had been haunting me recently had been positive, which reinforced my belief that I was where I was supposed to be.

However, I couldn't tell Connor this because I didn't even know how to explain it to him.

I knew him well enough to know that pure facts were the most important thing to him, whereas he downplayed superstition.

He was helping me then because of the bond of friendship that had formed between us over years of knowing each other, and spending time together in the police force.

Connor knew I needed his help now and supported me as best he could.

I was eternally grateful to him for that.

"I really think that's it; I can't explain it to you, but I feel like I need to go down that path." I confided.

"I understand, don't worry, we'll check it out, just be patient." He replied thoughtfully.

"Patience is my middle name." I joked.

"Sure, it's twenty past nine, I guess it's time to go home?"

"I think so, so what? Shall we go?" I replied, after which we both started to gather to leave.

I had to admit that my conscience had eased.

Talking to Connor had helped me a lot, especially as I knew, I could count on my friend to help me, and I continued to have his support. Maybe this support was a bit forced by me and my friend felt obliged to accompany me on a task, that fell on me without warning like a bolt from the blue. I had no choice but to see it through to the end, nevertheless, he proved once again what a great person he is.

What I didn't know that evening was that dinner at St Barnabas' House might be my last memory of time spent with my best friend, Declan O'Connor.

A memory that will stay with me, as I wait for someone to abruptly end my life on this earth.

As we walked together towards "Tottenham Court Road," tube station, dodging countless people on the street, a scenario of the next events began to take shape in my head.

I planned in my mind, what my next actions would be.

At first glance it all seemed easy, but there was nothing about it that could be considered "easy."

Above all, I was hoping that Connor would find the first person relatively quickly, so that I could try to set up another meeting and have another conversation.

But the future was going to be very different to what I thought it would be, and no matter what I planned, neither of these goals had the slightest chance of success.

My investigation was about to come to a sudden end, due to people I had gotten under the skin of by getting too close to the truth, so they decided to silence me.

Fortunately, I didn't have to worry about this predicament until the near future, and as they say - ignorance is bliss, so at this time I only had one problem to solve.

The hour was 09:35pm.

In the street I could hear the noise of cars and people shouting from all sides.

Given the rather late hour of the evening, it was no surprise that people under the influence of alcohol or other intoxicants, were returning from bars or heading to a club to party.

It was the "normal" atmosphere of a night out in Soho.

In a matter of minutes, we had reached the underground station. From there I was going to head down the stairs, Connor on the other hand, had to continue across the street to the bus stop, where his bus was leaving from.

"Don't forget to call Racheal, I'm sure she's worried about you." He said.

"I'll call her, she'll be fine if she waits a bit."

"Sure, see you tomorrow, I'll come and say goodbye to you before you leave."

"See you then." I replied, after which we exchanged handshakes, and went our separate ways.

As I walked down the stairs to Tottenham Court Road station I heard loud laughter from some women.

From where I could still only make out the noise, I could easily tell that there were several of them and they were drunk.

At first, I ignored this as I was used to annoying drunk people on the street and secondly, as I mentioned, it wasn`t unusual behaviour at that time of day, in this London district.

However, when I got to where I was passing the laughing women, one of them poked me with her arm in such a way that she almost fell over, if it hadn't been for her friend who continued to grab her arm while laughing incessantly.

"Excuse me." I said without thinking

"It's me who's sorry, handsome!" said the inebriated woman before she had time to look at me, which made the other three ladies burst out laughing. The moment she lifted her head, and we could see each other's faces, my brain quickly scanned the people I knew or remembered and then, let me know in a split second that I had already seen her.

In those few seconds that we were looking at each other, I saw the woman's expression change from joy to almost fear in a flash, and for some reason unknown to me at the time, a panic in her eyes had appeared.

"I'm sorry." She said again, this time without any kindness, after which she walked quickly away.

Her companions, still laughing loudly, followed her.

I stood stunned for a moment, before slowly moving further down the stairs.

It didn't take me long to remember, how I knew the unknown woman's face. "She is from North Hill..." I said under my breath. "...I'll have to see if I can find out her name."

Thus, Nattaly Swanson appeared on my radar for the first time, all thanks to a happy coincidence.

19

House of Cards.

'The more you are ready to give yourself to God and to others, the more you discover the authentic meaning of life.'

One day later, 9 June 2019, North Hill, 01:45pm.

The next day I came back to North Hill, the same way I'd left, by train. Before I left, I got a call from Connor, who regretfully told me that he wouldn't be able to meet me at the station, due to an emergency he had to attend to immediately.

He didn't say exactly what it was about, but I guessed it had something to do with his elderly parents, so I wished him well and said I would call him in the evening.

Overall, I was extremely pleased with the trip and considered it a 100% success.

So, once I was on the train, I had a pleasant feeling that my time in London had been used productively.

At that point, I had no reason to think that the time spent with a friend was something, that might never happen again.

From then on, my plan was somewhat simpler, as I had already had my first conversation with Ain Hailu, and the burden of finding another member of the other victims' families fell on Connor's shoulders.

Before we parted the previous evening, I had also left him a list of names of specific people I wanted to meet, which I thought would make his search easier.

Joanna Richardson.

Carolin Robert.

Christopher Wilson.

Alexandra Murphy.

Although I had arranged the names in the correct order from the first event to the last, not knowing the exact ages of these people, the order didn't really matter, the most important thing was simply to find someone from this list.

Now, I assumed it would be a long time before I heard from Connor again, so there was nothing left for me to do but get back to my daily routine, and keep my fingers crossed for my friend's success.

All I wanted to know when I returned to North Hill was, who was the woman who bumped into me on the steps of the London Underground?

I didn't even have to try very hard to remember that I mostly saw her in the town centre.

Although I hadn't paid much attention to her before, as she was just another person I saw on the street from time to time, I remembered that at one point I found her behaviour strange to say the least.

I had this impression because, as a police officer with many years of experience patrolling the streets of a large city, I paid close attention to people's behaviour.

Over time, this developed into a habit that I could not get rid of, sharpening my intuition.

It is something that is based on developed instincts as part of one's profession, such as the chef who stops at the window of a restaurant to read what is on the menu, or the hairdresser who knows perfectly which type of hair conditioner to recommend to a client.

My attention, on the other hand, was always drawn to the body language of strangers.

At the time, however, I couldn't remember exactly what made my gaze focus on this woman.

But whatever it was, it must have made her stand out significantly from other passers-by, although at the same time it was not so serious, that I had to intervene in any way.

In any case, the decision was made; because of the incident on the underground steps, I had to find out the name of the mystery woman and, if I was lucky, something more about her.

But before I could do anything about that, I had first, get back home. I still had an hour left on the train, so this time, too, I decided to relax with some music, but before I did, I set the alarm on my phone for 50 minutes ahead.

"This time I won't fall asleep like last time." I said to myself and closed my eyes.

11 June 2019, 01:54pm.

Two days later, Danny was driving to his appointment with Dr Susan McKane, as he did every Wednesday.

This was his fourteenth appointment with the kind psychologist, since he and Rachel had moved to North Hill, so he was used to this turn of events. This meeting was going to be a little different from the others, however, because Danny, despite Susan's previous reluctance to answer questions about the events in North Hill, was going to ask if she knew the woman, who had fallen on him on the steps of a London Underground station. According to the retired police officer, the unknown woman was probably the same age as the psychologist.

Therefore, if they attended the same school in North Hill, even if they were in different classes, Susan would have to know something about her, especially, as they both still live in the same town.

She was the first-person Danny decided to ask about it, the next in line was Mark Brown, whom he was due to meet the following afternoon.

Danny turned up at Susan's office, a few minutes before 2pm.

The psychologist was, of course, already waiting for him and, as usual, she greeted him warmly, with a smile on her face.

"Mr Davis, hello." She welcomed him.

The conversation took place, as always, in a friendly and caring atmosphere.

Danny decided to ask the question, which was bothering him, only at the very end of the meeting, so as not to disrupt the therapy.

As usual, Susan asked about his mood, the past week, his feelings or his attitude to his surroundings, and then gave him time to answer. They spent the last twenty minutes together meditating, practising to relaxing music.

Danny was initially reluctant to undertake meditation, but over time he realised that he really did feel much better, at the end of the therapy. The clock was approaching 3pm, which meant it was time to end the session.

Before this happened, Susan helped Danny out of his light trance, so that he had time to recover, before leaving the office and getting into the car.

"Three... Two... One... And you're back." Susan said.

He slowly opened his eyes at this point, then surreptitiously yawned.

"How are you feeling, Mr Davis?"

"Fine, thank you." He replied getting up from the sofa.

"I'm glad to hear that."

"I've tried meditating at home on my own, but I must admit, it doesn't work as well as it does here." Danny confessed.

"Oh, it's a matter of practice..." smiled Susan. "...Please keep trying and I guarantee, you will eventually succeed."

"Of course." Danny got up from the sofa and walked over to the coat rack where his coat was hanging, then took it off the hook and hung it over his right forearm.

Meanwhile, the psychologist moved her chair back to its original place under her desk.

She then walked over and sat down at it, simultaneously waking up her dormant computer with a mouse.

Susan's desk was immaculately tidy, with a modern flat-screen computer that didn't take up much space, a wireless keyboard and mouse, a pen stand, a desk lamp and three picture frames.

Danny had never seen those pictures before, because they were facing Susan and only from her side, behind the desk, could you see what they represented.

They were private, so it didn't even occur to him to look at them. "I'd like to ask you, one more question." Danny said suddenly, coming closer to where she was sitting.

The woman tore her gaze away from the computer screen and peered at him, curiously.

"Of course, I'm listening, how can I help you?" she asked.

"Being in London a few days ago, I met a woman who is most likely from North Hill..." Danny started to develop the thread.

Susan squinted her eyes slightly in anticipation of what he was getting at.

"... Long brown hair, medium height, slim figure, always very smartly dressed, I don't know much about designer stuff, but probably something like "Dior" or "Versace", a young person, my guess is thirty-something years old, does that description tell you anything?"

"Hmmm, yes, I think it does, after that description only one person comes to mind, do you mean Nattaly Swanson?"

"Nattaly Swanson..." he repeated after her. "...Probably yes, but I still need to confirm it."

"If you don't mind me asking, what do you need this information for?" she stared at him intrigued.

Her expression changed from one of curiosity to one of suspicion, as she recalled the unfortunate encounter of a drunken Nattaly at the hotel, when she unexpectedly bumped into her in the bar in the middle of the night. Back then, Nattaly had shouted incomprehensible suspicions to Susan about Danny Davis being a "spy."

And now, Danny was standing in front of her in her office, asking about Nattaly's identity, it was all a bit strange.

"Actually, for nothing..." he lied. "...I was just curious, because she bumped into me on the underground stairs, and I almost fell over because of her."

"Oh, I understand, an unpleasant incident?"

"Indeed..." he nodded. "...Okay, I'll be on my way, thanks again for your help."

he added and extended his right hand, on which his coat hung, towards Susan in a friendly farewell.

"Goodbye." The woman said and shook his hand.

As Danny started to back away, his coat awkwardly snagged on one of the picture frames, which tipped over and fell off the desk onto the floor.

"Oh, I'm so sorry." He said embarrassed and quickly bent down to pick it up.

Once he had the frame in his hand, he quickly looked it over to see if it was intact.

Surprisingly, he found that despite the fall, the glass had not broken and there was no damage.

Conducting a quick visual inspection, Danny couldn't help but notice the photo inside.

It showed a smiling Susan, a few years younger at the time the photograph was taken, with a little girl in her arms.

The child was no more than five years old, but there was something else on it.

One small detail, which momentarily caught the attention of the observant police officer and caused his mind to start a rapid process, of recalling the information stored there commonly known as "memory."

All thanks to a seemingly innocent bracelet the child had pinned on the left wrist.

Especially the little figures, resembling dolphins.

Danny had seen a similar bracelet before, of course, at this point he was unable to determine that it was the same jewellery he had in mind, as there could have been hundreds, if not thousands, just like this one. What's more, at this point he couldn't even remember where or when he had seen it, but his intuition was ringing alarm bells, and he had to quickly recall the circumstances in which he had come across a similar ornament. While he held the photo in his hand and looked at it, Susan also observed him, carefully.

The uncommonly intelligent woman noticed the change of expression on his face, clearly something he was looking at was of great interest to him. She did not take her eyes off him, meticulously registering the man's every move.

"Once again, I'm very sorry, I'm glad it didn't break...." he repeated putting the photo down on the desk. "...Lovely girl."

Susan smiled broadly and moved the photo closer to herself, so she could see it better.

"It's alright, don't worry..." she said. "...Yes, that's my Nicole, she's ten years old now." She added staring at the photograph.

"Congratulations, she is beautiful, very much like you."

"Oh, you are a flatterer." She laughed, casually approaching the subject.

"I must go now, see you next Wednesday."

"I'll see you then." She replied.

Danny had only managed to take a few steps towards the door, when he heard Susan's voice, which made him stop as if paralysed, unable to go any further.

"Yes, this is my Nicole, Nicole Denice." These words of Susan froze the blood in his veins, the man turned around without delay.

"Excuse me, what did you say?" he asked immediately.

"Excuse me?" Susan looked at him confused.

"Nicole Denise?" he repeated after her.

"Oh yes, that's my daughter's name, not Denise but Denice, Nicole Denice McKane." Susan replied.

Danny stood still and felt as if a tornado had passed through his head, all his thoughts began to tangle with each other, like a huge funnel of powerful air that stirred everything together, creating one all-encompassing chaos.

...Denise... Nicole Denice... Ten years... Nicole... Denice... Denise Randal... Ten years...words that also interspersed scenes from memories taken out of context.

...The sight of a drugged man with a gun held to a child's head... The weeping face of Denise Randal... Views from beyond the fog, Denise walking beside the stretcher on which Danny was being wheeled to the ambulance... Her ghost standing at the foot of the bed in the middle of the night, before dissolving into thin air... Things moving by themselves... Phones ringing for no reason... As is usually the case in such situations, the whole event lasted only a few seconds.

However, to the person experiencing the flashback, which only takes place in his or her mind, it may seem as if a considerable amount of time has just passed, although in fact the exact opposite is true.

Danny has experienced unexpected flashbacks in the past, but not on this scale.

This was usually triggered by a word or circumstance that was particularly familiar to him, because of its similarity and personal proximity to a similar event in the past.

And so, it was in this case, only much more intense.

At a certain point, the overabundance of things related to the trauma of a retired police officer fell on him like a ton of bricks, causing his mental resilience to collapse and opening the door, to all the nightmarish and unwanted memories.

But there was something useful in it, something Danny needed to discover, sooner or later.

Namely, it was about the last memory that flashed through his mind. The memory of the last time he had looked at a picture of Magda Richardson, on the computer screen in his London flat.

Because, he had seen the dolphin bracelet then, that was why the decoration on Susan McKane's daughter's hand now seemed so familiar to him.

It was his next clue and then he realised it.

"Are you feeling alright?" Susan's voice snapped him out of his reverie. Danny 'woke up' quickly, and realised even more quickly, how stupid he looked standing there motionless with his mouth open.

"Yes, yes, I`m fine, sorry..." he replied. "... I got distracted."

"Because of something I said? I was under the impression that I had knocked you off balance with something?" asked the psychologist, constantly looking at him curiously.

"No, I'm fine, my mind sometimes plays tricks on me..." he tried to explain himself. "...You know what they say, old age is no joy."

"Well then, take care of yourself, especially when driving, I really don't want any tragedy to happen."

"Of course, don't worry, it doesn't happen to me very often, despite appearances..." he assured her. "... See you on Wednesday." He added, then left the office closing the door behind him.

"Damn it!" Danny chastised himself when he was in the corridor.

His heart continued to pound like a hammer, and he had to calm his nerves before he headed for the exit and further down the street to his car. When Susan was left alone, she picked up the photograph he had turned over.

She squinted in concentration, then began to search for the reason why Danny Davis's behaviour had changed so dramatically.

"What made you so interested? What did you notice?" she said aloud, scanning the picture, piece by piece.

03:15pm.

Danny got into his car and headed towards home, as quickly as possible. Completely forgetting in the process that his wife had asked him to pick up a few things from the shop, after his session with Susan.

All he could think about now was the bracelet, which he was seeing for the second time in his life, he wanted to find and compare it as soon as possible.

To do this, he immediately had to check the archive of photos he kept stored in the memory of his laptop.

Since, unfortunately, he had no way of putting the two photos together and finding a resemblance, he had to rely on the fact that he had managed to remember the pendant well enough, to compare it with the one on Magda Richardson's wrist, from the photocopy from the archive newspaper. The whole thing was made easier by the fact that it was a simple, most likely silver bracelet, decorated with small, attached dolphin patterns, of which there were no more than six.

After ten minutes of driving, he parked the vehicle next to Rachel's car in the driveway, in front of the house's garage.

Then, wasting no time, he got out of it and moved quickly to the front door. Rachel was in the kitchen when she heard the door slam, which surprised her a little as she didn't expect to see Danny, for at least another hour. She took three steps back to get a better view of the hallway and the door of the house, but saw no one, which worried her even more. "Hello, Danny?" she called out into the depths of the flat.

She waited a few seconds and when she received silence in response, she called out again.

"Is that you, Danny!"

"Yes, yes, it's me." She heard her husband's voice, somewhere upstairs.

The woman breathed a sigh of relief at the sound of the familiar voice. "You scared the hell out of me! What are you doing home so early? Did you buy what I asked you to?" she asked loudly from the kitchen.

By this time, Danny was already sitting in front of his desk, going through the photos he had saved on his computer over the years.

It was only when he heard Rachel's words that he remembered that he had indeed, promised her that he would go shopping.

But it didn't matter now, the priority now was finding the old photograph.

"Danny…?! DANNY!!" Rachel wasn't giving up.

"I'll go out again! I just came back for my wallet!" He lied to get his wife to leave him alone.

"Alright!" she replied and went back to her chores.

"Where, are, you? I know it was somewhere here…" he said to himself, scrolling down the screen hurriedly. "…There it is!" he said in a triumphant voice, at the sight of the page from the article he read for the first time on 19 October 2018.

When he first saw Magda Richardson's face on his computer screen in 2018, an inexplicable phenomenon occurred.

He noticed what he could call "tears" falling from the child's eyes on the screen.

The droplets resembled tears, except that they had no right to appear in such a place, as it was happening on a glass monitor.

But when he touched them, they were wet.

The photograph showed Magda Richardson, standing in the garden opposite the house where she lived with her mother Joanna at the time. He squinted slightly and zoomed in on a not-so-clear archive shot of the girl's forearm, which did indeed have a bracelet on it, very similar to the one he had seen earlier in Dr Susan McKane's office.

But it was difficult to draw any conclusions from this, as, of course, it could have been another pure coincidence, and Susan's daughter simply owned a very similar piece of jewellery that Magda Richardson had once owned, and there were probably hundreds of them.

However, if this was not the case, then where did the psychologist and her daughter fit in this puzzle?

With no hard evidence and guided only by circumstantial events, Danny had no choice but to, metaphorically, lump everything he could find into one bag, and then try to make some sense out of it.

Now, he had found what he was looking for, the excitement subsided slightly and Danny, already at ease, began to piece together the successive facts he had assimilated that day.

Without any concrete facts, only by guesswork.

"Susan McKane's daughter's name is Nicole Denice..." he said to himself under his breath. "...As Susan said, Denice not Denise, she is now ten years old, Denise Randal was ten when she died, both girls are namesakes of the same age, on top of that there is also a certain, Nattaly Swanson..." he wondered aloud.

The man took a deep breath and straightened up in his chair.

"For the love of God, Denise..." he said letting the air out of his lungs. "...What are you trying to tell me?"

As soon as he said these words, the screen of his laptop was flooded with horizontal lines, it looked like interference on old television sets. The man noticed this and squirmed in surprise.

Suddenly, after a few seconds, the error stopped as quickly as it had appeared, and in its place was the face of Nicole Denice McKane.

The same face, he had seen in the photo in Susan's office.

"What the hell...?" Danny couldn't believe what he was seeing. "...How did this happen?" he felt his heart start to accelerate again.

Especially when "tears" started to run down the screen again, just as they had from Magda's photo.

This time the unexpected liquid was red.

Danny reached out to touch the droplets, picked one up from the monitor with his index finger and then, rubbed it to check its consistency.

"Dear God, is that blood…?" he said in concern. "...Is she going to be, the next victim?"

05:05pm, London, "Bradley and Brad Lettings" agency office.

Matthiew Braddock sat at his desk nervously tapping his fingers on the tabletop, holding the phone to his ear.

He was nervous, even though there had been no alarming news from North Hill that day.

"...If you think this is the only way out, so be it..." he said into the receiver. "...It's going to be risky, but if we plan everything right, it should work." He added, then listened in silence to the person on the other end of the line.

Once again, the conversation was about Danny Davis, who Matthiew had been hearing about more and more recently.

This made his anxiety gradually grow, until his measure of patience began to exceed its limits.

Matthiew remembered him and Rachel; from the time he made a deal with them to buy a house in North Hill.

What he didn't expect was that he was an ex-policeman and as time went on, he would start causing more and more problems, for the agency. Warnings came from Simon Edwards, who was tasked with keeping an eye on the man and who also reported, that Danny had recently been in London to meet Ain Hailu.

366

And that he and his partner, were gathering more information regarding the "missing four."

In other words, Danny Davis was meddling in other people's business and was beginning to pose a serious threat, to the organisation's interests. The situation was becoming increasingly dangerous, and it was necessary to intervene before it was too late.

"...I agree..." Matthiew said. "...I will notify Harry and Simon to start preparing, I will call you when they confirm they are ready..." he spoke with pauses.

"...If that's what you want, that's what we'll do, we'll strike two birds with one stone, you expose him and they'll take care of the rest and that's it, you don't have to stick your neck out anymore, this will be the last action, I'll contact you soon." He added in conclusion and put the phone on the desk.

With this conversation, a death sentence was passed on Danny Davis and... Nicole Denice McKane.

05:10pm, North Hill, Nattaly Swanson's flat.

Meanwhile, Nattaly Swanson was nervously carrying on a phone conversation, as well.

"...We need to do something about him..." she said. "...He's following me, I'm more than sure he knows something about us..." she continued, her voice almost hysterical.

The person on the other side was clearly trying to calm her down, as she took breaks between tasks, listened carefully and breathed slowly. However, the situation was not looking good, the woman was a bundle of nerves and there was no indication that anything would change. "...He followed me to London! Do you understand!

I saw him! You must resolve this somehow or I'm out!" she threatened the person she was talking to.

This was an unacceptable statement, and she knew it, she understood she was too deep into this matter to be able to walk away from it.

She saw and knew too much about the organisation, which was a huge risk in a business, where in reality no one trusts anyone, this was also the case with Nattaly.

She was only trying to draw attention to the seriousness of the situation, rather than making real threats.

She simply wanted to emphasise her concern in a way that could not be ignored, and sometimes the best defence is an attack.

"...You need to sort this out, talk to whoever you need to talk to, and do something about this guy, he's all over the place and any minute now the police are going to knock on my door, then I'm going to tell them everything I know, just because you let it happen." She added seriously.

In shady deals, the biggest panic is always the real fear that everything could collapse like a house of cards, when the person who knows too many starts talking to the police and law enforcement.

That's when all involved end their rich, pleasant lives then swap their luxury cars and flats for police cars and prison cells

It is a game where their job is to stay at large, for as long as possible, so that they can enjoy the fruits of their shenanigans.

Therefor the person Nattaly spoke to, took her premise seriously and had no choice but to do something about the situation.

So that one day, in the not-too-distant future, someone doesn't knock to his door and say: "Game over, you've lost."

20

Judgement Day.

'Each of you, young friends, also finds in life some of your Westerplatte. Some measure of the tasks it must undertake and fulfil. Some righteous cause for which you cannot fail to fight. A duty, a responsibility that cannot be dodged. You cannot desert.

18 August 2019.

Amsterdam police headquarters, Elandsgracht 117, 1016 TT, the Netherlands, 06:00am European time.

An international police operation, planned for months and conducted on an international scale, was just beginning.

Aimed at, tracking down and arresting heroin smugglers.

Investigators from the Netherlands, France and England were involved in the operation.

The Amsterdam smugglers had been under surveillance by the local police for some time, but due to the scale of the operation, no major raids were carried out on suspicious locations, so as not to deter the major bosses involved in the crimes.

Thanks to intensive police work, it was established that the drugs had travelled from Amsterdam via France and England.

In each of these countries, there was at least one high-ranking person in the hierarchy that the police wanted to catch at all costs.

After countless hours of cooperation between these countries and a carefully devised strategy, everything was buttoned up.

Then, after receiving the green light from the most senior officers, the operating group of the united police officers, was to hit the drug traffickers with unprecedented force and then, raze once and for all the places where the deadly product was produced.

As a result of this day, many arrests were to be made and the ranks of criminals, who had hitherto felt unpunished, seriously weakened.

The whole thing was supposed to start at 07:00 in the morning.

In the meantime, all the initiated officers were meticulously preparing for the operation, thinking that they were in for a long and hard day. But as everyone knows, there are two sides to the coin, so the criminals also had their work cut out for them in the day ahead, but their time of freedom was inexorably coming to an end with every second of the clock approaching 07:00am... Tick-tock.

Nattaly Swanson's flat, 08:15am,

Nattaly was also about to have an eventful day.

Since her return to North Hill two months ago, she hadn't met Danny once and business was also back to normal, going better than before.

Therefore, the first task on her to-do list for the next 24 hours was to arrive at the port in the early afternoon, but she waited patiently for the exact time, not putting her mobile phone down for a moment.

Since her tense conversation with her London partner, she had managed to contain her emotions, convinced that the problem of the inconveniently nosy policeman would soon be solved, as she had been promised at the time.

Nattaly had no choice, but to believe her business partner's words of reassurance and continue with the task as usual.

But she had something completely different planned for this afternoon, as she had no intention of staying in North Hill for the rest of the day. Yes, she was going to undertake the first phase of the task according to the original scenario, but she wanted to do the second part of it in a way, that she herself thought would be more effective.

So, she was to pick up the package at the port, but instead of shipping it on or sending it back under the guise of car parts, Nattaly decided to drive it to London in person.

The woman loved the city, it was the only place where she felt free and safe, among hundreds of thousands of people, she could be herself and not be afraid that someone was watching her.

She was a vein person and valued her freedom, so she had no intention of restricting it or allowing anyone, to come between her and her whims.

It was an extremely self-destructive mindset for a young, spoilt woman, and one that would soon lead to her losing everything, including her beloved freedom.

But no matter what decision she made that morning, the threat to her and the entire operation was inexorably approaching, nothing could change that.

But at the time, she was clueless about this, excited for another trip out of town.

Nattaly was happy she'd finally be back in London soon.

Susan and Nicole Denice McKane's, home 12:15pm.

Susan McKane was in a strange mood; she had mixed feelings and did not know how to treat yesterday's conversation with Mark Brown. The previous day, the commander had unexpectedly turned up at her house and insisted on speaking to her face to face.

The woman let her visitor into the house and offered him coffee, but when Mark began to discuss the specific purpose of his visit, she felt confused, and this mood followed her throughout the night and into the next day. Mark had warned her in a serious tone, that she should be particularly careful with her ten-year-old daughter.

He also convinced her, there was a suspicion that her child might be in danger.

But he could not specify his concerns or even tell her, where he got the idea that there was a real risk.

This was because he had promised Danny, he would not reveal to her that it was the retired police officer, who had sensed the impending disaster. The commander had to heavily manoeuvre around the subject and choose his words carefully, to ensure that the psychologist did not guess the truth. But he did so bluntly and eventually the woman took the warning to heart.

Telling someone that your child may be in danger is no easy task, but to do so without backing it up with any evidence, borders on the miraculous.

Throughout the conversation, Mark was aware that she would probably have kicked him out if it wasn't for the fact that he was an authority figure in North Hill, which made her respect him as such.

Nonetheless, Dr Susan McKane had been in a fluctuating mood since the morning, not knowing quite what she should think about it.

This day was going to prove particularly difficultfor her, especially as the commander's words were going to come true in the next few hours.

Danny's fears that something sinister was hovering in the air, were entirely justified.

However, neither of them knew the most important fact in the matter at the time, something that was about to change before the next morning.

Time: 03:30pm, Danny and Rachel Davis's house.

Rachel wanted to spend the evening with a friend she'd met during a certain outing with Danny downtown.

The woman's name was Cailee, and she lived on the other side of town, with her husband Charles.

Rachel visited them from time to time, where she also helped Cailee with her persistent back pain, as she was an experienced physiotherapist. Danny used this time to be alone, which was good for their relationship, as they each had the opportunity to be away from their partner for a while.

However, he had no plans to occupy his day in any way.

Everything he could do up to that point had already been done, and Connor continued his search, so all that was left was to wait and see what would happen.

Initially, he considered going to London, as it would be the first anniversary of Denise Randal's death in two months' time.

He wasn't sure if he would have the opportunity to visit her grave on that day, but he wanted to light a candle there and lay a fresh bouquet of flowers in honour of the girl's untimely death.

In the end, given the circumstances, he decided to stay in North Hill, as he expected his presence there would be needed soon.

In addition, not knowing how the situation would develop effectively tied his hands, making it impossible for him to plan anything in advance. Declan O'Connor had been given another name to check a few weeks earlier, thanks to his access to the police database.

Danny also suggested to his friend, that he thought, "Nattaly Swanson," was someone who needed to be investigated more thoroughly.

Connor wasted no time and immediately checked the police register for the woman, but to no avail, which indicated that this person had never been in trouble with the law before.

However, this did not mean that this situation would remain unchanged, and that Nattaly had a clear conscience.

Danny lamented the fact that he had not been able to share with Connor the experience, he had during the search for Magda Richardson's photographs.

All he had discussed with his friend, was that he had a hunch about another potential victim in North Hill.

Connor then advised him to notify the local authorities, which of course he later discussed with Mark Brown, who expressed his unconditional support if necessary.

He also assured him, that he would take exceptional care of Nicole Denice and Susan McKane.

Unfortunately, he was unable to answer the Commander's questions as to why he suspected such things, saying only, "it's really important" and "please trust me."

It never occurred to him for a moment, that revealing the immediate source of his concerns would be better, than trying to avoid the subject. This was not easy to explain to someone, who had never encountered a similar phenomenon before, and it would be difficult to believe the words of someone, who has regular contact with the paranormal.

For many people, this type of subject matter falls into the realm of fantasy books, films, stories told by a liar or mentally ill person. Danny was not going to risk falling into any of these categories. The episode with the drops of blood running down the monitor screen, continually lingered deep in his mind, along with the belief that something terrible was about to happen.

The man knew, he had this gif for a reason, but he had no idea what to do with it.

He could not tell anyone about it, lest he be considered mad, but on the other hand, he was aware that it had been given to him for a specific purpose.

The whole situation looked like a cruel joke that someone had played on a retired police officer.

However, from his point of view, everything was very real and only he could foresee the impending misfortune.

So, he decided to keep in close contact with Susan McKane for as long as possible, to prevent anything from happening.

This was not an easy mission, as Susan was a very secretive person and did not allow her patients, to get too close to her private life.

The case was further complicated by the fact that Danny could not tell her directly about his concerns about her daughter, without being immediately on the list of suspects.

All he could do was wait, watch and be vigilant.

Canary Wharf, London, office "Bradley and Brad Lettings", 17:58pm.

Matthiew Braddock was sitting at his desk, talking to Simon Edwards on the phone.

"Everything is in place, we are ready."

"Okay, stick around, I'll let you know soon, when you can move." Matthiew replied.

"I hope you know what you're doing, I don't think I need to remind you, what consequences await you, if you fuck this up." Simon was not patient with his boss.

"You guys' better worry about not fucking something up yourselves, you know damn well I can wash my hands of anything."

"It's going to be hard for you to wash anything, if I cut your hands off , better pray that this partner of yours, prepares everything as agreed."

"Just do what you're being paid a lot of money for!" Matthiew couldn't stand it and nervously ended the call.

"FUCK!!!" he shouted with all his might, hurling the phone against the desktop in the process, his voice spreading around the room.

Matthiew had a very bad feeling about this.

In his opinion everything could stay as it was, business was going well and there was no need to change it.

Unfortunately, it was not up to him to have the last word, and he had to give in to the decision made by Nattaly.

However, it was comforting to know that the woman had never failed in her plans before, so he saw no reason why that should change this time. Still, Matthiew understood Simon's nervousness, but he couldn't show weakness to the people he was employing.

He decided that the best way out of the situation was to just grit his teeth, stick to the plan and hope that everything went well, after which he wouldn't have to go back to it.

So, he picked up the phone and assessed its damage, the screen was intact, then searched for Nattaly's number and pressed the green button.

After a few beeps the call was connected.

"We're ready, we're waiting for a sign." He said.

"We'll start in an hour." The voice in the receiver answered and immediately hung up.

The man got up from his desk and walked over to the liquor bar hidden in the sideboard.

He pulled a glass from the shelf and half-filled it with Scotch whisky, then took a large sip.

He squirmed slightly and went back to his desk, to pick up the phone. It was just after 6pm when he sent a text to Simon:

1H.

He tipped his glass of whisky and swallowed its contents in one gulp, then returned to the bar and this time, instead of pouring himself a glass, he grabbed the whole bottle.

"Fuck..." he cursed under his breath. "...It's going to be a long day."

Danny and Rachel Davis's house, 6:10pm.

I was sitting on the couch and dully staring at the TV, when Rachel walked into the living room.

"I'm going out..." She announced. "...I'll probably be back around eleven." She added, putting on her coat.

"Of course, I'll be home at that time." I replied.

"There's no need to rush, if you want, it can be later." She encouraged me. "I'm not a teenager anymore to come back home in the middle of the night, besides, I doubt Mark will want to stay out longer either, we'll most likely talk for a couple of hours, have a bite to eat and that's it."

"Whatever you want, take care of yourself, my old man." Rachel came over to give me a kiss goodbye.

"You too and drive carefully." I replied stupidly and waved to my beloved, as she walked away towards the exit.

If I had known then that this might be the last time I would see the love of my life, I would have walked up to her, hugged her as tightly as I could and told her, that she was the best thing that ever happened to me, and I couldn't imagine life without her.

Unfortunately, no one can predict the future, so I had no idea that I would be sitting on the ground a few hours later, tied up, waiting for someone to probably put a bullet in my head, thus ending my existence.

I saw no way out of this hopeless situation for myself, a few kilometres from humanity, bound and defenceless, among people who would unscrupulously pull the trigger and watch with satisfaction, as I gave my last breath.

This is the world in which we live; man will literally do anything for money. In doing so, he is prepared to sacrifice his personal pride, conscience and soul.

Just to be able to enjoy the wealth, often only for a short period of time, without considering the further, often inevitable and harsh consequences of these actions.

Greed is a terrible disease, but I'd rather sleep peacefully at night without remorse, than pursue wealth while destroying my soul in the process. I found it pointless to have a lot of money in my bank account and be afraid, that one day I will have to answer where I got it from.

Everyone chooses their own path in life, I was walking mine, but fate would have it that my path, had to cross with these horrible people.

However, at this point, all I had in mind was a meeting with Mark Brown, to discuss a few things.

I didn't have to deal with the rest of the problems, which were already very close, until later in the evening.

20:30pm,

I met Mark at 7pm in the café and the conversation was going extremely well, so before I knew it, an hour and a half had passed.

I looked at my watch and thought to stay another thirty minutes, and then go home.

"Any progress with Connor?" he asked.

"He hasn't told me anything about it yet, so that means there's nothing new. They've been very busy for a few weeks, as they're getting ready with the squad for a bigger drug operation, so he hasn't had much time..." I replied. "...But Connor is a smart guy, I think it's only a matter of time before he comes up with something."

"I understand, I've ordered regular patrols around the McKane property, every thirty minutes, the uniformed officers practically never let it out of their sight." He said and his face saddened, I could clearly see, how tired this situation was making him.

"I can't explain it to you Mark, but I really think something is going to happen there, of course, I'm keeping my fingers crossed that I'm wrong."

"I'll tell you honestly, I'm not sure what I'd prefer in this situation, on the one hand I'd like peace, which has been going on for over a year and a half, on the other hand, if something happened again we'd reopen the investigation and maybe, finally catch whoever is behind it, but I can't have the McKane's being watched forever either."

"Obviously it doesn't look good either way, but there's a chance we'll get them." I replied and at that moment Mark's phone, which had been lying quietly on the table until then, began to ring.

The commander picked it up in one movement and, without looking to see who was calling him, answered it.

"This is Mark Brown." He said.

Of course, I couldn't hear what was said to him.

But judging by his expression and the look in his eyes, which pierced me with such force that it could have knocked me and my chair over onto my back if it had been possible, I could imagine it.

The conversation lasted no more than ten seconds, after which Mark rose from where he was sitting.

"I'm on my way!" he said.

"I wasn't wrong though, is this about Nicole?" I asked, also getting up from the table.

Mark only nodded, confirming my guess.

I had no doubt that it was about her, I didn't even need his confirmation, I just knew it was.

"Shall we go together?" I suggested.

"I'm sorry, but I can't take you with me, at least not now..." he said firmly.

"...Uniformed officers are at the McKane house, Susan called them, but they can't find her anywhere either, I think she's gone to look for her daughter." He added after which he almost ran out of the café, without giving me a chance to add anything more.

I was left alone with confusion in my head, completely unsure of what I should do.

After a moment of uncertainty, struggling with my own thoughts, I decided to go near to the McKane house.

Of course, I knew that, no longer having a consultant's pass, I was a civilian and there was no way I could get permission to go inside, or even get closer to the property.

But I could drive slowly down the street and have a look, from a distance. Without thinking twice, I got up from the table and headed towards my car parked nearby.

I got into the car, started the engine and was about to drive away, when my phone rang.

I immediately thought it was probably Rachel calling to check on me, but when I looked at the display, I was overwhelmed with surprise.

The incoming call number was signed as: Dr McKane.

With a slightly trembling hand from a surge of emotion, I answered.

"Hello?"

"DANNY! OH DANNY, I NEED YOUR HELP!!! I'M NEAR YOUR HOUSE, IN THE WOODS!!!" the woman shouted, in a frightened voice.

"In the woods...???" I asked puzzled. "...What are you doing there??? Did you call the police???"

"YES! I CALLED! THEY'RE ON THEIR WAY HERE! NICOLE IS HERE

SOMEWHERE! I KNOW SHE'S HERE SOMEWHERE! I CAN'T SEE ANYTHING IN THIS DARKNESS! HELP ME! GET THE FLASHLIGHTS FROM HOME AND COME TO ME! HELP ME DANNY PLEASE!!!"

"Okay, I'm on my way to you now! Don't move from there, I'm coming to you!" I shouted into the phone and pressed the accelerator so hard, that I left wheel tracks on the street.

20:55pm.

Normally it would have taken me about 20 minutes to get home, but that evening I covered the distance in ten.

I ran inside in a hurry, leaving the front door open behind me.

I quickly ran up to the first floor and, in the bedroom wardrobe where I kept various useful gadgets, I found two torches and the batteries for them and checked, that they worked for sure.

When everything appeared to be in order, I put on my mackintosh and ordinary tracksuit trousers.

Until now I was dressed in a suit, it was not a practical outfit for a walk in the woods at this late hour.

Quickly changing, I left my phone and spare "mini" on the bedside table where, in the chaos, I forgot to take it later.

I tucked the two torches into my jacket pocket, grabbed one phone and was about to go downstairs, when I heard the front door slam, which made me stop for a moment.

I listened to the sound, slightly confused and had no idea who might have closed the door.

Rachel wasn't due home for at least an hour and a half.

I glanced at my phone screen, which showed 9:02pm and cautiously, headed towards the stairs.

When I was halfway down the stairs a figure began to appear, starting from the legs at and moving up, as I was approaching the first step.

"Hello! Who are you and what are you doing in my house!" I called out, but the individual remained silent.

Once I was on the ground floor, I saw a man standing by the door, wearing a black hoodie and black sweatpants.

He looked at me in response, at that point, I recognised his face.

It was the same man I had met when Rachel and I, first visited the "BnBL" agency.

I recalled him leaving the office with another man, as I remembered his terrifying look, when we had made an eye contact for a few seconds.

I thought then, I saw death in his eyes.

"I SAID, WHAT ARE YOU DOING HERE!!!"

He didn't answer, instead a smile appeared on his face, he turned his gaze away from me and directed it at something behind me, then nodded. I realised that this gesture was a sign, which made me immediately look behind in panic.

At that moment the other guy, already standing behind my back, surprised me with a powerful right hook to the chin.

It was a textbook example of a knockout, after which more than one heavyweight boxer had no right to doubt himself...The next stage of such a blow was only a close encounter with the ring surface, and the lights out for at least a few seconds.

I had no chance of avoiding the ambush, but the worst part of it all was that I could no longer help Nicole Denice, Susan or even myself.... I had failed.

London, Lewisham, 21:39pm.

Connor and his squad were called out to assist a drugs unit in the Peckham area of southeast London.

Initial indications were that as much support as possible was required from uniformed officers, to synchronise investigative efforts to prevent the distribution of hard drugs from the area to most areas of south London. The drugs unit blocked o all streets around "Peckham Rye" station at 9.30pm sharp and intended to hit pre-determined targets.

Connor arrived at "Rye Lane" a few minutes after receiving the order, over the radio from Lewisham Police HQ.

On arrival, he saw that the operation had only just begun and heavily armed special officers, wearing black uniforms, were beginning to move the first suspects out of nearby buildings.

Connor, along with his partner, immediately joined in to assist in the seizure of those previously arrested.

Two masked police officers led a handcuffed woman to them, Connor grabbed her under the arm and then sat her in the back seat of his police car.

He sat back behind the wheel and activated the on-board computer, with the intention of establishing her identity.

"Name, please." He said.

The woman sat quietly with her head down, clearly in no mood to talk, or make his task any easier.

Fortunately, the officer who had just brought the woman, returned with her handbag.

"It belongs to her." He said briefly, and then immediately returned to carry out further activities.

Given the unique circumstances of the arrest, Connor opened the handbag without hesitation and started looking for documents, that would reveal the identity of the person in the back seat.

It didn't take him long, because her ID was in her wallet.

"Oh fuck..." he cursed under his breath, not believing his eyes. "...Nattaly Swanson." He read the woman's name aloud.

North Hill, 21:45pm.

Rachel Davis was driving her car, back from her friends,

Before she got into the vehicle, she called Danny to let him know she would be home soon.

She wasn't too concerned when he didn't answer, thinking he'd fallen asleep on the couch, which sometimes happened to him, or hadn't heard the ringtone.

There were times when, for various reasons, he didn't see someone calling him, but he had a habit of quickly calling back later, as soon as he realised it.

This time Rachel thought she wouldn't disturb her husband, as she would be meeting him at home soon anyway.

The road was dark, and she drove very carefully through built-up areas. However, the next part of the route took her through the forest, where she could afford to accelerate slightly.

With the pleasant music filling the interior of the car, she felt relaxed and calm.

Then, out of the corner of her eye, she saw that the screen of her phone, which was lying on the passenger seat, lit up, signalling that someone was trying to contact her.

She had been looking straight ahead for the entire drive, until now. After making sure the street was empty, she looked down for a few seconds to pick up the phone.

But when she lifted her gaze back up, she saw a man appear out of nowhere in the middle of the street of an unpopulated area.

He was standing just less than a metre in front of her speeding car, and a collision was inevitable.

Rachel immediately put her foot on the brake pedal and closed her eyes in anticipation of the inevitable collision.

The car stopped with a squeal of tyres a moment later, but to her surprise she did not hear her car hitting any object.

The woman promptly got out of the car with her heart in her throat, then intuitively approached the bonnet of the vehicle, in search of the hit man. There was no spark of hope in her mind, that he had managed to jump away in time from the speeding vehicle in a split second, certainly not with such a short distance separating them at the time.

She was sure that she had just hit someone, and her consciousness was still filled by the fact that, after all, she had not heard any sound confirming the accident.

The woman stood in front of her vehicle and realised that the front of it was intact, her heart still beating at an accelerated rate, due to the adrenaline rush, she began frantically looking around for signs of the mystery man.

It took her a few seconds to see that he was standing behind her car. He was in the same place she had driven through, evidence of which could be seen in the long and black tyre tracks, left by the sudden braking. "Oh my God...!!" Rachel shouted in a trembling voice. "...Are you alright!?" she added running up to the stranger.

When she took a closer look at him, she saw an average looking man, medium height in a black suit with short, cropped hair.

The only thing that could undoubtedly distinguish him from other people, was his complexion as he was unnaturally pale.

A phrase filled the woman's mind - pale as a corpse.

"Danny..." he said suddenly as she faced him.

"I beg your pardon?" Rachel squirmed in surprise.

"...You need to call..."

The woman looked at him confused, it was dark, but at times she had the impression that the man's lips were not moving, even though she could hear his voice, which also seemed to come to her ears as if from afar.

"Do you know my husband?" she asked.

"...You must save him...."

"Is this some kind of strange joke? I am very sorry about this situation, but what are you doing in the middle of the road, in a place like this? Have you got a death wish?" she was irritated.

"...You need to make a call, a second phone..."

"Sir, who are you? What's your name?"

"...Danny, you must make a call, second phone, save them..." the man's voice became increasingly indistinct, quite as if he was moving away slowly, although he himself had not moved an inch.

"Are you drunk? I'm not calling anyone until I know who you are!?"

"... John... John McKane..." she heard in reply.

"Can I give you a lift somewhere, help you somehow?" she offered to calm things down a bit.

"...You can't help me, I'm already dead."

Rachel lowered her head and smiled slightly, taking it as a silly joke. However, when she raised it a moment later ready to answer him, the man was gone.

The woman quickly looked around, but she was alone, surrounded by a forest, in the middle of the road and a car with its lights on.

There was no sign of the mystery man or even any idea, how he could have left so quickly.

Rachel returned to the car, stunned, and reached for her phone. That's when she saw a message from Connor, which had arrived minutes before the incident:

"Rachel, where is Danny? I need to speak to him immediately, it's very important! Call me as soon as possible."

After reading the text and adding the strange conversation of a few seconds ago, the woman had no doubt that she should report the matter to the police.

Fortunately, she knew Mark Brown personally, thanks to Danny she had his private phone number.

So, she decided to contact the commander directly, rather than waste time making emergency calls, and explaining everything to the officers on duty. The woman sat behind the wheel of her car, dialled the number for Mark and put the phone to her ear.

However, when she heard the voicemail after a few rings, slightly disappointed, she hung up and waited a few moments before trying again. This time she also had to wait a few seconds for the call to connect but was lucky when the man answered. "Commander Mark Brown speaking."

"Mark! Thank goodness..." she was pleased. "...Is Danny with you?" she asked directly.

"No, he's not here, we got separated in the cafe about half an hour ago..." Mark replied. "...Rachel, I can't talk to you too right now, we have a serious situation here, call him.

"I called and he's not answering, something very strange has happened." She was having difficulty gathering her thoughts.

"It's okay, calm down, what's the matter? Why are you so upset?" he became anxious.

"Listen, I met a man on the way home who told me to save Danny." Rachel mouthed.

"That you should save him? What kind of nonsense is that? Who is this man?"

"He said his name was John McKane, but I don't know him personally. He jumped out of nowhere in front of my car in the middle of the street, I nearly hit him!" she explained, then fell silent, waiting for a reply, but instead she heard silence and Mark's breathing on the phone.

"I got out of the car to check he was fine, and then he told me to call Danny, on an emergency number to save them! I don't understand any of this."

"Can you repeat what he said his name was?" the commander suddenly asked.

"John, he said his name was John McKane."

"Are you sure of that?"

"Of course, I am sure! When I asked who he was, he said my name was John McKane...!" she got angry. "...Mark, what the hell is going on here! Do you know this man?"

The commander was gathering himself to answer, holding Rachel in suspense.

"Yes, I used to know him, but he died, nine years ago." He replied in a serious voice.

"...You can't help me... I am already dead..." the words spoken by the mysterious man resounded in her head.

"...Tell me where you are now, I'm coming to get you." Mark added after a moment.

Currently, North Hill suburb, 10:10pm.

"IS THAAAAAT HEEEER...YES...YES... THAT IS HEEEEER...!!! SHEEE IS HERE..." silent, afterlife whispers reached Danny's ears from everywhere and only he could hear them.

The voices of the dead carried on the wind, driven by anger, gathering invisible energy with a force equal to a hurricane.

This caused the trees around them to sway more and more, in all directions.

Danny also saw distant, barely visible, dark and almost completely transparent figures approaching them slowly, as if cautiously and uncertainly.

"Susan...??" he asked in disbelief, at the same turned over his head to hide, from the car's refractors, in Susan shadow "...What the hell are you doing here!?"

"You're the reason I'm here, I wouldn't be here today if you hadn't made me do it."

"And Nicole? Where is Nicole Denice! WHAT HAVE YOU DONE TO HER!!!!"

"Me, I didn't do anything..." Susan replied calmly. "...Do you see that wooden fishing shack? I built it with my stepfather, when he used to take me fishing here, when I was a child, at that time we were the only ones who knew about this place, it was our escape from reality, our common refuge..."

She said, pointing her finger deep into the woods.

Danny looked over his shoulder and recognised the place she was talking about.

There was a lamp shining in the middle of a small and dingy hut, which barely illuminated the room from the inside, but enough to be seen from a short distance.

At this point, the man realised that the fisherman's hut was not the only thing he recognised in the area.

He immediately realised that he knew the place well, remembered both the hut and the entire surroundings.

He had been here many times in his dreams, when Denise Randal had led him there, holding his hand.

Then everything became clear, he now knew why Denise's soul had led him, step by step, to this place for the last few months.

His mission was to find the missing four children and he had succeeded in doing so.

Unfortunately, he stumbled at the finish line, being so close to finally solving this mystery.

However, he could not have foreseen that he himself would fall into the trap, set for him by these ruthless people.

Especially as one of these people, was to turn out to be someone, who had gained his almost complete trust.

Danny Davis accepted the challenge, but his luck ran out, as it sometimes does in life.

"...THAT`S HEEEER...SHEEEE IS HEEEERE...!!!"

"...There's Nicole, over there, inside." She added.

"She's your daughter, how could you? What do you want to do with her!" he wanted to know.

"Mr Davis, let me explain something to you..." she began to speak calmly. "...My mother gave me away to an orphanage when I was still an infant, then, I was raised by foster parents, for years I knew I was different from everyone else, my parents thought it had to do with my high intelligence quotient, but I knew it wasn't about that, I just could not experience feelings like other people, no matter how hard I tried, something in my head wasn't working the way it should..." she said. "...I turned eighteen and I already had enough knowledge to diagnose myself, it's alexithymia, to put it simply, I don't have the same feelings and emotions as the rest of the people, but I always try to evoke or find them in myself and if necessary, I can simulate them perfectly..." the woman walked up to him and squatted down. Danny looked deeply into her eyes, there was no hint of remorse in them. "...Then, my biological mother somehow found me and after that one meeting with her, I found out where to find my father, George Bradley, I got in touch with him, that was probably the only time in my life that I thought I could have genuine affection for someone..."

"...YEEEEES...SHEEEEE IS HEEEEERE...!!!"

"...I've spent a lot of time studying the human mind, just to find out what's wrong with me. I've had a career, I've got married, I've had a baby, all in the hope that eventually something would change in me, but it never did..." The woman got up on her feet and Danny kept his eyes on her.

"...Then my biological father died, leaving me most of the shares in the housing agency he set up, then I unofficially took my mother's name Nattaly Kemp, translating from the French Noelle Kemp, as a quiet owner I began to manage the business, my identity known only to my lawyer in London.

"Bradley and Brad Lettings..." Danny interjected.

"I know you are familiar with the agency."

"...But where do the Voodoo dolls come from? Why the kidnappings?" as for the kidnappings and black magic it was Matthiew's idea, when it succeeded the first time and then the second, why not continue?"

"Just to make money from buying back houses from these poor, mentally damaged people? What kind of monster do you have to be to do something so disgusting!"

"Mr Davis, I don't see it that way, but I too am tired of it all, after today I will finally have a free pass to leave this town, I will sell my house like everyone else, and no one will hold it against me."

"Why are you telling me all this?"

"Honestly? I like talking to you, I've got used to our meetings and I'll miss them a bit, besides, you deserve some explanations, I've never told anyone about this, and I wanted to see how it would affect me, you know yourself, it's good to talk to someone from time to time."

"And what, did it help?"

...IS THAT HEEEER??? YEEEEES....YEEEES.... THAT`S HEEEER....SHEEEE IS HEEEERE...!!!

The whispers were getting clearer and clearer, along with them the wind was also getting stronger.

"Not really, but that wasn't the point..." she replied briefly, then added. "...Well, Mr Davis, it is time for me to go, I leave you in the company of these two gentlemen, I am afraid, here our acquaintance has come to an end, so farewell." She pointed to Simon and Harry.

...THAT IS HEEEER!!! SHEEEE!!! SHEEEE IS HEEEEERE...!!!

392

The wind was picking up, the huge trees standing nearby were bending under an invisible weight at which Susan, looked around her anxiously. Faintly visible black figures were already all around her, she was surrounded without even knowing it, even though, they were standing literally, at her fingertips.

Danny watched everything, all the while sitting on the ground leaning against Simon and Harry's car, waiting for events to unfold.

Watching her behaviour he understood, she now had realised, she was in danger.

The hunter had become hunted.

The woman's hair began to blow chaotically in the wind in all directions, and she tried to walk towards her car to get in and drive away, as quickly as possible.

However, she was unable to overcome the forces of nature, that were pushing against her with tremendous force.

The two men who were still sitting in the car, also realised that something unexpected was happening.

As Simon quickly got out of the driver's seat to check what was happening, Susan was pulled backwards with such force that she landed several metres away.

She fell straight into the pit that had been dug, without a shadow of a doubt, to bury Danny in.

It happened so suddenly and quickly; the woman didn't even manage to make a sound.

At one point, it looked as if someone had literally grabbed her by the stomach and then, jerked her with all their might in such a way that, as she flew backwards.

Her arms and legs straightened horizontally in the air, like a rag doll being pulled by someone on strings, to create the illusion that the toy was alive.

...SHEEEE IS HEEEER!!! SHEEEE!!! SHEEE!!! SHEEEE IS HEEERE!!!...

Simon, who was standing next to the car at the time, watched the whole event with his mouth open, not believing his eyes.

But he didn't even have the chance to explain to himself what was happening, let alone try to help her.

For at that very moment, he heard the loud crack of breaking branches, one after the other and all at once, coming from above, seeming to get closer and closer to him.

When he turned his gaze towards the source of the noise, he was filled with horror at the sight of the huge tree leaning ever faster towards him. In the circumstances that lasted a few seconds, there was no time to even think that his partner Harry was still in the car, which now was between him and the falling heavy tree.

At the same moment, the man was desperately trying to open the passenger door, jerking it open in a panic.

His huge figure was now playing against him, as he was too big to simply move to the next seat and thus free himself from the trap.

In the moment Simon got out of the vehicle, the door slammed shut for no apparent reason, imprisoning him inside.

There was nothing Simon could do to save his friend.

Within seconds, the tree fell to the ground, and he miraculously managed to jump away enough to crush only his leg but save his life. "AAAAAAAA!!!!" shouted Harry just before he was crushed.

The sound of breaking branches mingled with the crackle of metal and glass and the man's bones breaking.

The force of the impact was so powerful that blood gushed through the cracks and fell several metres away, like chunks of watermelon smashed with a 20-pound hammer, creating a gruesome sight.

Danny settled flat on the ground and then rolled away from the wreckage to a safer distance, uninjured by the incident.

...SHEEEEE...!!! SHEEEEE IS HEEEERE...!!! THAT IS HEEEER...!!!

Susan lay down and heard everything that was happening on the surface, hysterically rolling her eyes, unable to move.

Breathing rapidly, she tried to regain control of her body, but was paralysed, and then soil began to fall on her.

The pile of earth, originally coming from where the woman was now, began to return to where it had come from.

Slowly at first, but gaining momentum with each passing moment, burying her alive.

Susan watched helplessly as the soil fell on her, breathing heavily and desperately, trying to move from side to side in vain.

Then another portion of debris landed straight on her face, and then another and another, until the pit was filled to the brim again.

From Danny's point of view, it looked very different, as he first heard the sirens of the approaching rescue units from afar and then, watched as the pile of earth moved towards the pit, as if by an invisible bulldozer.

The whole situation happened very quickly.

No more than thirty seconds elapsed, from the moment the gusty wind started to blow, through the fall of the tree until the landslide was over.

As the wind died down and he finally got to his feet, he saw that the figures, previously dark and indistinct, had become bright and visible, taking on human form.

A calm and friendly aura was emanating from them.

As the sirens of the police cars grew louder, they positioned themselves around the spot where Susan McKane lay.

Eventually he could see their faces, two girls, Magda Richardson and Jessica Murphy, and two boys, David Roberts and Oliver Wilson, the missing four from North Hill.

The souls of the children stood still and looked straight at Danny, smiling slightly at him.

Suddenly, each of them flashed with a bright and brilliant light, like rays of sunlight, it was beautiful as well as pleasant to watch.

It seemed as if, each of them gained full power and then disappeared in a flash, ending the show unexpectedly.

Danny was left alone and for the first time in ten months, he felt an inner peace.

"You are free." He said in an emotional voice.

But there was someone else, who had not completed unfinished business yet.

A fifth figure, now clear and pleasant, approached the man and he recognised her immediately.

"Hello Denise." He said.

The girl's almost transparent face smiled, and he felt the good aura surrounding the child's soul warm his heart, bringing tears to his eyes.

Denise pointed to the wooden shed, reminding him why they were here.

"Unchain me!" he shouted to the only survivor, Simon.

The man was still lying on the ground, from where he had jumped to save himself from the tree.

However, Danny noticed that he couldn't move, because his right leg was under a large branch.

However, the cu s came loose and fell o his sore wrists, which brought a smile to his face, as he knew who to thank for this.

Denise Randal, this ten-year-old posthumously saved not only me, but other distraught souls; what started as a nightmare turned into a miraculous story. He thought.

Individual emergency vehicles began to arrive and line up in available locations, and the area lit up in red and blue.

But Danny, ignoring the arriving people, opened his hand for Denise to grab it, then together, they set off towards the wooden shed.

It was an expedition they had often made together in his dreams, so he felt like he knew every step before he even took it.

The only difference was, this time he knew why he was here and, who he would find inside.

This time was different, it was no longer a dream, and the man knew that he was covering this distance for the last time and that his task, would soon come to an end.

Rachel, who had also arrived with Mark Brown, got out of the car and saw

her husband calmly walking away towards the woods. "Danny!!!" she called out with all her might.

The man turned around hearing his wife's voice, then pointed with his hand to a spot near them.

"Dig there! That's where Susan McKane is!" he said and moved on. Mark and Rachel first looked at each other in surprise and then in the direction he had marked out for them.

Officers and services from the medical centre had arrived and were scattering around looking for injured people.

What attracted the most attention, of course, was the huge fallen tree and the crushed car beneath it.

"Attention everyone!!!" shouted Mark, standing on the doorstep of the car, to be more visible.

"...Start digging here immediately!!! Someone is underground!!!" he added, pointing to a distinct area.

His subordinates and the people who felt obliged to help, immediately ran to the patch of ground.

Then, desperately and with everything they could, including their bare hands, they started digging the debris out of the pit.

Fortunately, one of the officers found two shovels lying nearby, previously belonging to Simon and Harry, which greatly accelerated the excavation process.

"Mark, where is he going?" asked Rachel, in an exasperated voice.

"I think he's going after Nicole Denice." He replied calmly.

At first, she felt like running after him, but decided she would let him make the journey on his own.

As she watched him disappear into the depths of the dingy shed, she subconsciously felt a sense of calm, she knew that was exactly what he needed.

Danny looked around the room, it was old and dusty, and the air was filled with the sour smell of rotten boards.

The first thing that caught his eye were the old and rusty tools lying around, as well as the remains of long unused fishing equipment.

When he looked to his left, he saw a blanket lying on the ground, under which there was clearly something.

"Nicole Denice..." he said quietly and walked closer.

He then removed the old cloth from the child, revealing her face.

The girl was unconscious but breathing.

"Thank God..." he sighed in relief and took her in his arms.

"...You are safe now." He added in a trembling voice, then heard behind him:

"My dear Denice, thank you."

As he slowly turned around, he saw Denise Randal standing next to a transparent man dressed in a suit, she was holding his hand.

"Your daughter, you are Susan's husband." Danny stated.

"John McKane." The figure replied.

Danny remembered last Christmas, when he had hosted a medium with whom he had conducted a spiritualist séance.

At the time, a woman had spoken in the voice of someone who introduced himself as John McKane, but only now did Danny see the point.

John McKane, Susan's late husband, could not be at peace after his death, knowing what kind of person his wife really was.

He knew that his only child, was in mortal danger at the hands of her own mother, and he could not leave until she was saved.

Denise Randal, also posthumously, wanted to help the children of North Hill, trapped and lost in purgatory.

In a way known only to her, she knew exactly when, another innocent child would die for reasons that can only be described in one word: greed.

It was never about revenge for not being able to save her life.

He could only guess that it was because all these children were of a similar age when they left this world prematurely.

But in Nicole Denice's case, it could also have been because she was her namesake or simply, it was the right time to end the senseless terror and havoc being wreaked on the innocent citizens of the town of North Hill, in the name of profit and unbridled greed.

Either way, Danny was proud to be the one who had the honour of putting an end to tragedy and freeing the anguished souls of the people, who had been harmed in the process.

John McKane and Denis Randal, like the other souls of the children, departed in a strong and pleasantly bright light and Danny Davis left the shed, carrying Nicole Denice in his arms.

It was with a great sense of satisfaction and relief that a situation that seemed hopeless from his perspective, had turned in his favour and he had emerged unscathed from serious trouble.

And it was all thanks to the North Hill missing four, who had finally received justice for the harm done to them.

Simon Edwards lay arrested in one of the ambulances that arrived, where he was attended to by medics.

He had broken his right leg because of being crushed by a tree and su ered multiple injuries, but his life was not in danger.

He was undoubtedly luckier than his companions, with Harry Green dying on the spot crushed in his car and Susan McKane, buried alive, fighting for her life while being resuscitated.

Police officers and medical volunteers worked hard to get her out from under the ground, as quickly as possible.

When they finally succeeded, she was immediately transferred to an ambulance where attempts to restore her breathing began. At the same time Mark, accompanied by Rachel and two uniformed officers, was looking at the wrecked car.

"You'd better not come over here." The commander turned to her, when he saw the bloodied body of a man in the wreckage of the vehicle.

Rachel took a few steps back and saw Danny approaching them, so she immediately moved towards him.

Mark also stopped what he was doing and focused his attention on him.

The two police officers who were examining the scene of the accident, could not understand why the tree had fallen.

"Look at the roots..." said one of them. "...See how long they are? This is a healthy and strong tree, how on earth, could it have fallen so suddenly?" one wondered.

"I agree, it literally looks like a hurricane, at least 10 on the Beaufort scale, or some giant has uprooted it." The other replied.

"Call me crazy, but I might agree with the second version, after all, it's only one tree and the rest are intact."

"Indeed, this guy did not have the slightest chance of survival." Summed up the partner.

Rachel ran up to Danny and wanted to throw herself around his neck but was held back, by the baby leaning on his shoulder.

"Is she alright?" she asked instead and hugged him around the waist. "Yes, she'll be fine..." He replied. "... But let's take her to the ambulance, let the professionals take care of her." He added caringly. "What happened Danny?" Rachel tried to pull his tongue.

"We'll talk about it later, better tell me, how did you manage to find us here?"

"What do you mean?" Rachel was baffled.

"How did you find this place? Susan confessed that only she and her stepfather knew about it." He explained.

"I called you on the mini and you picked up, you just didn't say anything, it was like you picked up by accident, and then Mark and I listened to your conversation with Susan while I was riding in the police car with him..." she explained. "...Mark ordered at head office that they contact the operator, who allowed us to track you via GPS."

"Mini? But I left it at home, did you hear everything she said?" Danny tried to put it all together in his head.

"Of course, we didn't just hear it, Mark recorded a significant part of it." She replied.

The truth was that Danny had left the device behind, as he hurriedly dressed to rush to Susan's aid.

But he had forgotten an important detail, namely that his guardian angel, Denis Randal, had been always watching over him and would never have allowed him to be left completely defenceless.

That is why, when he was put unconscious in the boot, his spare phone was already there.

Precisely so that it would be activated at the crucial moment

Moments later, Mark joined them when they were already halfway back. Along with him came two officers who immediately picked up the girl and then quickly carried her to the nearest ambulance, so she could be checked by specialists.

"Come on, I'll take you both home, we'll talk there..." Mark suggested. "...You did well Danny, you need to rest, you've had a tough day." He added.

However, Danny was feeling unexpectedly well, considering the events he had faced over the last few hours.

The feeling of tiredness was replaced by relief that Nicole Denice had been rescued.

But most of all, the knowledge that thanks to him, the nightmare in North

Hill was over and everyone would be able to sleep peacefully, from now on.

19 August 2019, London, Lewisham, 07:00am.

The next day, things went downhill.

As a result of the events in North Hill, an avalanche was set in motion that would ultimately bury the "Bradley and Brad Lettings" agencies.

Officers from North Hill Police, in conjunction with London Metropolitan Police, worked through the night to formally issue charges and arrest warrants.

An unsuspecting Matthiew Braddock was awoken at 7 am by a loud knock on the door.

Drowsy and disoriented, with a headache caused by a night of heavy drinking, he went to see who was knocking so insistently, on his flat door in the early morning.

Although, he did not receive the usual confirmation from Simon that the job was done, he found solace in a bottle of whisky, and quickly forgot an important detail.

...BUMBUMBUM!!!

"I'm coming!! FOR FUCK'S SAKE!!!" he shouted indignantly.

As he walked to the door and looked through the peephole, he sobered up momentarily and the hair on the back of his neck rose.

...BUMBUMBUM!!! "This is the police! Please open the door!" one of the uniformed men called out.

"On what matter!"

"Please open immediately! We have a warrant!" the officer replied. Reluctantly, but seeing no other option, Matthew slowly turned the key in the door, and it gave way with a quiet click. At this sound the officers without waiting for the man to let them in, burst in and placed him face against the wall, whilst placing handcuffs on his hands.

"Matthiew Braddock, you are under arrest on suspicion of conspiracy to obtain property assets and accessory to murder, you have the right to remain silent, anything you say..." the officer began to dictate his Miranda rights, when the man interrupted him. "When do I get to call a lawyer?" he asked.

"There will be time for that, for now you will come with us." The policeman replied and grabbed him by the arm, pressing him so that it did not even occur to him to resist.

The day before, Matthiew had a premonition that something might go wrong this time.

From the outset, he didn't think it was necessary to eliminate Danny Davis or get rid of Nicole Denice, but he had to listen to Susan McKane a.k.a. Nattaly Kemp because she had the final say, and she was adamant that Danny was becoming more and more of a threat.

Rightly so, because the man was hanging around wherever he could and sooner or later, he would discover the truth about her.

Susan "Nattaly" McKane realised that Danny had discovered something the moment he looked at the photo of her and Nicole Denice, in her office. She noticed that his facial expression and body language had changed, and when he left the building, she also looked at the same photo and discovered that the dolphin bracelet had originally belonged to Magda Richardson.

She associated this fact, only after much thought.

Then, she recalled the moment Magda's mother, Joanna Richardson, whom she knew well at the time, showed her the bracelet, boasting about what a nice gift she had bought her daughter for her birthday.

From there, she had to slowly, step by step, analyse the jewellery's journey before it came into Nicole Denice's possession.

Through deductive reasoning, she realised that either Simon or Harry had taken the ornament from the child's wrist, but it must have later ended up in Matthiew's possession.

He was the one who had sent her daughter the seventh birthday present, that included the bracelet.

She suspected two reasons why this happened, and both scenarios can be described in one word: greed.

Firstly, Matthiew's subordinates were too stingy to simply dispose of the jewellery, so they kept it to give to their boss later.

Secondly, Matthiew, while in possession of the bracelet, was too lazy to buy anything from the shop and, despite his good intentions, sent her evidence of the crime.

Either way, she decided that day that she was done with her role at North

Hill.

Before that, she needed to get rid of Danny Davis and Nicole Denice so that she could sell the house that John McKane had left to his daughter, then leave the country and hide out in some safe corner of the world. However, all plans fell apart and there was no extenuating circumstances left.

Nattaly Swanson was also in big trouble.

She was arrested for being part of an organised crime group, involved in smuggling heroin from France by sea and distributing it in England. She received and paid for shipments of illegal substances from smugglers who transported them by sea, attached to the ships below the surface of the water to avoid capture.

Sometimes these were regular fishing boats, as well as private yachts.

Her job was to pick them up and then send them to London, where her partner would take them over and distribute them.

Both she and the father of her child were arrested and faced a long and difficult trial, that they could not win.

So, they had to get used to the idea, they would undoubtedly spend at least quite a few years behind bars, and Nattaly's son, Yaqub, would be taken care of by her parents.

Epilogue

Two months later.

19 October 2019.

The afternoon news reported a court hearing involving Susan McKane, Matthiew Braddock and Simon Edwards.

Although the subject of Magda Richardson's disappearance had been avoided for ten years, with few articles written about it in the media, each subsequent event had been skilfully swept under the carpet and avoided national attention.

This time, the issue again made national headlines, especially when the solemn funeral of the four missing children from North Hill broadcast seven weeks earlier.

Several thousand people from all over the country came to say goodbye to the dead, including, of course, the children's parents.

Also present were Danny, Rachel, Mark and Connor, as people deserving special recognition for their part in solving the case.

The whole ceremony concluded late in the evening as the sun went down, hundreds of white lanterns were released into the air and a beautiful spectacle was created in the sky.

Susan McKane, who was barely resuscitated on 18 August 2019, was sentenced to life imprisonment without the possibility of parole.

Matthiew Braddock and Simon Edwards also received life without parole.

Although, only the second man had direct involvement in the murders.

Harry Green, died because of his injuries.

Susan McKane's solicitor asked for clemency for her client, arguing that she has a rare mental disorder called alexithymia, which meant she is technically insane.

Matthiew also explained his behaviour was allegedly caused by alcohol and substance abuse.

Only Simon Edwards had the courage to admit his guilt and accept the punishment with humility.

He also testified, tormented by remorse, that he and Harry had received orders together with instructions directly from Matthiew.

Who also gave them precise descriptions of the targets, addresses, dates and times they were to strike.

True to Matthiew's word, Simon Edwards', was to receive fifty thousand pounds to share with his partner for each mission accomplished, i.e. for each child kidnapped.

He also admitted to dropping o Voodoo dolls and bloody parcels at addresses he had previously, received and to vandalising the Hailu family home in 2008.

He also admitted fuelling the hate speech to ultimately get the Ethiopian banker to abandon the house in favour of the agency, buying it at a reduced price.

The man confessed that they had initially planned to send the kidnapped abroad in the form of human trafficking.

But when Magda Richardson, previously drugged with chloroform, failed to wake up, they went to plan B and were forced to take her to some remote location.

That's when they got Matthiew's directions to a remote place in the woods, by a river, where they were to go regularly thereafter. Each subsequent child, after being sedated with chloroform, would receive a lethal dose of fast-acting insulin, directly into the bloodstream and not wake up again. The only consolation was that none of the victims suffered, before dying.

Simon also recounted how such a task was carried out, explaining in subsections:

Firstly: Matthiew called him and told him that they had to start preparing.

Then they knew what he expected of them, so they didn't leave North Hill. Second: He would give them an address, a date and a description of the destination.

They would then find the place and the person the boss had described.

Third: when the day came, they would wait for confirmation of the exact time they could start.

This meant that the area was clear, and the target was easiest to reach.

They then used chloroform to immobilise the victim, given that Matthiew Braddock was in command of the operation up to that point, but after that he didn't care what they did with the abductee.

Furthermore, as the first kidnapped child had sadly died during the task, they decided to make sure that the others would also not wake up, from their chloroform-induced sleep.

It was therefore assumed that the least cruel way to achieve this, would be to inject the victims with a large amount of insulin, because of which they would die in their sleep without feeling anything.

The Simon Edwards' testimony completely buried Matthiew, but he did not say a word about Susan McKane.

The explanation, however, was astonishingly simple, neither Simon Edwards nor Harry Green knew about her, they only knew that some woman from North Hill, was working with their boss and nothing more.

During the trial, the judge dismissed all mitigating circumstances that could theoretically explain the defendants' actions.

This came after the solicitor of George Bradley, acting for Susan McKane, was called upon to produce all documents relating to the estate agency. George clearly wrote there that "...The sole heir to the estate I own is my daughter Susan McKane, who, for the sake of anonymity, goes by the name of her mother Noelle Kemp, known as Nattaly in English..."

All the indications were that Susan did in fact own most of the shares in the housing agency and, as a result, it was she who made, either on her own or through her lawyer, the final decisions about the business.

At the time, the court undoubtedly found Susan and Matthiew guilty of conspiracy to enrich themselves by terrorising innocent people through buying properties for sometimes half their actual value.

However, it was Susan who received particularly harsh treatment. After the investigation revealed that she personally knew all the victims' families, she synchronised her actions, informing Matthiew Braddock of their every move.

She knew exactly where, on what day and at what time they would be.

During this time, she often hosted them in her office.

Then, using her authority and profession, under the guise of therapy sessions, she persuaded emotionally unstable people, to leave town and sell their properties at the same time.

In his closing speech, the judge noted that "...What we have witnessed here, is an exceptionally abhorrent crime..."

This was undoubtedly the only and correct statement, as Susan McKane had worked with the affected parents as a psychologist, before and long after the tragedies they suffered at her hands, without even knowing it. When she met them face to face, she lied, manipulated without compassion and, instead of helping them cope with the tragedy, which was her profession, she encouraged them to sell their homes and move. In addition to the convictions, the guilty parties were also ordered to pay compensation to the affected families, five hundred thousand pounds each.

Nicole Denice McKane, in turn, was to live with John's parents, until she reached the age of majority.

North Hill, Danny and Rachel's home, 01:45pm.

Danny and Rachel listened to the final verdict on TV but were not surprised at what the decision was.

Danny had only one word in his head throughout the broadcast: guilty. The day before, they had returned from London, where they had gone to visit Denise Randal's grave on the first anniversary of her death. There they met Clare Randal, with whom they had an interesting conversation.

The woman looked much better and admitted that she recognised Danny's picture from an article on the internet, about a closed case of four missing children from North Hill.

She also told him that on the night of 18 August, when the incident occurred, she had a dream about her daughter, who told her that everything would be fine from then on and that she had already found peace.

She went on to talk about how Denise had travelled to North Hill to visit her grandparents for the holidays, every year since she was six years old. There she met Nicole Denice, and the two girls became very fond of each other.

Denise texted her and they often spoke on the phone and when the holidays came around, she couldn't wait to see her friend.

An exceptionally pleasant conversation ended with Clare affectionately hugging Danny and Rachel, allowing the man to add the final piece of the puzzle.

No question went unanswered.

"Come on..." Rachel said, getting up from the sofa. "...let's go."

"Sure, I'm ready." Danny joined her.

They both went out into the corridor, where they took freshly cut bouquets of flowers from a vase that had been left there earlier, and then dressed warmly before going outside.

They got into the car and started down the street towards the nearby cemetery.

When they got there, Danny got out of the car and waited for his wife to do the same, opened the boot and picked up the bouquets of fragrant flowers.

Rachel came up to him and grabbed him under the arm, and together they moved slowly towards the resting place of the missing four from North Hill. When they stood in front of the four graves side by side, they both said their prayer first, then Danny carefully arranged the flowers on each of them. He then reached into his pocket, pulled out a dolphin bracelet and knelt in front of Magda Richardson's plaque, placed the jewellery under the cross with her name on it and said:

You must be strong with the power of love, which is mightier than death... You must be a love that is patient, is gracious...

www.ingramcontent.com/pod-product-compliance
Lightning Source LLC
Chambersburg PA
CBHW030351030726
47497CB00002B/279

* 9 7 8 1 9 6 6 5 3 4 5 4 9 *